Rhododendrons in the mist

Books by Ruskin Bond

Fiction

A Gallery of Rascals: My Favourite Tales of Rogues, Rapscallions and Ne'er-do-wells
Unhurried Tales: My Favourite Novellas
Small Towns, Big Stories
Upon an Old Wall Dreaming
A Gathering of Friends
Tales of Fosterganj
The Room on the Roof & Vagrants in the Valley
The Night Train at Deoli and Other Stories
Time Stops at Shamli and Other Stories
Our Trees Still Grow in Dehra
A Season of Ghosts
When Darkness Falls and Other Stories
A Flight of Pigeons
Delhi is Not Far
A Face in the Dark and Other Hauntings
The Sensualist
A Handful of Nuts
Maharani
Secrets

Non-fiction

Rain in the Mountains
Scenes from a Writer's Life
A Book of Simple Living
Love among the Bookshelves
Landour Days
Notes from a Small Room
The India I Love

Anthologies

Classic Ruskin Bond: Complete and Unabridged
Classic Ruskin Bond Volume 2: The Memoirs
Dust on the Mountain: Collected Stories
The Best of Ruskin Bond
Friends in Small Places
Indian Ghost Stories (ed.)
Indian Railway Stories (ed.)
Ghost Stories from the Raj
Tales of the Open Road
Ruskin Bond's Book of Nature
Ruskin Bond's Book of Humour
A Town Called Dehra
The Writer on the Hill

Poetry

Ruskin Bond's Book of Verse
Hip-Hop Nature Boy & Other Poems

Rhododendrons in the mist

MY FAVOURITE TALES OF THE HIMALAYA

RUSKIN BOND

ALEPH

ALEPH

ALEPH BOOK COMPANY
An independent publishing firm
promoted by *Rupa Publications India*

First published in India in 2019
by Aleph Book Company
7/16 Ansari Road, Daryaganj
New Delhi 110 002

ISBN: 978-81-942337-6-3

1 3 5 7 9 10 8 6 4 2

Printed by Parksons Graphics Pvt. Ltd., Mumbai.

CONTENTS

INTRODUCTION

Most of the stories in this collection were written after I came to live in the hills, and over the period from the late 1960s to the present. Naturally, they describe life in a hill station and the hills and valleys that surround it. As in much of my writing, the personal element is always present, and stories like 'The Cherry Tree', 'Love is a Sad Song' and 'The Playing Fields of Simla' are almost factual. In 'The Blue Umbrella' and 'A Long Walk for Bina' I have dwelt on village life, and in some tales the supernatural plays a part.

The selection was made by my publisher David Davidar, and it's a good mix. As the stories can be largely said to revolve around two distinctive themes—suspense and mystery and the drama of everyday life—this book is divided into sections entitled 'The Dark Side of Mountains' and 'Himalayan Drama' respectively. Besides old favourites, my publisher insisted that I write three new stories for the book. And so, last February, a bleak and bitterly cold month in Landour, I sat beside the bottle and wrote the title story of this collection, as well as 'The Garden of Dreams' and 'Breakfast at Barog', the last being a little tribute to my father.

I am very fortunate to be still writing stories and memories in my eighty-fifth year, enjoying the process as much as I ever did, and hopefully giving pleasure to a widening circle of readers. Living in the hills might have something to do with it. The mountains give you a feeling of freedom. And the constant care and attention I receive from my grandchildren, Rakesh and Beena, means that I am free to read and write and dream and watch the clouds roll by, to my heart's delight!

Ruskin Bond
Landour, Mussoorie
September 2019

PART I

The Dark Side of Mountains

RHODODENDRONS IN THE MIST

Blood-red, the fallen blossoms lay on the snow, even more striking when laid bare. On the trees they blended with the foliage. On the ground, on those patches of recent snow, they seemed to be bleeding.

It had been a harsh winter in the hills, and it was still snowing at the end of March. But this was flowering time for the rhododendron trees, and they blossomed in sun, snow, or pelting rain. By mid-afternoon the hill station was shrouded in a heavy mist, and the trees stood out like ghostly sentinels.

The hill station wasn't Simla, where I had gone to school, or Mussoorie, where I was to settle later on. It was Dalhousie, a neglected and almost forgotten hill station in the western Himalaya. But Dalhousie had the best rhododendron trees, and they grew all over the mountain, showing off before the colourless oaks and drooping pines.

But I wasn't in Dalhousie for the rhododendrons. It was 1959, and the Dalai Lama had just fled from Tibet, seeking sanctuary in India. Thousands of his followers and fellow-Tibetans had fled with him, and these refugees had to be settled somewhere. Dalhousie, with its many empty houses, was ideal for this purpose, and a carpet-weaving centre had been set up on one of the estates. The Tibetans made beautiful rugs and carpets. I know nothing about carpet-weaving, but I was working for CARE, an American relief organization, and I had been sent to Dalhousie (with the approval of the Government of India) to assess the needs of the refugees.

This is not the story of my tryst with the Tibetans, although I did suffer greatly from drinking large quantities of butter tea, which travels very slowly down the gullet and feels like lead by the time it reaches your stomach. The carpet-weaving centre became a great success, and I went on to work for CARE for several years; but that's another story. Out of one experience came another experience, as often happens during our peregrinations on planet earth, and it was during my stay in Dalhousie that I had a strange and rather unsettling experience.

I was staying at a small hotel which was quite empty as no one visited Dalhousie in those days and certainly not at the end of March. The hill station had been convenient for visitors from Lahore, but Partition had put an end to that.

∽

The hotel had a small garden, bare at this time of the year. But on the second day of my stay, returning from the carpet-weaving centre, I noticed that there was a gardener working on the flower beds, digging around and transplanting some seedlings. He looked up as I passed, and for a moment I thought I knew him. There was something familiar about his features—the slit eyes, the broad, flattened nose, the harelip—yes, the cleft lip was very noticeable—but he wasn't anyone I knew or had known, at least I didn't think so.... He was just a likeness to someone I had seen somehow, somewhere else. It was a bit of a tease.

And it would have remained just that if he hadn't looked up and met my gaze.

A flood of recognition crossed his face. But then he looked away, almost as though he did not want to recognize me; or be recognized.

I passed him. It was curious, but it didn't bother me. We keep bumping into people who look slightly familiar. It is said that everyone has a double somewhere on this planet. I had yet to meet mine—God forbid!—but perhaps I was seeing someone else's double.

I was relaxing in the veranda later that evening, browsing through an old magazine, when the gardener passed me on his way to the garden shed to put away his tools. There

was something about his walk that brought back an image
from the past. He had a slight limp. And when he looked
at me again, his harelip registered itself on my memory.
And now I recognized him. And of course he knew me.

I was the man who'd caught him rifling through my
landlady's cupboards and drawers in Dehradun, some three
years previously. I had exposed him, reported him, suggested
she dismiss him; but the old lady, a widow, had grown quite
fond of the youth, and had kept him in her service. He was
good at running about and making himself useful, and, in
spite of his cleft lip, he was not unattractive.

When I left Dehradun to take up my job in Delhi, I
had forgotten the matter, almost forgotten the young man
and my landlady; it was another tenant who informed me
that the youth—his name was Sohan—had stabbed the old
lady and made off with the contents of her jewel case and
other valuables. She had died in hospital a few days later.

Sohan hadn't been caught. He had obviously left the
town and taken to the hills or a large city. The police had
made sporadic attempts to locate him, but as time passed
the case lost its urgency. The victim was not a person of
importance. The criminal was a stranger, a shadowy figure
of no known background.

But here he was three years later, staring me in the
face. What was I to do about him? Or what was he to
do about me?

∽

After Sohan had gone to his quarters, somewhere behind
the hotel, I went in search of the manager. I would tell him
what I knew and together we could decide on a course of
action. But he had gone to a marriage and would be back
late. The hotel was in charge of the cook who, a little
drunk, served dinner in a hurry and retired to his quarters.
'Don't you have a night-watchman?' I asked him before he
took off. 'Yes, of course,' he replied, 'Sohan, the gardener.

He's the chowkidar too!'

An early retirement seemed the best thing all round, especially as I had to leave the next day. So I went to my room and made sure all the doors and windows were locked. I pushed the inside bolts all the way. I made sure the antiquated window frames were locked. As I peered out of the window, I noticed that a heavy mist had descended on the hillside. The trees stood out like ghostly apparitions, here and there a rhododendron glowing like the embers of a small fire. Then darkness enveloped the hillside. I felt cold, and wondered how much of it was fear.

I went to the bathroom and bolted the back door. Now no one could get in. Even so, I felt uneasy. Sohan was still a fugitive from the law, I had recognized him, and I was a threat to his freedom. He had killed once—perhaps more than once—and he could kill again.

I read for some time, then put out the light and tried to sleep. From a distance came the strains of music from a wedding band. Someone knocked on the door. I switched on the light and looked at my watch. It was only 10 p.m. Perhaps the manager had returned.

There was another knock, and I went to the door and was about to open it when some childhood words of warning from my grandmother came to mind: 'Never open the door unless you know who's there!'

'Who's there?' I called.

No answer. Just another knock.

'Who's there?' I called again.

There was a cough, a double-rap on the door.

'I'm sleeping,' I said. 'Come in the morning.' And I returned to my bed. The knocking continued but I ignored it, and after some time the person went away.

I slept a little. A couple of hours must have passed when I was woken by further knocking. But it did not come from the door. It was above me, high up on the wall. I'd forgotten there was a skylight.

I switched on the light and looked up. A face was outlined against the glass of the skylight. I could make out the flat rounded face and the harelip. It appeared to be grinning at me—rather like the disembodied head of the Cheshire cat in *Alice in Wonderland*.

The skylight was very small and I knew he couldn't crawl through the opening. But he could show me a knife—and that was what he did. It was a small clasp knife and he held it between his teeth as he peered down at me. I felt very vulnerable on the bed. So I switched off the light and moved to an old sofa at the far end of the room, where I couldn't be seen. There didn't seem to be any point in shouting for help. So I just sat there, waiting.... And presumably, without a sound, he slipped away, and I remained on the sofa until the first glimmer of dawn penetrated the drawn window curtains.

∽

The manager was apologetic. 'You should have rung the bell,' he said, 'someone would have come.'

'The bell doesn't work. And someone did come...'

'I'm sorry, I'm sorry. The fellow's a villain, no doubt about it. And he's missing this morning. Your presence here must have frightened him off. So he's wanted for theft and murder. Well, we shall inform the police. Perhaps they can pick him up before he leaves the town.'

And we did inform the police. But Sohan had already taken off. The milkman had seen him boarding the early morning bus to Pathankot.

Pathankot was a busy little town on the plain below Dehradun. From there one road goes to Jammu, another to Dharamsala, a narrow-gauge railway to Kangra, and the main railway to Amritsar or Delhi. Sohan could have taken any of those routes. And no one was going to go looking for him. A police alert would be put out—a mere formality. He wasn't on their list of current criminals.

That afternoon I took a taxi to Pathankot and whiled away the evening at the railway station. My train, an overnight express to Delhi, left at 8 p.m. There was no rush at that time of the year. I had a first-class compartment to myself.

In those days our trains were somewhat different from what they are today. A first, second or third class compartment was usually a single carriage, or bogey. We did not have corridor trains. Bogeys were connected by steel couplings, otherwise you were not connected in any way to the other compartments. But there was an emergency cord above the upper berths, and if you pulled it, the train might stop. There were always troublemakers on the trains, just as there are today, and sometimes the chain was pulled out of mischief. As a result it was often ignored.

As the train began moving out of the station I went to all the windows and made sure that they were fastened. Then I bolted the carriage door. I was becoming adept at bolting doors and windows. Sohan was probably hiding out in some distant town or village, but I wasn't taking any chances.

The train gathered speed. The lights of Pathankot receded as we plunged into a dark and moonless night. I had a pillow and a blanket with me, and I stretched out on one of the bunks and tried to think about pleasant things such as scarlet geraniums, fragrant sweet peas, and the beautiful Nimmi, star of the silver screen; but instead I kept seeing the grinning face of a young man with a harelip. All the same, I drifted into sleep. The rocking movement of the carriage, the rhythm of the wheels on the rails, have always had a soothing effect on my nerves. I sleep well in trains and rocking chairs.

But not that night.

I woke to the sound of that familiar tapping; not at the door, but on the window glass not far from my head. The insistent tapping of someone who wanted to get in.

It was common enough for ticketless travellers to hang on to the carriage of a moving train, in the hope that someone would let them in. But they usually chose the crowded second or third-class compartments; a first-class traveller, often alone, was unlikely to let in a stranger who might well turn out to be a train robber.

I raised my head from my pillow, and there he was, clinging to the fast-moving train, his face pressed to the glass, his harelip revealing part of a broken tooth.... I pulled down the shutters, blotting out his face. But, agile as a cat, he moved to the next window, the sneer still on his face. I pulled down that shutter too.

I pulled down all the shutters on his side of the carriage. He couldn't get in, bodily. But mentally, he was all over me.

Mind over matter. Well, I could apply my mind too. I shut my eyes and willed my tormentor to fall off the train!

No one fell off the train (at least no one was reported to have done so), but presently we slowed to a gradual stop and, when I pulled up the shutters of the window, I saw that we were at a station. Jalandhar, I think. The platform was brightly lit and there was no sign of Sohan. He must have jumped off the train as it slowed down. It was about one in the morning. A vendor brought me a welcome glass of hot tea, and life returned to normal.

∽

I did not see Sohan in the years that followed. Or rather, I saw many Sohans. For two or three years I was pursued by my 'familiar'. Wherever I went—and my work took me to different parts of the country—I found myself encountering young men with harelips and a menacing look. Pure imagination, of course. He had every reason to stay as far from me as possible.

Gradually, the 'sightings' died down. Young men with harelips became extremely rare. Perhaps they were all going in for corrective surgery.

The years passed, and I had forgotten my familiar. I had given up my job in Delhi and moved to the hills. I was a moderately successful writer, and a familiar figure on Mussoorie's Mall Road. Sometimes other writers came to see me, in my cottage under the deodars. One of them invited me to have dinner with him at the old Regal hotel, where he was staying. Before dinner, he took me to the bar for a drink.

'What will you have, whisky or vodka?'

No one seemed to drink anything else. I asked for some dark rum, and the barman went off in search of a bottle. When he returned and began pouring my drink, I noticed something slightly familiar about his features, his stance. He was almost bald, and he had a grey, drooping moustache which concealed most of his upper lip. He glanced at me and our eyes met. There was no sign of recognition. He smiled politely as he poured my drink. No, it definitely wasn't Sohan. He was too refined, for one thing. And he went about his duties without another glance in my direction.

Dinner over, I thanked my writer friend for his hospitality, and took the long walk home to my cottage. It was a dark, moonless night. No one followed me, no one came tapping on my bedroom window.

∽

Mussoorie had its charms. In my mind, every hill station is symbolized by a particular tree, even if it's not the dominant one. Dalhousie has its rhododendrons, Simla its deodars, Kasauli its pines, and Mussoorie its horse chestnuts. The monkeys would do their best to destroy the chestnuts, but I would collect those that were whole and plant them in people's gardens, whether they wanted them or not. The horse chestnut is a lovely tree to look at, even if you can't do anything with it!

My walks took me to the Regal from time to time, and occasionally I would relax in the bar, chatting to an old resident or a casual visitor, while the barman poured me a rum and soda. He never looked twice at me. And I never saw him outside that barroom. He appeared to be as much of a fixture as the moth-eaten antler-head on the wall, only he wasn't quite as moth-eaten.

'Efficient chap,' said Colonel Bhushan indicating the barman. 'And a great favourite with his mistress.'

'You mean the owner of this place?' I had only a vague idea of who owned what in the town. And in some cases the ownership was rather vague. But in the case of the Regal—Mrs Kapoor, a wealthy widow in her fifties, was very much in charge, all too visible an owner; well fleshed-out, ample-bosomed, with arms like rolling pins. Her staff trembled at her approach; but not, it seemed, the bartender, who led a charmed life, incapable of doing any wrong.

The lights went out, as they frequently do in this technological age, and the barman brought over our next round of drinks by candlelight.

By the light of a candle I caught a glimpse of the barman's features as he hovered over me. There was only the hint of a harelip, and the candle lit up his slanting eyes and prominent cheekbones. This was the only time I had a really close look at him.

∽

A week later I met Colonel Bhushan on the Mall. This was where all the gossip took place.

'Have you heard what happened last night at the Regal?' He wasted no time in getting to the news of the day.

A twinge of fear, of anticipation, ran through me. 'Nothing too terrible, I hope?'

'That barman chap—always thought he was a bit too smooth—stabbed the old lady, stabbed her two or three times, then plundered her room and made off with jewellery worth lakhs—as well as all the cash he could find!'

'How's the lady?'

'She'll survive. Tough old buffalo. But the rascal got away. By now he must be in Sirmur, or even across the Nepal border. Probably belongs to some criminal tribe.'

Yes, I thought, possibly a descendant of one of those robber gangs who harassed pilgrims on their way to the sacred shrines, or plundered traders from Tibet, or caravans to Samarkand.... To rob and plunder still runs in the blood of the most harmless looking people.

So the barman at the Regal was the same man I'd known in Dehradun and then encountered in Dalhousie. The passing of time had altered his features but not his way of life. By now he would probably be far from Mussoorie. But I had a feeling I'd see him again—if not here, then somewhere else. Each one of us had a 'familiar'—a presence we would rather do without—an unwelcome and menacing guest—and for me it is Sohan.

Where does he come from, where does he go? I doubt if I shall ever know.

But I have a feeling he'll turn up again one of these days. And then?

A FACE IN THE DARK

Mr Oliver, an Anglo-Indian teacher, was returning to his school late one night, on the outskirts of the hill station of Simla. From before Kipling's time, the school had been run on English public-school lines and the boys, most of them from wealthy Indian families, wore blazers, caps and ties. *Life* magazine, in a feature on India, had once called it the 'Eton of the East'. Mr Oliver had been teaching in the school for several years.

The Simla bazaar, with its cinemas and restaurants, was about three miles from the school and Mr Oliver, a bachelor, usually strolled into the town in the evening, returning after dark, when he would take a shortcut through the pine forest.

When there was a strong wind, the pine trees made sad, eerie sounds that kept most people to the main road. But Mr Oliver was not a nervous or imaginative man. He carried a torch and its gleam—the batteries were running out—moved fitfully down the narrow forest path. When its flickering light fell on the figure of a boy who was sitting alone on a rock, Mr Oliver stopped. Boys were not supposed to be out after dark.

'What are you doing out here, boy?' asked Mr Oliver sharply, moving closer so that he could recognize the miscreant. But even as he approached the boy, Mr Oliver sensed that something was wrong. The boy appeared to be crying. His head hung down, he held his face in his hands and his body shook convulsively. It was a strange, soundless weeping and Mr Oliver felt distinctly uneasy.

'Well, what's the matter?' he asked, his anger giving way to concern. 'What are you crying for?' The boy would not answer or look up. His body continued to be racked with silent sobbing.

'Come on, boy, you shouldn't be out here at this hour.

Tell me the trouble. Look up!' The boy looked up. He took his hands from his face and looked up at his teacher. The light from Mr Oliver's torch fell on the boy's face—if you could call it a face.

It had no eyes, ears, nose or mouth. It was just a round smooth head—with a school cap on top of it! And that's where the story should end. But for Mr Oliver it did not end here.

The torch fell from his trembling hand. He turned and scrambled down the path, running blindly through the trees and calling for help. He was still running blindly towards the school buildings when he saw a lantern swinging in the middle of the path. Mr Oliver stumbled up to the watchman, gasping for breath. 'What is it, sahib?' asked the watchman. 'Has there been an accident? Why are you running?'

'I saw something—something horrible—a boy weeping in the forest—and he had no face!'

'No face, sahib?'

'No eyes, nose, mouth—nothing!'

'Do you mean it was like this, sahib?' asked the watchman and raised the lamp to his own face. The watchman had no eyes, no ears, no features at all—not even an eyebrow! And that's when the wind blew the lamp out.

EYES OF THE CAT

Her eyes seemed flecked with gold when the sun was on them. And as the sun set over the mountains, drawing a deep red wound across the sky, there was more than gold in Binya's eyes. There was anger; for she had been cut to the quick by some remarks her teacher had made—the culmination of weeks of insults and taunts.

Binya was poorer than most of the girls in her class and could not afford the tuitions that had become almost obligatory if one was to pass and be promoted. 'You'll have to spend another year in the ninth,' said Madam. 'And if you don't like that, you can find another school—a school where it won't matter if your blouse is torn and your tunic is old and your shoes are falling apart.' Madam had shown her large teeth in what was supposed to be a good-natured smile, and all the girls had tittered dutifully. Sycophancy had become part of the curriculum in Madam's private academy for girls.

On the way home in the gathering gloom, Binya's two companions commiserated with her. 'She's a mean old thing,' said Usha. 'She doesn't care for anyone but herself.'

'Her laugh reminds me of a donkey braying,' said Sunita, who was more forthright.

But Binya wasn't really listening. Her eyes were fixed on some point in the far distance, where the pines stood in silhouette against a night sky that was growing brighter every moment. The moon was rising, a full moon, a moon that meant something very special to Binya, that made her blood tingle and her skin prickle and her hair glow and send out sparks. Her steps seemed to grow lighter, her limbs more sinewy as she moved gracefully, softly over the mountain path.

Abruptly she left her companions at a fork in the road.

'I'm taking the shortcut through the forest,' she said.

Her friends were used to her sudden whims. They knew she was not afraid of being alone in the dark. But Binya's moods made them feel a little nervous, and now, holding hands, they hurried home along the open road.

The shortcut took Binya through the dark oak forest. The crooked, tormented branches of the oaks threw twisted shadows across the path. A jackal howled at the moon; a nightjar called from urgency, and her breath came in short, sharp gasps. Bright moonlight bathed the hillside when she reached her home on the outskirts of the village.

Refusing her dinner, she went straight to her small room and flung the window open. Moonbeams crept over the windowsill and over her arms which were already covered with golden hair. Her strong nails had shredded the rotten wood of the windowsill.

Tail swishing and ears pricked, a tawny leopard came swiftly outside the window, crossed the open field behind the house and melted into the shadows.

A little later it padded silently through the forest.

Although the moon shone brightly on the tin-roofed town, the leopard knew where the shadows were deepest and merged beautifully with them. An occasional intake of breath, which resulted in a short rasping cough, was the only sound it made.

Madam was returning from dinner at a ladies' club, called the Kitten Club as a sort of foil to the husbands' club affiliations. There were still a few people in the street, and while no one could help noticing Madam, who had the contours of a steamroller, none saw or heard the predator who had slipped down a side alley and reached the steps of the teacher's house. It sat there silently, waiting with all the patience of an obedient schoolgirl.

When Madam saw the leopard on her steps, she dropped her handbag and opened her mouth to scream; but her voice would not materialize. Nor would her tongue ever be used again, either to savour chicken biryani or to pour scorn upon her pupils, for the leopard had sprung at her throat, broken her neck and dragged her into the bushes.

In the morning, when Usha and Sunita set out for school, they stopped as usual at Binya's cottage and called out to her.

Binya was sitting in the sun, combing her long black hair.

'Aren't you coming to school today, Binya?' asked the girls.

'No, I won't bother to go today,' said Binya. She felt lazy, but pleased with herself, like a contented cat.

'Madam won't be pleased,' said Usha. 'Shall we tell her you're sick?'

'It won't be necessary,' said Binya, and gave them one of her mysterious smiles. 'I'm sure it's going to be a holiday.'

STRYCHNINE IN THE COGNAC

Sick was she on Thursday,
Dead was she on Friday,
Glad was Tom on Saturday night
To bury his wife on Sunday.

Miss Bean was reclining in a cane chair in a corner of the hotel's Beer Garden, reciting old nursery rhymes to herself, when Mr Lobo, the resident pianist, walked over and placed a glass of lemon juice beside her.

'Oranges and lemons,' he said, sitting down beside her. 'Which do you prefer?'

'Both,' she said. 'Oranges for the complexion, lemons for the digestion.'

'Words of wisdom. But that nursery rhyme sounded a bit wicked. I can only remember the innocent ones like Jack and Jill.'

'Not so innocent. "Jack fell down and broke his crown"—he wouldn't have survived a broken head. Maybe Jill pushed him over a cliff—and went tumbling after!'

'Like the judge who fell into the Kempty Waterfall. Was he pushed, or did he fall?'

'We shall never know. No witnesses. But here comes the Roys—what a handsome couple!'

The Roys were, indeed, a handsome couple, as you would expect them to be. Dilip Roy was in his mid-forties, but still a name to be reckoned with in Bollywood. He was greying a little at the temples, just below the edges of his wig; but he remained lean and athletic looking, and the meaty romantic roles still came his way. His wife, Rosie Roy, was two or three years younger than him, but inclined to plumpness. When she was in her late twenties and early thirties she had starred in several very popular films—two of them opposite Dilip Roy, whom she had married while on location with him in Kashmir—but of late she had been having some difficulty in getting parts to her liking. She hadn't been feeling very well and had taken to sleeping late in the mornings. Her doctor had suspected diabetes and had advised a complete check-up, but she kept putting off the necessary tests.

'You need change,' said Dilip, always concerned about her health. 'A change from Bombay. A fortnight in the hills will do wonders for you. I'll spend a few days with you too, before I start shooting in Switzerland. Where would you like to go—Simla, Mussoorie, Darjeeling, Ooty?'

'Why not Switzerland?'

Dilip laughed uneasily. 'It wouldn't be much of a holiday. I'd be shooting all the time and you'd be pestered by hangers-on and loads of admirers.'

'Former admirers.'

'Well, better an old admirer than none at all. And I'm still jealous.'

They settled on Mussoorie—partly because Dilip Roy's father was an old friend of Nandu, the owner of the hotel, and partly because Rosie had spent an idyllic summer there as a girl, staying with an aunt in Barlowganj. When the couple arrived at the hotel, the first person they encountered was Miss Bean, watering the potted aspidistras in the porch of the hotel.

'Hello,' said Rosie, smiling curiously at Miss Bean. 'Are you the new gardener?'

'I'm the old gardener,' said Miss Bean. 'A long-time resident, actually. But the gardener never waters these aspidistras—he thinks they are hardy enough to go without. But plants are like humans—they need a little attention from time to time, otherwise they die of neglect. I've seen you somewhere, haven't I?'

'Only if you go to the movies,' said Rosie. And added, 'Old movies.'

'You're Rosie Roy,' said Miss Bean. 'I saw you in *Cobra Lady.*'

'Wasn't it terrible?'

'It was so bad that I enjoyed every moment of it. And this must be the great Dilip Roy,' observed Miss Bean, as the well-known actor joined them, followed by room boys loaded with luggage. 'The hero of *Love in Kathmandu*,' said Miss Bean, but the hero ignored her.

Dilip Roy did not stop to gossip, but continued up the steps to the lobby, followed by his wife and the room boys. Miss Bean gave her attention to the aspidistras.

'Friendly heroine but not so friendly hero,' she said to the nearest potted plant. The aspidistra appeared to agree.

∽

The couple settled in, and over the next few days Miss Bean saw quite a lot of them although she took care not to intrude in any way, for it was obvious that the Roys were not looking for company.

In the evenings Dilip Roy would plant himself on a bar stool, and work his way through several whiskies, occasionally answering polite questions from the bartender or a casual customer, but always rather morosely, his mind obviously elsewhere. In the background, Mr Lobo, the hotel pianist, would play popular numbers but without receiving any encouragement or applause.

Rosie did not join her husband in the bar. But occasionally a martini was served to her in her room—sometimes two martinis—it was obvious that she liked a gin and vermouth cocktail now and then. Nandu presented her with a bottle of cognac, and she kept it on her dresser, intending to open it only when her husband was in the mood to drink with her.

They went out for quiet walks together, avoiding the Mall where they would quickly be recognized by both locals and tourists. Sometimes they passed Miss Bean, who was herself a great walker. As they were fellow residents of the hotel they would stop to exchange comments on the weather, the view, the hotel, the town, sometimes even the country and the rest of the world. But from the quiet of the mountains the rest of the world can seem very far away.

Rosie Roy liked the look of Miss Bean and was always ready to stop and talk. Dilip Roy was polite but brusque. The local gossip did not interest him, and he thought Miss Bean a rather quaint and rather foolish bit of flotsam surviving from the days of the British Raj. But then (as Rosie argued) the hotel, the cottages, the winding footpaths, the hill station itself, were all survivors of the Raj, and if their old-world atmosphere did not please you, it might have been better to holiday in Goa—and soak up the Portuguese atmosphere!

India would always be haunted by its history...

∽

One day the Roys had a violent quarrel. Miss Bean was no eavesdropper but she couldn't help overhearing every word that was spoken. Her favourite place was a bench situated behind a tall hibiscus hedge. It looked out upon the snows, and Miss Bean liked to spend a half hour there with a book while Fluff, her little terrier, investigated the hillside, looking for rats' holes. You couldn't see the bench from the Beer Garden, and it was in the Beer Garden that Rosie and Dilip Roy were confronting each other.

'You're off because of that woman in Bandra.' Rosie's voice was quite shrill. 'A week away from her and you're beginning to look like a real Majnu—all pale and melancholy.'

'Don't make up things.' Dilip Roy sounded impatient rather than melancholy. 'You know they start shooting on the new film next week. And it's in Switzerland, not Bandra.'

'You're not the star. They can do without you. You've been getting too fat for leading roles. And you're drinking too much.'

'I'll end up an alcoholic if I stay here much longer. The doctors advised rest for you, not for me. You've given yourself ulcers and you won't get any better if you worry over trifles.'

Here the couple were interrupted by a group of youngsters seeking autographs, and Miss Bean took advantage of the diversion to slip away, taking a roundabout path to her room. Fluff enjoyed the extended walk.

That evening Dilip Roy opened the bottle of cognac. He was leaving the next morning, and he was in a mood to celebrate. But he was not particularly fond of cognac, and did most of his celebrating with his favourite Scotch. Rosie poured herself a glass of cognac, then put the bottle away on the dresser in their room. There it remained all night.

Dilip Roy breakfasted alone in the dining room, then sent for a taxi to take him down to Dehradun. Rosie did not see him off.

'She's sleeping late,' explained Dilip. 'She has a headache. Don't disturb her.'

'Enjoy yourself in Switzerland,' said Nandu, the affable proprietor.

'Look after Rosie,' said Dilip Roy. 'Let her get plenty of rest.'

And everyone did their best to make Rosie comfortable and welcome, because she was much the more gracious of the two. The manager and staff fussed over her, and Mr Lobo played her favourite tunes, especially the one she always requested:

The future is hard to see,
Whatever will be will be...

Even Miss Bean was drawn towards Rosie and joined her on an inspection of the garden, for they were both fond of flowers, and in late summer the grounds were awash with bright yellow marigolds, petunias, larkspur and climbing roses. They had coffee together and Rosie recalled her parents and happy childhood days spent in Mussoorie; she did not talk about her marriage.

As evening came on, Rosie would retire to her room and send for a martini; it would be followed by a second. She would have a light supper in her room—usually a chicken or mushroom soup with toast—followed by a few sips of cognac as a nightcap...and then to bed.

This routine continued for three or four days, and the cognac bottle was still half full because Rosie preferred martinis. Dilip Roy made a couple of calls from Bombay— the crew would be off to Switzerland any day, and meanwhile they were shooting some scenes in Lonavala.

He had been away for almost a week when Rosie suddenly fell ill. At about ten o'clock after her dinner she rang her bell. A room boy answered her summons, found her on her bed, still dressed, and having a fit of sorts. He ran for the manager. The manager hurried to the room, followed by a concerned Mr Lobo. They found her still having convulsions.

'I'll go get Dr Bisht,' said Lobo, and hurried from the room. Minutes later they heard the splutter of his scooter as he took the winding driveway down to the Mall. Dr Bisht had a scooter too—it was the Age of the Scooter—and he arrived in time to give Rosie some basic first aid and arrange for her to be taken to the local hospital. He was cautious in his diagnosis. 'Looks like food poisoning,' he said, and then his eye fell on the open bottle of cognac, of which about half remained. There was still some liquor in a glass, and he sniffed at it and made a face. 'Or something else.... We'd better have this bottle examined.' But that would take time.

A call was put through to Dilip Roy's studio in Bombay; but the actor was in Switzerland, and air flights were not very frequent those days. It would be two or three days before he could return.

Miss Bean visited Rosie Roy every day, and so, occasionally, did Nandu and Mr Lobo. To everyone's relief and amazement, Rosie made a good recovery. There were crystals of strychnine at the bottom of that bottle, but they had only just begun to dissolve. Another evening's drinking and Rosie would have reached the fatal dose lying in wait for her. For it was obvious that someone had placed the poison in the bottle, and that someone could only have been Dilip Roy, before he had left Mussoorie. Far away at the time of his wife's expiry, he would have the perfect alibi.

Of course, nothing could be proven—all was surmise and conjecture—but Rosie was certain in her own mind that her husband had intended to do away with her in absentia, so to speak—and had very nearly succeeded.

She and Miss Bean had become fast friends, and Rosie found herself confiding all her fears and suspicions to the older person, and turning to her for advice and guidance.

∽

They sat together on the lawns of the Savoy, Rosie reclining in an easy chair, Miss Bean quite at ease on a wooden bench. From indoors came the tinkle of a piano as Mr Lobo played 'September Song'. Miss Bean sang the words softly, almost to herself:

But it's a long time from May to December,
And the days grown short when we reach September.
'That's a pretty song,' said Rosie. 'A little sad, though.'

'September is a sad month,' said Miss Bean musingly. 'The end of summer, the end of all those lovely picnics. Holding hands and paddling in mountain streams. Hot sunny days. And then all that rain—weeks of endless rain and mist. September brings back the sunshine if only for a short time, and then those icy winds will start coming down from the snows.'

'How romantic!' exclaimed Rosie. 'You are lucky to have lived here most of your life. Well, perhaps I'll come and join you when I've finished with that wretched husband of mine in Bombay.'

'What do you intend to do, my dear? Put arsenic in his vodka?'

'Arsenic is too slow. But if he eats enough of those chocolate-coated hazelnuts of which he is so fond, he could well come to a sticky end.'

'What do you mean, dear?'

'This is only for your ears, Auntie May.'

She addressed Miss Bean by her first name whenever she became trustful and confiding. 'I know you won't give me away—just in case something happens.'

'What could happen now?'

'Well, during the last two years I've been so miserable that I've always kept a little cyanide pill with me, just so that I can put an end to my life if it becomes too unbearable.'

'Oh, dear. Do throw it away. Don't even think of doing away with yourself.'

'Well, actually I did throw it away—got rid of it. I took the pill and gave it a nice coating of chocolate and then mixed it up with all the little hazelnut chocolates in the tin that Dilip always carries around.'

'Oh, but that was wicked of you. Quite diabolical! Understandable though, when you think of what he tried to do to you. But he could get to that chocolate pill any day. Pop it into his mouth, and then—'

'Pop off?' added Rosie, a glint in her hazel eyes.

'But it's been some time, hasn't it? Almost three weeks since he left. Someone else might have helped himself or herself to a chocolate—'

Just then they saw Nandu advancing across the lawn. It wasn't his usual amble, he looked very purposeful.

'Bad news,' he said, when he reached their sunny corner. 'I've just had a call from Dilip's manager. Your husband died last night. Suicide, it appears. Cyanide. He must have been feeling very guilty about what happened to you. I'm sorry for your loss, Rosie...'

∽

That evening Miss Bean dined with Rosie in the old
ballroom. It was the end of the season, and only a few
tables were occupied. Mr Lobo was at the piano, playing
nostalgic numbers.

'What will you have, Auntie May? You're my special
guest today. It's not that I want to celebrate or anything
like that—'

'I quite understand, my dear.'

'So you must have a decent wine, instead of that dreadful
crème-de-menthe you make in your room. Here's the wine
list.'

Miss Bean ran her eye down the wine list. She was no
blackmailer, but she couldn't help feeling a little surge of
power as she made her choice. And it was such a long time
since she'd enjoyed a really good wine. So she plumped
for the most expensive wine on the list, and sat back in
anticipation.

THE LAST TRUCK RIDE

[Twice a day Pritam Singh takes his battered old truck on the narrow, mountainous roads to the limestone quarry. He is in the habit of driving fast. The brakes of his truck are in good condition. What happens when a stray mule suddenly appears on the road?]

A horn blared, shattering the silence of the mountains, and a truck came round the bend in the road. A herd of goats scattered left and right.

The goatherds cursed as a cloud of dust enveloped them, and then the truck had left them behind and was rattling along the stony, unpaved hill road.

At the wheel of the truck, stroking his grey moustache, sat Pritam Singh, a turbaned Sikh. It was his own truck. He did not allow anyone else to drive it. Every day he made two trips to the limestone quarries, carrying truckloads of limestone back to the depot at the bottom of the hill. He was paid by the trip and he was always anxious to get in two trips every day.

Sitting beside him was Nathu, his cleaner-boy. Nathu was a sturdy boy, with a round cheerful face. It was difficult to guess his age. He might have been twelve or he might have been fifteen—he did not know himself, since no one in his village had troubled to record his birthday—but the hard life he led probably made him look older than his years. He belonged to the hills, but his village was far away, on the next range.

Last year the potato crop had failed. As a result there was no money for salt, sugar, soap and flour, and Nathu's parents and small brothers and sisters couldn't live entirely on the onions and artichokes which were about the only crops that had survived the drought. There had been no rain that summer. So Nathu waved goodbye to his people and came down to the town in the valley to look for work. Someone directed him to the limestone depot. He was too young to work at the quarries, breaking stones and loading them on the trucks; but Pritam Singh, one of the older drivers, was looking for someone to clean and look after his truck. Nathu looked like a bright, strong boy, and he was brought on board at ten rupees a day.

That had been six months ago, and now Nathu was an experienced hand at looking after trucks, riding in them and even sleeping in them. He got on well with Pritam Singh, the grizzled, fifty-year-old Sikh, who had well-to-do sons in Punjab, but whose sturdy independence kept him on the road in his battered old truck.

Pritam Singh pressed hard on his horn. Now there was no one on the road—no animals, no humans—but Pritam was fond of his horn and liked blowing it. It was music to his ears.

'One more year on this road,' said Pritam. 'Then I'll sell my truck and retire.'

'Who will buy this truck? said Nathu. 'It will retire before you do.'

'Don't be cheeky, boy. She's only twenty years old. There are still a few years left in her!' And as though to prove it, he blew his horn again. Its strident sound echoed and re-echoed down the mountain gorge. A pair of wild fowl, disturbed by the noise, flew out from the bushes and glided across the road in front of the truck.

Pritam Singh's thoughts went to his dinner. 'Haven't had a good meal for days,' he grumbled.

'Haven't had a good meal for weeks,' said Nathu, although he looked quite well fed.

'Tomorrow I'll give you dinner,' said Pritam. 'Tandoori chicken and pulao.'

'I'll believe it when I see it,' said Nathu.

Pritam Singh sounded his horn again before slowing

down. The road had become narrow and precipitous, and trotting ahead of them was a train of mules. As the horn blared, one mule ran forward, one ran backwards. One went uphill, one went downhill. Soon there were mules all over the place.

'You can never tell with mules,' said Pritam, after he had left them behind.

The hills were bare and dry. Much of the forest had long since disappeared. Just a few scraggy old oaks still grew on the steep hillside. This particular range was rich in limestone, and the hills were scarred by quarrying.

'Are your hills as bare as these?' asked Pritam.

'No, they have not started blasting there as yet,' said Nathu.

'We still have a few trees. And there is a walnut tree in front of our house, which gives us two baskets of walnuts every year'.

'And do you have water?'

'There is a stream at the bottom of the hill. But for the fields, we have to depend on the rainfall. And there was no rain last year.'

'It will rain soon,' said Pritam. 'I can smell rain. It is coming from the north.'

'It will settle the dust.'

The dust was everywhere. The truck was full of it. The leaves of the shrubs and the few trees were thick with it. Nathu could feel the dust near his eyelids and on his lips. As they approached the quarries, the dust increased—but it was a different kind of dust now—whiter, stinging the eyes, irritating the nostrils—limestone dust, hanging in the air.

The blasting was in progress.

Pritam Singh brought the truck to a halt. 'Let's wait a bit,' he said.

They sat in silence, staring through the windscreen at the scarred cliffs about a hundred yards down the road. There was no sign of life around them.

Suddenly, the hillside blossomed outwards, followed by a sharp crack of explosives. Earth and rock hurtled down the hillside.

Nathu watched in awe as shrubs and small trees were flung into the air. It always frightened him—not so much the sight of the rocks bursting asunder, but the trees being flung aside and destroyed. He thought of his own trees at home—the walnut, the pines—and wondered if one day they would suffer the same fate and whether the mountains would all become a desert like this particular range. No trees, no grass, no water—only the choking dust of the limestone quarries.

Pritam Singh pressed hard on his horn again to let the people at the site know he was coming. Soon they were parked outside a small shed, where the contractor and the overseer were sipping cups of tea. A short distance away some labourers were hammering at chunks of rock, breaking them up into manageable blocks. A pile of stones stood ready for loading, while the rock that had just been blasted lay scattered about the hillside.

'Come and have a cup of tea,' called out the contractor.

'Get on with the loading,' said Pritam. 'I can't hang about all afternoon. There's another trip to make and it gets dark early these days.'

But he sat down on a bench and ordered two cups of tea from the stall owner. The overseer strolled over to the group of labourers and told them to start loading. Nathu let down the grid at the back of the truck.

Nathu stood back while the men loaded the truck with limestone rocks. He was glad that he was chubby: thin people seemed to feel the cold much more—like the contractor, a skinny fellow who was shivering in his expensive overcoat.

To keep himself warm, Nathu began helping the labourers with the loading.

'Don't expect to be paid for that,' said the contractor, for whom every extra paise spent was a paisa off his profits.

'Don't worry,' said Nadhu, 'I don't work for contractors. I work for Pritam Singh.'

'That's right,' called out Pritam. 'And mind what you say to Nathu—he's nobody's servant!'

It took them almost an hour to fill the truck with stones. The contractor wasn't happy until there was no space left for a single stone. Then four of the six labourers climbed on the pile of stones. They would ride back to the depot on the truck. The contractor, his overseer and the others would follow by jeep. 'Let's go!' said Pritam, getting behind the steering wheel. 'I want to be back here and then home by eight o'clock. I'm going to a marriage party tonight!'

Nathu jumped in beside him, banging his door shut. It never opened at a touch. Pritam always joked that his truck was held together with Sellotape.

He was in good spirits. He started his engine, blew his horn and burst into a song as the truck started out on the return journey.

The labourers were singing too, as the truck swung round the sharp bends of the winding mountain road. Nathu was feeling quite dizzy. The door beside him rattled on its hinges.

'Not so fast,' he said.

'Oh,' said Pritam, 'And since when did you become nervous about fast driving?'

'Since today,' said Nathu.

'And what's wrong with today?'

'I don't know. It's just that kind of day, I suppose.'

'You are getting old,' said Pritam. That's your trouble.'

'Just wait till you get to be my age,' said Nathu.

'No more cheek,' said Pritam, and stepped on the accelerator and drove faster. As they swung round a bend, Nathu looked out of his window. All he saw was the sky above and the valley below. They were very near the edge. But it was always like that on this narrow road. After a few more hairpin bends, the road started descending steeply to the valley.

'I'll just test the brakes,' said Pritam and jammed down on there so suddenly that one of the labourers almost fell off at the back.

They called out in protest.

'Hang on!' shouted Pritam.

'You're nearly home!'

'Don't try any shortcuts,' said Nathu.

Just then a stray mule appeared in the middle of the road. Pritam swung the steering wheel over to his right; but the road turned left, and the truck went straight over the edge.

As it tipped over, hanging for a few seconds on the edge of the cliff, the labourers leapt from the back of the truck.

The truck pitched forward, bouncing over the rocks, turning over on its side and rolling over twice before coming to rest against the trunk of a scraggy old oak tree. Had it missed the tree, the truck would have plunged a few hundred feet down to the bottom of the gorge.

Two labourers sat on the hillside, stunned and badly shaken.

The other two had picked themselves up and were running back to the quarry for help.

Nathu had landed in a bed of nettles. He was smarting all over, but he wasn't really hurt.

His first impulse was to get up and run back with the labourers. Then he realized that Pritam was still in the truck. If he wasn't dead, he would certainly be badly injured.

Nathu skidded down the steep slope, calling out, 'Pritam, Pritam, are you all right?

There was no answer.

Then he saw Pritam's arm and half his body jutting out of the open door of the truck. It was a strange position to be in, half in and half out. When Nathu came nearer, he saw Pritam was jammed in the driver's seat, held there by the steering wheel which was pressed hard against his chest. Nathu thought he was dead. But as he was about to turn away and clamber back up the hill, he saw Pritam open one blackened swollen eye. It looked straight up at Nathu.

'Are you alive?' whispered Nathu, terrified.

'What do you think?' muttered Pritam. He closed his eye again.

When the contractor and his men arrived, it took them almost an hour to get him to a hospital in the town. He had a broken collarbone, a dislocated shoulder and several fractured ribs. But the doctors said he was repairable—which was more than what could be said for his truck.

'The truck's finished,' said Pritam, when Nathu came to see him a few days later. 'Now 'I'll have to go home and live with my sons. But you can get work on another truck.'

'No,' said Nathu. 'I'm going home too.'

'And what will you do there?'

'I'll work on the land. It's better to grow things on the land than to blast things out of it.'

They were silent for some time.

'Do you know something?' said Pritam finally. 'But for that tree, the truck would have ended up at the bottom of the hill and I wouldn't be here, all bandaged up and talking to you. It was the tree that saved me. Remember that, boy.'

'I'll remember,' said Nathu.

PANTHER'S MOON

I

In the entire village, he was the first to get up. Even the dog, a big hill mastiff called Sheroo, was asleep in a corner of the dark room, curled up near the cold embers of the previous night's fire. Bisnu's tousled head emerged from his blanket. He rubbed the sleep from his eyes and sat up on his haunches. Then, gathering his wits, he crawled in the direction of the loud ticking that came from the battered little clock which occupied the second most honoured place in a niche in the wall. The most honoured place belonged to a picture of Ganesha, the god of learning, who had an elephant's head and a fat boy's body. Bringing his face close to the clock, Bisnu could just make out the hands. It was five o'clock. He had half an hour in which to get ready and leave.

He got up, in vest and underpants, and moved quietly towards the door. The soft tread of his bare feet woke Sheroo and the big black dog rose silently and padded behind the boy. The door opened and closed and then the boy and the dog were outside in the early dawn. The month was June and the nights were warm, even in the Himalayan valleys; but there was fresh dew on the grass. Bisnu felt the dew beneath his feet. He took a deep breath and began walking down to the stream.

The sound of the stream filled the small valley. At that early hour of the morning, it was the only sound; but Bisnu was hardly conscious of it. It was a sound he lived with and took for granted. It was only when he had crossed the hill, on his way to the town—and the sound of the stream grew distant—that he really began to notice it. And it was only when the stream was too far away to be heard that he really missed its sound.

He slipped out of his underclothes, gazed for a few moments at the goose pimples rising on his flesh, and then dashed into the shallow stream. As he went further in, the cold mountain water reached his loins and navel and he gasped with shock and pleasure. He drifted slowly with the current, swam across to a small inlet which formed a fairly deep pool and plunged into the water. Sheroo hated cold water at this early hour. Had the sun been up, he would not have hesitated to join Bisnu. Now he contented himself with sitting on a smooth rock and gazing placidly at the slim brown boy splashing about in the clear water, in the widening light of dawn.

Bisnu did not stay long in the water. There wasn't time. When he returned to the house, he found his mother up, making tea and chapattis. His sister, Puja, was still asleep. She was a little older than Bisnu, a pretty girl with large black eyes, good teeth and strong arms and legs. During the day, she helped her mother in the house and in the fields. She did not go to the school with Bisnu. But when he came home in the evenings, he would try teaching her some of the things he had learnt. Their father was dead. Bisnu, at twelve, considered himself the head of the family.

He ate two chapattis, after spreading butter-oil on them. He drank a glass of hot sweet tea. His mother gave two thick chapattis to Sheroo and the dog wolfed them down in a few minutes. Then she wrapped two chapattis and a gourd curry in some big green leaves and handed these to Bisnu. This was his lunch packet. His mother and Puja would take their meal afterwards.

When Bisnu was dressed, he stood with folded hands before the picture of Ganesha. Ganesha is the god who blesses all beginnings. The author who begins to write a new book, the banker who opens a new ledger, the traveller who starts on a journey, all invoke the kindly help of Ganesha. And as Bisnu made a journey every day, he never left without the goodwill of the elephant-headed god.

How, one might ask, did Ganesha get his elephant's head? When born, he was a beautiful child. Parvati, his mother, was so proud of him that she went about showing him to everyone.

Unfortunately she made the mistake of showing the child to that envious planet, Saturn, who promptly burnt off poor Ganesha's head. Parvati in despair went to Brahma, the Creator, for a new head for her son. He had no head to give her but advised her to search for some man or animal caught in a sinful or wrong act. Parvati wandered about until she came upon an elephant sleeping with its head the wrong way, that is, to the south. She promptly removed the elephant's head and planted it on Ganesha's shoulders, where it took root.

Bisnu knew this story. He had heard it from his mother. Wearing a white shirt and black shorts and a pair of worn white keds, he was ready for his long walk to school, five miles up the mountain.

His sister woke up just as he was about to leave. She pushed the hair away from her face and gave Bisnu one of her rare smiles.

'I hope you have not forgotten,' she said.

'Forgotten?' said Bisnu, pretending innocence. 'Is there anything I am supposed to remember?'

'Don't tease me. You promised to buy me a pair of bangles, remember? I hope you won't spend the money on sweets, as you did last time.'

'Oh, yes, your bangles,' said Bisnu. 'Girls have nothing better to do than waste money on trinkets. Now, don't lose your temper! I'll get them for you. Red and gold are the colours you want?'

'Yes, Brother,' said Puja gently, pleased that Bisnu had remembered the colours.

'And for your dinner tonight we'll make you something special. Won't we, Mother?'

'Yes. But hurry up and dress. There is some ploughing to be done today. The rains will soon be here, if the gods are kind.'

'The monsoon will be late this year,' said Bisnu. 'Mr Nautiyal, our teacher, told us so. He said it had nothing to do with the gods.'

'Be off, you are getting late,' said Puja, before Bisnu could begin an argument with his mother. She was diligently winding the old clock. It was quite light in the room. The sun would be up any minute.

Bisnu shouldered his school bag, kissed his mother, pinched his sister's cheeks and left the house. He started climbing the steep path up the mountainside. Sheroo bounded ahead; for he, too, always went with Bisnu to school.

Five miles to school. Every day, except Sunday, Bisnu walked five miles to school; and in the evening, he walked home again. There was no school in his own small village of Manjari, for the village consisted of only five families. The nearest school was at Kemptee, a small township on the bus route through the district of Garhwal. A number of boys walked to school, from distances of two or three miles; their villages were not quite as remote as Manjari. But Bisnu's village lay right at the bottom of the mountain, a drop of over two thousand feet from Kemptee. There was no proper road between the village and the town.

In Kemptee there was a school, a small mission hospital, a post office and several shops. In Manjari village there were none of these amenities. If you were sick, you stayed at home until you got well; if you were very sick, you walked or were carried to the hospital, up the five-mile path. If you wanted to buy something, you went without it; but if you wanted it very badly, you could walk the five miles to Kemptee.

Manjari was known as the Five-Mile Village.

Twice a week, if there were any letters, a postman came

to the village. Bisnu usually passed the postman on his way to and from school.

There were other boys in Manjari village, but Bisnu was the only one who went to school. His mother would not have fussed if he had stayed at home and worked in the fields. That was what the other boys did; all except lazy Chittru, who preferred fishing in the stream or helping himself to the fruit off other people's trees. But Bisnu went to school. He went because he wanted to. No one could force him to go; and no one could stop him from going. He had set his heart on receiving a good schooling. He wanted to read and write as well as anyone in the big world, the world that seemed to begin only where the mountains ended. He felt cut off from the world in his small valley. He would rather live at the top of a mountain than at the bottom of one. That was why he liked climbing to Kemptee, it took him to the top of the mountain; and from its ridge he could look down on his own valley to the north and to the wide endless plains stretching towards the south.

The plainsman looks to the hills for the needs of his spirit but the hillman looks to the plains for a living. Leaving the village and the fields below him, Bisnu climbed steadily up the bare hillside, now dry and brown. By the time the sun was up, he had entered the welcome shade of an oak and rhododendron forest. Sheroo went bounding ahead, chasing squirrels and barking at langurs.

A colony of langurs lived in the oak forest. They fed on oak leaves, acorns and other green things and usually remained in the trees, coming down to the ground only to play or bask in the sun. They were beautiful, supple-limbed animals, with black faces and silver-grey coats and long, sensitive tails. They leapt from tree to tree with great agility. The young ones wrestled on the grass like boys.

A dignified community, the langurs did not have the cheekiness or dishonest habits of the red monkeys of the plains; they did not approach dogs or humans. But they had grown used to Bisnu's comings and goings and did not fear him. Some of the older ones would watch him quietly, a little puzzled. They did not go near the town, because the Kemptee boys threw stones at them. And anyway, the oak forest gave them all the food they required. Emerging from the trees, Bisnu crossed a small brook. Here he stopped to drink the fresh clean water of a spring. The brook tumbled down the mountain and joined the river a little below Bisnu's village. Coming from another direction was a second path and at the junction of the two paths Sarru was waiting for him. Sarru came from a small village about three miles from Bisnu's and closer to the town. He had two large milk cans slung over his shoulders. Every morning he carried this milk to town, selling one can to the school and the other to Mrs Taylor, the lady doctor at the small mission hospital. He was a little older than Bisnu but not as well built.

They hailed each other and Sarru fell into step beside Bisnu. They often met at this spot, keeping each other company for the remaining two miles to Kemptee.

'There was a panther in our village last night,' said Sarru.

This information interested but did not excite Bisnu. Panthers were common enough in the hills and did not usually present a problem except during the winter months, when their natural prey was scarce. Then, occasionally, a panther would take to haunting the outskirts of a village, seizing a careless dog or a stray goat.

'Did you lose any animals?' asked Bisnu.

'No. It tried to get into the cowshed but the dogs set up an alarm. We drove it off.'

'It must be the same one which came around last winter. We lost a calf and two dogs in our village.'

'Wasn't that the one the shikaris wounded? I hope it hasn't become a cattle lifter.'

'It could be the same. It has a bullet in its leg. These hunters are the people who cause all the trouble. They think it's easy to shoot a panther. It would be better if they missed altogether but they usually wound it.'

'And then the panther's too slow to catch the barking deer and starts on our own animals.'

'We're lucky it didn't become a man-eater. Do you remember the man-eater six years ago? I was very small then. My father told me all about it. Ten people were killed in our valley alone. What happened to it?'

'I don't know. Some say it poisoned itself when it ate the headman of another village.'

Bisnu laughed. 'No one liked that old villain. He must have been a man-eater himself in some previous existence!' They linked arms and scrambled up the stony path. Sheroo began barking and ran ahead. Someone was coming down the path. It was Mela Ram, the postman.

II

'Any letters for us?' asked Bisnu and Sarru together. They never received any letters but that did not stop them from asking. It was one way of finding out who had received letters.

'You're welcome to all of them,' said Mela Ram, 'if you'll carry my bag for me.'

'Not today,' said Sarru. 'We're busy today. Is there a letter from Corporal Ghanshyam for his family?'

'Yes, there is a postcard for his people. He is posted on the Ladakh border now and finds it very cold there.'

Postcards, unlike sealed letters, were considered public property and were read by everyone. The senders knew that too, and so Corporal Ghanshyam Singh was careful to mention that he expected a promotion very soon. He wanted everyone in his village to know it.

Mela Ram, complaining of sore feet, continued on his way and the boys carried on up the path. It was eight o'clock when they reached Kemptee. Dr Taylor's outpatients were just beginning to trickle in at the hospital gate. The doctor was trying to prop up a rose creeper which had blown down during the night. She liked attending to her plants in the mornings, before starting on her patients. She found this helped her in her work. There was a lot in common between ailing plants and ailing people.

Dr Taylor was fifty, white-haired but fresh in the face and full of vitality. She had been in India for twenty years and ten of these had been spent working in the hill regions.

She saw Bisnu coming down the road. She knew about the boy and his long walk to school and admired him for his keenness and sense of purpose. She wished there were more like him.

Bisnu greeted her shyly. Sheroo barked and put his paws up on the gate.

'Yes, there's a bone for you,' said Dr Taylor. She often put aside bones for the big black dog, for she knew that Bisnu's people could not afford to give the dog a regular diet of meat—though he did well enough on milk and chapattis.

She threw the bone over the gate and Sheroo caught it before it fell. The school bell began ringing and Bisnu broke into a run.

Sheroo loped along behind the boy.

When Bisnu entered the school gate, Sheroo sat down on the grass of the compound. He would remain there until the lunch break. He knew of various ways of amusing himself during school hours and had friends among the bazaar dogs. But just then he didn't want company. He had his bone to get on with.

Mr Nautiyal, Bisnu's teacher, was in a bad mood. He was a keen rose grower and only that morning, on getting up and looking out of his bedroom window, he had been horrified to see a herd of goats in his garden. He had chased them down the road with a stick but the damage had already been done. His prize roses had all been consumed.

Mr Nautiyal had been so upset that he had gone without his breakfast. He had also cut himself whilst shaving. Thus, his mood had gone from bad to worse. Several times during the day, he brought down his ruler on the knuckles of any boy who irritated him. Bisnu was one of his best pupils. But even Bisnu irritated him by asking too many questions about a new sum which Mr Nautiyal didn't feel like explaining.

That was the kind of day it was for Mr Nautiyal. Most schoolteachers know similar days.

'Poor Mr Nautiyal,' thought Bisnu. 'I wonder why he's so upset. It must be because of his pay. He doesn't get much money. But he's a good teacher. I hope he doesn't take another job.'

But after Mr Nautiyal had eaten his lunch, his mood improved (as it always did after a meal) and the rest of the day passed serenely. Armed with a bundle of homework, Bisnu came out from the school compound at four o'clock and was immediately joined by Sheroo. He proceeded down the road in the company of several of his class-fellows. But he did not linger long in the bazaar. There were five miles to walk and he did not like to get home too late. Usually, he reached his house just as it was beginning to get dark.

Sarru had gone home long ago and Bisnu had to make the return journey on his own. It was a good opportunity to memorize the words of an English poem he had been asked to learn. Bisnu had reached the little brook when he remembered the bangles he had promised to buy for his sister.

'Oh, I've forgotten them again,' he said aloud. 'Now I'll catch it—and she's probably made something special for my dinner!'

Sheroo, to whom these words were addressed, paid no attention but bounded off into the oak forest. Bisnu looked around for the monkeys but they were nowhere to be seen.

'Strange,' he thought, 'I wonder why they have disappeared.'

He was startled by a sudden sharp cry, followed by a fierce yelp. He knew at once that Sheroo was in trouble. The noise came from the bushes down the khud, into which the dog had rushed but a few seconds previously.

Bisnu jumped off the path and ran down the slope

towards the bushes. There was no dog and not a sound. He whistled and called but there was no response. Then he saw something lying on the dry grass. He picked it up. It was a portion of a dog's collar, stained with blood. It was Sheroo's collar and Sheroo's blood.

Bisnu did not search further. He knew, without a doubt, that Sheroo had been seized by a panther. No other animal could have attacked so silently and swiftly and carried off a big dog without a struggle. Sheroo was dead—must have been dead within seconds of being caught and flung into the air. Bisnu knew the danger that lay in wait for him if he followed the blood trail through the trees. The panther would attack anyone who interfered with its meal.

With tears starting in his eyes, Bisnu carried on down the path to the village. His fingers still clutched the little bit of bloodstained collar that was all that was left to him of his dog.

III

Bisnu was not a very sentimental boy but he sorrowed for his dog who had been his companion on many a hike into the hills and forests. He did not sleep that night but turned restlessly from side to side, moaning softly. After some time he felt Puja's hand on his head. She began stroking his brow. He took her hand in his own and the clasp of her rough, warm familiar hand gave him a feeling of comfort and security.

Next morning, when he went down to the stream to bathe, he missed the presence of his dog. He did not stay long in the water. It wasn't as much fun when there was no Sheroo to watch him.

When Bisnu's mother gave him his food, she told him to be careful and hurry home that evening. A panther, even if it is only a cowardly lifter of sheep or dogs, is not to be trifled with. And this particular panther had shown some daring by seizing the dog even before it was dark.

Still, there was no question of staying away from school. If Bisnu remained at home every time a panther put in an appearance, he might just as well stop going to school altogether.

He set off even earlier than usual and reached the meeting of the paths long before Sarru. He did not wait for his friend because he did not feel like talking about the loss of his dog. It was not the day for the postman and so Bisnu reached Kemptee without meeting anyone on the way. He tried creeping past the hospital gate unnoticed, but Dr Taylor saw him and the first thing she said was: 'Where's Sheroo? I've got something for him.'

When Dr Taylor saw the boy's face, she knew at once that something was wrong.

'What is it, Bisnu?' she asked. She looked quickly up and down the road. 'Is it Sheroo?'

He nodded gravely.

'A panther took him,' he said.

'In the village?'

'No, while we were walking home through the forest. I did not see anything—but I heard.'

Dr Taylor knew that there was nothing she could say that would console him and she tried to conceal the bone which she had brought out for the dog, but Bisnu noticed her hiding it behind her back and the tears welled up in his eyes. He turned away and began running down the road.

His school-fellows noticed Sheroo's absence and questioned Bisnu. He had to tell them everything. They were full of sympathy but they were also quite thrilled at what had happened and kept pestering Bisnu for all the details. There was a lot of noise in the classroom, and Mr Nautiyal had to call for order. When he learnt what had happened, he patted Bisnu on the head and told him that he need not attend school for the rest of the day. But Bisnu did not want to go home. After school, he got into a fight with one of the boys, and that helped him forget.

IV

The panther that plunged the village into an atmosphere of gloom and terror may not have been the same panther that took Sheroo. There was no way of knowing and it would have made no difference, because the panther that came by night and struck at the people of Manjari was that most feared of wild creatures, a man-eater.

Nine-year-old Sanjay, son of Kalam Singh, was the first child to be attacked by the panther.

Kalam Singh's house was the last in the village and nearest the stream. Like the other houses, it was quite small, just a room above and a stable below, with steps leading up from outside the house. He lived there with his wife, two sons (Sanjay was the youngest) and little daughter Basanti, who had just turned three.

Sanjay had brought his father's cows home after grazing them on the hillside in the company of other children. He had also brought home an edible wild plant, which his mother cooked into a tasty dish for their evening meal. They had their food at dusk, sitting on the floor of their single room, and soon after settled down for the night. Sanjay curled up in his favourite spot, with his head near the door, where he got a little fresh air. As the nights were warm, the door was usually left a little ajar. Sanjay's mother piled ash on the embers of the fire and the family was soon asleep.

No one heard the stealthy padding of a panther approaching the door, pushing it wider open. But suddenly there were sounds of a frantic struggle, and Sanjay's stifled cries were mixed with the grunts of the panther. Kalam Singh leapt to his feet with a shout. The panther had dragged Sanjay out of the door and was pulling him down the steps, when Kalam Singh started battering at the animal with a large stone. The rest of the family screamed in terror, rousing the entire village. A number of men came to Kalam Singh's assistance and the panther was driven off. But Sanjay lay unconscious.

Someone brought a lantern and the boy's mother screamed when she saw her small son with his head lying in a pool of blood. It looked as if the side of his head had been eaten off by the panther. But he was still alive, and as Kalam Singh plastered ash on the boy's head to stop the bleeding, he found that though the scalp had been torn off one side of the head, the bare bone was smooth and unbroken.

'He won't live through the night,' said a neighbour. 'We'll have to carry him down to the river in the morning.'

The dead were always cremated on the banks of a small river which flowed past Manjari village.

Suddenly the panther, still prowling about the village, called out in rage and frustration, and the villagers rushed to their homes in panic and barricaded themselves in for the night.

Sanjay's mother sat by the boy for the rest of the night, weeping and watching. Towards dawn he started to moan and show signs of coming round. At this sign of returning consciousness, Kalam Singh rose determinedly and looked around for his stick.

He told his elder son to remain behind with the mother and daughter, as he was going to take Sanjay to Dr Taylor at the hospital.

'See, he is moaning and in pain,' said Kalam Singh. 'That means he has a chance to live if he can be treated at once.'

With a stout stick in his hand, and Sanjay on his back, Kalam Singh set off on the two miles of hard mountain track to the hospital at Kemptee. His son, a bloodstained cloth around his head, was moaning but still unconscious. When at last Kalam Singh climbed up through the last fields below the hospital, he asked for the doctor and stammered out an account of what had happened.

It was a terrible injury, as Dr Taylor discovered. The bone over almost one-third of the head was bare and the scalp was torn all round. As the father told his story, the doctor cleaned and dressed the wound, and then gave Sanjay a shot of penicillin to prevent sepsis. Later, Kalam Singh carried the boy home again.

V

After this, the panther went away for some time. But the people of Manjari could not be sure of its whereabouts. They kept to their houses after dark and shut their doors. Bisnu had to stop going to school, because there was no one to accompany him and it was dangerous to go alone. This worried him because his final exam was only a few weeks away and he would be missing important classwork. When he wasn't in the fields, helping with the sowing of rice and maize, he would be sitting in the shade of a chestnut tree, going through his well-thumbed second-hand schoolbooks. He had no other reading, except for a copy of the Ramayana and a Hindi translation of *Alice in Wonderland*. These were well-preserved, read only in fits and starts and usually kept locked in his mother's old tin trunk.

Sanjay had nightmares for several nights and woke up screaming. But with the resilience of youth, he quickly recovered. At the end of the week he was able to walk to the hospital, though his father always accompanied him. Even a desperate panther will hesitate to attack a party of two. Sanjay, with his thin little face and huge bandaged head, looked a pathetic figure, but he was getting better and the wound looked healthy.

Bisnu often went to see him, and the two boys spent long hours together near the stream. Sometimes Chittru would join them, and they would try catching fish with a homemade net. They were often successful in taking home one or two mountain trout. Sometimes, Bisnu and Chittru wrestled in the shallow water or on the grassy banks of the stream. Chittru was a chubby boy with a broad chest, strong legs and thighs, and when he used his weight he got

Bisnu under him. But Bisnu was hard and wiry and had very strong wrists and fingers. When he had Chittru in a vice, the bigger boy would cry out and give up the struggle. Sanjay could not join in these games.

He had never been a very strong boy and he needed plenty of rest if his wounds were to heal well.

The panther had not been seen for over a week and the people of Manjari were beginning to hope that it might have moved on over the mountain or further down the valley.

'I think I can start going to school again,' said Bisnu. 'The panther has gone away.'

'Don't be too sure,' said Puja. 'The moon is full these days and perhaps it is only being cautious.'

'Wait a few days,' said their mother. 'It is better to wait. Perhaps you could go the day after tomorrow when Sanjay goes to the hospital with his father. Then you will not be alone.'

And so, two days later, Bisnu went up to Kemptee with Sanjay and Kalam Singh. Sanjay's wound had almost healed over. Little islets of flesh had grown over the bone. Dr Taylor told him that he need come to see her only once a fortnight, instead of every third day.

Bisnu went to his school and was given a warm welcome by his friends and by Mr Nautiyal.

'You'll have to work hard,' said his teacher. 'You have to catch up with the others. If you like, I can give you some extra time after classes.'

'Thank you, sir, but it will make me late,' said Bisnu. 'I must get home before it is dark, otherwise my mother will worry. I think the panther has gone but nothing is certain.'

'Well, you mustn't take risks. Do your best, Bisnu. Work hard and you'll soon catch up with your lessons.'

Sanjay and Kalam Singh were waiting for him outside the school. Together they took the path down to Manjari, passing the postman on the way. Mela Ram said he had heard that the panther was in another district and that there was nothing to fear. He was on his rounds again.

Nothing happened on the way. The langurs were back in their favourite part of the forest. Bisnu got home just as the kerosene lamp was being lit. Puja met him at the door with a winsome smile.

'Did you get the bangles?' she asked.

But Bisnu had forgotten again.

VI

There had been a thunderstorm and some rain—a short, sharp shower which gave the villagers hope that the monsoon would arrive on time. It brought out the thunder lilies— pink, crocus-like flowers which sprang up on the hillsides immediately after a summer shower.

Bisnu, on his way home from school, was caught in the rain. He knew the shower would not last, so he took shelter in a small cave and, to pass the time, began doing sums, scratching figures in the damp earth with the end of a stick.

When the rain stopped, he came out from the cave and continued down the path. He wasn't in a hurry. The rain had made everything smell fresh and good. The scent from fallen pine needles rose from the wet earth. The leaves of the oak trees had been washed clean and a light breeze turned them about, showing their silver undersides. The birds, refreshed and high-spirited, set up a terrific noise. The worst offenders were the yellow-bottomed bulbuls who squabbled and fought in the blackberry bushes. A barbet, high up in the branches of a deodar, set up its querulous, plaintive call. And a flock of bright green parrots came swooping down the hill to settle on a wild plum tree and feast on the unripe fruit. The langurs, too, had been revived by the rain. They leapt friskily from tree to tree, greeting Bisnu with little grunts.

He was almost out of the oak forest when he heard a faint bleating. Presently, a little goat came stumbling up the path towards him. The kid was far from home and must have strayed from the rest of the herd. But it was not yet conscious of being lost. It came to Bisnu with a hop, skip and a jump and started nuzzling against his legs like a cat.

'I wonder who you belong to,' mused Bisnu, stroking the little creature. 'You'd better come home with me until someone claims you.'

He didn't have to take the kid in his arms. It was used to humans and followed close at his heels. Now that darkness was coming on, Bisnu walked a little faster.

He had not gone very far when he heard the sawing grunt of a panther.

The sound came from the hill to the right and Bisnu judged the distance to be anything from a hundred to two hundred yards. He hesitated on the path, wondering what to do. Then he picked the kid up in his arms and hurried on in the direction of home and safety.

The panther called again, much closer now. If it was an ordinary panther, it would go away on finding that the kid was with Bisnu. If it was the man-eater, it would not hesitate to attack the boy, for no man-eater fears a human. There was no time to lose and there did not seem much point in running. Bisnu looked up and down the hillside. The forest was far behind him and there were only a few trees in his vicinity. He chose a spruce.

The branches of the Himalayan spruce are very brittle and snap easily beneath a heavy weight. They were strong enough to support Bisnu's light frame. It was unlikely they would take the weight of a full-grown panther. At least that was what Bisnu hoped.

Holding the kid with one arm, Bisnu gripped a low branch and swung himself up into the tree. He was a good climber. Slowly but confidently he climbed halfway up the tree, until he was about twelve feet above the ground. He couldn't go any higher without risking a fall.

He had barely settled himself in the crook of a branch when the panther came into the open, running into the clearing at a brisk trot. This was no stealthy approach, no wary stalking of its prey. It was the man-eater, all right. Bisnu felt a cold shiver run down his spine. He felt a little sick.

The panther stood in the clearing with a slight thrusting forward of the head. This gave it the appearance of gazing intently and rather short-sightedly at some invisible object in the clearing. But there is nothing short-sighted about a panther's vision. Its sight and hearing are acute.

Bisnu remained motionless in the tree and sent up a prayer to all the gods he could think of. But the kid began bleating. The panther looked up and gave its deep-throated, rasping grunt—a fearsome sound, calculated to strike terror in any tree-borne animal. Many a monkey, petrified by a panther's roar, has fallen from its perch to make a meal for Mr Spots. The man-eater was trying the same technique on Bisnu. But though the boy was trembling with fright, he clung firmly to the base of the spruce tree.

The panther did not make any attempt to leap into the tree. Perhaps, it knew instinctively that this was not the type of tree that it could climb. Instead, it described a semicircle round the tree, keeping its face turned towards Bisnu. Then it disappeared into the bushes.

The man-eater was cunning. It hoped to put the boy off his guard, perhaps entice him down from the tree. For, a few seconds later, with a half-pitched growl, it rushed back into the clearing and then stopped, staring up at the boy in some surprise. The panther was getting frustrated. It snarled, and putting its forefeet up against the tree trunk, began scratching at the bark in the manner of an ordinary domestic cat. The tree shook at each thud of the beast's paw.

Bisnu began shouting for help.

The moon had not yet come up. Down in Manjari village, Bisnu's mother and sister stood in their lighted doorway, gazing anxiously up the pathway. Every now and then, Puja would turn to take a look at the small clock.

Sanjay's father appeared in a field below. He had a

kerosene lantern in his hand.

'Sister, isn't your boy home as yet?' he asked.

'No, he hasn't arrived. We are very worried. He should have been home an hour ago. Do you think the panther will be about tonight? There's going to be a moon.'

'True, but it won't be dark for another hour. I will fetch the other menfolk and we will go up the mountain for your boy. There may have been a landslide during the rain. Perhaps the path has been washed away.'

'Thank you, brother. But arm yourselves, just in case the panther is about.'

'I will take my spear,' said Kalam Singh. 'I have sworn to spear that devil when I find him. There is some evil spirit dwelling in the beast and it must be destroyed!'

'I am coming with you,' said Puja.

'No, you cannot go,' said her mother. 'It's bad enough that Bisnu is in danger. You stay at home with me. This work is for men.'

'I shall be safe with them,' insisted Puja. 'I am going, Mother!'

And she jumped down the embankment into the field and followed Sanjay's father through the village.

Ten minutes later, two men armed with axes had joined Kalam Singh in the courtyard of his house and the small party moved silently and swiftly up the mountain path. Puja walked in the middle of the group, holding the lantern. As soon as the village lights were hidden by a shoulder of the hill, the men began to shout—both to frighten the panther, if it was about, and to give themselves courage.

Bisnu's mother closed the front door and turned to the image of Ganesha for comfort and help.

Bisnu's calls were carried on the wind and Puja and the men heard him while they were still half a mile away. Their own shouts increased in volume and, hearing their voices, Bisnu felt strength return to his shaking limbs. Emboldened by the approach of his own people, he began shouting insults at the snarling panther, then throwing twigs and small branches at the enraged animal. The kid added its bleats to the boy's shouts, the birds took up the chorus. The langurs squealed and grunted, the searchers shouted themselves hoarse and the panther howled with rage. The forest had never before been so noisy.

As the search party drew near, they could hear the panther's savage snarls, and hurried, fearing that perhaps Bisnu had been seized. Puja began to run.

'Don't rush ahead, girl,' said Kalam Singh. 'Stay between us.'

The panther, now aware of the approaching humans, stood still in the middle of the clearing, head thrust forward in a familiar stance. There seemed too many men for one panther. When the animal saw the light of the lantern dancing between the trees, it turned, snarled defiance and hate, and without another look at the boy in the tree, disappeared into the bushes. It was not yet ready for a showdown.

VII

Nobody turned up to claim the little goat, so Bisnu kept it. A goat was a poor substitute for a dog, but, like Mary's lamb, it followed Bisnu wherever he went, and the boy couldn't help being touched by its devotion. He took it down to the stream, where it would skip about in the shallows and nibble the sweet grass that grew on the banks.

As for the panther, frustrated in its attempt on Bisnu's life, it did not wait long before attacking another human.

It was Chittru who came running down the path one afternoon, bubbling excitedly about the panther and the postman.

Chittru, deeming it safe to gather ripe bilberries in the daytime, had walked about half a mile up the path from the village, when he had stumbled across Mela Ram's mailbag lying on the ground. Of the postman himself there was no sign. But a trail of blood led through the bushes.

Once again, a party of men headed by Kalam Singh and accompanied by Bisnu and Chittru, went out to look for the postman. But though they found Mela Ram's bloodstained clothes, they could not find his body. The panther had made no mistake this time.

It was to be several weeks before Manjari had a new postman.

A few days after Mela Ram's disappearance, an old woman was sleeping with her head near the open door of her house. She had been advised to sleep inside with the door closed but the nights were hot and anyway the old woman was a little deaf, and in the middle of the night, an hour before moonrise, the panther seized her by the throat. Her strangled cry woke her grown-up son, and all the men in the village woke up at his shouts and came running.

The panther dragged the old woman out of the house and down the steps, but left her when the men approached with their axes and spears, and made off into the bushes. The old woman was still alive and the men made a rough stretcher of bamboo and vines and started carrying her up the path. But they had not gone far when she began to cough, and because of her terrible throat wounds, her lungs collapsed and she died.

It was the 'dark of the month'—the week of the new moon when nights are darkest.

Bisnu, closing the front door and lighting the kerosene lantern, said, 'I wonder where that panther is tonight!'

The panther was busy in another village: Sarru's village.

A woman and her daughter had been out in the evening bedding the cattle down in the stable. The girl had gone into the house and the woman was following. As she bent down to go in at the low door, the panther sprang from the bushes. Fortunately, one of its paws hit the doorpost and broke the force of the attack, or the woman would have been killed. When she cried out, the men came round shouting and the panther slunk off. The woman had deep scratches on her back and was badly shocked.

The next day, a small party of villagers presented themselves in front of the magistrate's office at Kemptee and demanded that something be done about the panther. But the magistrate was away on tour and there was no one else in Kemptee who had a gun. Mr Nautiyal met the villagers and promised to write to a well-known shikari but said that it would be at least a fortnight before the shikari would be able to come.

Bisnu was fretting because he could not go to school. Most boys would be only too happy to miss school, but when you are living in a remote village in the mountains and having an education is the only way of seeing the world, you look forward to going to school, even if it is five miles from home. Bisnu's exams were only two weeks off and he didn't want to remain in the same class while the others were promoted. Besides, he knew he could pass even though he had missed a number of lessons. But he had to sit for the exams. He couldn't miss them.

'Cheer up, brother,' said Puja, as they sat drinking glasses of hot tea after their evening meal. 'The panther may go away once the rains break.'

'Even the rains are late this year,' said Bisnu. 'It's so hot and dry. Can't we open the door?'

'And be dragged down the steps by the panther?' said his mother. 'It isn't safe to have the window open, let alone the door.'

And she went to the small window—through which a cat would have found difficulty in passing—and bolted it firmly.

With a sigh of resignation, Bisnu threw off all his clothes except his underwear and stretched himself out on the earthen floor.

'We will be rid of the beast soon,' said his mother. 'I know it in my heart. Our prayers will be heard, and you shall go to school and pass your exams.'

To cheer up her children, she told them a humorous story

which had been handed down to her by her grandmother. It was all about a tiger, a panther and a bear, the three of whom were made to feel very foolish by a thief hiding in the hollow trunk of a banyan tree. Bisnu was sleepy and did not listen very attentively. He dropped off to sleep before the story was finished.

When he woke, it was dark and his mother and sister were asleep on the cot. He wondered what it was that had woken him. He could hear his sister's easy breathing and the steady ticking of the clock. Far away an owl hooted— an unlucky sign, his mother would have said; but she was asleep and Bisnu was not superstitious.

And then he heard something scratching at the door, and the hair on his head felt tight and prickly. It was like a cat scratching, only louder. The door creaked a little whenever it felt the impact of the paw—a heavy paw, as Bisnu could tell from the dull sound it made.

'It's the panther,' he muttered under his breath, sitting up on the hard floor.

The door, he felt, was strong enough to resist the panther's weight. And if he set up an alarm, he could rouse the village. But the middle of the night was no time for the bravest of men to tackle a panther.

In a corner of the room stood a long bamboo stick with a sharp knife tied to one end, which Bisnu sometimes used for spearing fish. Crawling on all fours across the room, he grasped the homemade spear, and then scrambling on to a cupboard, he drew level with the skylight window. He could get his head and shoulders through the window.

'What are you doing up there?' said Puja, who had woken up at the sound of Bisnu shuffling about the room.

'Be quiet,' said Bisnu. 'You'll wake Mother.'

Their mother was awake by now. 'Come down from there, Bisnu. I can hear a noise outside.'

'Don't worry,' said Bisnu, who found himself looking down on the wriggling animal which was trying to get its paw in under the door. With his mother and Puja awake, there was no time to lose.

He had got the spear through the window, and though he could not manoeuvre it so as to strike the panther's head, he brought the sharp end down with considerable force on the animal's rump.

With a roar of pain and rage the man-eater leapt down from the steps and disappeared into the darkness. It did not pause to see what had struck it. Certain that no human could have come upon it in that fashion, it ran fearfully to its lair, howling until the pain subsided.

VIII

A panther is an enigma. There are occasions when it proves itself to be the most cunning animal under the sun and yet the very next day it will walk into an obvious trap that no self-respecting jackal would ever go near. One day a panther will prove itself to be a complete coward and run like a hare from a couple of dogs and the very next it will dash in amongst half a dozen men sitting round a campfire and inflict terrible injuries on them.

It is not often that a panther is taken by surprise, as its power of sight and hearing are very acute. It is a master at the art of camouflage and its spotted coat is admirably suited for the purpose. It does not need heavy jungle to hide in. A couple of bushes and the light and shade from surrounding trees are enough to make it almost invisible.

Because the Manjari panther had been fooled by Bisnu, it did not mean that it was a stupid panther. It simply meant that it had been a little careless. And Bisnu and Puja, growing in confidence since their midnight encounter with the animal, became a little careless themselves.

Puja was hoeing the last field above the house and Bisnu, at the other end of the same field, was chopping up several branches of green oak, prior to leaving the wood to dry in the loft. It was late afternoon and the descending sun glinted in patches on the small river. It was a time of day when only the most desperate and daring of man-eaters would be likely to show itself.

Pausing for a moment to wipe the sweat from his brow, Bisnu glanced up at the hillside and his eye caught sight of a rock on the brow of the hill which seemed unfamiliar to him. Just as he was about to look elsewhere, the round rock began to grow and then alter its shape, and Bisnu watching in fascination was at last able to make out the head and forequarters of the panther. It looked enormous from the angle at which he saw it and for a moment he thought it was a tiger. But Bisnu knew instinctively that it was the man-eater.

Slowly, the wary beast pulled itself to its feet and began to walk round the side of the great rock. For a second it disappeared and Bisnu wondered if it had gone away. Then it reappeared and the boy was all excitement again. Very slowly and silently the panther walked across the face of the rock until it was in direct line with the corner of the field where Puja was working.

With a thrill of horror Bisnu realized that the panther was stalking his sister. He shook himself free from the spell which had woven itself round him and shouting hoarsely ran forward.

'Run, Puja, run!' he called. 'It's on the hill above you!'

Puja turned to see what Bisnu was shouting about. She saw him gesticulate to the hill behind her, looked up just in time to see the panther crouching for his spring.

With great presence of mind, she leapt down the banking of the field and tumbled into an irrigation ditch.

The springing panther missed its prey, lost its foothold on the slippery shale banking and somersaulted into the ditch a few feet away from Puja. Before the animal could recover from its surprise, Bisnu was dashing down the slope, swinging his axe and shouting, 'Maro, maro!'

Two men came running across the field. They, too, were

armed with axes. Together with Bisnu they made a half-circle around the snarling animal, which turned at bay and plunged at them in order to get away. Puja wriggled along the ditch on her stomach. The men aimed their axes at the panther's head and Bisnu had the satisfaction of getting in a well-aimed blow between the eyes. The animal then charged straight at one of the men, knocked him over and tried to get at his throat. Just then Sanjay's father arrived with his long spear. He plunged the end of the spear into the panther's neck.

The panther left its victim and ran into the bushes, dragging the spear through the grass and leaving a trail of blood on the ground.

The men followed cautiously—all except the man who had been wounded and who lay on the ground, while Puja and the other womenfolk rushed up to help him.

The panther had made for the bed of the stream and Bisnu, Sanjay's father and their companion were able to follow it quite easily. The water was red where the panther had crossed the stream and the rocks were stained with blood. After they had gone downstream for about a furlong, they found the panther lying still on its side at the edge of the water. It was mortally wounded but it continued to wave its tail like an angry cat. Then, even the tail lay still.

'It is dead,' said Bisnu. 'It will not trouble us again in this body.'

'Let us be certain,' said Sanjay's father and he bent down and pulled the panther's tail.

There was no response.

'It is dead,' said Kalam Singh. 'No panther would suffer such an insult were it alive!'

They cut down a long piece of thick bamboo and tied the panther to it by its feet. Then, with their enemy hanging upside down from the bamboo pole, they started back for the village.

'There will be a feast at my house tonight,' said Kalam

Singh. 'Everyone in the village must come. And tomorrow we will visit all the villages in the valley and show them the dead panther, so that they may move about again without fear.'

'We can sell the skin in Kemptee,' said their companion. 'It will fetch a good price.'

'But the claws we will give to Bisnu,' said Kalam Singh, putting his arm around the boy's shoulders. 'He has done a man's work today. He deserves the claws.'

A panther's or tiger's claws are considered to be lucky charms.

'I will take only three claws,' said Bisnu. 'One each for my mother and sister, and one for myself. You may give the others to Sanjay and Chittru and the smaller children.'

As the sun set, a big fire was lit in the middle of the village of Manjari and the people gathered round it, singing and laughing. Kalam Singh killed his fattest goat and there was meat for everyone.

IX

Bisnu was on his way home. He had just handed in his first paper, arithmetic, which he had found quite easy. Tomorrow it would be algebra, and when he got home he would have to practice square roots and cube roots and fractional coefficients.

Mr Nautiyal and the entire class had been happy that he had been able to sit for the exams. He was also a hero to them for his part in killing the panther. The story had spread through the villages with the rapidity of a forest fire, a fire which was now raging in Kemptee town.

When he walked past the hospital, he was whistling cheerfully.

Dr Taylor waved to him from the veranda steps.

'How is Sanjay now?' she asked.

'He is well,' said Bisnu.

'And your mother and sister?'

'They are well,' said Bisnu.

'Are you going to get yourself a new dog?'

'I am thinking about it,' said Bisnu. 'At present I have a baby goat—I am teaching it to swim!'

He started down the path to the valley. Dark clouds had gathered and there was a rumble of thunder. A storm was imminent.

'Wait for me!' shouted Sarru, running down the path behind Bisnu, his milk pails clanging against each other. He fell into step beside Bisnu.

'Well, I hope we don't have any more man-eaters for some time,' he said. 'I've lost a lot of money by not being able to take milk up to Kemptee.'

'We should be safe as long as a shikari doesn't wound another panther. There was an old bullet wound in the man-eater's thigh. That's why it couldn't hunt in the forest. The deer were too fast for it.'

'Is there a new postman yet?'

'He starts tomorrow. A cousin of Mela Ram's.'

When they reached the parting of their ways, it had begun to rain a little.

'I must hurry,' said Sarru. It's going to get heavier any minute.'

'I feel like getting wet,' said Bisnu. 'This time it's the monsoon, I'm sure.'

Bisnu entered the forest on his own and at the same time the rain came down in heavy opaque sheets. The trees shook in the wind and the langurs chattered with excitement.

It was still pouring when Bisnu emerged from the forest, drenched to the skin. But the rain stopped suddenly, just as the village of Manjari came into view. The sun appeared through a rift in the clouds. The leaves and the grass gave out a sweet, fresh smell.

Bisnu could see his mother and sister in the field transplanting the rice seedlings. The menfolk were driving the yoked oxen through the thin mud of the fields while the children hung on to the oxen's tails, standing on the plain wooden harrows, and with weird cries and shouts sending the animals almost at a gallop along the narrow terraces.

Bisnu felt the urge to be with them, working in the fields. He ran down the path, his feet falling softly on the wet earth. Puja saw him coming and waved at him. She met him at the edge of the field.

'How did you find your paper today?' she asked.

'Oh, it was easy.' Bisnu slipped his hand into hers and together they walked across the field. Puja felt something smooth and hard against her fingers, and before she could see what Bisnu was doing, he had slipped a pair of bangles on her wrist.

'I remembered,' he said with a sense of achievement.

Puja looked at the bangles and blurted out: 'But they are blue, Bhai, and I wanted red and gold bangles!' And then, when she saw him looking crestfallen, she hurried on: 'But they are very pretty and you did remember.... Actually, they are just as nice as red and gold bangles! Come into the house when you are ready. I have made something special for you.'

'I am coming,' said Bisnu, turning towards the house. 'You don't know how hungry a man gets, walking five miles to reach home!'

WILSON'S BRIDGE

The old wooden bridge has gone, and today an iron suspension bridge straddles the Bhagirathi as it rushes down the gorge below Gangotri. But villagers will tell you that you can still hear the hooves of Wilson's horse as he gallops across the bridge he had built 150 years ago. The legend of Wilson and his pretty hill bride, Gulabi, is still well known in this region.

I had joined some friends in the old forest rest house near the river. There were the Rays, recently married, and the Duttas, married many years. The younger Rays quarrelled frequently; the older Duttas looked on with more amusement than concern. I was a part of their group and yet something of an outsider. As a single man, I was a person of no importance. And as a marriage counsellor, I wouldn't have been of any use to them.

I spent most of my time wandering along the riverbanks or exploring the thick deodar and oak forests that covered the slopes. It was these trees that had made a fortune for Wilson and his patron, the Raja of Tehri. They had exploited the great forests to the full, floating huge logs downstream to the timber yards in the plains.

Returning to the rest house late one evening, I was halfway across the bridge when I saw a figure at the other end, emerging from the mist. Presently I made out a woman, wearing the plain dhoti of the hills; her hair fell loose over her shoulders. She appeared not to see me, and reclined against the railing of the bridge, looking down at the rushing waters far below. And then, to my amazement and horror, she climbed over the railing and threw herself into the river.

I ran forward, calling out, but I reached the railing only to see her fall into the foaming waters below, from where she was carried swiftly downstream.

The watchman's cabin stood a little way off. The door was open. The watchman, Ram Singh, was reclining on his bed, smoking a hookah.

'Someone just jumped off the bridge,' I said breathlessly. 'She's been swept down the river!'

The watchman was unperturbed. 'Gulabi again,' he said, almost to himself; and then to me, 'Did you see her clearly?'

'Yes, a woman with long loose hair—but I didn't see her face very clearly.'

'It must have been Gulabi. Only a ghost, my dear sir. Nothing to be alarmed about. Every now and then someone sees her throw herself into the river. Sit down,' he said, gesturing towards a battered old armchair, 'be comfortable and I'll tell you all about it.'

I was far from comfortable, but I listened to Ram Singh tell me the tale of Gulabi's suicide. After making me a glass of hot sweet tea, he launched into a long, rambling account of how Wilson, a British adventurer seeking his fortune, had been hunting musk deer when he encountered Gulabi on the path from her village. The girl's grey-green eyes and peach-blossom complexion enchanted him, and he went out of his way to get to know her people. Was he in love with her, or did he simply find her beautiful and desirable? We shall never really know. In the course of his travels and adventures he had known many women, but Gulabi was different, childlike and ingenuous, and he decided he would marry her. The humble family to which she belonged had no objection. Hunting had its limitations and Wilson found it more profitable to tap the region's great forest wealth. In a few years, he had made a fortune. He built a large timbered house at Harsil, another in Dehradun and a third at Mussoorie. Gulabi had all she could have wanted, including two robust little sons. When he was away on work, she looked after their children and their large apple orchard at Harsil.

And then came the evil day when Wilson met the

Englishwoman, Ruth, on the Mussoorie Mall, and decided
that she should have a share of his affections and his wealth.
A fine house was provided for her, too. The time he spent
at Harsil with Gulabi and his children dwindled. 'Business
affairs'—he was now one of the owners of a bank—kept
him in the fashionable hill resort. He was a popular host
and took his friends and associates on shikar parties in
the Doon.

Gulabi brought up her children in village style. She heard
stories of Wilson's dalliance with the Mussoorie woman
and, on one of his rare visits, she confronted him and
voiced her resentment, demanding that he leave the other
woman. He brushed her aside and told her not to listen
to idle gossip. When he turned away from her, she picked
up the flintlock pistol that lay on the gun table and fired
one shot at him. The bullet missed him and shattered her
looking glass. Gulabi ran out of the house, through the
orchard and into the forest, then down the steep path to
the bridge built by Wilson only two or three years before.
When he had recovered his composure, he mounted his horse
and came looking for her. It was too late. She had already
thrown herself off the bridge into the swirling waters far
below. Her body was found a mile or two downstream,
caught between some rocks.

This was the tale that Ram Singh told me, with various
flourishes and interpolations of his own. I thought it would
make a good story to tell my friends that evening, before the
fireside in the rest house. They found the story fascinating,
but when I told them I had seen Gulabi's ghost, they thought
I was doing a little embroidering of my own. Mrs Dutta
thought it was a tragic tale. Young Mrs Ray thought Gulabi
had been very silly. 'She was a simple girl,' opined Mr Dutta.
'She responded in the only way she knew...'; 'Money can't
buy happiness,' said Mr Ray. 'No,' said Mrs Dutta, 'but it
can buy you a great many comforts.' Mrs Ray wanted to
talk of other things, so I changed the subject. It can get a

little confusing for a bachelor who must spend the evening with two married couples. There are undercurrents which he is aware of but not equipped to deal with.

I would walk across the bridge quite often after that. It was busy with traffic during the day, but after dusk there were only a few vehicles on the road and seldom any pedestrians. A mist rose from the gorge below and obscured the far end of the bridge. I preferred walking there in the evening, half expecting, half hoping to see Gulabi's ghost again. It was her face that I really wanted to see. Would she still be as beautiful as she was fabled to be?

It was on the evening before our departure that something happened that would haunt me for a long time afterwards.

There was a feeling of restiveness as our days there drew to a close. The Rays had apparently made up their differences, although they weren't talking very much. Mr Dutta was anxious to get back to his office in Delhi and Mrs Dutta's rheumatism was playing up. I was restless too, wanting to return to my writing desk in Mussoorie.

That evening I decided to take one last stroll across the bridge to enjoy the cool breeze of a summer's night in the mountains. The moon hadn't come up, and it was really quite dark, although there were lamps at either end of the bridge providing sufficient light for those who wished to cross over.

I was standing in the middle of the bridge, in the darkest part, listening to the river thundering down the gorge, when I saw the sari-draped figure emerging from the lamplight and making towards the railings.

Instinctively I called out, 'Gulabi!'

She half turned towards me, but I could not see her clearly. The wind had blown her hair across her face and all I saw was wildly staring eyes. She raised herself over the railing and threw herself off the bridge. I heard the splash as her body struck the water far below.

Once again I found myself running towards the part of the railing where she had jumped. And then someone was running towards the same spot, from the direction of the rest house. It was young Mr Ray.

'My wife!' he cried out. 'Did you see my wife?'

He rushed to the railing and stared down at the swirling waters of the river.

'Look! There she is!' He pointed at a helpless figure bobbing about in the water.

We ran down the steep bank to the river but the current had swept her on. Scrambling over rocks and bushes, we made frantic efforts to catch up with the drowning woman. But the river in that defile is a roaring torrent, and it was over an hour before we were able to retrieve poor Mrs Ray's body, caught in driftwood about a mile downstream.

She was cremated not far from where we found her and we returned to our various homes in gloom and grief, chastened but none the wiser for the experience.

If you happen to be in that area and decide to cross the bridge late in the evening, you might see Gulabi's ghost or hear the hoof beats of Wilson's horse as he canters across the old wooden bridge looking for her. Or you might see the ghost of Mrs Ray and hear her husband's anguished cry. Or there might be others. Who knows?

ON FAIRY HILL

Those little green lights that I used to see, twinkling away on Pari Tibba—there had to be a scientific explanation for them, I was sure. After dark we see or hear many things that seem mysterious, irrational. And then by the clear light of day we find that the magic, the mystery has an explanation after all.

But I did see those lights occasionally—late at night, when I walked home from town to my little cottage at the edge of the forest. They moved too fast for them to be torches or lanterns carried by people. And as there were no roads on Pari Tibba, they could not have been cycle or cart lamps. Someone told me there was phosphorus in the rocks, and that this probably accounted for the luminous glow emanating from the hillside late at night. Possibly; but I was not convinced.

My encounter with the little people happened by the light of day.

One morning, early in April, purely on an impulse I decided to climb to the top of Pari Tibba and look around for myself. It was springtime in the Himalayan foothills. The sap was rising—in the trees, in the grass, in the wild flowers, in my own veins. I took the path through the oak forest, down to the little steam at the bottom of the hill, and then up the steep slope of Pari Tibba, hill of the fairies.

It was quite a scramble getting to the top. The path ended at the stream. After that, I had to clutch at brambles and tufts of grass to make the ascent. Fallen pine needles, slippery underfoot, made it difficult to get a foothold. But finally I made it to the top—a grassy plateau fringed by pines and a few wild medlar trees now clothed in white blossom.

It was a pretty spot. And as I was hot and sweaty, I removed most of my clothing and lay down under a medlar to rest. The climb had been quite tiring. But a fresh breeze soon brought me back to life. It made a soft humming sound in the pines. And the grass, sprinkled with yellow buttercups, buzzed with the sound of crickets and grasshoppers.

After some time I stood up and surveyed the scene. To the north, Landour with its rusty red-roofed cottages; to the south, the wide valley and a silver stream flowing towards the Ganga. To the west, rolling hills, patches of forest, and a small village tucked into a fold of the mountain.

Disturbed by my presence, a barking deer ran across the clearing and down the opposite slope. A band of long-tailed blue magpies rose from the oak trees, glided across the knoll and settled in another strand of oaks.

I was alone. Alone with the wind and the sky. It had probably been months, possibly years, since any human had passed that way. The soft lush grass looked most inviting. I lay down again on the sun-warmed sward. Pressed and bruised by my weight, catmint and clover gave out a soft fragrance. A ladybird climbed up my leg and began to explore my body. A swarm of white butterflies fluttered around me.

I slept.

I have no idea how long I slept, but when I awoke it was to experience an unusual, soothing sensation all over my limbs, as though they were being gently stroked with rose petals.

All lethargy gone, I opened my eyes to find a little girl—or was it a woman?—about two inches high, sitting cross-legged on my chest and studying me intently. Her hair fell in long black tresses. Her skin was the colour of honey. Her firm little breasts were like tiny acorns. She held a buttercup, larger than her hand, and with it she was stroking my tingling flesh.

I was tingling all over. A sensation of sensual joy surged through my limbs.

A tiny boy—or man—completely naked, now joined the

elfin girl, and they held hands and looked into my eyes, smiling, their teeth little pearls, their lips soft petals of apricot blossom. Were these the nature spirits, the flower fairies I had often dreamt of? I raised my head and saw that there were scores of little people all over me—exploring my legs, thighs, waist and arms. Delicate, caring, gentle, caressing creatures. They wanted to love me!

Some of them were laving me with dew or pollen or some soft essence. I closed my eyes. Waves of pure physical pleasure swept over me. I had never known anything like it. My limbs turned to water. The sky revolved around me, and I must have fainted.

When I awoke, perhaps an hour later, the little people had gone. A fragrance of honeysuckle lingered in the air. A deep rumble overhead made me look up. Dark clouds had gathered, threatening rain. Had the thunder frightened them away, to their abode beneath the rocks and tree roots? Or had they simply tired of sporting with a strange newcomer? Mischievous they were; for when I looked around for my clothes I could not find them anywhere.

A wave of panic surged over me. I ran here and there, looking behind shrubs and tree trunks, but to no avail. My clothes had disappeared, along with the fairies—if, indeed, they were fairies!

It began to rain. Large drops cannoned off the dry rocks. Then it hailed and soon the slope was covered with ice. There was no shelter. Naked, I ran down the path to the stream. There was no one to see me—only a wild mountain goat, speeding away in the opposite direction. Gusts of wind slashed rain and hail across my face and body. Panting and shivering, I took shelter beneath an overhanging rock until the storm had passed. By then it was almost dusk and I was able to ascend the path to my cottage without encountering anyone, apart from a band of startled langurs, who chattered excitedly on seeing me.

I couldn't stop shivering, so I went straight to bed. I

slept a deep, dreamless sleep and woke up the next morning with a high fever.

Mechanically I dressed, made myself some breakfast and tried to get through the morning's chores. When I took my temperature I found it was a hundred and four. So I swallowed a tablet and went back to bed.

There I lay until late afternoon, when the postman's knocking woke me. I left my letters unopened on my desk (that in itself was unusual) and returned to my bed.

The fever lasted almost a week and left me weak and half-starved. I couldn't have climbed Pari Tibba again, even if I'd wanted to; but I reclined on my window seat and looked at the clouds drifting over that desolate hill. Desolate it seemed, and yet strangely inhabited. When it grew dark, I waited for those little green fairy lights to appear; but these, it seemed, were now to be denied to me.

And so I returned to my desk, my typewriter, my newspaper articles and correspondence. It was a lonely period in my life. My marriage hadn't worked out: my wife, fond of high society and averse to living with an unsuccessful writer in a remote cottage in the woods, was following her own, more successful career in Mumbai. I had always been rather half-hearted in my approach to making money, whereas she had always wanted more and more of it. She left me—left me with my books and my dreams...

Had it all been a dream, that strange episode on Pari Tibba? Had an overactive imagination conjured up those aerial spirits, those siddhas of the upper air? Or were they underground people, living deep within the bowels of the hill? If I was going to keep my sanity I knew I had better get on with the more mundane aspects of living—such as going into town to buy my groceries, mending the leaking roof, paying the electricity bill, plodding up to the post office and remembering to deposit the odd cheque that came my way. All the mundane things that made life so dull and dreary.

The truth is, what we commonly call life is not life at all.

Its routine and settled ways are the curse of life and we will do almost anything to get away from the trivial, even if it is only for a few hours of forgetfulness in alcohol, drugs, forbidden sex or golf. Some of us would even go underground with the fairies, those little people who have sought refuge in Mother Earth from mankind's killing ways; for they are as vulnerable as butterflies and flowers. All things beautiful are easily destroyed.

I am sitting at my window in the gathering dark, penning these stray thoughts, when I see them coming—hand in hand, walking on a swirl of mist, radiant, suffused with all the colours of the rainbow. For a rainbow has formed a bridge from them, from Pari Tibba, to the edge of my window.

I am ready to go, to love and be loved, in their secret lairs or in the upper air—far from the stifling confines of the world in which we toil...

Come, fairies, carry me away, to love me as you did that summer's day!

THE CHAKRATA CAT

Chakrata is a small hill station I roughly trek from one hill station to another, sometimes alone, sometimes in company. It would take me about five days to cover the distance. I was a leisurely walker. You couldn't enjoy a hike if you felt you had to catch a train at the end of it.

At Chakrata there was an old forest rest house where I would sometimes spend the night. Don't go looking for it now. It has fallen into disuse and been replaced by a new building closer to the tour.

Towards sunset, late that summer, I trudged up to the rest house and called out for the chowkidar. I forget his name. He was a grizzled old man, uncommunicative. If you told him you had just been chased by a bear, he would simply nod and say, 'You'd better rest, then. You must be tired.' Nothing about the bear!

Anyway, he opened up one of the bedrooms for me, prepared a modest meal (which I enjoyed, having eaten little all day) and offered to make a fire in the old fireplace.

Chakrata can be cold, even in September, and I offered to pay for the firewood if he would fetch some. He switched on the bedroom and veranda lights and then walked to the rear of the building to fetch some wood.

That was when I saw the cat.

It was a large black cat, and it was sitting before the fireplace, almost as though expecting a fire to be lit. I hadn't noticed it entering the room, and it did not pay much attention to me, just kept staring into the fireplace. Then, when it heard the chowkidar returning, it got up and left the room.

'You have a cat?' I asked, trying to make conversation while he lit the fire.

He shook his head. 'Cats come for rats,' he said, which

left me no wiser. And he took off, promising to bring me a cup of tea early next morning. There was a small bookshelf in a corner of the room, and I found an old favourite, *A Warning to the Curious* by M. R. James. These haunting stories of ghosts in old colleges kept me awake for a couple of hours; then I put out the light and got into bed.

I had forgotten about the cat.

Now I heard a soft purring as the cat jumped on to the bed and curled up near my feet. I am not particularly fond of cats and my first impulse was to kick it off the bed. Then I thought, well, it's probably used to sleeping in this room, especially with the fire lit. I'll let it be, as long as it doesn't start chasing rats in the middle of the night! And all it did was come a little closer to me, advancing from my feet to my knees, and purring loudly, as though quite satisfied with the situation.

I fell asleep and slept soundly. In fact, I must have slept for a couple of hours before I awoke to a feeling of wetness under my armpit. My vest was wet and something was sucking away at my flesh.

It was with a feeling of horror that I realized that the cat had crawled into bed with me, that it was now stretched out beside me and that it was licking away at my armpit with a certain amount of relish. For the purring was louder than ever.

I sat up in bed, flung the cat from me and made a dash for the light switch. As the light came on, I saw the cat standing at the foot of the bed, tail erect and hair on end. It was very angry. And then, for the space of five seconds at the most, its appearance changed and its head was that of a human—a woman, black-browed with flaring nostrils and large crooked ears, her lips full and drenched with blood—my blood!

The moment passed and it was a cat's head once again. She let out a howl, sprang from the bed and disappeared through the bathroom door.

My shirt and vest were soaked with blood. For over an hour the cat had been licking and sucking at my fragile skin, wearing it away until the blood oozed out. Cat or vampire or witches revenant? Or a combination of all three.

I went to the bathroom. The cat had taken off through an open window. I closed the window, bathed my wound and examined myself in the mirror.

I had not been bitten. There were no teeth marks, no scratches. The tongue, and constant licking, had done the damage.

I found some cotton-wool in my haversacks and used it to stop the trickle of blood from my armpit. Then I changed my vest and shirt and sat down on an easy chair to wait for dawn. It was three in the morning. I felt weak and fell asleep in my chair, to be awakened by the chowkidar knocking on my door with a cup of tea.

Chakrata is a lovely place, prettier than most hill stations, but I had no desire to stay there any longer. There was a bus to Dehradun at eight o'clock. I decided to cut my trek short and take the bus.

'Where's that cat of yours?' I asked the chowkidar before I left. He knew nothing about a cat. He did not care for cats. They were unlucky, the companions of evil spirits, creatures of the world of dead.

I did not stop to argue, but thanked him for his hospitality and took my leave.

The wound, if you can call it that, took some time to heal. The skin beneath my armpit was all crinkly for a few weeks, but the body heals itself, if given a chance to do so.

But what remains on my skin is a bright red mark, the size and shape of a cat's tongue. It's been there all these years and won't go away. I'll show it to you the next time you come to see me.

THE MONKEYS

I couldn't be sure, next morning, if I had been dreaming or if I had really heard dogs barking in the night and had seen them scampering about on the hillside below the cottage. There had been a golden cocker, a retriever, a peke, a dachshund, a black Labrador and one or two nondescripts. They had woken me with their barking shortly after midnight and had made so much noise that I had got out of bed and looked out of the open window. I saw them quite plainly in the moonlight, five or six dogs rushing excitedly through the bracket and long monsoon grass.

It was only because there had been so many breeds among the dogs that I felt a little confused. I had been in the cottage only a week, and I was already on nodding or speaking terms with most of my neighbours. Colonel Fanshawe, retired from the Indian army, was my immediate neighbour. He did keep a cocker, but it was black. The elderly Anglo-Indian spinsters who lived beyond the deodars kept only cats. (Though why cats should be the prerogative of spinsters, I have never been able to understand.) The milkman kept a couple of mongrels. And the Punjabi industrialist who had bought a former prince's palace—without ever occupying it—left the property in charge of a watchman who kept a huge Tibetan mastiff.

None of these dogs looked like the ones I had seen in the night.

'Does anyone here keep a retriever?' I asked Colonel Fanshawe, when I met him taking his evening walk.

'No one that I know of,' he said and gave me a swift, penetrating look from under his bushy eyebrows. 'Why, have you seen one around?'

'No, I just wondered. There are a lot of dogs in the area, aren't there?'

'Oh, yes. Nearly everyone keeps a dog here. Of course, every now and then a panther carries one off. Lost a lovely little terrier myself only last winter.'

Colonel Fanshawe, tall and red-faced, seemed to be waiting for me to tell him something more—or was he just taking time to recover his breath after a stiff uphill climb?

That night I heard the dogs again. I went to the window and looked out. The moon was at the full, silvering the leaves of the oak trees.

The dogs were looking up into the trees and barking. But I could see nothing in the trees, not even an owl.

I gave a shout, and the dogs disappeared into the forest.

Colonel Fanshawe looked at me expectantly when I met him the following day. He knew something about those dogs, of that I was certain; but he was waiting to hear what I had to say. I decided to oblige him.

'I saw at least six dogs in the middle of the night,' I said. 'A cocker, a retriever, a peke, a dachshund and two mongrels. Now, Colonel, I'm sure you must know whose they are.'

The Colonel was delighted. I could tell by the way his eyes glinted that he was going to enjoy himself at my expense. 'You've been seeing Miss Fairchild's dogs,' he said with smug satisfaction.

'Oh, and where does she live?'

'She doesn't, my boy. Died fifteen years ago.'

'Then what are her dogs doing here?'

'Looking for monkeys,' said the Colonel. And he stood back to watch my reaction.

'I'm afraid I don't understand,' I said.

'Let me put it this way,' said the Colonel. 'Do you believe in ghosts?'

'I've never seen any,' I said.

'But you have, my boy, you have. Miss Fairchild's dogs died years ago—a cocker, a retriever, a dachshund, a peke and two mongrels. They were buried on a little knoll under the oaks. Nothing odd about their deaths, mind you. They were all quite old, and didn't survive their mistress very long. Neighbours looked after them until they died.'

'And Miss Fairchild lived in the cottage where I stay? Was she young?'

'She was in her mid-forties, an athletic sort of woman, fond of the outdoors. Didn't care much for men. I thought you knew about her.'

'No, I haven't been here very long, you know. But what was it you said about monkeys? Why were the dogs looking for monkeys?'

'Ah, that's the interesting part of the story. Have you seen the langur monkeys that sometimes come to eat oak leaves?'

'No.'

'You will, sooner or later. There has always been a band of them roaming these forests. They're quite harmless really, except that they'll ruin a garden if given half a chance.... Well, Miss Fairchild fairly loathed those monkeys. She was very keen on her dahlias—grew some prize specimens—but the monkeys would come at night, dig up the plants and eat the dahlia bulbs. Apparently they found the bulbs much to their liking. Miss Fairchild would be furious. People who are passionately fond of gardening often go off balance when their best plants are ruined—that's only human, I suppose. Miss Fairchild set her dogs on the monkeys whenever she could, even if it was in the middle of the night. But the monkeys simply took to the trees and left the dogs barking.

'Then one day—or rather one night—Miss Fairchild took desperate measures. She borrowed a shotgun and sat up near a window. And when the monkeys arrived, she shot one of them dead.'

The Colonel paused and looked out over the oak trees which were shimmering in the warm afternoon sun.

'She shouldn't have done that,' he said.

'Never shoot a monkey. It's not only that they're sacred

to Hindus—but they are rather human, you know. Well, I must be getting on. Good day!' And the Colonel, having ended his story rather abruptly, set off at a brisk pace through the deodars.

I didn't hear the dogs that night. But the next day I saw the monkeys—the real ones, not ghosts. There were about twenty of them, young and old, sitting in the trees munching oak leaves. They didn't pay much attention to me, and I watched them for some time.

They were handsome creatures, their fur a silver-grey, their tails long and sinuous. They leapt gracefully from tree to tree and were very polite and dignified in their behaviour towards each other—unlike the bold, rather crude red monkeys of the plains. Some of the younger ones scampered about on the hillside, playing and wrestling with each other like schoolboys.

There were no dogs to molest them—and no dahlias to tempt them into the garden.

But that night, I heard the dogs again. They were barking more furiously than ever.

'Well, I'm not getting up for them this time,' I mumbled, and pulled the blanket over my ears.

But the barking grew louder and was joined by other sounds, a squealing and a scuffling.

Then suddenly, the piercing shriek of a woman rang through the forest. It was an unearthly sound, and it made my hair stand up.

I leapt out of bed and dashed to the window.

A woman was lying on the ground, three or four huge monkeys were on top of her, biting her arms and pulling at her throat. The dogs were yelping and trying to drag the monkeys off, but they were being harried from behind by others. The woman gave another bloodcurdling shriek, and I dashed back into the room, grabbed hold of a small axe and ran into the garden.

But everyone—dogs, monkeys and shrieking woman—

had disappeared, and I stood alone on the hillside in my pyjamas, clutching an axe and feeling very foolish.

The Colonel greeted me effusively the following day.

'Still seeing those dogs?' he asked in a bantering tone.

'I've seen the monkeys too,' I said.

'Oh, yes, they've come around again. But they're real enough, and quite harmless.'

'I know—but I saw them last night with the dogs.'

'Oh, did you really? That's strange, very strange.' The Colonel tried to avoid my eye, but I hadn't quite finished with him.

'Colonel,' I said. 'You never did get around to telling me how Miss Fairchild died.'

'Oh, didn't I? Must have slipped my memory. I'm getting old, don't remember people as well as I used to. But, of course, I remember about Miss Fairchild, poor lady. The monkeys killed her. Didn't you know? They simply tore her to pieces...'

His voice trailed off, and he looked thoughtfully at a caterpillar that was making its way up his walking stick. 'She shouldn't have shot one of them,' he said. 'Never shoot a monkey—they're rather human, you know...'

THE OVERCOAT

It was clear frosty weather, and as the moon came up over the Himalayan peaks, I could see that patches of snow still lay on the roads of the hill station. I would have been quite happy in bed, with a book and a hot-water bottle at my side, but I'd promised the Kapadias that I'd go to their party and I felt it would be churlish of me to stay away. I put on two sweaters, an old football scarf and an overcoat and set off down the moonlit road.

It was a walk of just over a mile to the Kapadias' house and I had covered about half the distance when I saw a girl standing in the middle of the road.

She must have been sixteen or seventeen. She looked rather old-fashioned—long hair, hanging to her waist, and a flummoxy sequined dress, pink and lavender, that reminded me of the photos in my Grandmother's family album. When I went closer, I noticed that she had lovely eyes and a winning smile.

'Good evening,' I said. 'It's a cold night to be out.'

'Are you going to the party?' she asked.

'That's right. And I can see from your lovely dress that you're going, too. Come along, we're nearly there.'

She fell into step beside me and we soon saw lights from the Kapadias' house shining brightly through the deodars. The girl told me her name was Julie. I hadn't seen her before but then, I'd only been in the hill station a few months.

There was quite a crowd at the party but no one seemed to know Julie. Everyone thought she was a friend of mine. I did not deny it. Obviously she was someone who was feeling lonely and wanted to be friendly with people. And she was certainly enjoying herself. I did not see her do much eating or drinking, but she flitted about from one group to another, talking, listening, laughing; and when the music began, she was dancing almost continuously, alone or with partners, it didn't matter which, she was completely wrapped up in the music.

It was almost midnight when I got up to go. I had drunk a fair amount of punch, and I was ready for bed. As I was saying goodnight to my hosts and wishing everyone a merry Christmas, Julie slipped her arm into mine and said she'd be going home, too.

When we were outside I said, 'Where do you live, Julie?'

'At Wolfsburn,' she said. 'At the top of the hill.'

'There's a cold wind,' I said. 'And although your dress is beautiful, it doesn't look very warm. Here, you'd better wear my overcoat. I've plenty of protection.'

She did not protest and allowed me to slip my overcoat over her shoulders. Then we started out on the walk home. But I did not have to escort her all the way. At about the spot where we had met, she said, 'There's a shortcut from here. I'll just scramble up the hillside.'

'Do you know it well?' I asked. 'It's a very narrow path.'

'Oh, I know every stone on the path. I use it all the time. And besides, it's a really bright night.'

'Well, keep the coat on,' I said. 'I can collect it tomorrow.'

She hesitated for a moment, then smiled and nodded at me. She then disappeared up the hill, and I went home alone.

The next day I walked up to Wolfsburn. I crossed a little brook, from which the house had probably got its name, and entered an open iron gate. But of the house itself little remained. Just a roofless ruin, a pile of stones, a shattered chimney, a few Doric pillars where a veranda had once stood.

Had Julie played a joke on me? Or had I found the wrong house?

I walked around the hill to the mission house where the Taylors lived, and asked old Mrs Taylor if she knew a girl called Julie.

'No, I don't think so,' she said. 'Where does she live?'

'At Wolfsburn, I was told. But the house is just a ruin.'

'Nobody has lived at Wolfsburn for over forty years. The Mackinnons lived there. One of the old families who settled here. But when their girl died...' She stopped and gave me a queer look. 'I think her name was Julie.... Anyway, when she died, they sold the house and went away. No one ever lived in it again, and it fell into decay. But it couldn't be the same Julie you're looking for. She died of consumption—there wasn't much you could do about it in those days. Her grave is in the cemetery, just down the road.'

I thanked Mrs Taylor and walked slowly down the road to the cemetery: not really wanting to know any more, but propelled forward almost against my will.

It was a small cemetery under the deodars. You could see the eternal snows of the Himalaya standing out against the pristine blue of the sky. Here lay the bones of forgotten Empire-builders—soldiers, merchants, adventurers, their wives and children. It did not take me long to find Julie's grave. It had a simple headstone with her name clearly outlined on it:

Julie Mackinnon
1923–39
With us one moment,
Taken the next
Gone to her Maker,
Gone to her rest.

Although many monsoons had swept across the cemetery wearing down the stones, they had not touched this little tombstone.

I was turning to leave when I caught a glimpse of something familiar behind the headstone. I walked round to where it lay.

Neatly folded on the grass was my overcoat.

TOPAZ

It seemed strange to be listening to the strains of 'The Blue Danube' while gazing out at the pine-clad slopes of the Himalaya, worlds apart. And yet the music of the waltz seemed singularly appropriate. A light breeze hummed through the pines and the branches seemed to move in time to the music. The record player was new but the records were old, picked up in a junk shop behind the Mall.

Below the pines there were oaks, and one oak tree in particular caught my eye. It was the biggest of the lot and stood by itself on a little knoll below the cottage. The breeze was not strong enough to lift its heavy old branches, but *something* was moving, swinging gently from the tree, keeping time to the music of the waltz, dancing...

It was someone hanging from the tree.

A rope oscillated in the breeze, the body turned slowly, turned this way and that, and I saw the face of a girl, her hair hanging loose, her eyes sightless, hands and feet limp; just turning, turning, while the waltz played on.

I turned off the player and ran downstairs.

Down the path through the trees and on to the grassy knoll where the big oak stood.

A long-tailed magpie took fright and flew out from the branches, swooping low across the ravine. In the tree there was no one, nothing. A great branch extended halfway across the knoll, and it was possible for me to reach up and touch it. A girl could not have reached it without climbing the tree.

As I stood there, gazing up into the branches, someone spoke behind me.

'What are you looking at?'

I swung round. A girl stood in the clearing, facing me. A girl of seventeen or eighteen; alive, healthy, with bright eyes and a tantalizing smile. She was lovely to look at. I hadn't seen such a pretty girl in years.

'You startled me,' I said. 'You came up so unexpectedly.'

'Did you see anything—in the tree?' she asked.

'I thought I saw someone from my window. That's why I came down. Did *you* see anything?'

'No.' She shook her head, the smile leaving her face for a moment. 'I don't see anything. But other people do—sometimes.'

'What do they see?'

'My sister.'

'Your *sister*?'

'Yes. She hanged herself from this tree. It was many years ago. But sometimes you can see her hanging there.'

She spoke matter-of-factly: whatever had happened seemed very remote to her.

We both moved some distance away from the tree. Above the knoll, on a disused private tennis court (a relic from the hill station's colonial past) was a small stone bench. She sat down on it: and, after a moment's hesitation, I sat down beside her.

'Do you live close by?' I asked.

'Further up the hill. My father has a small bakery.'

She told me her name—Hameeda. She had two younger brothers.

'You must have been quite small when your sister died.'

'Yes. But I remember her. She was pretty.'

'Like you.'

She laughed in disbelief. 'Oh, I am nothing to her. You should have seen my sister.'

'Why did she kill herself?'

'Because she did not want to live. That's the only reason, no? She was to have been married but she loved someone else, someone who was not of our own community. It's an old story and the end is always sad, isn't it?'

'Not always. But what happened to the boy—the one

she loved? Did he kill himself too?'

'No, he took a job in some other place. Jobs are not easy to get, are they?'

'I don't know. I've never tried for one.'

'Then what do you do?'

'I write stories.'

'Do people *buy* stories?'

'Why not? If your father can sell bread, I can sell stories.'

'People must have bread. They can live without stories.'

'No, Hameeda, you're wrong. People can't live without stories.'

∽

Hameeda! I couldn't help loving her. Just loving her. No fierce desire or passion had taken hold of me. It wasn't like that. I was happy just to look at her, watch her while she sat on the grass outside my cottage, her lips stained with the juice of wild bilberries. She chatted away—about her friends, her clothes, her favourite things.

'Won't your parents mind if you come here every day?' I asked.

'I have told them you are teaching me.'

'Teaching you what?'

'They did not ask. You can tell me stories.'

So I told her stories.

It was midsummer.

The sun glinted on the ring she wore on her third finger: a translucent golden topaz, set in silver.

'That's a pretty ring,' I remarked.

'You wear it,' she said, impulsively removing it from her hand. 'It will give you good thoughts. It will help you to write better stories.'

She slipped it on to my little finger.

'I'll wear it for a few days,' I said. 'Then you must let me give it back to you.'

On a day that promised rain I took the path down to

the stream at the bottom of the hill. There I found Hameeda gathering ferns from the shady places along the rocky ledges above the water.

'What will you do with them?' I asked.

'This is a special kind of fern. You can cook it as a vegetable.'

'Is it tasty?'

'No, but it is good for rheumatism.'

'Do you suffer from rheumatism?'

'Of course not. They are for my grandmother, she is very old.'

'There are more ferns further upstream,' I said. 'But we'll have to get into the water.'

We removed our shoes and began paddling upstream. The ravine became shadier and narrower, until the sun was almost completely shut out. The ferns grew right down to the water's edge. We bent to pick them but instead found ourselves in each other's arms; and sank slowly, as in a dream, into the soft bed of ferns, while overhead a whistling thrush burst out in a dark sweet song.

'It isn't time that's passing by,' it seemed to say. 'It is you and I. It is you and I...'

I waited for her the following day, but she did not come.

Several days passed without my seeing her.

Was she sick? Had she been kept at home? Had she been sent away? I did not even know where she lived, so I could not ask. And if I had been able to ask, what would I have said?

Then one day I saw a boy delivering bread and pastries at the little tea shop about a mile down the road. From the upward slant of his eyes, I caught a slight resemblance to Hameeda. As he left the shop, I followed him up the hill. When I came abreast of him, I asked: 'Do you have your own bakery?'

He nodded cheerfully, 'Yes. Do you want anything— bread, biscuits, cakes? I can bring them to your house.'

'Of course. But don't you have a sister? A girl called Hameeda?'

His expression changed. He was no longer friendly. He looked puzzled and slightly apprehensive.

'Why do you want to know?'

'I haven't seen her for some time.'

'We have not seen her either.'

'Do you mean she has gone away?'

'Didn't you know? You must have been away a long time. It is many years since she died. She killed herself. You did not hear about it?'

'But wasn't that her sister—your other sister?'

'I had only one sister—Hameeda—and she died, when I was very young. It's an old story, ask someone else about it.'

He turned away and quickened his pace, and I was left standing in the middle of the road, my head full of questions that couldn't be answered.

That night there was a thunderstorm. My bedroom window kept banging in the wind. I got up to close it and, as I looked out, there was a flash of lightning and I saw that frail body again, swinging from the oak tree.

I tried to make out the features, but the head hung down and the hair was blowing in the wind.

Was it all a dream?

It was impossible to say. But the topaz on my hand glowed softly in the darkness. And a whisper from the forest seemed to say, 'It isn't time that's passing by, my friend. It is you and I....'

GHOSTS OF THE SAVOY

The clock over the Savoy Bar is stationary at 8.20 and has been like that since the atomic bomb was dropped on Hiroshima fifty years ago. That's what Nandu tells me and I have no reason to disbelieve him. Many of his more outlandish statements often turn out to be true.

Almost any story about this old hotel in Mussoorie has a touch of the improbable about it, even when supported by facts. A previous owner, Mr McClintock, had a false nose—according to Nandu, who never saw it. So I checked with old Negi, who first came to work in the hotel as a room boy back in 1932 (a couple of years before I was born) and who, sixty years and two wives later, looks after the front office. Negi tells me it's quite true.

'I used to take McClintock-sahib his cup of cocoa last thing at night. After leaving his room I'd dash around to one of the windows and watch him until he went to bed. The last thing he did, before putting the light out, was to remove his false nose and place it on the bedside table. He never slept with it on. I suppose it bothered him whenever he turned over or slept on his face. First thing in the morning, before having his cup of tea, he'd put it on again. A great man, McClintock-sahib.'

'But how did he lose his nose in the first place?' I asked.

'Wife bit it off,' said Nandu.

'No, sir,' said Negi, whose reputation for telling the truth is proverbial. 'It was shot away by a German bullet during World War I. He got the Victoria Cross as compensation.'

'And when he died, was he wearing his nose?' I asked.

'No, sir,' said old Negi, continuing his tale with some relish. 'One morning when I took the sahib his cup of tea, I found him stone dead, *without his nose*! It was lying on the bedside table. I suppose I should have left it there, but

McClintock-sahib was a good man, I could not bear to have the whole world knowing about his false nose. So I stuck it back on his face and then went and informed the manager. A natural death, just a sudden heart attack. But I made sure that he went into his coffin with his nose attached!'

We all agreed that Negi was a good man to have around, especially in a crisis.

Mr McClintock's ghost is supposed to haunt the corridors of the hotel, but I have yet to encounter it. Will the ghost be wearing its nose? Old Negi thinks not (the false nose being man-made), but then he hasn't seen the ghost at close quarters, only receding into the distance between the two giant deodars on the edge of the Beer Garden. Those deodars have been there a couple of hundred years, before the hotel was built, before the hill station came up.

A lot of people who enter the bar look pretty far gone and sometimes I have difficulty distinguishing the living from the dead. But the real ghosts are those who manage to slip away without paying for their drinks.

I don't have to slip away. In the five or six years during which I have helped to prop up the Savoy Bar, I have seldom paid for a drink. That's the kind of friend I have in Nandu. You won't find a harsh word about him in these pages. I think he decided long ago that I was an adornment to the bar, and that, draped over a bar stool, I looked like Ray Milland in *The Lost Weekend*. (He won an Oscar for that, remember?)

As for the Man-from-Sail, who is usually parked on the next bar stool, he's no adornment, in spite of the Jackie Shroff-moustache. But I have to admit that he's skilful at pouring drinks, mixing cocktails and showing tipsy ladies to the powder room. He doesn't pay for his drinks either.

How, then, does dear Nandu survive? Obviously there are some real customers in the wings, and we help them feel at home, chatting them up and encouraging them to try the Royal Salute or even a glass of Beaujolais. I can rattle off the history of the hotel for anyone who wants to hear it; and as for the Man-from-Sail, he provides a free ambulance service for those who can't handle the hotel's hospitality. The Man-from-Sail is the town's number one blood donor, so if you come away from your transfusion with a bad hangover, you'll know whose blood is coursing around in your veins. But it's real Scotch, not the stuff they make at the bottom of the Sail mountain.

Nandu tells me that Pearl S. Buck, the Nobel laureate, stayed here for a few days in the early fifties. I looked up the hotel register and found that he was right as usual. As far as I know, Miss Buck did not record her impressions of the hotel or the town in any of her books. It's the sort of place people usually have something to say about. Like the correspondent of the *Melbourne Age* who complained because the roof had blown off his room during one of our equinoxal storms. A frivolous sort of complaint, to say the least. Nandu placated him by saying, 'Sir, in Delhi you can only get a five-star room. From your room here you can see all the stars!' And so he could, once the clouds had rolled away.

It's a windy sort of mountain, and in cyclonic storms our corrugated iron roofs are frequently blown away. Old Negi recalls that a portion of the Savoy roof once landed on St George's School, five miles away, at the height of the midsummer storm. In its flight it decapitated an early-morning fitness freak. Had anyone else told me the story, I wouldn't have believed it. But Negi's word is the real thing—as good as a sip of Johnnie Walker Blue Label.

And here's a limerick I wrote for Nandu and the Man-from-Sail:

> *There was a young man who could fix*
> *Anything in five minutes or six;*
> *His statue is found*
> *On Savoy's hallowed ground,*
> *With Nandu beside him, transfix'd!*

THE SKULL

I am not normally bothered by skeletons and old bones—they are, after all, just the chalky remains of the long dead—so when my nephew Anil came back from medical college with a well-preserved skull, it was no cause for alarm. He was a second year student, at times a bit of a prankster.

'I hope you didn't take it without permission,' I said, taking the skull in my hands and admiring its symmetry but without philosophizing upon it like Hamlet.

'Oh, the college is full of them,' said Anil. 'I just borrowed it for the vacation.' He placed it on the mantelpiece, among some of the awards and mementos (cheap brassware mostly) that had accumulated over the years, and I must say it livened up the shelf a little.

Anil had placed the skull at one end of the mantelpiece, and there it stood until we'd had our dinner. He settled down with a book while I poured myself a small glass of cognac before settling into an easy chair with a notebook on my knee. It was midsummer and the window was open, so that we could hear the crickets singing in the oak trees. My cottage was on the outskirts of Mussoorie, surrounded by Himalayan oak and maple.

I had been making some notes for an article on wild flowers. When I had finished my notes and my cognac, I looked up and noticed that the skull now stood in the centre of the mantelpiece.

'Did you move the skull?' I asked.

'No,' said Anil, looking up. 'I placed it at the end of the shelf.'

'Well, it's now in the middle. How did it get there?'

'You must have moved it yourself, without noticing. That was a stiff cognac you drank, Uncle.'

I let it pass, it did not seem important.

∽

People often dropped in to see me. Schoolteachers, visitors to the hill station, students, other writers, neighbours. During that week I had a number of visitors and of course everyone noticed the skull on the mantelpiece. Some were intrigued and wanted to know whose skull it was. One or two lady teachers were frightened by it. A fellow writer thought it was in bad taste, displaying human remains in my sitting room. One visitor offered to buy it.

I would gladly have sold the wretched thing but it belonged to Anil and he intended to take it back to Meerut. But when the time came to leave he forgot about the skull, his mind no doubt taken up with other matters—such as the daily phone calls he received from a girl student in Delhi. After seeing him off at the bus stop, I came home to find that the skull was still occupying pride of place on the mantelpiece.

I ignored it for a few days, and the skull didn't seem to mind that. It was receiving plenty of attention from visitors during the day.

But it was beginning to get on my nerves. Every evening, when I sat down to enjoy a whisky or a cognac, I would feel its empty eye sockets staring at me. And on one occasion, when I tried to change its position, my hand got caught in its jawbone and it was with some difficulty that I withdrew it.

Getting fed up of its presence, I decided to lock the thing away where it wouldn't be seen.

There was a wall cupboard in the room, where I kept my manuscripts, notebooks and writing materials, and there was plenty of space there for the skull. So I shifted it to the cupboard and made sure the doors were locked.

That evening I enjoyed my drink without being watched by that remnant of a human head. The crickets were singing, a nightjar was calling and a zephyr of a wind moved softly through the trees. I finished my article and went to bed in a happy frame of mind.

In the middle of the night I woke to a loud rattling sound. At first I thought it was a loose door latch or a wobbly drainpipe, then realized the noise was coming from the wall cupboard. A rat, perhaps? But no. As soon as I opened the cupboard door, out popped the skull, landing near my feet and bouncing away right across the drawing room.

For the sake of peace and quiet, I returned it to the mantelpiece. If a skull could smile, it would probably have done so. I went back to my bed and slept like a baby. It takes more than a dancing skull to keep me from enjoying a good night's sleep.

The next morning I got to work making up a parcel. Normally, I hate making parcels, they usually fall apart. But for once I took pleasure in making a parcel. I wrapped the skull in a plastic bag, then placed it in a strong cardboard box, wrapped this in brown parcel paper, used a liberal amount of Sellotape and addressed the package to Dr Anil at his medical college. Then I walked into town and handed it over to the registration clerk at the post office.

Rubbing my hands with satisfaction, I treated myself to fish and chips and an ice cream before setting out on the walk down the hill to my cottage.

I was about halfway down the steep path that leads to one of our famous schools when I heard something rattling down the slope behind me. At first I thought it was an empty tin but then I recognized my boon companion, that wretched skull, embellished with bits of wrapping paper and Sellotape, bouncing down the hill towards me. How did the skull get out of that parcel? I shall never know. Perhaps a nosy postal clerk had opened it to check the contents. I hope he got the fright of his life. I broke into a run, making a dash for the cottage door. But it was there before me, grinning up at me from a pot full of flowering petunias.

So back it went to its favourite place on the mantelpiece.

And there it remained for several weeks.

∽

The school's playing field was situated just above the path
to the cottage and during the football season I could hear
the boys kicking a football around.

One day a football escaped from the field and came
bouncing down the hillside, landing on a flower bed. The
match was over and no one bothered to come down to
retrieve the ball. But it gave me an idea. I removed the
bladder, stuffed the skull into the leather interior and tied it
up firmly. Then I had the football delivered to the school's
games master, with my compliments.

Nothing happened for a couple of days. There was no
shortage of footballs. Then in the middle of the game against
St George's College, a ball went out of the grounds and a
spare one was required.

The replacement did not bounce quite as well as the
previous one and it was inclined to spin around a lot and take
off in directions opposite to those intended. Also, it squeaked
whenever it received a kick and sometimes those squeaks
sounded a bit like screams of protest. The goalkeepers at
either end found the ball difficult to hold, it did its best to
elude their grasp. And more goals were scored by accident
rather than design. Finally, this eccentric ball was kicked
out of play and was replaced by another.

What happens to old footballs? I expect they finally fall
apart and end up in a dustbin.

In this case, the football found a new owner, for the
sports master was a kind man who gave away old bats,
balls and other worn-out stuff to the poor children of the
locality. A boy from a village near Rajpur was the recipient
of the battered football, and he and his friends carried it
away with a cheer, kicking it all the way down the steep
path, making so much noise that they did not hear the
groans of protest that issued from the battered old football.

Well, weeks passed, months passed, without the skull making a reappearance. But then something strange began to happen. I found myself missing that troublesome skull!

It had, after all, been company of a sort for a lonely writer living on his own on the edge of the forest. And when you have lived with someone for a long time, then, no matter how much you may quarrel or get on each other's nerves, a bond is formed and the strength of that bond can only be known when it is broken.

The skull had been sharing my life for over a year and now that it was gone, seemingly forever, my life seemed rather empty.

So I began searching for the skull. I enquired amongst the children down in Rajpur but they had long since lost the football. I made a round of all the junk shops in Dehradun, without any luck. There were lots of old footballs lying around, but not the one I wanted. And no, they didn't buy or sell human skulls.

Young Anil, the doctor, paid me a brief visit and found me looking depressed.

'What's the trouble?' he asked. 'You look as though you've just lost a friend.'

'I have, indeed,' I said. 'I miss that skull you gave me. It was company of a sort.'

'Well, I'll get you another. No shortage of skulls in my college.'

'No, I don't want another. I want the same skull. It had a personality of its own.'

Anil looked at me as though he thought I was going off my rocker. And perhaps I was.

And then one day, as I was walking down a busy street in neighbouring Saharanpur, I noticed a fortune teller plying his trade on the pavement. I don't believe in fortune telling but everyone has to make a living and telling fortunes seems to me a harmless way of doing it. And then I noticed that he had a skull beside him and that he would consult it before handing his customer a slip of paper with words of advice or encouragement written on it. It looked a bit like my skull but I couldn't be sure. All the kicking and manhandling it had received had possibly altered its appearance.

But, anyway, I gave the fortune teller some money and asked him for a prediction. He chanted something, then extracted a slip of paper from beneath the skull and handed it to me with a flourish.

I read the words printed neatly on the paper.

'Ullu ka patha', went the message, followed by 'Gadhe ka baccha!'

It was definitely my skull! Only an old friend could abuse me like that.

So I pleaded and haggled with the fortune teller, paid him a hundred rupees for the skull and carried it home in triumph.

And there it is today, decorating my mantelpiece, a little the worse for wear and with a silly grin on its skeletal face. To improve its looks I have placed an old cricket cap on its head.

Sometimes we don't value our friends until we lose them.

PART II

Himalayan Drama

BREAKFAST AT BAROG

It's well over seventy years that I actually breakfasted at Barog, that little railway station on the Kalka–Simla line; but last night I dreamt of it—dreamt of the station, the dining room, the hillside, and the long dark Barog tunnel—which meant that it had been present in my subconscious all these years and was now striving to come to the fore and revive a few poignant memories.

Should I go there again? The station is still there, and so is the tunnel. I'm told that the area has been built up over the years, so that it is now almost a mini hill station. That wouldn't surprise me. Our villages have become towns, our towns have become cities, and in a few years' time our country will be one vast megacity with a few parks here and there to remind us that this was once a green planet.

I don't remember any dwellings around Barog, just that one little station and its one little restaurant with a cook and a waiter and its one little stationmaster. No, such a small station couldn't have had someone as important as a stationmaster. Someone quite junior must have been in charge.

Never mind. It was the breakfast that was important. And that I was with my father and on my way to Simla and a boarding school. The boarding school was the least desirable part of the journey. It was almost two years since I had been in a school and I was perfectly happy to continue living in an ideal world where schools need not exist. The breakup of my parents' marriage had resulted in my being withdrawn from a convent school in Mussoorie and taken over by my father who was on active service with the RAF It was 1942 and World War II was at its peak. Against all regulations he kept me with him, but to do this he had to rent a flat in New Delhi. Most of the day he was at work and I would have the flat to myself, surrounded by books, gramophone records and stamp albums. Evenings I would help him with his stamp collection, for he was an avid collector. On weekends he would take me to see Delhi's historic monuments; there was no dearth of them. From the stamps I learned geography, from the monuments history, from the books literature. I learnt more in two years at home than I did in a year at school.

But finally he was transferred—first Colombo, then Karachi, then Calcutta—and it was no longer possible for me to share his quarters. I was admitted to Bishop Cotton's in Simla.

We took the railcar from Kalka. It glided over the rails without any of the huffing and puffing of the steam engine that dragged the little narrow gauge train up the steep mountain. I would be travelling in that train in the years to come, but on this, my first to Simla, I was given the luxury of the railcar.

It glided into the Barog station punctually at 10 a.m., in time for breakfast.

The Barog breakfast was already well known and I did full justice to it. I skipped the cornflakes and concentrated on the scrambled eggs and buttered toasts. There was bacon too, and honey and marmalade.

'Tuck in, Ruskin,' said my father, 'School breakfasts won't be half as good.'

He didn't eat much himself. There was a lot on his mind in those days, apart from his work. There was his estranged wife, my mother; my invalid sister, now with his mother in Calcutta; his frequent transfers; his own frequent attacks of malaria; and our future in India, once the War was over—for India's Independence was just around the corner.

'When do we get to Simla?' I asked, quite happy to remain in Barog forever.

'In a little over an hour. But first we go through the longest of all the tunnels on this line. It will take about five minutes. Time for you to make a wish.'

The railcar plunged into the tunnel and we were enveloped in the darkness of the mountain. I held my father's hand. A couple of soldiers sitting behind us broke into a song from an earlier war.

> *'Pack up your troubles in your old kitbag,*
> *And smile, smile, smile!'*

A glimmer of daylight appeared at the end of the tunnel and then we were out in the sunshine and the pine-scented air.

'Did you make your wish?' asked my father.

I nodded, 'I wished that my mother would come back.'

He was silent for a few moments. 'Do you miss her a lot?'

'I don't miss her,' I said firmly. 'I'm always happy with you. But you miss her all the time. I don't like to see you so sad.'

'I've often asked her to come back,' he said. 'But it's up to her. She wants a different kind of life.'

And that was true. She was still very young—in her late twenties—and she enjoyed parties and dances and a busy social life. My father was in his forties. He liked staying at home, listening to classical music. When he took a holiday, he went in search of rare butterflies. My mother was a butterfly too—pretty, merry, fluttering here and there—but most unwilling to be displayed in a butterfly museum.

I suppose for most of us, big or small, life is just a succession of making mistakes and we spend most of our time trying to rectify them. Marriage was a mistake for both my parents. And I was a product of that mistake!

In the time he had, my father did his best for me. And how proud I was of him when he accompanied me down to my new school! He was wearing his dark blue RAF uniform with its flying officer's stripes, and uniforms, especially officers' uniforms, made a great impression amongst schoolboys in those wartime days. I was received with respect and curiosity. Word went around that my father was a fighter pilot and that he'd shot down dozens of Japanese planes! He was another Biggles, that fictional aviator. Nothing could have been further from reality. My father did not fly at all. He worked for a unit called Codes and Cyphers, helping to create new codes or breaking down enemy codes. It was important work and secret work but there was no glamour about it.

Not that I was averse to the glamour of being Biggles Junior. In my previous school I'd been something of an outsider and the Irish nuns hadn't cared much for a quiet, sensitive boy. Here I was made to feel I belonged and in no time at all I made a number of friends. It was already halfway through the school year but I had no difficulty in catching up with my classmates.

This was 'prep' school—junior school—and certainly more fun than senior school, still a couple of years away, would ever be.... Still, I was always looking forward to the winter break, when I would be with my father again, for at least three months. And there he was, waiting at the Old Delhi railway station, as my train drew alongside the platform. He was still in Delhi, at Air Headquarters, and I made the most of my time with him. Connaught Place was close by, and two or three evenings every week, we would go to the cinema. There were four to choose from—the Regal, the Rivoli, the Odeon and the Plaza, all very new and smart and showing the latest films from Hollywood. I became a regular film buff. The bookshops were there too, and the record shops, and Wenger's with its confectionery and the Milk Bar with its milkshakes and Kwality with its ice creams. It was hard to believe that there was a world war going on in Europe and Asia and North Africa and the Pacific; or that the Quit India movement was at its height and that my father and I might have to leave the country in the near future. He spoke about it sometimes and of the possibility of my going to a school in England. We did not talk about my mother, but I noticed that he still kept a photograph of her in his desk drawer.

It was back to school in March, when the rhododendrons were in bloom. This time I went up with the school party, in the small train with its steam engine chugging slowly up the steep inclines. The journey took all day. We did stop briefly at Barog, but we were not allowed to get down from the train; one or two boys were certain to be left behind. I looked longingly at the little restaurant on the far side of the platform; but it was already teatime. Breakfast was for the railcar!

The school year rolled on. My father was transferred to Karachi and then to Calcutta. He had grown up in Calcutta and knew the city well. He wrote to me every week and in his last letter he told me what I could look forward to during the winter holidays—the New Market with its bookshops, the botanical gardens with its ancient banyan tree, the zoo, the riverfront, the great maidan where hundreds of people would be taking in the evening air.... I was hoping he would come up to see me during the autumn break, but instead I had news of another kind.

It must be difficult for a young schoolmaster, as yet untouched by tragedy, to tell a ten-year-old that he has just lost his father. Mr Murtough was given this onerous duty. And he did his best, mumbling something ridiculous about God needing my father more than I did and so on and so on...

My friends were more natural in expressing this sympathy—giving me their sweets or chocolates, offering to play games with me, talking to me in the middle of the night when they discovered I wasn't asleep.... For the future did look bleak. I wasn't sure where I would be going next—my Calcutta granny or my Dehra granny, or my mother and stepfather.... I did receive a letter from my mother, telling me that my father had died of the malaria that had plagued him for years; but it was an unemotional letter and it did little to bring me comfort.

But I did go to her when school closed for the winter and I was to spend the next few years in my stepfather's home. But that's another story.

I continued my school in Simla, and every year in March, the small train would take me and my schoolmates up the mountain, through numerous tunnels and winding gradients, forests of pine and deodar, and we always stopped at Barog, before the biggest tunnel of all. But I never made another wish when passing through that tunnel.

That was over seventy years ago.

Is the railcar still running on that line? And do they still serve breakfast at Barog?

They say you should see Venice before you die. Or better still, Varanasi. But I'll settle for that little station among the pines. And if my father is standing on the platform, waiting for me, ready to take me by the hand, I'll be a small boy again and that railcar will take us to a different destination altogether.

THE BLUE UMBRELLA

I

'Neelu! Neelu!' cried Binya.

She scrambled barefoot over the rocks, ran over the short summer grass, up and over the brow of the hill, all the time calling 'Neelu, Neelu!' Neelu—Blue—was the name of the blue-grey cow. The other cow, which was white, was called Gori, meaning Fair One. They were fond of wandering off on their own, down to the stream or into the pine forest, and sometimes they came back by themselves and sometimes they stayed away—almost deliberately, it seemed to Binya.

If the cows didn't come home at the right time, Binya would be sent to fetch them. Sometimes her brother, Bijju, went with her, but these days he was busy preparing for his exams and didn't have time to help with the cows.

Binya liked being on her own, and sometimes she allowed the cows to lead her into some distant valley, and then they would all be late coming home. The cows preferred having Binya with them, because she let them wander. Bijju pulled them by their tails if they went too far.

Binya belonged to the mountains, to this part of the Himalaya known as Garhwal. Dark forests and lonely hilltops held no terrors for her. It was only when she was in the market town, jostled by the crowds in the bazaar, that she felt rather nervous and lost. The town, five miles from the village, was also a pleasure resort for tourists from all over India.

Binya was probably ten. She may have been nine or even eleven, she couldn't be sure because no one in the village kept birthdays; but her mother told her she'd been born during a winter when the snow had come up to the windows, and that was just over ten years ago, wasn't it?

Two years later, her father had died, but his passing had made no difference to their way of life. They had three tiny terraced fields on the side of the mountain, and they grew potatoes, onions, ginger, beans, mustard and maize: not enough to sell in the town, but enough to live on.

Like most mountain girls, Binya was quite sturdy, fair of skin, with pink cheeks and dark eyes and her black hair tied in a pigtail. She wore pretty glass bangles on her wrists, and a necklace of glass beads. From the necklace hung a leopard's claw. It was a lucky charm, and Binya always wore it. Bijju had one, too, only his was attached to a string.

Binya's full name was Binyadevi, and Bijju's real name was Vijay, but everyone called them Binya and Bijju. Binya was two years younger than her brother.

She had stopped calling for Neelu; she had heard the cowbells tinkling, and knew the cows hadn't gone far. Singing to herself, she walked over fallen pine needles into the forest glade on the spur of the hill. She heard voices, laughter, the clatter of plates and cups, and stepping through the trees, she came upon a party of picnickers.

They were holidaymakers from the plains. The women were dressed in bright saris, the men wore light summer shirts, and the children had pretty new clothes. Binya, standing in the shadows between the trees, went unnoticed; for some time she watched the picnickers, admiring their clothes, listening to their unfamiliar accents, and gazing rather hungrily at the sight of all their food. And then her gaze came to rest on a bright blue umbrella, a frilly thing for women, which lay open on the grass beside its owner.

Now Binya had seen umbrellas before, and her mother had a big black umbrella which nobody used anymore because the field rats had eaten holes in it, but this was the first time Binya had seen such a small, dainty, colourful umbrella and she fell in love with it. The umbrella was like a flower, a great blue flower that had sprung up on the dry brown hillside.

She moved forward a few paces so that she could see the umbrella better. As she came out of the shadows into the sunlight, the picnickers saw her.

'Hello, look who's here!' exclaimed the older of the two women. 'A little village girl!'

'Isn't she pretty?' remarked the other. 'But how torn and dirty her clothes are!' It did not seem to bother them that Binya could hear and understand everything they said about her.

'They're very poor in the hills,' said one of the men.

'Then let's give her something to eat.' And the older woman beckoned to Binya to come closer.

Hesitantly, nervously, Binya approached the group.

Normally she would have turned and fled, but the attraction was the pretty blue umbrella. It had cast a spell over her, drawing her forward almost against her will.

'What's that on her neck?' asked the younger woman.

'A necklace of sorts.'

'It's a pendant—see, there's a claw hanging from it!'

'It's a tiger's claw,' said the man beside her. (He had never seen a tiger's claw.) 'A lucky charm. These people wear them to keep away evil spirits.' He looked to Binya for confirmation, but Binya said nothing.

'Oh, I want one too!' said the woman, who was obviously his wife.

'You can't get them in shops.'

'Buy hers, then. Give her two or three rupees, she's sure to need the money.'

The man, looking slightly embarrassed but anxious to please his young wife, produced a two-rupee note and offered it to Binya, indicating that he wanted the pendant in exchange. Binya put her hand to the necklace, half afraid that the excited woman would snatch it away from her. Solemnly she shook her head.

The man then showed her a five-rupee note, but again Binya shook her head.

'How silly she is!' exclaimed the young woman.

'It may not be hers to sell,' said the man. 'But I'll try again. How much do you want—what can we give you?' And he waved his hand towards the picnic things scattered about on the grass.

Without any hesitation Binya pointed to the umbrella.

'My umbrella!' exclaimed the young woman. 'She wants my umbrella. What cheek!'

'Well, you want her pendant, don't you?'

'That's different.'

'Is it?'

The man and his wife were beginning to quarrel with each other.

'I'll ask her to go away,' said the older woman.

'We're making such fools of ourselves.'

'But I want the pendant!' cried the other, petulantly.

And then, on an impulse, she picked up the umbrella and held it out to Binya.

'Here, take the umbrella!'

Binya removed her necklace and held it out to the young woman, who immediately placed it around her own neck. Then Binya took the umbrella and held it up. It did not look so small in her hands; in fact, it was just the right size.

She had forgotten about the picnickers, who were busy examining the pendant. She turned the blue umbrella this way and that, looked through the bright blue silk at the pulsating sun, and then, still keeping it open, turned and disappeared into the forest glade.

II

Binya seldom closed the blue umbrella. Even when she had it in the house, she left it lying open in a corner of the room. Sometimes Bijju snapped it shut, complaining that it got in the way. She would open it again a little later. It wasn't beautiful when it was closed.

Whenever Binya went out—whether it was to graze the

cows, or fetch water from the spring, or carry milk to the little tea shop on the Tehri road—she took the umbrella with her. That patch of skyblue silk could always be seen on the hillside.

Old Ram Bharosa (Ram the Trustworthy) kept the tea shop on the Tehri road. It was a dusty, un-metalled road. Once a day, the Tehri bus stopped near his shop and passengers got down to sip hot tea or drink a glass of curd. He kept a few bottles of Coca-Cola too, but as there was no ice, the bottles got hot in the sun and so were seldom opened. He also kept sweets and toffees, and when Binya or Bijju had a few coins to spare, they would spend them at the shop. It was only a mile from the village.

Ram Bharosa was astonished to see Binya's blue umbrella.

'What have you there, Binya?' he asked.

Binya gave the umbrella a twirl and smiled at Ram Bharosa. She was always ready with her smile, and would willingly have lent it to anyone who was feeling unhappy.

'That's a lady's umbrella,' said Ram Bharosa. 'That's only for memsahibs. Where did you get it?'

'Someone gave it to me—for my necklace.'

'You exchanged it for your lucky claw!'

Binya nodded.

'But what do you need it for? The sun isn't hot enough, and it isn't meant for the rain. It's just a pretty thing for rich ladies to play with!'

Binya nodded and smiled again. Ram Bharosa was quite right; it was just a beautiful plaything. And that was exactly why she had fallen in love with it.

'I have an idea,' said the shopkeeper. 'It's no use to you, that umbrella. Why not sell it to me? I'll give you five rupees for it.'

'It's worth fifteen,' said Binya.

'Well, then, I'll give you ten.'

Binya laughed and shook her head.

'Twelve rupees?' said Ram Bharosa, but without much hope.

Binya placed a five-paise coin on the counter.

'I came for a toffee,' she said.

Ram Bharosa pulled at his drooping whiskers, gave Binya a wry look, and placed a toffee in the palm of her hand. He watched Binya as she walked away along the dusty road. The blue umbrella held him fascinated, and he stared after it until it was out of sight.

The villagers used this road to go to the market town. Some used the bus, a few rode on mules and most people walked. Today, everyone on the road turned their heads to stare at the girl with the bright blue umbrella.

Binya sat down in the shade of a pine tree. The umbrella, still open, lay beside her. She cradled her head in her arms, and presently she dozed off. It was that kind of day, sleepily warm and summery.

And while she slept, a wind sprang up.

It came quietly, swishing gently through the trees, humming softly. Then it was joined by other random gusts, bustling over the tops of the mountains. The trees shook their heads and came to life. The wind fanned Binya's cheeks. The umbrella stirred on the grass.

The wind grew stronger, picking up dead leaves and sending them spinning and swirling through the air. It got into the umbrella and began to drag it over the grass. Suddenly it lifted the umbrella and carried it about six feet from the sleeping girl. The sound woke Binya.

She was on her feet immediately, and then she was leaping down the steep slope. But just as she was within reach of the umbrella, the wind picked it up again and carried it further downhill.

Binya set off in pursuit. The wind was in a wicked, playful mood. It would leave the umbrella alone for a few moments but as soon as Binya came near, it would pick up the umbrella again and send it bouncing, floating, dancing away from her.

The hill grew steeper. Binya knew that after twenty yards it would fall away in a precipice. She ran faster. And the wind ran with her, ahead of her, and the blue umbrella stayed up with the wind.

A fresh gust picked it up and carried it to the very edge of the cliff. There it balanced for a few seconds, before toppling over, out of sight.

Binya ran to the edge of the cliff. Going down on her hands and knees, she peered down the cliff face. About a hundred feet below, a small stream rushed between great boulders. Hardly anything grew on the cliff face—just a few stunted bushes, and, halfway down, a wild cherry tree growing crookedly out of the rocks and hanging across the chasm. The umbrella had stuck in the cherry tree.

Binya didn't hesitate. She may have been timid with strangers, but she was at home on a hillside. She stuck her bare leg over the edge of the cliff and began climbing down. She kept her face to the hillside, feeling her way with her feet, only changing her handhold when she knew her feet were secure. Sometimes she held on to the thorny bilberry bushes, but she did not trust the other plants, which came away very easily.

Loose stones rattled down the cliff. Once on their way, the stones did not stop until they reached the bottom of the hill; and they took other stones with them, so that there was soon a cascade of stones, and Binya had to be very careful not to start a landslide.

As agile as a mountain goat, she did not take more than five minutes to reach the crooked cherry tree. But the most difficult task remained—she had to crawl along the trunk of the tree, which stood out at right angles from the cliff. Only by doing this could she reach the trapped umbrella.

Binya felt no fear when climbing trees. She was proud of the fact that she could climb them as well as Bijju. Gripping the rough cherry bark with her toes, and using her knees as leverage, she crawled along the trunk of the projecting tree until she was almost within reach of the umbrella. She noticed with dismay that the blue cloth was torn in a couple of places.

She looked down, and it was only then that she felt afraid. She was right over the chasm, balanced precariously about eighty feet above the boulder-strewn stream. Looking down, she felt quite dizzy. Her hands shook, and the tree shook too. If she slipped now, there was only one direction in which she could fall—down, down, into the depths of that dark and shadowy ravine.

There was only one thing to do; concentrate on the patch of blue just a couple of feet away from her. She did not look down or up, but straight ahead, and willing herself forward, she managed to reach the umbrella.

She could not crawl back with it in her hands. So, after dislodging it from the forked branch in which it had stuck, she let it fall, still open, into the ravine below.

Cushioned by the wind, the umbrella floated serenely downwards, landing in a thicket of nettles.

Binya crawled back along the trunk of the cherry tree. Twenty minutes later, she emerged from the nettle clump, her precious umbrella held aloft. She had nettle stings all over her legs, but she was hardly aware of the smarting. She was as immune to nettles as Bijju was to bees.

III

About four years previously, Bijju had knocked a hive out of an oak tree, and had been badly stung on the face and legs. It had been a painful experience. But now, if a bee stung him, he felt nothing at all: he had been immunized for life!

He was on his way home from school. It was two o'clock and he hadn't eaten since six in the morning. Fortunately, the kingora bushes—the bilberries—were in fruit, and already Bijju's lips were stained purple with the juice of the wild, sour fruit.

He didn't have any money to spend at Ram Bharosa's shop, but he stopped there anyway to look at the sweets in their glass jars.

'And what will you have today?' asked Ram Bharosa.

'No money,' said Bijju.

'You can pay me later.'

Bijju shook his head. Some of his friends had taken sweets on credit, and at the end of the month they had found they'd eaten more sweets than they could possibly pay for! As a result, they'd had to hand over to Ram Bharosa some of their most treasured possessions—such as a curved knife for cutting grass, or a small hand-axe, or a jar for pickles, or a pair of earrings—and these had become the shopkeeper's possessions and were kept by him or sold in his shop.

Ram Bharosa had set his heart on having Binya's blue umbrella, and so naturally he was anxious to give credit to either of the children, but so far neither had fallen into the trap.

Bijju moved on, his mouth full of Kingora berries. Halfway home, he saw Binya with the cows. It was late evening, and the sun had gone down, but Binya still had the umbrella open. The two small rents had been stitched up by her mother.

Bijju gave his sister a handful of berries. She handed him the umbrella while she ate the berries.

'You can have the umbrella until we get home,' she said. It was her way of rewarding Bijju for bringing her the wild fruit.

Calling 'Neelu! Gori!' Binya and Bijju set out for home, followed at some distance by the cows.

It was dark before they reached the village, but Bijju still had the umbrella open.

෴

Most of the people in the village were a little envious of

Binya's blue umbrella. No one else had ever possessed one like it. The schoolmaster's wife thought it was quite wrong for a poor cultivator's daughter to have such a fine umbrella while she, a second-class BA, had to make do with an ordinary black one. Her husband offered to have their old umbrella dyed blue; she gave him a scornful look, and loved him a little less than before. The pujari, who looked after the temple, announced that he would buy a multi-coloured umbrella the next time he was in the town. A few days later he returned looking annoyed and grumbling that they weren't available except in Delhi. Most people consoled themselves by saying that Binya's pretty umbrella wouldn't keep out the rain, if it rained heavily; that it would shrivel in the sun, if the sun was fierce; that it would collapse in a wind, if the wind was strong; that it would attract lightning, if lightning fell near it; and that it would prove unlucky, if there was any ill luck going about. Secretly, everyone admired it.

Unlike the adults, the children didn't have to pretend. They were full of praise for the umbrella. It was so light, so pretty, so bright a blue! And it was just the right size for Binya. They knew that if they said nice things about the umbrella, Binya would smile and give it to them to hold for a little while—just a very little while!

Soon it was the time of the monsoon. Big black clouds kept piling up, and thunder rolled over the hills.

Binya sat on the hillside all afternoon, waiting for the rain. As soon as the first big drop of rain came down, she raised the umbrella over her head. More drops, big ones, came pattering down. She could see them through the umbrella silk, as they broke against the cloth.

And then there was a cloudburst, and it was like standing under a waterfall. The umbrella wasn't really a rain umbrella, but it held up bravely. Only Binya's feet got wet. Rods of rain fell around her in a curtain of shivered glass.

Everywhere on the hillside people were scurrying for

shelter. Some made for a charcoal burner's hut, others for a mule-shed, or Ram Bharosa's shop. Binya was the only one who didn't run. This was what she'd been waiting for—rain on her umbrella—and she wasn't in a hurry to go home. She didn't mind getting her feet wet. The cows didn't mind getting wet either.

Presently she found Bijju sheltering in a cave. He would have enjoyed getting wet, but he had his schoolbooks with him and he couldn't afford to let them get spoilt. When he saw Binya, he came out of the cave and shared the umbrella. He was a head taller than his sister, so he had to hold the umbrella for her, while she held his books.

The cows had been left far behind.

'Neelu, Neelu!' called Binya.

'Gori!' called Bijju.

When their mother saw them sauntering home through the driving rain, she called out: 'Binya! Bijju! Hurry up, and bring the cows in! What are you doing out there in the rain?'

'Just testing the umbrella,' said Bijju.

IV

The rains set in, and the sun only made brief appearances. The hills turned a lush green. Ferns sprang up on walls and tree trunks. Giant lilies reared up like leopards from the tall grass. A white mist coiled and uncoiled as it floated up from the valley. It was a beautiful season, except for the leeches.

Every day, Binya came home with a couple of leeches fastened to the flesh of her bare legs. They fell off by themselves just as soon as they'd had their thimbleful of blood, but you didn't know they were on you until they fell off, and then, later, the skin became very sore and itchy. Some of the older people still believed that to be bled by leeches was a remedy for various ailments. Whenever Ram Bharosa had a headache, he applied a leech to his throbbing temple.

Three days of incessant rain had flooded out a number of small animals who lived in holes in the ground. Binya's mother suddenly found the roof full of field rats. She had to drive them out; they ate too much of her stored-up wheat flour and rice. Bijju liked lifting up large rocks to disturb the scorpions who were sleeping beneath. And snakes came out to bask in the sun.

Binya had just crossed the small stream at the bottom of the hill when she saw something gliding out of the bushes and coming towards her. It was a long black snake. A clatter of loose stones frightened it. Seeing the girl in its way, it rose up, hissing, prepared to strike. The forked tongue darted out, the venomous head lunged at Binya.

Binya's umbrella was open as usual. She thrust it forward, between herself and the snake, and the snake's hard snout thudded twice against the strong silk of the umbrella. The reptile then turned and slithered away over the wet rocks, disappearing into a clump of ferns.

Binya forgot about the cows and ran all the way home to tell her mother how she had been saved by the umbrella. Bijju had to put away his books and go out to fetch the cows. He carried a stout stick, in case he met with any snakes.

∽

First the summer sun, and now the endless rain, meant that the umbrella was beginning to fade a little. From a bright blue it had changed to a light blue. But it was still a pretty thing, and tougher than it looked, and Ram Bharosa still desired it. He did not want to sell it; he wanted to own it. He was probably the richest man in the area—so why shouldn't he have a blue umbrella? Not a day passed without his getting a glimpse of Binya and the umbrella; and the more he saw the umbrella, the more he wanted it.

The schools closed during the monsoon, but this didn't mean that Bijju could sit at home doing nothing. Neelu and Gori were providing more milk than was required at home, so Binya's mother was able to sell a kilo of milk every day: half a kilo to the schoolmaster, and half a kilo (at reduced rate) to the temple pujari. Bijju had to deliver the milk every morning.

Ram Bharosa had asked Bijju to work in his shop during the holidays, but Bijju didn't have time—he had to help his mother with the ploughing and the transplanting of the rice seedlings. So Ram Bharosa employed a boy from the next village, a boy called Rajaram. He did all the washing-up, and ran various errands. He went to the same school as Bijju, but the two boys were not friends.

One day, as Binya passed the shop, twirling her blue umbrella, Rajaram noticed that his employer gave a deep sigh and began muttering to himself.

'What's the matter, Babuji?' asked the boy.

'Oh, nothing,' said Ram Bharosa. 'It's just a sickness that has come upon me. And it's all due to that girl Binya and her wretched umbrella.'

'Why, what has she done to you?'

'Refused to sell me her umbrella! There's pride for you. And I offered her ten rupees.'

'Perhaps, if you gave her twelve...'

'But it isn't new any longer. It isn't worth eight rupees now. All the same, I'd like to have it.'

'You wouldn't make a profit on it,' said Rajaram.

'It's not the profit I'm after, wretch! It's the thing itself. It's the beauty of it!'

'And what would you do with it, Babuji? You don't visit anyone—you're seldom out of your shop. Of what use would it be to you?'

'Of what use is a poppy in a cornfield? Of what use is a rainbow? Of what use are you, numbskull? Wretch! I, too, have a soul. I want the umbrella, because—because I want its beauty to be mine!'

Rajaram put the kettle on to boil, began dusting the

counter, all the time muttering: 'I'm as useful as an umbrella,' and then, after a short period of intense thought, said: 'What will you give me, Babuji, if I get the umbrella for you?'

'What do you mean?' asked the old man.

'You know what I mean. What will you give me?'

'You mean to steal it, don't you, you wretch? What a delightful child you are! I'm glad you're not my son or my enemy. But look, everyone will know it has been stolen, and then how will I be able to show off with it?'

'You will have to gaze upon it in secret,' said Rajaram with a chuckle. 'Or take it into Tehri, and have it coloured red! That's your problem. But tell me, Babuji, do you want it badly enough to pay me three rupees for stealing it without being seen?'

Ram Bharosa gave the boy a long, sad look. 'You're a sharp boy,' he said. 'You'll come to a bad end. I'll give you two rupees.'

'Three,' said the boy.

'Two,' said the old man.

'You don't really want it, I can see that,' said the boy.

'Wretch!' said the old man. 'Evil one! Darkener of my doorstep! Fetch me the umbrella, and I'll give you three rupees.'

V

Binya was in the forest glade where she had first seen the umbrella. No one came there for picnics during the monsoon. The grass was always wet and the pine needles were slippery underfoot. The tall trees shut out the light, and poisonous-looking mushrooms, orange and purple, sprang up everywhere. But it was a good place for porcupines, who seemed to like the mushrooms, and Binya was searching for porcupine quills.

The hill people didn't think much of porcupine quills, but far away in southern India, the quills were valued as charms and sold at a rupee each. So Ram Bharosa paid a tenth of a rupee for each quill brought to him, and he in turn sold the quills at a profit to a trader from the plains.

Binya had already found five quills, and she knew there'd be more in the long grass. For once, she'd put her umbrella down. She had to put it aside if she was to search the ground thoroughly.

It was Rajaram's chance.

He'd been following Binya for some time, concealing himself behind trees and rocks, creeping closer whenever she became absorbed in her search. He was anxious that she should not see him and be able to recognize him later.

He waited until Binya had wandered some distance from the umbrella. Then, running forward at a crouch, he seized the open umbrella and dashed off with it.

But Rajaram had very big feet. Binya heard his heavy footsteps and turned just in time to see him as he disappeared between the trees. She cried out, dropped the porcupine quills, and gave chase.

Binya was swift and sure-footed, but Rajaram had a long stride. All the same, he made the mistake of running downhill. A long-legged person is much faster going uphill than down. Binya reached the edge of the forest glade in time to see the thief scrambling down the path to the stream. He had closed the umbrella so that it would not hinder his flight.

Binya was beginning to gain on the boy. He kept to the path, while she simply slid and leapt down the steep hillside. Near the bottom of the hill the path began to straighten out, and it was here that the long-legged boy began to forge ahead again.

Bijju was coming home from another direction. He had a bundle of sticks which he'd collected for the kitchen fire. As he reached the path, he saw Binya rushing down the hill as though all the mountain spirits in Garhwal were after her.

'What's wrong?' he called. 'Why are you running?'

Binya paused only to point at the fleeing Rajaram.

'My umbrella!' she cried. 'He has stolen it!'

Bijju dropped his bundle of sticks, and ran after his sister. When he reached her side, he said, 'I'll soon catch him!' and went sprinting away over the lush green grass. He was fresh, and he was soon well ahead of Binya and gaining on the thief.

Rajaram was crossing the shallow stream when Bijju caught up with him. Rajaram was the taller boy, but Bijju was much stronger. He flung himself at the thief, caught him by the legs, and brought him down in the water. Rajaram got to his feet and tried to drag himself away, but Bijju still had him by a leg. Rajaram overbalanced and came down with a great splash. He had let the umbrella fall. It began to float away on the current. Just then Binya arrived, flushed and breathless, and went dashing into the stream after the umbrella.

Meanwhile, a tremendous fight was taking place. Locked in fierce combat, the two boys swayed together on a rock, tumbled on to the sand, rolled over and over the pebbled bank until they were again thrashing about in the shallows of the stream. The magpies, bulbuls and other birds were disturbed, and flew away with cries of alarm.

Covered with mud, gasping and spluttering, the boys groped for each other in the water. After five minutes of frenzied struggle, Bijju emerged victorious.

Rajaram lay flat on his back on the sand, exhausted, while Bijju sat astride him, pinning him down with his arms and legs.

'Let me get up!' gasped Rajaram. 'Let me go—I don't want your useless umbrella!'

'Then why did you take it?' demanded Bijju. 'Come on—tell me why!'

'It was that skinflint Ram Bharosa,' said Rajaram.

'He told me to get it for him. He said if I didn't fetch it, I'd lose my job.'

By early October, the rains were coming to an end. The leeches disappeared. The ferns turned yellow, and the sunlight on the green hills was mellow and golden, like the limes on the small tree in front of Binya's home. Bijju's days were happy ones as he came home from school, munching on roasted corn. Binya's umbrella had turned a pale milky blue, and was patched in several places, but it was still the prettiest umbrella in the village, and she still carried it with her wherever she went.

The cold, cruel winter wasn't far off, but somehow October seems longer than other months, because it is a kind month: the grass is good to be upon, the breeze is warm and gentle and pine-scented. That October, everyone seemed contented—everyone, that is, except Ram Bharosa.

The old man had by now given up all hope of ever possessing Binya's umbrella. He wished he had never set eyes on it. Because of the umbrella, he had suffered the tortures of greed, the despair of loneliness. Because of the umbrella, people had stopped coming to his shop!

Ever since it had become known that Ram Bharosa had tried to have the umbrella stolen, the village people had turned against him. They stopped trusting the old man; instead of buying their soap and tea and matches from his shop, they preferred to walk an extra mile to the shops near the Tehri bus stand. Who would have dealings with a man who had sold his soul for an umbrella? The children taunted him, twisted his name around. From 'Ram the Trustworthy' he became 'Trusty Umbrella Thief'.

The old man sat alone in his empty shop, listening to the eternal hissing of his kettle and wondering if anyone would ever again step in for a glass of tea. Ram Bharosa had lost his own appetite, and ate and drank very little. There was no money coming in. He had his savings in a bank in Tehri, but it was a terrible thing to have to dip into them! To save money, he had dismissed the blundering Rajaram. So he was left without any company. The roof leaked and the wind got in through the corrugated tin sheets, but Ram Bharosa didn't care.

Bijju and Binya passed his shop almost every day. Bijju went by with a loud but tuneless whistle. He was one of the world's whistlers; cares rested lightly on his shoulders. But, strangely enough, Binya crept quietly past the shop, looking the other way, almost as though she was in some way responsible for the misery of Ram Bharosa.

She kept reasoning with herself, telling herself that the umbrella was her very own, and that she couldn't help it if others were jealous of it. But had she loved the umbrella too much? Had it mattered more to her than people mattered? She couldn't help feeling that, in a small way, she was the cause of the sad look on Ram Bharosa's face ('His face is a yard long,' said Bijju) and the ruinous condition of his shop. It was all due to his own greed, no doubt, but she didn't want him to feel too bad about what he'd done, because it made her feel bad about herself; and so she closed the umbrella whenever she came near the shop, opening it again only when she was out of sight.

One day towards the end of October, when she had ten paise in her pocket, she entered the shop and asked the old man for a toffee.

She was Ram Bharosa's first customer in almost two weeks. He looked suspiciously at the girl. Had she come to taunt him, to flaunt the umbrella in his face? She had placed her coin on the counter. Perhaps it was a bad coin. Ram Bharosa picked it up and bit it; he held it up to the light; he rang it on the ground. It was a good coin. He gave Binya the toffee.

Binya had already left the shop when Ram Bharosa saw the closed umbrella lying on his counter. There it was, the blue umbrella he had always wanted, within his grasp at last! He had only to hide it at the back of his shop, and no one would know that he had it, no one could prove that Binya had left it behind.

He stretched out his trembling, bony hand, and took the umbrella by the handle. He pressed it open. He stood beneath it, in the dark shadows of his shop, where no sun or rain could ever touch it.

'But I'm never in the sun or in the rain,' he said aloud. 'Of what use is an umbrella to me?'

And he hurried outside and ran after Binya.

'Binya, Binya!' he shouted. 'Binya, you've left your umbrella behind!'

He wasn't used to running, but he caught up with her, held out the umbrella, saying, 'You forgot it—the umbrella!'

In that moment it belonged to both of them.

But Binya didn't take the umbrella. She shook her head and said, 'You keep it. I don't need it anymore.'

'But it's such a pretty umbrella!' protested Ram Bharosa. 'It's the best umbrella in the village.'

'I know,' said Binya. 'But an umbrella isn't everything.'

And she left the old man holding the umbrella, and went tripping down the road, and there was nothing between her and the bright blue sky.

VI

Well, now that Ram Bharosa has the blue umbrella—a gift from Binya, as he tells everyone—he is sometimes persuaded to go out into the sun or the rain, and as a result he looks much healthier. Sometimes he uses the umbrella to chase away pigs or goats. It is always left open outside the shop, and anyone who wants to borrow it may do so; and so in a way it has become everyone's umbrella. It is faded and patchy, but it is still the best umbrella in the village.

People are visiting Ram Bharosa's shop again. Whenever Bijju or Binya stop for a cup of tea, he gives them a little extra milk or sugar. They like their tea sweet and milky.

A few nights ago, a bear visited Ram Bharosa's shop. There had been snow on the higher ranges of the Himalaya, and the bear had been finding it difficult to obtain food; so it had come lower down, to see what it could pick up near the village. That night it scrambled on to the tin roof of Ram Bharosa's shop, and made off with a huge pumpkin which had been ripening on the roof. But in climbing off the roof, the bear had lost a claw.

Next morning Ram Bharosa found the claw just outside the door of his shop. He picked it up and put it in his pocket. A bear's claw was a lucky find.

A day later, when he went into the market town, he took the claw with him, and left it with a silversmith, giving the craftsman certain instructions. The silversmith made a locket for the claw, then he gave it a thin silver chain. When Ram Bharosa came again, he paid the silversmith ten rupees for his work.

The days were growing shorter, and Binya had to be home a little earlier every evening. There was a hungry leopard at large, and she couldn't leave the cows out after dark.

She was hurrying past Ram Bharosa's shop when the old man called out to her.

'Binya, spare a minute! I want to show you something.'

Binya stepped into the shop.

'What do you think of it?' asked Ram Bharosa, showing her the silver pendant with the claw.

'It's so beautiful,' said Binya, just touching the claw and the silver chain.

'It's a bear's claw,' said Ram Bharosa. 'That's even luckier than a leopard's claw. Would you like to have it?'

'I have no money,' said Binya.

'That doesn't matter. You gave me the umbrella, I give you the claw! Come, let's see what it looks like on you.'

He placed the pendant on Binya, and indeed it looked very beautiful on her.

Ram Bharosa says he will never forget the smile she gave him when she left the shop.

She was halfway home when she realized she had left

the cows behind.

'Neelu, Neelu!' she called. 'Oh, Gori!'

There was a faint tinkle of bells as the cows came slowly down the mountain path.

In the distance she could hear her mother and Bijju calling for her.

She began to sing. They heard her singing, and knew she was safe and near.

She walked home through the darkening glade, singing of the stars, and the trees stood still and listened to her, and the mountains were glad.

THE FUNERAL

'I don't think he should go,' said Aunt M.

'He's too small,' concurred Aunt B. 'He'll get upset and probably throw a tantrum. And you know Padre Lal doesn't like having children at funerals.'

The boy said nothing. He sat in the darkest corner of the darkened room, his face revealing nothing of what he thought and felt. His father's coffin lay in the next room, the lid fastened forever over the tired, wistful countenance of the man who had meant so much to the boy. Nobody else had mattered—neither uncles nor aunts nor the fond grandparents. Least of all the mother who was hundreds of miles away with another husband. He hadn't seen her since he was four—that was just over five years ago—and he did not remember her very well.

The house was full of people—friends, relatives, neighbours. Some had tried to fuss over him but had been discouraged by his silence, the absence of tears. The more understanding of them had kept their distance.

Scattered words of condolence passed back and forth like dragonflies on the wind. 'Such a tragedy!...' 'Only forty...' 'No one realized how serious it was...' 'Devoted to the child...'

It seemed to the boy that everyone who mattered in the hill station was present. And for the first time they had the run of the house for his father had not been a sociable man. Books, music, flowers and his stamp collection had been his main preoccupations, apart from the boy.

A small hearse, drawn by a hill pony, was led in at the gate and several able-bodied men lifted the coffin and manoeuvred it into the carriage. The crowd drifted away. The cemetery was about a mile down the road and those who did not have cars would have to walk the distance.

The boy stared through a window at the small procession passing through the gate. He'd been forgotten for the moment—left in care of the servants, who were the only ones to stay behind. Outside it was misty. The mist had crept up the valley and settled like a damp towel on the face of the mountain. Everyone was wet although it hadn't rained.

The boy waited until everyone had gone and then he left the room and went out on the veranda. The gardener, who had been sitting in a bed of nasturtiums, looked up and asked the boy if he needed anything. But the boy shook his head and retreated indoors. The gardener, looking aggrieved because of the damage done to the flower beds by the mourners, shambled off to his quarters. The sahib's death meant that he would be out of a job very soon. The house would pass into other hands. The boy would go to an orphanage. There weren't many people who kept gardeners these days. In the kitchen, the cook was busy preparing the only big meal ever served in the house. All those relatives, and the padre too, would come back famished, ready for a sombre but nevertheless substantial meal. He, too, would be out of a job soon; but cooks were always in demand.

The boy slipped out of the house by a back door and made his way into the lane through a gap in a thicket of dog roses. When he reached the main road, he could see the mourners wending their way round the hill to the cemetery. He followed at a distance.

It was the same road he had often taken with his father during their evening walks. The boy knew the name of almost every plant and wild flower that grew on the hillside. These, and various birds and insects, had been described and pointed out to him by his father.

Looking northwards, he could see the higher ranges of the Himalaya and the eternal snows. The graves in the cemetery were so laid out that if their incumbents did happen to rise one day, the first thing they would see would be the glint of the sun on those snow-covered peaks. Possibly the site had been chosen for the view. But to the boy it did not seem as if anyone would be able to thrust aside those massive tombstones and rise from their graves to enjoy the view. Their rest seemed as eternal as the snows. It would take an earthquake to burst those stones asunder and thrust the coffins up from the earth. The boy wondered why people hadn't made it easier for the dead to rise. They were so securely entombed that it appeared as though no one really wanted them to get out.

'God has need of your father...' With those words a well-meaning missionary had tried to console him.

And had God, in the same way, laid claim to the thousands of men, women and children who had been put to rest here in these neat and serried rows? What could he have wanted them for? Of what use are we to God when we are dead, wondered the boy.

The cemetery gate stood open but the boy leant against the old stone wall and stared down at the mourners as they shuffled about with the unease of a batsman about to face a very fast bowler. Only this bowler was invisible and would come up stealthily and from behind.

Padre Lal's voice droned on through the funeral service and then the coffin was lowered—down, deep down. The boy was surprised at how far down it seemed to go! Was that other, better world down in the depths of the earth? How could anyone, even a Samson, push his way back to the surface again? Superman did it in comics but his father was a gentle soul who wouldn't fight too hard against the earth and the grass and the roots of tiny trees. Or perhaps he'd grow into a tree and escape that way! 'If ever I'm put away like this,' thought the boy, 'I'll get into the root of a plant and then I'll become a flower and then maybe a bird will come and carry my seed away...I'll get out somehow!'

A few more words from the padre and then some of those present threw handfuls of earth over the coffin before moving away.

Slowly, in twos and threes, the mourners departed. The mist swallowed them up. They did not see the boy behind the wall. They were getting hungry.

He stood there until they had all gone. Then he noticed that the gardeners or caretakers were filling in the grave. He did not know whether to go forward or not. He was a little afraid. And it was too late now. The grave was almost covered.

He turned and walked away from the cemetery. The road stretched ahead of him, empty, swathed in mist. He was alone. What had his father said to him once? 'The strongest man in the world is he who stands alone.'

Well, he was alone, but at the moment he did not feel very strong.

For a moment he thought his father was beside him, that they were together on one of their long walks. Instinctively he put out his hand, expecting his father's warm, comforting touch. But there was nothing there, nothing, no one...

He clenched his fists and pushed them deep down into his pockets. He lowered his head so that no one would see his tears. There were people in the mist but he did not want to go near them, for they had put his father away.

'He'll find a way out,' the boy said fiercely to himself. 'He'll get out somehow!'

THE PLAYING FIELDS OF SIMLA

It had been a lonely winter for a twelve-year-old boy. I hadn't really got over my father's untimely death two years previously; nor had I as yet reconciled myself to my mother's marriage to the Punjabi gentleman who dealt in second-hand cars. The three-month winter break over, I was almost happy to return to my boarding school in Simla—that elegant hill station once celebrated by Kipling and soon to lose its status as the summer capital of the Raj in India.

It wasn't as though I had many friends at school. I had always been a bit of a loner, shy and reserved, looking out only for my father's rare visits—on his brief leaves from RAF duties—and to my sharing his tent or air force hutment outside Delhi or Karachi. Those unsettled but happy days would not come again. I needed a friend but it was not easy to find one among a horde of rowdy, pea-shooting fourth formers, who carved their names on desks and stuck chewing gum on the class teacher's chair. Had I grown up with other children, I might have developed a taste for schoolboy anarchy; but, in sharing my father's loneliness after his separation from my mother, I had turned into a premature adult. The mixed nature of my reading—Dickens, Richmal Crompton, Tagore and *Champion* and *Film Fun* comics—probably reflected the confused state of my life. A book reader was rare even in those pre-electronic times. On rainy days most boys played cards or Monopoly, or listened to Artie Shaw on the wind-up gramophone in the common room.

After a month in the fourth form I began to notice a new boy, Omar, and then only because he was a quiet, almost taciturn person who took no part in the form's feverish attempts to imitate the Marx Brothers at the circus. He showed no resentment at the prevailing anarchy nor did he make a move to participate in it. Once he caught me looking at him and he smiled ruefully, tolerantly. Did I sense another adult in the class? Someone who was a little older than his years?

Even before we began talking to each other, Omar and I developed an understanding of sorts, and we'd nod almost respectfully to each other when we met in the classroom corridors or the environs of the dining hall or dormitory. We were not in the same house. The house system practised its own form of apartheid, whereby a member of, say, Curzon House was not expected to fraternize with someone belonging to Rivaz or Lefroy! Those public schools certainly knew how to clamp you into compartments. However, these barriers vanished when Omar and I found ourselves selected for the School Colts' hockey team—Omar as a fullback, I as goalkeeper. I think a defensive position suited me by nature. In all modesty I have to say that I made a good goalkeeper, both at hockey and football. And fifty years on, I am still keeping goal. Then I did it between goalposts, now I do it off the field—protecting a family, protecting my independence as a writer...

The taciturn Omar now spoke to me occasionally and we combined well on the field of play. A good understanding is needed between goalkeeper and fullback. We were on the same wavelength. I anticipated his moves, he was familiar with mine. Years later, when I read Conrad's *The Secret Sharer,* I thought of Omar.

It wasn't until we were away from the confines of school, classroom and dining hall that our friendship flourished. The hockey team travelled to Sanawar on the next mountain range, where we were to play a couple of matches against our old rivals, the Lawrence Royal Military School. This had been my father's old school, but I did not know that in his time it had also been a military orphanage. Grandfather, who had been a private foot soldier—of the likes of Kipling's Mulvaney, Otheris and Learoyd—had joined the Scottish

Rifles after leaving home at the age of seventeen. He had died while his children were still very young, but my father's more rounded education had enabled him to become an officer.

Omar and I were thrown together a good deal during the visit to Sanawar, and in our more leisurely moments, strolling undisturbed around a school where we were guests and not pupils, we exchanged life histories and other confidences. Omar, too, had lost his father—had I sensed that before?— shot in some tribal encounter on the Frontier, for he hailed from the lawless lands beyond Peshawar. A wealthy uncle was seeing to Omar's education. The RAF was now seeing to mine.

We wandered into the school chapel, and there I found my father's name—A. A. Bond—on the school's roll of honour board: old boys who had lost their lives while serving during the two world wars.

'What did his initials stand for?' asked Omar.

'Aubrey Alexander.'

'Unusual names, like yours. Why did your parents call you Ruskin?'

'I am not sure. I think my father liked the works of John Ruskin, who wrote on serious subjects like art and architecture. I don't think anyone reads him now. They'll read me, though!' I had already started writing my first book. It was called *Nine Months* (the length of the school term, not a pregnancy), and it described some of the happenings at school and lampooned a few of our teachers. I had filled three slim exercise books with this premature literary project, and I allowed Omar to go through them. He must have been my first reader and critic. 'They're very interesting,' he said, 'but you'll get into trouble if someone finds them. Especially Mr Oliver.' And he read out an offending verse:

Olly, Olly, Olly, with his balls on a trolley,
And his arse all painted green!

I have to admit it wasn't great literature. I was better at hockey and football. I made some spectacular saves, and we won our matches against Sanawar. When we returned to Simla, we were school heroes for a couple of days and lost some of our reticence; we were even a little more forthcoming with other boys. And then Mr Fisher, my housemaster, discovered my literary opus, *Nine Months,* under my mattress, and took it away and read it (as he told me later) from cover to cover. Corporal punishment then being in vogue, I was given six of the best with a springy malacca cane, and my manuscript was torn up and deposited in Fisher's wastepaper basket. All I had to show for my efforts were some purple welts on my bottom. These were proudly displayed to all who were interested, and I was a hero for another two days.

'Will you go away too when the British leave India?' Omar asked me one day.

'I don't think so,' I said. 'My stepfather is Indian.'

'Everyone is saying that our leaders and the British are going to divide the country. Simla will be in India, Peshawar in Pakistan!'

'Oh, it won't happen,' I said glibly. 'How can they cut up such a big country?' But even as we chatted about the possibility, Nehru and Jinnah and Mountbatten and all those who mattered were preparing their instruments for major surgery.

Before their decision impinged on our lives and everyone else's, we found a little freedom of our own—in an underground tunnel that we discovered below the third flat.

It was really part of an old, disused drainage system, and when Omar and I began exploring it, we had no idea just how far it extended. After crawling along on our bellies for some twenty feet, we found ourselves in complete darkness. Omar had brought along a small pencil torch, and with its help we continued writhing forward (moving backwards would have been quite impossible) until we saw a glimmer of light at the end of the tunnel. Dusty, musty, very scruffy, we emerged at last on to a grassy knoll, a little way outside the school boundary.

It's always a great thrill to escape beyond the boundaries that adults have devised. Here we were in unknown territory. To travel without passports—that would be the ultimate in freedom!

But more passports were on their way and more boundaries.

Lord Mountbatten, viceroy and governor-general-to-be, came for our Founder's Day and gave away the prizes. I had won a prize for something or the other, and mounted the rostrum to receive my book from this towering, handsome man in his pinstripe suit. Bishop Cotton's was then the premier school of India, often referred to as the 'Eton of the East'. Viceroys and governors had graced its functions. Many of its boys had gone on to eminence in the civil services and armed forces. There was one 'old boy' about whom they maintained a stolid silence—General Dyer, who had ordered the massacre at Amritsar and destroyed the trust that had been building up between Britain and India.

Now Mountbatten spoke of the momentous events that were happening all around us—the war had just come to an end, the United Nations held out the promise of a world living in peace and harmony, and India, an equal partner with Britain, would be among the great nations...

A few weeks later, Bengal and Punjab provinces were bisected. Riots flared up across northern India, and there was a great exodus of people crossing the newly drawn frontiers of Pakistan and India. Homes were destroyed, thousands lost their lives.

The common-room radio and the occasional newspaper kept us abreast of events, but in our tunnel, Omar and I felt immune from all that was happening, worlds away from all the pillage, murder and revenge. And outside the tunnel, on the pine knoll below the school, there was fresh untrodden grass, sprinkled with clover and daisies, the only sounds the hammering of a woodpecker, the distant insistent call of the Himalayan barbet. Who could touch us there?

'And when all the wars are done,' I said, 'a butterfly will still be beautiful.'

'Did you read that somewhere?'

'No, it just came into my head.'

'Already you're a writer.'

'No, I want to play hockey for India or football for Arsenal. Only winning teams!'

'You can't win forever. Better to be a writer.'

When the monsoon rains arrived, the tunnel was flooded, the drain choked with rubble. We were allowed out to the cinema to see Laurence Olivier's *Hamlet*, a film that did nothing to raise our spirits on a wet and gloomy afternoon—but it was our last picture that year, because communal riots suddenly broke out in Simla's Lower Bazaar, an area that was still much as Kipling had described it—'a man who knows his way there can defy all the police of India's summer capital'—and we were confined to school indefinitely.

One morning after chapel, the headmaster announced that the Muslim boys—those who had their homes in what was now Pakistan—would have to be evacuated, sent to their homes across the border with an armed convoy.

The tunnel no longer provided an escape for us. The bazaar was out of bounds. The flooded playing field was deserted. Omar and I sat on a damp wooden bench and talked about the future in vaguely hopeful terms; but we didn't solve any problems. Mountbatten and Nehru and Jinnah were doing all the solving.

It was soon time for Omar to leave—he along with some fifty other boys from Lahore, Pindi and Peshawar. The rest of us—Hindus, Christians, Parsis—helped them load their luggage into the waiting trucks. A couple of boys broke down and wept. So did our departing school captain, a Pathan who had been known for his stoic and unemotional demeanour. Omar waved cheerfully to me and I waved back. We had vowed to meet again some day.

The convoy got through safely enough. There was only one casualty—the school cook, who had strayed into an off-limits area in the foothill town of Kalka and been set upon by a mob. He wasn't seen again.

Towards the end of the school year, just as we were all getting ready to leave for the school holidays, I received a letter from Omar. He told me something about his new school and how he missed my company and our games and our tunnel to freedom. I replied and gave him my home address, but I did not hear from him again. The land, though divided, was still a big one, and we were very small.

Some seventeen or eighteen years later I did get news of Omar, but in an entirely different context. India and Pakistan were at war and in a bombing raid over Ambala, not far from Simla, a Pakistani plane was shot down. Its crew died in the crash. One of them, I learnt later, was Omar.

Did he, I wonder, get a glimpse of the playing fields we knew so well as boys?

Perhaps memories of his schooldays flooded back as he flew over the foothills. Perhaps he remembered the tunnel through which we were able to make our little escape to freedom.

But there are no tunnels in the sky.

THE CHERRY TREE

One day, when Rakesh was six, he walked home from the Mussoorie bazaar eating cherries. They were a little sweet, a little sour; small, bright red cherries, which had come all the way from the Kashmir valley.

Here in the Himalayan foothills where Rakesh lived, there were not many fruit trees. The soil was stony and the dry cold winds stunted the growth of most plants. But on the more sheltered slopes there were forests of oak and deodar.

Rakesh lived with his grandfather on the outskirts of Mussoorie, just where the forest began. His father and mother lived in a small village fifty miles away, where they grew maize and rice and barley in narrow terraced fields on the lower slopes of the mountain. But there were no schools in the village and Rakesh's parents were keen that he should go to school. As soon as he was of school-going age, they sent him to stay with his grandfather in Mussoorie.

Grandfather was a retired forest ranger. He had a little cottage outside the town.

Rakesh was on his way home from school when he bought the cherries. He paid fifty paise for the bunch. It took him about half an hour to walk home, and by the time he reached the cottage, there were only three cherries left.

'Have a cherry, Grandfather,' he said, as soon as he saw his grandfather in the garden.

Grandfather took one cherry and Rakesh promptly ate the other two. He kept the last seed in his mouth for some time, rolling it round and round on his tongue until all the tang had gone. Then he placed the seed on the palm of his hand and studied it.

'Are cherry seeds lucky?' asked Rakesh.

'Of course.'

Then I'll keep it.'

'Nothing is lucky if you put it away. If you want luck, you must put it to some use.'

What can I do with a seed?'

'Plant it.'

So Rakesh found a small space and began to dig up a flower bed.

'Hey, not there,' said Grandfather, 'I've sown mustard in that bed. Plant it in that shady corner, where it won't be disturbed.'

Rakesh went to a corner of the garden where the earth was soft and yielding. He did not have to dig. He pressed the seed into the soil with his thumb and it went right in.

Then he had his lunch and ran off to play cricket with his friends, and forgot all about the cherry seed.

When it was winter in the hills, a cold wind blew down from the snows and went whoo-whoo-whoo in the deodar trees and the garden was dry and bare. In the evenings Grandfather and Rakesh sat around a charcoal fire and Grandfather told Rakesh stories—stories about people who turned into animals and ghosts who lived in trees and beans that jumped and stones that wept—and in turn Rakesh would read to him from the newspaper, Grandfather's eyesight being rather weak. Rakesh found the newspaper very dull—especially after the stories—but Grandfather wanted all the news...

They knew it was spring when the wild duck flew north again, to Siberia. Early in the morning, when he got up to chop wood and light a fire, Rakesh saw the V-shaped formation streaming northward, the calls of the birds carrying clearly through the thin mountain air.

One morning in the garden he bent to pick up what he thought was a small twig and found to his surprise that it was well rooted. He stared at it for a moment, then ran to fetch Grandfather, calling, 'Dada, come and look, the cherry tree has come up!'

'What cherry tree?' asked Grandfather, who had forgotten about it. 'The seed we planted last year—look, it's come up!'

Rakesh went down on his haunches, while Grandfather bent almost double and peered down at the tiny tree. It was about four inches high.

'Yes, it's a cherry tree,' said Grandfather. 'You should water it now and then.'

Rakesh ran indoors and came back with a bucket of water.

'Don't drown it!' said Grandfather.

Rakesh gave it a sprinkling and circled it with pebbles.

'What are the pebbles for?' asked Grandfather.

'For privacy,' said Rakesh.

He looked at the tree every morning but it did not seem to be growing very fast, so he stopped looking at it except quickly, out of the corner of his eye. And, after a week or two, when he allowed himself to look at it properly, he found that it had grown—at least an inch!

That year the monsoon rains came early and Rakesh plodded to and from school in raincoat and gum boots. Ferns sprang from the trunks of trees, strange-looking lilies came up in the long grass and even when it wasn't raining the trees dripped and mist came curling up the valley. The cherry tree grew quickly in this season.

It was about two feet high when a goat entered the garden and ate all the leaves. Only the main stem and two thin branches remained.

'Never mind,' said Grandfather, seeing that Rakesh was upset. 'It will grow again, cherry trees are tough.'

Towards the end of the rainy season new leaves appeared on the tree. Then a woman cutting grass scrambled down the hillside, her scythe swishing through the heavy monsoon foliage. She did not try to avoid the tree: one sweep, and the cherry tree was cut in two.

When Grandfather saw what had happened, he went

after the woman and scolded her; but the damage could not be repaired.

'Maybe it will die now,' said Rakesh.

'Maybe,' said Grandfather.

But the cherry tree had no intention of dying.

By the time summer came round again, it had sent out several new shoots with tender green leaves. Rakesh had grown taller too. He was eight now, a sturdy boy with curly black hair and deep black eyes. 'Blackberry eyes,' Grandfather called them.

That monsoon Rakesh went home to his village, to help his father and mother with the planting and ploughing and sowing. He was thinner but stronger when he came back to Grandfather's house at the end of the rains to find that the cherry tree had grown another foot. It was now up to his chest.

Even when there was rain, Rakesh would sometimes water the tree. He wanted it to know that he was there.

One day he found a bright green praying mantis perched on a branch, peering at him with bulging eyes. Rakesh let it remain there; it was the cherry tree's first visitor.

The next visitor was a hairy caterpillar, who started making a meal of the leaves. Rakesh removed it quickly and dropped it on a heap of dry leaves.

'Come back when you're a butterfly,' he said.

Winter came early. The cherry tree bent low with the weight of snow. Field mice sought shelter in the roof of the cottage. The road from the valley was blocked and for several days there was no newspaper and this made Grandfather quite grumpy. His stories began to have unhappy endings.

In February it was Rakesh's birthday. He was nine—and the tree was four, but almost as tall as Rakesh.

One morning, when the sun came out, Grandfather came into the garden, 'to let some warmth get into my bones,' as he put it. He stopped in front of the cherry tree, stared at it for a few moments and then called out, 'Rakesh! Come and look! Come quickly before it falls!'

Rakesh and Grandfather gazed at the tree as though it had performed a miracle. There was a pale pink blossom at the end of a branch.

The following year there were more blossoms. And suddenly the tree was taller than Rakesh, even though it was less than half his age. And then it was taller than Grandfather, who was older than some of the oak trees.

But Rakesh had grown too. He could run and jump and climb trees as well as most boys, and he read a lot of books, although he still liked listening to Grandfather's tales.

In the cherry tree, bees came to feed on the nectar in the blossoms and tiny birds pecked at the blossoms and broke them off. But the tree kept blossoming right through the spring and there were always more blossoms than birds.

That summer there were small cherries on the tree. Rakesh tasted one and spat it out.

'It's too sour,' he said.

They'll be better next year,' said Grandfather.

But the birds liked them—especially the bigger birds, such as the bulbuls and scarlet minivets—and they flitted in and out of the foliage, feasting on the cherries.

On a warm sunny afternoon, when even the bees looked sleepy, Rakesh was looking for Grandfather without finding him in any of his favourite places around the house. Then he looked out of the bedroom window and saw Grandfather reclining on a cane chair under the cherry tree.

There's just the right amount of shade here,' said Grandfather. 'And I like looking at the leaves.'

They're pretty leaves,' said Rakesh. 'And they are always ready to dance if there's a breeze.'

After Grandfather had come indoors, Rakesh went into the garden and lay down on the grass beneath the tree. He gazed up through the leaves at the great blue sky; and turning on his side, he could see the mountains striding away into the clouds. He was still lying beneath the tree when the evening shadows crept across the garden. Grandfather came back and sat down beside Rakesh, and they waited in silence until the stars came out and the nightjar began to call. In the forest below, the crickets and cicadas began tuning up; and suddenly the trees were full of the sound of insects.

'There are so many trees in the forest,' said Rakesh, What's so special about this tree? Why do we like it so much?'

'We planted it ourselves,' said Grandfather. That's why it's special.'

'Just one small seed,' said Rakesh, and he touched the smooth bark of the tree that he had grown. He ran his hand along the trunk of the tree and put his finger to the tip of a leaf. 'I wonder,' he whispered. 'Is this what it feels to be God?'

GETTING GRANNY'S GLASSES

Granny could hear the distant roar of the river and smell the pine needles beneath her feet, and feel the presence of her grandson, Mani; but she couldn't see the river or the trees; and of her grandson she could only make out his fuzzy hair, and sometimes, when he was very close, his blackberry eyes and the gleam of his teeth when he smiled.

Granny wore a pair of old glasses; she'd been wearing them for well over ten years, but her eyes had grown steadily weaker, and the glasses had grown older and were now scratched and spotted, and there was very little she could see through them. Still, they were better than nothing. Without them, everything was just a topsy-turvy blur.

Of course, Granny knew her way about the house and the fields, and on a clear day she could see the mountains—the mighty Himalayan snow peaks—striding away into the sky; but it was felt by Mani and his father that it was high time Granny had her eyes tested and got herself new glasses.

'Well, you know we can't get them in the village,' said Granny.

Mani said, 'You'll have to go to the eye hospital in Mussoorie. That's the nearest town.'

'But that's a two-day journey,' protested Granny. 'First I'd have to walk to Nain Market, twelve miles at least, spend the night there at your Uncle's place, and then catch a bus for the rest of the journey! You know how I hate buses. And it's ten years since I walked all the way to Mussoorie. That was when I had these glasses made.'

'Well, it's still there,' said Mani's father.

'What is still there?'

'Mussoorie.'

'And the eye hospital?'

'That too.'

'Well, my eyes are not too bad, really,' said Granny, looking for excuses. She did not feel like going far from the village; in particular, she did not want to be parted from Mani. He was eleven and quite capable of looking after himself, but Granny had brought him up ever since his mother had died when he was only a year old. She was his Nani (maternal grandmother), and had cared for boy and father, and cows and hens and household, all these years, with great energy and devotion.

'I can manage quite well,' she said. As long as I can see what's right in front of me, there's no problem. I know you got a ball in your hand, Mani; please don't bounce it off the cow.'

'It's not a ball, Granny; it's an apple.'

'Oh, is it?' said Granny, recovering quickly from her mistake. 'Never mind, just don't bounce it off the cow. And don't eat too many apples!'

'Now listen,' said Mani's father sternly, 'I know you don't want to go anywhere. But we're not sending you off on your own. I'll take you to Mussoorie.'

'And leave Mani here by himself? How could you even think of doing that?'

'Then I'll take you to Mussoorie,' said Mani eagerly. 'We can leave Father on his own, can't we? I've been to Mussoorie before, with my school friends. I know where we can stay. But—' He paused a moment and looked doubtfully from his father to his grandmother. 'You wouldn't be able to walk all the way to Nain, would you, Granny?'

'Of course I can walk,' said Granny. 'I may be going blind, but there's nothing wrong with my legs!'

That was true enough. Only day before they'd found Granny in the walnut tree, tossing walnuts, not very accurately, into a large basket on the ground.

'But you're seventy, Granny.'

'What has that got to do with it? And besides, it's downhill to Nain.'

'And uphill coming back.'

'Uphill's easier!' said Granny.

Now that she knew Mani might be accompanying her, she was more than ready to make the journey.

The monsoon rains had begun, and in front of the small stone house a cluster of giant dahlias reared their heads. Mani had seen them growing in Nain and had brought some bulbs home. 'These are big flowers, Granny,' he'd said. 'You'll be able to see them better.'

She could indeed see the dahlias, splashes of red and yellow against the old stone of the cottage walls.

Looking at them now, Granny said, 'While we're in Mussoorie, we'll get some seeds and bulbs. And a new bell for the white cow. And a pullover for your father. And shoes for you. Look, there's nothing much left of the ones you're wearing.'

'Now just a minute,' said Mani's father. 'Are you going there to get your eyes tested, or are you going on a shopping expedition? I've got only a hundred rupees to spare. You'll have to manage with that.'

'We'll manage,' said Mani. 'We'll sleep at the bus shelter.'

'No, we won't,' said Granny. 'I've got fifty rupees of my own. We'll stay at a hotel!'

Early next morning, in a light drizzle, Granny and Mani set out on the path to Nain.

Mani carried a small bedding roll on his shoulder; Granny carried a large cloth shopping bag and an umbrella. The path went through fields and around the brow of the hill and then began to wind here and there, up and down and around, as though it had a will of its own and no intention of going anywhere in particular. Travellers new to the area often left the path, because they were impatient or in a hurry, and thought there were quicker, better ways of reaching their destinations. Almost immediately they found themselves lost. For it was a wise path and a good path, and had found the right way of crossing the mountains after centuries of trial and error.

'Whenever you feel tired, we'll take a rest,' said Mani.

'We've only just started out,' said Granny. 'We'll rest when you're hungry!'

They walked at a steady pace, without talking too much. A flock of parrots whirled overhead, flashes of red and green against the sombre sky. High in a spruce tree a barbet called monotonously. But there were no other sounds, except for the hiss and gentle patter of the rain.

Mani stopped to pick wild blackberries from a bush. Granny wasn't fond of berries and didn't slacken her pace. Mani had to run to catch up with her. Soon his lips were purple with the juice from the berries.

The rain stopped and the sun came out. Below them, the light green of the fields stood out against the dark green of the forests, and the hills were bathed in golden sunshine.

Mani ran ahead.

'Can you see all right, Granny?' he called.

'I can see the path and I can see your white shirt. That's enough for now.'

'Well, watch out, there are some mules coming down the road.'

Granny stepped aside to allow the mules to pass. They clattered by, the mule-driver urging them on with a romantic song; but the last mule veered toward Granny and appeared to be heading straight for her. Granny saw it just in time. She knew that mules and ponies always preferred going around objects, if they could see what lay ahead of them, so she held out her open umbrella and the mule cantered round it without touching her.

Granny and Mani ate their light meal on the roadside, in the shade of a whispering pine, and drank from a spring a little further down the path.

By late afternoon they were directly above Nain.

'We're almost there,' said Mani. 'I can see the temple near Uncle's house.'

'I can't see a thing,' said Granny.

'That's because of the mist. There's a thick mist coming up the valley.'

It started raining heavily as they entered the small market town on the banks of the river. Granny's umbrella was leaking badly. But they were soon drying themselves in Uncle's house, and drinking glasses of hot sweet milky tea.

Mani got up early the next morning and ran down the narrow street to bathe in the river. The swift but shallow mountain river was a tributary of the sacred Ganges, and its waters were held sacred too. As the sun rose, people thronged the steps leading down to the river, to bathe or pray or float flower offerings downstream.

As Mani dressed, he heard the blare of a bus horn. There was only one bus to Mussoorie. He scampered up the slope, wondering if they'd miss it. But Granny was waiting for him at the bus stop. She had already bought their tickets.

The motor road followed the course of the river, which thundered a hundred feet below. The bus was old and rickety, and rattled so much that the passengers could barely hear themselves speaking.

One of them was pointing to a spot below, where another bus had gone off the road a few weeks back, resulting in many casualties.

The driver appeared to be unaware of the accident. He drove at some speed, and whenever he went round a bend, everyone in the bus was thrown about. In spite of all the noise and confusion, Granny fell asleep; her head resting against Mani's shoulder.

Suddenly the bus came to a grinding halt. People were thrown forward in their seats. Granny's glasses fell off and had to be retrieved from the folds of someone else's umbrella.

'What's happening?' she asked. 'Have we arrived?'

'No, something is blocking the road,' said Mani.

'It's a landslide!' exclaimed someone, and all the passengers put their heads out of the windows to take a look.

It was a big landslide. Sometime in the night, during the heavy rain, earth and trees and bushes had given way and come crashing down, completely blocking the road. Nor was it over yet. Debris was still falling. Mani saw rocks hurtling down the hill and into the river.

'Not a suitable place for a bus stop,' observed Granny, who couldn't see a thing.

Even as she spoke, a shower of stones and small rocks came clattering down on the roof of the bus. Passengers cried out in alarm. The driver began reversing, as more rocks came crashing down.

'I never did trust motor roads,' said Granny.

The driver kept backing until they were well away from the landslide. Then everyone tumbled out of the bus. Granny and Mani were the last to get down.

They were told that it would take days to clear the road, and most of the passengers decided to return to Nain with the bus. But a few bold spirits agreed to walk to Mussoorie, taking a shortcut up the mountain which would bypass the landslide.

'It's only ten miles from here by the footpath,' said one of them. 'A stiff climb, but we can make it by evening.'

Mani looked at Granny. 'Shall we go back?'

'What's ten miles?' said Granny. 'We did that yesterday.'

So they started climbing a narrow path, little more than a goat-track, which went steeply up the mountainside. But there was much huffing and puffing, and pausing for breath and by the time they got to the top of the mountain Granny and Mani were on their own. They could see a few stragglers far below; the rest had retreated to Nain.

Granny and Mani stood on the summit of the mountain. They had it all to themselves. Their village was hidden by the range to the north. Far below rushed the river. Far above circled a golden eagle.

In the distance, on the next mountain, the houses of Mussoorie were white specks on the dark green hillside.

'Did you bring any food from Uncle's house?' asked Mani.

'Naturally,' said Granny. 'I knew you'd soon be hungry. There are pakoras and buns, and peaches from Uncle's garden.'

'Good!' said Mani, forgetting his tiredness. 'We'll eat as we go along. There's no need to stop.'

'Eating or walking?'

'Eating, of course. We'll stop when you're tired, Granny.'

'Oh, I can walk forever,' said Granny, laughing. 'I've been doing it all my life. And one day I'll just walk over the mountains and into the sky. But not if it's raining. This umbrella leaks badly.'

Down again they went, and up the next mountain, and over bare windswept hillsides, and up through a dark gloomy deodar forest. And then just as it was getting dark, they saw the lights of Mussoorie twinkling ahead of them.

As they came nearer, the lights increased, until presently they were in a brightly lit bazaar, swallowed up by crowds of shoppers, strollers, tourists and merrymakers. Mussoorie seemed a very jolly sort of place for those who had money to spend. Jostled in the crowd, Granny kept one hand firmly on Mani's shoulder so that she did not lose him.

They asked around for the cheapest hotel. But there were no cheap hotels. So they spent the night in a dharamsala adjoining the temple, where other pilgrims had taken shelter.

Next morning, at the eye hospital, they joined a long queue of patient patients. The eye specialist, a portly man in a suit and tie who himself wore glasses, dealt with the patients in a brisk but kind manner. After an hour's wait, Granny's turn came.

The doctor took one horrified look at Granny's glasses and dropped them in a wastebasket. Then he fished them out and placed them on his desk and said, 'On second thought, I think I'll send them to a museum. You should have changed your glasses years ago. They've probably done more harm than good.'

He examined Granny's eyes with a strong light, and said, 'Your eyes are very weak, but you're not going blind. We'll fit you up with a stronger pair of glasses.' Then he placed her in front of a board covered with letters in English and Hindi, large and small, and asked Granny if she could make them out.

'I can't even see the board,' said Granny.

'Well, can you see me?' asked the doctor.

'Some of you,' said Granny.

'I want you to see all of me,' said the doctor, and he balanced a wire frame on Granny's nose and began trying out different lenses.

Suddenly Granny could see much better. She saw the board and the biggest letters on it.

'Can you see me now?' asked the doctor.

'Most of you,' said Granny. And then added, by way of being helpful: 'There's quite a lot of you to see.'

'Thank you,' said the doctor. 'And now turn around and tell me if you can see your grandson.'

Granny turned, and saw Mani clearly for the first time in many years.

'Mani!' she exclaimed, clapping her hands with joy. 'How nice you look! What a fine boy I've brought up! But you do need a haircut. And a wash. And buttons on your shirt. And a new pair of shoes. Come along to the bazaar!'

'First have your new glasses made,' said Mani, laughing. 'Then we'll go for shopping!'

A day later they were in a bus again, although no one knew how far it would be able to go. Sooner or later they would have to walk.

Granny had a window seat, and Mani sat beside her. He had new shoes and Granny had a new umbrella and they had also bought a thick woollen Tibetan pullover for Mani's father. And seeds and bulbs and a cowbell.

As the bus moved off, Granny looked eagerly out of the

window. Each bend in the road opened up new vistas for her, and she could see many things that she hadn't seen for a long time—distant villages, people working in the fields, milkmen on the road, two dogs rushing along beside the bus, monkeys in the trees, and, most wonderful of all, a rainbow in the sky.

She couldn't see perfectly, of course, but she was very pleased with the improvement.

'What a large cow!' she remarked, pointing at a beast grazing on the hillside.

'It's not a cow, Granny,' said Mani. 'It's a buffalo.'

Granny was not to be discouraged. 'Anyway, I saw it,' she insisted.

While most of the people on the bus looked weary and bored, Granny continued to gaze out of the window, discovering new sights.

Mani watched for some time and listened to her excited chatter. Then his head began to nod. It dropped against Granny's shoulder, and remained there, comfortably supported. The bus swerved and jolted along the winding mountain road, but Mani was fast asleep.

THE PROSPECT OF FLOWERS

Fern Hill, The Oaks, Hunter's Lodge, The Parsonage, The Pines, Dumbarnie, Mackinnon's Hall and Windermere. These are the names of some of the old houses that still stand on the outskirts of one of the smaller Indian hill stations. Most of them have fallen into decay and ruin. They are very old, of course—built over a hundred years ago by Britons who sought relief from the searing heat of the plains. Today's visitors to the hill stations prefer to live near the markets and cinemas and many of the old houses, set amidst oak and maple and deodar, are inhabited by wild cats, bandicoots, owls, goats and the occasional charcoal burner or mule driver.

But amongst these neglected mansions stands a neat, whitewashed cottage called Mulberry Lodge. And in it, up to a short time ago, lived an elderly English spinster named Miss Mackenzie.

In years Miss Mackenzie was more than 'elderly', being well over eighty. But no one would have guessed it. She was clean, sprightly, and wore old-fashioned but well-preserved dresses. Once a week, she walked the two miles to town to buy butter and jam and soap and sometimes a small bottle of eau de cologne.

She had lived in the hill station since she had been a girl in her teens, and that had been before the First World War. Though she had never married, she had experienced a few love affairs and was far from being the typical frustrated spinster of fiction. Her parents had been dead thirty years; her brother and sister were also dead. She had no relatives in India and she lived on a small pension of forty rupees a month and the gift parcels that were sent out to her from New Zealand by a friend of her youth.

Like other lonely old people, she kept a pet—a large

black cat with bright yellow eyes. In her small garden she grew dahlias, chrysanthemums, gladioli and a few rare orchids. She knew a great deal about plants and about wild flowers, trees, birds and insects. She had never made a serious study of these things, but having lived with them for so many years had developed an intimacy with all that grew and flourished around her.

She had few visitors. Occasionally, the padre from the local church called on her, and once a month the postman came with a letter from New Zealand or her pension papers. The milkman called every second day with a litre of milk for the lady and her cat. And sometimes she received a couple of eggs free, for the egg seller remembered a time when Miss Mackenzie, in her earlier prosperity, had bought eggs from him in large quantities. He was a sentimental man. He remembered her as a ravishing beauty in her twenties when he had gazed at her in round-eyed, nine-year-old wonder and consternation.

Now it was September and the rains were nearly over and Miss Mackenzie's chrysanthemums were coming into their own. She hoped the coming winter wouldn't be too severe because she found it increasingly difficult to bear the cold.

One day, as she was pottering about in her garden, she saw a schoolboy plucking wild flowers on the slope above the cottage.

'Who's that?' she called. 'What are you up to, young man?'

The boy was alarmed and tried to dash up the hillside, but he slipped on pine needles and came slithering down the slope on to Miss Mackenzie's nasturtium bed.

When he found there was no escape, he gave a bright disarming smile and said, 'Good morning, miss.'

He belonged to the local English-medium school and wore a bright red blazer and a red and black striped tie. Like most polite Indian schoolboys, he called every woman 'miss'.

'Good morning,' said Miss Mackenzie severely. 'Would you mind moving out of my flower bed?'

The boy stepped gingerly over the nasturtiums and looked up at Miss Mackenzie with dimpled cheeks and appealing eyes. It was impossible to be angry with him.

'You're trespassing,' said Miss Mackenzie.

'Yes, miss.'

'And you ought to be in school at this hour.'

'Yes, miss.'

'Then what are you doing here?'

'Picking flowers, miss.' And he held up a bunch of ferns and wild flowers.

'Oh,' Miss Mackenzie was disarmed. It was a long time since she had seen a boy taking an interest in flowers and, what was more, playing truant from school in order to gather them.

'Do you like flowers?' she asked.

'Yes, miss. I'm going to be a botan—a botantist?'

'You mean a botanist.'

'Yes, miss.'

'Well, that's unusual. Most boys at your age want to be pilots or soldiers or perhaps engineers. But you want to be a botanist. Well, well. There's still hope for the world, I see. And do you know the names of these flowers?'

'This is a bukhilo flower,' he said, showing her a small golden flower. 'That's a Pahari name. It means puja or prayer. The flower is offered during prayers. But I don't know what this is...'

He held out a pale pink flower with a soft, heart-shaped leaf.

'It's a wild begonia,' said Miss Mackenzie. 'And that purple stuff is salvia, but it isn't wild. It's a plant that escaped from my garden. Don't you have any books on flowers?'

'No, miss.'

'All right, come in and I'll show you a book.'

She led the boy into a small front room, which was

crowded with furniture and books and vases and jam jars, and offered him a chair. He sat awkwardly on its edge. The black cat immediately leapt on to his knees and settled down on them, purring loudly.

'What's your name?' asked Miss Mackenzie, as she rummaged through her books.

'Anil, miss.'

'And where do you live?'

'When school closes, I go to Delhi. My father has a business.'

'Oh, and what's that?'

'Bulbs, miss.'

'Flower bulbs?'

'No, electric bulbs.'

'Electric bulbs! You might send me a few, when you get home. Mine are always fusing and they're so expensive, like everything else these days. Ah, here we are!' She pulled a heavy volume down from the shelf and laid it on the table. '*Flora Himaliensis,* published in 1892, and probably the only copy in India. This is a very valuable book, Anil. No other naturalist has recorded so many wild Himalayan flowers. And let me tell you this, there are many flowers and plants which are still unknown to the fancy botanists who spend all their time with microscopes instead of in the mountains. But perhaps, *you'll* do something about that, one day.'

'Yes, miss.'

They went through the book together, and Miss Mackenzie pointed out many flowers that grew in and around the hill station while the boy made notes of their names and seasons. She lit a stove and put the kettle on for tea. And then the old English lady and the small Indian boy sat side by side over cups of hot sweet tea, absorbed in a book on wild flowers.

'May I come again?' asked Anil, when finally he rose to go.

'If you like,' said Miss Mackenzie. 'But not during school hours. You mustn't miss your classes.'

After that, Anil visited Miss Mackenzie about once a week, and nearly always brought a wild flower for her to identify. She found herself looking forward to the boy's visits—and sometimes, when more than a week passed and he didn't come, she was disappointed and lonely and would grumble at the black cat.

Anil reminded her of her brother, when the latter had been a boy. There was no physical resemblance. Andrew had been fair-haired and blue-eyed. But it was Anil's eagerness, his alert, bright look and the way he stood—legs apart, hands on hips, a picture of confidence—that reminded her of the boy who had shared her own youth in these same hills.

And why did Anil come to see her so often? Partly because she knew about wild flowers and he really did want to become a botanist. And partly because she smelt of freshly baked bread and that was a smell his own grandmother had possessed. And partly because she was lonely and sometimes a boy of twelve can sense loneliness better than an adult. And partly because he was a little different from other children.

By the middle of October, when there was only a fortnight left for the school to close, the first snow had fallen on the distant mountains. One peak stood high above the rest, a white pinnacle against the azure blue sky. When the sun set, this peak turned from orange to gold to pink to red.

'How high is that mountain?' asked Anil.

'It must be over twelve thousand feet,' said Miss Mackenzie. 'About thirty miles from here, as the crow flies. I always wanted to go there, but there was no proper road. At that height, there'll be flowers that you don't get here—the blue gentian and the purple columbine, the anemone and the edelweiss.'

'I'll go there one day,' said Anil.

'I'm sure you will, if you really want to.'

The day before his school closed, Anil came to say goodbye to Miss Mackenzie.

'I don't suppose you'll be able to find many wild flowers in Delhi,' she said. 'But have a good holiday.'

'Thank you, miss.'

As he was about to leave, Miss Mackenzie, on an impulse, thrust the *Flora Himaliensis* into his hands.

'You keep it,' she said. 'It's a present for you.'

'But I'll be back next year,and I'll be able to look at it then. It's so valuable.'

'I know it's valuable and that's why I've given it to you. Otherwise it will only fall into the hands of the junk dealers.'

'But, miss...'

'Don't argue. Besides, I may not be here next year.'

'Are you going away?'

'I'm not sure. I may go to England.'

She had no intention of going to England; she had not seen the country since she was a child, and she knew she would not fit in with the life of post-war Britain. Her home was in these hills, among the oaks and maples and deodars. It was lonely but at her age it would be lonely anywhere.

The boy tucked the book under his arm, straightened his tie, stood stiffly to attention and said, 'Goodbye, Miss Mackenzie.' It was the first time he had spoken her name.

Winter set in early and strong winds brought rain and sleet and soon there were no flowers in the garden or on the hillside. The cat stayed indoors, curled up at the foot of Miss Mackenzie's bed. Miss Mackenzie wrapped herself up in all her old shawls and mufflers but still she felt the cold. Her fingers grew so stiff that she took almost an hour to open a can of baked beans. And then it snowed and for several days the milkman did not come. The postman arrived with her pension papers but she felt too tired to take them up to town to the bank.

She spent most of the time in bed. It was the warmest place. She kept a hot-water bottle at her back and the cat kept her feet warm. She lay in bed, dreaming of the spring and summer months. In three months' time the primroses would be out and with the coming of spring the boy would return.

One night the hot-water bottle burst and the bedding was soaked through. As there was no sun for several days, the blanket remained damp. Miss Mackenzie caught a chill and had to keep to her cold, uncomfortable bed. She knew she had a fever but there was no thermometer with which to take her temperature. She had difficulty breathing.

A strong wind sprang up one night and the window flew open and kept banging all night. Miss Mackenzie was too weak to get up and close it and the wind swept the rain and sleet into the room. The cat crept into the bed and snuggled close to its mistress's warm body. But towards morning that body had lost its warmth and the cat left the bed and started scratching about on the floor.

As a shaft of sunlight streamed through the open window, the milkman arrived. He poured some milk into the cat's saucer on the doorstep and the cat leapt down from the windowsill and made for the milk.

The milkman called a greeting to Miss Mackenzie, but received no answer. Her window was open and he had always known her to be up before sunrise. So he put his head in at the window and called again. But Miss Mackenzie did not answer. She had gone away to the mountain where the blue gentian and purple columbine grew.

A LONG WALK FOR BINA

I

A leopard, lithe and sinewy, drank at the mountain stream and then lay down on the grass to bask in the late February sunshine. Its tail twitched occasionally and the animal appeared to be sleeping. At the sound of distant voices it raised its head to listen, then stood up and leapt lightly over the boulders in the stream, disappearing among the trees on the opposite bank.

A minute or two later, three children came walking down the forest path. They were a girl and two boys and they were singing in their local dialect an old song they had learnt from their grandparents.

Five more miles to go!
We climb through rain and snow.
A river to cross...
A mountain to pass...
Now we've four more miles to go!

Their school satchels looked new, their clothes had been washed and pressed. Their loud and cheerful singing startled a spotted forktail. The bird left its favourite rock in the stream and flew down the dark ravine.

'Well, we have only three more miles to go,' said the bigger boy, Prakash, who had been this way hundreds of times. 'But first we have to cross the stream.'

He was a sturdy twelve-year-old with eyes like black currants and a mop of bushy hair that refused to settle down on his head. The girl and her small brother were taking this path for the first time.

'I'm feeling tired, Bina,' said the little boy.

Bina smiled at him and Prakash said, 'Don't worry,

Sonu, you'll get used to the walk. There's plenty of time.' He glanced at the old watch he'd been given by his grandfather. It needed constant winding. 'We can rest here for five or six minutes.'

They sat down on a smooth boulder and watched the clear water of the shallow stream tumbling downhill. Bina examined the old watch on Prakash's wrist. The glass was badly scratched and she could barely make out the figures on the dial. 'Are you sure it still gives the right time?' she asked.

'Well, it loses five minutes every day, so I put it ten minutes ahead at night. That means by morning it's quite accurate! Even our teacher, Mr Mani, asks me for the time. If he doesn't ask, I tell him! The clock in our classroom keeps stopping.'

They removed their shoes and let the cold mountain water run over their feet. Bina was the same age as Prakash. She had pink cheeks, soft brown eyes and hair that was just beginning to lose its natural curls. Hers was a gentle face but a determined little chin showed that she could be a strong person. Sonu, her younger brother, was ten. He was a thin boy who had been sickly as a child but was now beginning to fill out. Although he did not look very athletic, he could run like the wind.

II

Bina had been going to school in her own village of Koli, on the other side of the mountain. But it had been a primary school, finishing at Class 5. Now, in order to study in Class 6, she would have to walk several miles every day to Nauti, where there was a high school going up to Class 8. It had been decided that Sonu would also shift to the new school, to give Bina company. Prakash, their neighbour in Koli, was already a pupil at the Nauti school. His mischievous nature, which sometimes got him into trouble, had resulted in his having to repeat a year.

But this didn't seem to bother him. 'What's the hurry?' he had told his indignant parents. 'You're not sending me to a foreign land when I finish school. And our cows aren't running away, are they?'

'You would prefer to look after the cows, wouldn't you?' asked Bina, as they got up to continue their walk.

'Oh, school's all right. Wait till you see old Mr Mani. He always gets our names mixed up, as well as the subjects he's supposed to be teaching. At our last lesson, instead of maths, he gave us a geography lesson!'

'More fun than maths,' said Bina.

'Yes, but there's a new teacher this year. She's very young they say, just out of college. I wonder what she'll be like.'

Bina walked faster and Sonu had some trouble keeping up with them. She was excited about the new school and the prospect of different surroundings. She had seldom been outside her own village, with its small school and single ration shop. The day's routine never varied—helping her mother in the fields or with household tasks like fetching water from the spring or cutting grass and fodder for the cattle. Her father, who was a soldier, was away for nine months in the year and Sonu was still too small for the heavier tasks.

As they neared Nauti Village, they were joined by other children coming from different directions. Even where there were no major roads, the mountains were full of little lanes and shortcuts. Like a game of snakes and ladders, these narrow paths zigzagged around the hills and villages, cutting through fields and crossing narrow ravines until they came together to form a fairly busy road along which mules, cattle and goats joined the throng.

Nauti was a fairly large village, and from here a broader but dustier road started for Tehri. There was a small bus, several trucks and (for part of the way) a roadroller. The road hadn't been completed because the heavy diesel roller couldn't take the steep climb to Nauti. It stood on the roadside halfway up the road from Tehri.

Prakash knew almost everyone in the area and exchanged greetings and gossip with other children as well as with muleteers, bus drivers, milkmen and labourers working on the road. He loved telling everyone the time, even if they weren't interested.

'It's nine o'clock,' he would announce, glancing at his wrist. 'Isn't your bus leaving today?'

'Off with you!' the bus driver would respond, 'I'll leave when I'm ready.'

As the children approached Nauti, the small flat school buildings came into view on the outskirts of the village, fringed by a line of long-leaved pines. A small crowd had assembled on the one playing field. Something unusual seemed to have happened. Prakash ran forward to see what it was all about. Bina and Sonu stood aside, waiting in a patch of sunlight near the boundary wall.

Prakash soon came running back to them. He was bubbling over with excitement.

'It's Mr Mani!' he gasped. 'He's disappeared! People are saying a leopard must have carried him off!'

III

Mr Mani wasn't really old. He was about fifty-five and was expected to retire soon. But for the children, most adults over forty seemed ancient! And Mr Mani had always been a bit absent-minded, even as a young man.

He had gone out for his early morning walk, saying he'd be back by eight o'clock, in time to have his breakfast and be ready for class. He wasn't married, but his sister and her husband stayed with him. When it was past nine o'clock his sister presumed he'd stopped at a neighbour's house for breakfast (he loved tucking into other people's breakfast) and that he had gone on to school from there. But when the school bell rang at ten o'clock and everyone but Mr Mani was present, questions were asked and guesses were made.

No one had seen him return from his walk and enquiries made in the village showed that he had not stopped at anyone's house. For Mr Mani to disappear was puzzling; for him to disappear without his breakfast was extraordinary.

Then a milkman returning from the next village said he had seen a leopard sitting on a rock on the outskirts of the pine forest. There had been talk of a cattle-killer in the valley, of leopards and other animals being displaced by the construction of a dam. But as yet no one had heard of a leopard attacking a man. Could Mr Mani have been its first victim? Someone found a strip of red cloth entangled in a blackberry bush and went running through the village showing it to everyone. Mr Mani had been known to wear red pyjamas. Surely he had been seized and eaten! But where were his remains? And why had he been in his pyjamas?

Meanwhile Bina and Sonu and the rest of the children had followed their teachers into the school playground. Feeling a little lost, Bina looked around for Prakash. She found herself facing a dark, slender young woman wearing spectacles, who must have been in her early twenties—just a little too old to be another student. She had a kind, expressive face and she seemed a little concerned by all that had been happening.

Bina noticed that she had lovely hands; it was obvious that the new teacher hadn't milked cows or worked in the fields!

'You must be new here,' said the teacher, smiling at Bina. 'And is this your little brother?'

'Yes, we've come from Koli Village. We were at school there.'

'It's a long walk from Koli. You didn't see any leopards, did you? Well, I'm new too. Are you in the Class 6?'

'Sonu is in the third. I'm in the sixth.'

'Then I'm your new teacher. My name is Tania Ramola. Come along, let's see if we can settle down in our classroom.'

꙾

Mr Mani turned up at twelve o'clock, wondering what all the fuss was about. No, he snapped, he had not been attacked by a leopard; and yes, he had lost his pyjamas and would someone kindly return them to him?

'How did you lose your pyjamas, sir?' asked Prakash.

'They were blown off the washing line!' snapped Mr Mani.

After much questioning, Mr Mani admitted that he had gone further than he had intended and that he had lost his way coming back. He had been a bit upset because the new teacher, a slip of a girl, had been given charge of the sixth, while he was still with the fifth, along with that troublesome boy Prakash, who kept on reminding him of the time! The headmaster had explained that as Mr Mani was due to retire at the end of the year, the school did not wish to burden him with a senior class. But Mr Mani looked upon the whole thing as a plot to get rid of him. He glowered at Miss Ramola whenever he passed her. And when she smiled back at him, he looked the other way!

Mr Mani had been getting even more absent-minded of late—putting on his shoes without his socks, wearing his homespun waistcoat inside out, mixing up people's names and, of course, eating other people's lunches and dinners. His sister had made a mutton broth for the postmaster, who was down with 'flu', and had asked Mr Mani to take it over in a thermos. When the postmaster opened the thermos, he found only a few drops of broth at the bottom—Mr Mani had drunk the rest somewhere along the way.

When sometimes Mr Mani spoke of his coming retirement, it was to describe his plans for the small field he owned just behind the house. Right now, it was full of potatoes, which did not require much looking after; but he had plans for growing dahlias, roses, French beans and other fruits and flowers.

The next time he visited Tehri, he promised himself, he would buy some dahlia bulbs and rose cuttings. The monsoon season would be a good time to put them down. And meanwhile, his potatoes were still flourishing.

IV

Bina enjoyed her first day at the new school. She felt at ease with Miss Ramola, as did most of the boys and girls in her class. Tania Ramola had been to distant towns such as Delhi and Lucknow—places they had only heard about—and it was said that she had a brother who was a pilot and flew planes all over the world. Perhaps he'd fly over Nauti some day!

Most of the children had of course seen planes flying overhead, but none of them had seen a ship, and only a few had been on a train. Tehri mountain was far from the railway and hundreds of miles from the sea. But they all knew about the big dam that was being built at Tehri, just forty miles away.

Bina, Sonu and Prakash had company for part of the way home, but gradually the other children went off in different directions. Once they had crossed the stream, they were on their own again.

It was a steep climb all the way back to their village. Prakash had a supply of peanuts which he shared with Bina and Sonu, and at a small spring they quenched their thirst.

When they were less than a mile from home, they met a postman who had finished his round of the villages in the area and was now returning to Nauti.

'Don't waste time along the way,' he told them. 'Try to get home before dark.'

'What's the hurry?' asked Prakash, glancing at his watch. 'It's only five o'clock.'

'There's a leopard around. I saw it this morning, not far from the stream. No one is sure how it got here. So don't take any chances. Get home early.'

'So, there really is a leopard,' said Sonu.

They took his advice and walked faster, and Sonu forgot to complain about his aching feet.

They were home well before sunset.

There was a smell of cooking in the air and they were hungry.

'Cabbage and roti,' said Prakash gloomily. 'But I could eat anything today.' He stopped outside his small slate-roofed house and Bina and Sonu waved goodbye and carried on across a couple of ploughed fields until they reached their small stone house.

'Stuffed tomatoes,' said Sonu, sniffing just outside the front door.

'And lemon pickle,' said Bina, who had helped cut, sun and salt the lemons a month previously.

Their mother was lighting the kitchen stove. They greeted her with great hugs and demands for an immediate dinner. She was a good cook who could make even the simplest of dishes taste delicious. Her favourite saying was, 'Home-made bread is better than roast meat abroad,' and Bina and Sonu had to agree.

Electricity had yet to reach their village, and they took their meal by the light of a kerosene lamp. After the meal, Sonu settled down to do a little homework, while Bina stepped outside to look at the stars.

Across the fields, someone was playing a flute. 'It must be Prakash,' thought Bina. 'He always breaks off on the high notes.' But the flute music was simple and appealing and she began singing softly to herself in the dark.

V

Mr Mani was having trouble with the porcupines. They had been getting into his garden at night and digging up and eating his potatoes. From his bedroom window—left open now that the mild April weather had arrived—he could listen to them enjoying the vegetables he had worked hard to grow. Scrunch, scrunch! katar, katar, as their sharp teeth sliced through the largest and juiciest of potatoes. For Mr Mani it was as though they were biting through his own flesh. And the sound of them digging industriously as they rooted up those healthy, leafy plants made him tremble with rage and indignation. The unfairness of it all!

Yes, Mr Mani hated porcupines. He prayed for their destruction, their removal from the face of the earth. But, as his friends were quick to point out, 'The creator made porcupines too,' and in any case you could never see the creatures or catch them, they were completely nocturnal.

Mr Mani got out of bed every night, torch in one hand, a stout stick in the other but, as soon as he stepped into the garden, the crunching and digging stopped and he was greeted by the most infuriating of silences. He would grope around in the dark, swinging wildly with the stick, but not a single porcupine was to be seen or heard. As soon as he was back in bed, the sounds would start all over again— scrunch, scrunch, katar, katar...

Mr Mani came to his class tired and dishevelled, with rings under his eyes and a permanent frown on his face. It took some time for his pupils to discover the reason for his misery, but when they did, they felt sorry for their teacher and took to discussing ways and means of saving his potatoes from the porcupines.

It was Prakash who came up with the idea of a moat or water ditch. 'Porcupines don't like water,' he said knowledgeably.

'How do you know?' asked one of his friends.

'Throw water on one and see how it runs! They don't like getting their quills wet.'

There was no one who could disprove Prakash's theory and the class fell in with the idea of building a moat, especially as it meant getting most of the day off.

'Anything to make Mr Mani happy,' said the Headmaster, and the rest of the school watched with envy as the pupils of Class 5, armed with spades and shovels collected from all parts of the village, took up their positions around Mr Mani's potato field and began digging a ditch.

By evening the moat was ready, but it was still dry and the porcupines got in again that night and had a great feast.

'At this rate,' said Mr Mani gloomily, 'there won't be any potatoes left to save.'

But the next day, Prakash and the other boys and girls managed to divert the water from a stream that flowed past the village. They had the satisfaction of watching it flow gently into the ditch. Everyone went home in a good mood. By nightfall, the ditch had overflowed, the potato field was flooded and Mr Mani found himself trapped inside his house. But Prakash and his friends had won the day. The porcupines stayed away that night!

∽

A month had passed, and wild violets, daisies and buttercups now sprinkled the hill slopes and, on her way to school, Bina gathered enough to make a little posy. The bunch of flowers fitted easily into an old inkwell. Miss Ramola was delighted to find this little display in the middle of her desk.

'Who put these here?' she asked in surprise.

Bina kept quiet and the rest of the class smiled secretively. After that, they took turns bringing flowers for the classroom.

On her long walks to school and home again, Bina became aware that April was the month of new leaves. The oak leaves were bright green above and silver beneath, and when they rippled in the breeze they were clouds of silvery green. The path was strewn with old leaves, dry and crackly. Sonu loved kicking them around.

Clouds of white butterflies floated across the stream. Sonu was chasing a butterfly when he stumbled over something dark and repulsive. He went sprawling on the grass. When he got to his feet, he looked down at the remains of a small animal.

'Bina! Prakash! Come quickly!' he shouted.

It was part of a sheep, killed some days earlier by a much larger animal.

'Only a leopard could have done this,' said Prakash.

'Let's get away, then,' said Sonu. 'It might still be around!'

'No, there's nothing left to eat. The leopard will be hunting elsewhere by now. Perhaps it's moved on to the next valley.'

'Still, I'm frightened,' said Sonu. 'There may be more leopards!'

Bina took him by the hand. 'Leopards don't attack humans!' she said.

'They will, if they get a taste for people!' insisted Prakash.

'Well, this one hasn't attacked any people as yet,' said Bina, although she couldn't be sure. Hadn't there been rumours of a leopard attacking some workers near the dam? But she did not want Sonu to feel afraid, so she did not mention the story. All she said was, 'It has probably come here because of all the activity near the dam.'

All the same, they hurried home. And for a few days, whenever they reached the stream, they crossed over very quickly, unwilling to linger too long at that lovely spot.

VI

A few days later, a school party was on its way to Tehri to see the new dam that was being built.

Miss Ramola had arranged to take her class, and Mr Mani, not wishing to be left out, insisted on taking his class as well. That meant there were about fifty boys and girls taking part in the outing. The little bus could only take thirty. A friendly truck driver agreed to take some children if they were prepared to sit on sacks of potatoes. And Prakash persuaded the owner of the diesel roller to turn it around and head it back to Tehri—with him and a couple of friends up on the driving seat.

Prakash's small group set off at sunrise, as they had to walk some distance in order to reach the stranded roadroller. The bus left at 9 a.m. with Miss Ramola and her class, and Mr Mani and some of his pupils. The truck was to follow later.

It was Bina's first visit to a large town, and her first bus ride.

The sharp curves along the winding, downhill road made several children feel sick. The bus driver seemed to be in a tearing hurry. He took them along at a rolling, rollicking speed, which made Bina feel quite giddy. She rested her head on her arms and refused to look out of the window. Hairpin bends and cliff edges, pine forests and snow-capped peaks, all swept past her, but she felt too ill to want to look at anything. It was just as well—those sudden drops, hundreds of feet to the valley below, were quite frightening. Bina began to wish that she hadn't come—or that she had joined Prakash on the roadroller instead!

Miss Ramola and Mr Mani didn't seem to notice the lurching and groaning of the old bus. They had made this journey many times. They were busy arguing about the advantages and disadvantages of large dams—an argument that was to continue on and off for much of the day.

Meanwhile, Prakash and his friends had reached the roller. The driver hadn't turned up, but they managed to reverse it and get it going in the direction of Tehri. They were soon overtaken by both bus and truck but kept moving along at a steady chug. Prakash spotted Bina at the window of the bus and waved cheerfully. She responded feebly.

Bina felt better when the road levelled out near Tehri. As they crossed an old bridge over the wide river, they were startled by a loud bang which made the bus shudder. A cloud of dust rose above the town.

'They're blasting the mountain,' said Miss Ramola.

'End of a mountain,' said Mr Mani, mournfully.

While they were drinking cups of tea at the bus stop, waiting for the potato truck and the roadroller, Miss Ramola and Mr Mani continued their argument about the dam. Miss Ramola maintained that it would bring electric power and water for irrigation to large areas of the country, including the surrounding area. Mr Mani declared that it was a menace, as it was situated in an earthquake zone. There would be a terrible disaster if the dam burst! Bina found it all very confusing. And what about the animals in the area, she wondered, what would happen to them?

The argument was becoming quite heated when the potato truck arrived. There was no sign of the roadroller, so it was decided that Mr Mani should wait for Prakash and his friends while Miss Ramola's group went ahead.

∽

Some eight or nine miles before Tehri, the roadroller had broken down, and Prakash and his friends were forced to walk. They had not gone far, however, when a mule train came along—five or six mules that had been delivering sacks of grain in Nauti. A boy rode on the first mule, but the others had no loads.

'Can you give us a ride to Tehri?' called Prakash.

'Make yourselves comfortable,' said the boy.

There were no saddles, only gunny sacks strapped on to the mules with rope. They had a rough but jolly ride down to the Tehri bus stop. None of them had ever ridden mules; but they had saved at least an hour on the road.

Looking around the bus stop for the rest of the party, they could find no one from their school. And Mr Mani, who should have been waiting for them, had vanished.

VII

Tania Ramola and her group had taken the steep road to the hill above Tehri. Half an hour's climbing brought them to a little plateau which overlooked the town, the river and the dam site.

The earthworks for the dam were only just coming up, but a wide tunnel had been bored through the mountain to divert the river into another channel. Down below, the old town was still spread out across the valley and from a distance it looked quite charming and picturesque.

'Will the whole town be swallowed up by the waters of the dam?' asked Bina.

'Yes, all of it,' said Miss Ramola. 'The clock tower and the old palace. The long bazaar and the temples, the schools and the jail, and hundreds of houses, for many miles up the valley. All those people will have to go—thousands of them! Of course they'll be resettled elsewhere.'

'But the town's been here for hundreds of years,' said Bina. 'They were quite happy without the dam, weren't they?'

'I suppose they were. But the dam isn't just for them— it's for the millions who live further downstream, across the plains.'

'And it doesn't matter what happens to this place?'

'The local people will be given new homes somewhere else.' Miss Ramola found herself on the defensive and decided to change the subject. 'Everyone must be hungry. It's time we had our lunch.'

Bina kept quiet. She didn't think the local people would want to go away. And it was a good thing, she mused, that there was only a small stream and not a big river running past her village. To be uprooted like this—a town and hundreds of villages—and put down somewhere on the hot, dusty plains—seemed to her unbearable.

'Well, I'm glad I don't live in Tehri,' she said.

She did not know it, but all the animals and most of the birds had already left the area. The leopard had been among them.

∽

They walked through the colourful, crowded bazaar, where

fruit sellers did business beside silversmiths and pavement vendors sold everything from umbrellas to glass bangles. Sparrows attacked sacks of grain, monkeys made off with bananas and stray cows and dogs rummaged in refuse bins, but nobody took any notice. Music blared from radios. Buses blew their horns. Sonu bought a whistle to add to the general din but Miss Ramola told him to put it away. Bina had kept five rupees aside and now she used it to buy a cotton headscarf for her mother.

As they were about to enter a small restaurant for a meal, they were joined by Prakash and his companions; but of Mr Mani there was still no sign.

'He must have met one of his relatives,' said Prakash. 'He has relatives everywhere.'

After a simple meal of rice and lentils, they walked the length of the bazaar without finding Mr Mani. At last, when they were about to give up the search, they saw him emerge from a by-lane, a large sack slung over his shoulder.

'Sir, where have you been?' asked Prakash. 'We have been looking for you everywhere.'

On Mr Mani's face was a look of triumph.

'Help me with this bag,' he said breathlessly.

'You've bought more potatoes, sir,' said Prakash.

'Not potatoes, boy. Dahlia bulbs!'

VIII

It was dark by the time they were all back in Nauti. Mr Mani had refused to be separated from his sack of dahlia bulbs and had been forced to sit in the back of the truck with Prakash and most of the boys.

Bina did not feel so ill on the return journey. Going uphill was definitely better than going downhill! But by the time the bus reached Nauti it was too late for most of the children to walk back to the more distant villages. The boys were put up in different homes, while the girls were given beds in the school veranda.

The night was warm and still. Large moths fluttered around the single bulb that lit the veranda. Counting moths, Sonu soon fell asleep. But Bina stayed awake for some time, listening to the sounds of the night. A nightjar went tonk-tonk in the bushes and somewhere in the forest an owl hooted softly. The sharp call of a barking deer travelled up the valley from the direction of the stream. Jackals kept howling. It seemed that there were more of them than ever before.

Bina was not the only one to hear the barking deer. The leopard, stretched full length on a rocky ledge, heard it too. The leopard raised its head and then got up slowly. The deer was its natural prey. But there weren't many left, and that was why the leopard, robbed of its forest by the dam, had taken to attacking dogs and cattle near the villages.

As the cry of the barking deer sounded nearer, the leopard left its lookout point and moved swiftly through the shadows towards the stream.

IX

In early June the hills were dry and dusty, and forest fires broke out, destroying shrubs and trees, killing birds and small animals. The resin in the pines made these trees burn more fiercely, and the wind would take sparks from the trees and carry them into the dry grass and leaves, so that new fires would spring up before the old ones had died out. Fortunately, Bina's village was not in the pine belt; the fires did not reach it. But Nauti was surrounded by a fire that raged for three days, and the children had to stay away from school.

And then, towards the end of June, the monsoon rains arrived and there was an end to forest fires. The monsoon lasts three months and the lower Himalaya would be drenched in rain, mist and cloud for the next three months.

The first rain arrived while Bina, Prakash and Sonu were returning home from school. Those first few drops on the dusty path made them cry out with excitement. Then the rain grew heavier and a wonderful aroma rose from the earth.

'The best smell in the world!' exclaimed Bina.

Everything suddenly came to life. The grass, the crops, the trees, the birds. Even the leaves of the trees glistened and looked new.

That first wet weekend, Bina and Sonu helped their mother plant beans, maize and cucumbers. Sometimes, when the rain was very heavy, they had to run indoors. Otherwise they worked in the rain, the soft mud clinging to their bare legs.

Prakash now owned a dog, a black dog with one ear up and one ear down. The dog ran around getting in everyone's way, barking at cows, goats, hens and humans, without frightening any of them. Prakash said it was a very clever dog, but no one else seemed to think so. Prakash also said it would protect the village from the leopard, but others said the dog would be the first to be taken—he'd run straight into the jaws of Mr Spots!

In Nauti, Tania Ramola was trying to find a dry spot in the quarters she'd been given. It was an old building and the roof was leaking in several places. Mugs and buckets were scattered about the floor in order to catch the drips.

Mr Mani had dug up all his potatoes and presented them to the friends and neighbours who had given him lunches and dinners. He was having the time of his life, planting dahlia bulbs all over his garden.

'I'll have a field of many-coloured dahlias!' he announced. 'Just wait till the end of August!'

'Watch out for those porcupines,' warned his sister. 'They eat dahlia bulbs too!'

Mr Mani made an inspection tour of his moat, no longer in flood, and found everything in good order. Prakash had done his job well.

Now, when the children crossed the stream, they found that the water level had risen by about a foot. Small cascades had turned into waterfalls. Ferns had sprung up on the banks. Frogs chanted.

Prakash and his dog dashed across the stream. Bina and Sonu followed more cautiously. The current was much stronger now and the water was almost up to their knees. Once they had crossed the stream, they hurried along the path, anxious not to be caught in a sudden downpour.

By the time they reached school, each of them had two or three leeches clinging to their legs. They had to use salt to remove them. The leeches were the most troublesome part of the rainy season. Even the leopard did not like them. It could not lie in the long grass without getting leeches on its paws and face.

One day, when Bina, Prakash and Sonu were about to cross the stream they heard a low rumble, which grew louder every second. Looking up at the opposite hill, they saw several trees shudder, tilt outwards and begin to fall. Earth and rocks bulged out from the mountain, then came crashing down into the ravine.

'Landslide!' shouted Sonu.

'It's carried away the path,' said Bina. 'Don't go any further.'

There was a tremendous roar as more rocks, trees and bushes fell away and crashed down the hillside.

Prakash's dog, who had gone ahead, came running back, tail between his legs.

They remained rooted to the spot until the rocks had stopped falling and the dust had settled. Birds circled the area, calling wildly. A frightened barking deer ran past them.

'We can't go to school now,' said Prakash. 'There's no way around.'

They turned and trudged home through the gathering mist.

In Koli, Prakash's parents had heard the roar of the

landslide. They were setting out in search of the children when they saw them emerge from the mist, waving cheerfully.

X

They had to miss school for another three days, and Bina was afraid they might not be able to take their final exams. Although Prakash was not really troubled at the thought of missing exams, he did not like feeling helpless just because their path had been swept away. So he explored the hillside until he found a goat-track going around the mountain. It joined up with another path near Nauti. This made their walk longer by a mile, but Bina did not mind. It was much cooler now that the rains were in full swing.

The only trouble with the new route was that it passed close to the leopard's lair. The animal had made this area its own since being forced to leave the dam area.

One day Prakash's dog ran ahead of them barking furiously. Then he ran back whimpering.

'He's always running away from something,' observed Sonu. But a minute later he understood the reason for the dog's fear.

They rounded a bend and Sonu saw the leopard standing in their way. They were struck dumb—too terrified to run. It was a strong, sinewy creature. A low growl rose from its throat. It seemed ready to spring.

They stood perfectly still, afraid to move or say a word. And the leopard must have been equally surprised. It stared at them for a few seconds, then bounded across the path and into the oak forest.

Sonu was shaking. Bina could hear her heart hammering. Prakash could only stammer: 'Did you see the way he sprang? Wasn't he beautiful?'

He forgot to look at his watch for the rest of the day.

A few days later, Sonu stopped and pointed to a large outcrop of rock on the next hill.

The leopard stood far above them, outlined against

the sky. It looked strong, majestic. Standing beside it were two young cubs.

'Look at those little ones!' exclaimed Sonu.

'So it's a female, not a male,' said Prakash.

'That's why she was killing so often,' said Bina. 'She had to feed her cubs too.'

They remained still for several minutes, gazing up at the leopard and her cubs. The leopard family took no notice of them.

'She knows we are here,' said Prakash, 'but she doesn't care. She knows we won't harm them.'

'We are cubs too!' said Sonu.

'Yes,' said Bina. 'And there's still plenty of space for all of us. Even when the dam is ready there will still be room for leopards and humans.'

XI

The school exams were over. The rains were nearly over too. The landslide had been cleared, and Bina, Prakash and Sonu were once again crossing the stream.

There was a chill in the air, for it was the end of September.

Prakash had learnt to play the flute quite well and he played on the way to school and then again on the way home. As a result he did not look at his watch so often. One morning they found a small crowd in front of Mr Mani's house.

'What could have happened?' wondered Bina. 'I hope he hasn't got lost again.'

'Maybe he's sick,' said Sonu.

'Maybe it's the porcupines,' said Prakash.

But it was none of these things.

Mr Mani's first dahlia was in bloom and half the village had turned up to look at it! It was a huge red double dahlia, so heavy that it had to be supported with sticks. No one had ever seen such a magnificent flower!

Mr Mani was a happy man. And his mood only improved over the coming week, as more and more dahlias flowered—crimson, yellow, purple, mauve, white—button dahlias, pom-pom dahlias, spotted dahlias, striped dahlias... Mr Mani had them all! A dahlia even turned up on Tania Ramola's desk—he got along quite well with her now—and another brightened up the headmaster's study.

A week later, on their way home—it was almost the last day of the school term—Bina, Prakash and Sonu talked about what they might do when they grew up.

'I think I'll become a teacher,' said Bina. 'I'll teach children about animals and birds, and trees and flowers.'

'Better than maths!' said Prakash.

'I'll be a pilot,' said Sonu. 'I want to fly a plane like Miss Ramola's brother.'

'And what about you, Prakash?' asked Bina.

Prakash just smiled and said, 'Maybe I'll be a flute player,' and he put the flute to his lips and played a sweet melody.

'Well, the world needs flute players too,' said Bina, as they fell into step beside him.

The leopard had been stalking a barking deer. She paused when she heard the flute and the voices of the children. Her own young ones were growing quickly, but the girl and the two boys did not look much older.

They had started singing their favourite song again.

Five more miles to go!
We climb through rain and snow.
A river to cross...
A mountain to pass...
Now we've four more miles to go!

The leopard waited until they had passed, before returning to the trail of the barking deer.

MRS ROBERTS

Elsie Roberts had been quite a beauty in her twenties and thirties—one of those fair Anglo-Indians who passed for European until their accents gave them away. Elsie, it was said, did her best to remain fair, staying out of the sun as much as possible. In her later years, she was seldom seen during the day but by then she had lost her looks and taken to drink; she slept by day and lived by night.

In her heyday Elsie (nee MacGowan) was a dancing partner to Roberts, a good-looking French Jew who had made his way to India just before World War II broke out. They danced in Cabaret at the Imperial and Swiss in Delhi and at Hakman's in Mussoorie and Filetto's in Lahore. They made an elegant pair—they danced beautifully. Inevitably, they were compared to Fred Astaire and Ginger Rogers, the dancing sensation of the silver screen. They married and continued to partner each other until the war ended. Then, Roberts made a trip to France to claim and collect some compensation due to him as a war refugee. As he stood at the cashier's counter, waiting for the first instalment to be handed over to him, he collapsed and died of a heart attack. Chance gives and takes away, and sometimes gives again, but human life is equally unpredictable.

However, Elsie, as his widow, was entitled to the proceeds. She gave up her dancing career and took to breeding dogs. I first saw her when she came to see my mother in New Delhi, sometime in 1958. My mother was breeding Poms, and Elsie bought a small black Pom. She was still very attractive (Elsie, not the Pom) and was escorted by a gentleman who owned a small restaurant in Mussoorie.

'He's after the money,' said my mother later and she was right, as the gentleman in question wheedled a large sum of money out of her and then deserted her.

Elsie transferred her affections to her dogs. She rented a house outside Mussoorie and provided board and lodging to a large variety of canines. There was considerable inbreeding. Poms wed dachshunds, Samoyeds wed spaniels and Labradors wed German shepherds. The resultant mixture was undistinguished, to say the least. Elsie didn't care. She had become devoted to her dogs and had no desire to sell them, with or without pedigree. She fed them well and the local butcher proclaimed that she was his best customer.

Of course, strays and village dogs also found their way on to the premises. When there are free lunches to be had, dogs and humans are no different. Word soon gets around and everyone drops in for the wedding feast.

They were not a ferocious lot. Like their owner, they were wary of humans, quite paranoid about them. They'd bark furiously but scatter at the approach of anything on two legs.

When I came to live in Mussoorie in the mid-1960s, I thought I'd pay a casual visit to Mrs Roberts; my mother had asked me to look her up. She was then living near Barlowganj where she had a huge bungalow to herself, most of it occupied by some twenty to thirty dogs.

At first she refused to see me but when I told her who I was, she let me in. 'So you're Edie's son,' she said. 'How is your mother?'

'Not too well, I'm afraid.'

'Does she still have her Poms?'

'Several of them.' I refrained from adding that they were a bloody nuisance. Try sharing a Delhi flat with half a dozen snapping, yapping, highly strung, hysterical Poms—my least favourite breed!

Mrs Roberts showed me around. The house was filthy. She was equally unkempt—her dress soiled, hands and feet unwashed, hair all over the place. Only traces of her former beauty remained. She was in her late forties and fading fast.

But she was to live another twenty years.

The next time I saw her, about five years later, she was in considerable distress. Two or three of her dogs were suffering from mange and had to be put down. But the vet's injections hadn't worked properly (it was probably some spurious stuff) and the dogs died slowly and painfully. Mrs Roberts went further into her shell and moved with her companions to the top of the mountain, near Sister's bazaar. Old-timers in that area still remember her.

She would emerge from her house once a month to collect her money from the local bank. The rest of the time she would remain locked up with her dogs, emerging only to receive the butcher or the milkman, who also brought her the local brew, a potent distillation made from mysterious ingredients. At the time we were going through a period of Prohibition (it was Morarji's government), but Mrs Roberts and the local villagers had beaten the system.

I, too, had come to rely on the local milkman as a source of supply. 'English wines and spirits' having been taken off the market. Kachi-sharab, the special from Kotti, Kanda and other gaons, was the only alternative. My milkman used my hot-water bottle to bring me the stuff. Unfortunately, the hot-water bottle stank for weeks afterwards and could no longer be used for legitimate purposes. No matter. Those were desperate times.

Mrs Roberts had been on the stuff for years and was apparently none the worse for it. Prohibition came and went and politicians came and went and while frail creatures such as I returned to mere whisky and water; tougher souls, such as Elsie Roberts, continued with the local stuff, which was certainly more potent.

Two or three years passed and I had forgotten Mrs Roberts and her dog, when one morning the local missionary doctor, Dr Olsen, dropped in to tell me she had died in the night (of double pneumonia) and did I know if she had any relatives.

'None that I know of,' I had to say, 'just those dogs.'

She was given a pauper's burial in the little burial ground below Woodstock, where some of the school's Christian servants were laid to rest. No tombstones there. As a beautiful young dancer she'd been the toast of Mussoorie. That had been over forty years ago. Now, friendless, she had been swept away like a dead leaf.

And what of the dogs?

Bereft of their benefactor and bewildered by her absence, they ran wild. Some fled into the forest and perished. A few survived, along with the many street dogs that proliferate around the hill station.

If you see a dog that looks especially weird (bits of terrier, spaniel, Pom and dachshund), you'll know it's descended from one of Mrs Roberts' pets. She did leave us a legacy of sorts.

LOVE IS A SAD SONG

I sit against this grey rock, beneath a sky of pristine blueness, and think of you, Sushila. It is November and the grass is turning brown and yellow. Crushed, it still smells sweet. The afternoon sun shimmers on the oak leaves and turns them a glittering silver. A cricket sizzles its way through the long grass. The stream murmurs at the bottom of the hill—that stream where you and I lingered on a golden afternoon in May.

I sit here and think of you and try to see your slim brown hand resting against this rock, feeling its warmth. I am aware again of the texture of your skin, the coolness of your feet, the sharp tingle of your fingertips. And in the pastures of my mind I run my hand over your quivering mouth and crush your tender breasts. Remembered passion grows sweeter with the passing of time.

You will not be thinking of me now, as you sit in your home in the city, cooking or sewing or trying to study for examinations. There will be men and women and children circling about you, in that crowded house of your grandmother's, and you will not be able to think of me for more than a moment or two. But I know you do think of me sometimes, in some private moment which cuts you off from the crowd. You will remember how I wondered what it is all about, this loving, and why it should cause such an upheaval. You are still a child, Sushila—and yet you found it so easy to quieten my impatient heart.

On the night you came to stay with us, the light from the street lamp shone through the branches of the peach tree and made leaf patterns on the walls. Through the glass panes of the front door I caught a glimpse of little Sunil's face, bright and questing, and then—a hand—a dark, long-fingered hand that could only have belonged to you.

It was almost a year since I had seen you, my dark and slender girl. And now you were in your sixteenth year. And Sunil was twelve; and your uncle, Dinesh, who lived with me, was twenty-three. And I was almost thirty—a fearful and wonderful age, when life becomes dangerous for dreamers.

I remember that when I left Delhi last year, you cried. At first I thought it was because I was going away. Then I realized that it was because you could not go anywhere yourself. Did you envy my freedom—the freedom to live in a poverty of my own choosing, the freedom of the writer? Sunil, to my surprise, did not show much emotion at my going away. This hurt me a little because during that year he had been particularly close to me and I felt for him a very special love. But separations cannot be of any significance to small boys of twelve who live for today, tomorrow and—if they are very serious—the day after.

Before I went away with Dinesh, you made us garlands of marigolds. They were orange and gold, fresh and clean and kissed by the sun. You garlanded me as I sat talking to Sunil. I remember you both as you looked that day— Sunil's smile dimpling his cheeks, while you gazed at me very seriously, your expression very tender. I loved you even then...

Our first picnic.

The path to the little stream took us through the oak forest, where the flashy blue magpies played follow-my-leader with their harsh, creaky calls. Skirting an open ridge (the place where I now sit and write), the path dipped through oak, rhododendron and maple, until it reached a little knoll above the stream. It was a spot unknown to the tourists and summer visitors. Sometimes a milkman or woodcutter crossed the stream on the way to town or village but no one lived beside it. Wild roses grew on the banks.

I do not remember much of that picnic. There was a lot of dull conversation with our neighbours, the Kapoors, who had come along too. You and Sunil were rather bored.

Dinesh looked preoccupied. He was fed up with college. He wanted to start earning a living, wanted to paint. His restlessness often made him moody, irritable.

Near the knoll the stream was too shallow for bathing, but I told Sunil about a cave and a pool further downstream and promised that we would visit the pool another day.

That same night, after dinner, we took a walk along the dark road that goes past the house and leads to the burning ghat. Sunil, who had already sensed the intimacy between us, took my hand and put it in yours. An odd, touching little gesture!

'Tell us a story,' you said.

'Yes, tell us,' said Sunil.

I told you the story of the pure in heart. A shepherd boy found a snake in the forest and the snake told the boy that it was really a princess who had been bewitched and turned into a snake and that it could only recover its human form if someone who was truly pure in heart gave it three kisses on the mouth. The boy put his lips to the mouth of the snake and kissed it thrice. And the snake was transformed into a beautiful princess. But the boy lay cold and dead.

'You always tell sad stories,' complained Sunil.

'I like sad stories,' you said. 'Tell us another.'

'Tomorrow night. I'm sleepy.'

We were woken in the night by a strong wind which went whistling round the old house and came rushing down the chimney, humming and hawing and finally choking itself.

Sunil woke up and cried out, 'What's that noise, Uncle?'

'Only the wind,' I said.

'Not a ghost?'

'Well, perhaps the wind is made up of ghosts. Perhaps this wind contains the ghosts of all the people who have lived and died in this old house and want to come in again from the cold.'

You told me about a boy who had been fond of you

in Delhi. Apparently he had visited the house on a few occasions and had sometimes met you on the street while you were on your way home from school. At first, he had been fond of another girl but later he switched his affections to you. When you told me that he had written to you recently and that before coming up you had replied to his letter, I was consumed by jealousy—an emotion which I thought I had grown out of long ago. It did not help to be told that you were not serious about the boy, that you were sorry for him because he had already been disappointed in love.

'If you feel sorry for everyone who has been disappointed in love,' I said, 'you will soon be receiving the affections of every young man over ten.'

'Let them give me their affections,' you said, 'and I will give them my chappal over their heads.'

'But spare my head,' I said.

'Have you been in love before?'

'Many times. But this is the first time.'

'And who is your love?'

'Haven't you guessed?'

Sunil, who was following our conversation with deep interest, seemed to revel in the situation. Probably he fancied himself playing the part of Cupid, or Kamadeva, and delighted in watching the arrows of love strike home. No doubt I made it more enjoyable for him. Because I could not hide my feelings. Soon Dinesh would know, too—and then?

A year ago my feelings about you were almost paternal! Or so I thought…. But you are no longer a child and I am a little older too. For when, the night after the picnic, you took my hand and held it against your soft warm cheek, it was the first time that a girl had responded to me so readily, so tenderly. Perhaps it was just innocence but that one action of yours, that acceptance of me, immediately devastated my heart.

Gently, fervently, I kissed your eyes and forehead, your small round mouth and the lobes of your ears and your long smooth throat; and I whispered, 'Sushila, I love you, I love you, I love you,' in the same way that millions and millions of love-smitten young men have whispered since time immemorial. What else can one say? I love you, I love you. There is nothing simpler; nothing that can be made to mean any more than that. And what else did I say? That I would look after you and work for you and make you happy; and that too had been said before, and I was in no way different from anyone. I was a man and yet I was a boy again.

We visited the stream again, a day or two later, early in the morning. Using the rocks as stepping stones, we wandered downstream for about a furlong until we reached a pool and a small waterfall and a cool dark cave. The rocks were mostly grey but some were yellow with age and some were cushioned with moss. A forktail stood on a boulder in the middle of the stream, uttering its low pleasant call. Water came dripping down from the sides of the cave, while sunlight filtered through a crevice in the rock ceiling, dappling your face. A spray of water was caught by a shaft of sunlight and at intervals it reflected the colours of the rainbow.

'It is a beautiful place,' you said.

'Come, then,' I said, 'let us bathe.'

Sunil and I removed our clothes and jumped into the pool while you sat down in the shade of a walnut tree and watched us disport ourselves in the water. Like a frog, Sunil leapt and twisted about in the clear, icy water; his eyes shone, his teeth glistened white, his body glowed with sunshine, youth and the jewels made by drops of water glistening in the sun.

Then we stretched ourselves out beside you and allowed the sun to sink deep into our bodies.

Your feet, laved with dew, stood firm on the quickening grass. There was a butterfly between us, its wings red and gold and heavy with dew. It could not move because of the weight of moisture. And as your foot came nearer and I saw that you would crush it, I said, 'Wait. Don't crush the butterfly, Sushila. It has only a few days in the sun and we have many.'

'And if I spare it,' you said, laughing, 'what will you do for me, what will you pay?'

'Why, anything you say.'

'And will you kiss my foot?'

'Both feet,' I said and did so willingly. For they were no less than the wings of butterflies.

Later, when you ventured near the water, I dragged you in with me. You cried out, not in alarm but with the shock of the cold water, and then, wrenching yourself from my arms, clambered on to the rocks, your thin dress clinging to your thighs, your feet making long patterns on the smooth stone.

Though we tired ourselves out that day, we did not sleep at night. We lay together, you and Sunil on either side of me. Your head rested on my shoulders, your hair lay pressed against my cheek. Sunil had curled himself up into a ball but he was far from being asleep. He took my hand, and he took yours, and he placed them together. And I kissed the tender inside of your hand.

I whispered to you, 'Sushila, there has never been anyone I've loved so much. I've been waiting all these years to find you. For a long time I did not even like women. But you are so different. You care for me, don't you?'

You nodded in the darkness. I could see the outline of your face in the faint moonlight that filtered through the skylight. You never replied directly to a question. I suppose that was a feminine quality; coyness, perhaps.

'Do you love me, Sushila?'

No answer.

'Not now. When you are a little older. In a year or two.'

Did you nod in the darkness or did I imagine it?

'I know it's too early,' I continued. 'You are still too

young. You are still at school. But already you are much wiser than me. I am finding it too difficult to control myself, but I will, since you wish it so. I'm very impatient, I know that, but I'll wait for as long as you make me—two or three or a hundred years. Yes, Sushila, a hundred years!'

Ah, what a pretty speech I made! Romeo could have used some of it; Majnu, too.

And your answer? Just a nod, a little pressure on my hand. I took your fingers and kissed them one by one. Long fingers, as long as mine.

After some time I became aware of Sunil nudging me.

'You are not talking to me,' he complained. 'You are only talking to her. You only love her.'

'I'm terribly sorry. I love you too, Sunil.'

Content with this assurance, he fell asleep; but towards morning, thinking himself to be in the middle of the bed, he rolled over and landed with a thump on the floor. He didn't know how it had happened and accused me of pushing him out.

'I know you don't want me in the bed,' he said.

It was a good thing Dinesh, in the next room, didn't wake up.

∽

'Have you done any work this week?' asked Dinesh with a look of reproach.

'Not much,' I said.

'You are hardly ever in the house. You are never at your desk. Something seems to have happened to you.'

'I have given myself a holiday, that's all. Can't writers take holidays too?'

'No. You have said so yourself. And anyway, you seem to have taken a permanent holiday.'

'Have you finished that painting of the Tibetan woman?' I asked, trying to change the subject.

'That's the third time you've asked me that question,

even though you saw the completed painting a week ago. You're getting very absent-minded.'

There was a letter from your old boyfriend; I mean your young boyfriend. It was addressed to Sunil but I recognized the sender's name and knew it was really for you.

I assumed a look of calm detachment and handed the letter to you. But both you and Sunil sensed my dismay. At first you teased me and showed me the boy's photograph, which had been enclosed (he was certainly good-looking in a flashy way); then, finding that I became gloomier every minute, you tried to make amends, assuring me that the correspondence was one-sided and that you no longer replied to his letters.

And that night, to show me that you really cared, you gave me your hand as soon as the lights were out. Sunil was fast asleep.

We sat together at the foot of your bed. I kept my arm about you while you rested your head against my chest. Your feet lay in repose upon mine. I kept kissing you. And when we lay down together, I loosened your blouse and kissed your small firm breasts and put my lips to your nipples and felt them grow hard against my mouth.

The shy responsiveness of your kisses soon turned to passion. You clung to me. We had forgotten time and place and circumstance. The light of your eyes had been drowned in that lost look of a woman who desires. For a space we both struggled against desire. Suddenly I had become afraid of myself—afraid for you. I tried to free myself from your clasping arms. But you cried in a low voice, 'Love me! Love me! I want you to love me.'

∽

Another night you fell asleep with your face in the crook of my arm and I lay awake a long time, conscious of your breathing, of the touch of your hair on my cheek, of the soft warm soles of your feet, of your slim waist and legs.

And in the morning, when the sunshine filled the room, I watched you while you slept—your slim body in repose, your face tranquil, your thin dark hands like sleeping butterflies and then, when you woke, the beautiful untidiness of your hair and the drowsiness in your eyes. You lay folded up like a kitten, your limbs as untouched by self-consciousness as the limbs of a young and growing tree. And during the warmth of the day a bead of sweat rested on your brow like a small pearl.

I tried to remember what you looked like as a child. Even then, I had always been aware of your presence. You must have been nine or ten when I first saw you—thin, dark, plain-faced, always wearing the faded green skirt that was your school uniform. You went about barefoot. Once, when the monsoon arrived, you ran out into the rain with the other children, naked, exulting in the swish of the cool rain. I remembered your beautiful straight legs and thighs, your swift smile, your dark eyes. You say you do not remember playing naked in the rain but that is because you did not see yourself.

I did not notice you growing. Your face did not change very much. You must have been thirteen when you gave up skirts and started wearing the salwar kameez. You had few clothes but the plainness of your dress only seemed to bring out your own radiance. And as you grew older, your eyes became more expressive, your hair longer and glossier, your gestures more graceful. And then, when you came to me in the hills, I found that you had been transformed into a fairy princess of devastating charm.

∽

We were idling away the afternoon on our beds and you were reclining in my arms when Dinesh came in unexpectedly. He said nothing, merely passed through the room and entered his studio. Sunil got a fright and you were momentarily confused. Then you said, 'He knows already,' and I said,

'Yes, he must know.'

Later I spoke to Dinesh. I told him that I wanted to marry you; that I knew I would have to wait until you were older and had finished school—probably two or three years—and that I was prepared to wait although I knew it would be a long and difficult business. I asked him to help me.

He was upset at first, probably because he felt I had been deceptive (which was true), and also because of his own responsibility in the matter. You were his niece and I had made love to you while he had been preoccupied with other things. But after a little while when he saw that I was sincere and rather confused he relented.

'It has happened too soon,' he said. 'She is too young for all this. Have you told her that you love her?'

'Of course. Many times.'

'You're a fool, then. Have you told her that you want to marry her?'

'Yes.'

'Fool again. That's not the way it is done. Haven't you lived in India long enough to know that?'

'But I love her.'

'Does she love you?'

'I think so.'

'You think so. Desire isn't love, you must know that. Still, I suppose she does love you, otherwise she would not be holding hands with you all day. But you are quite mad, falling in love with a girl half your age.'

'Well, I'm not exactly an old man. I'm thirty.'

'And she's a schoolgirl.'

'She isn't a girl any more, she's too responsive.'

'Oh, you've found that out, have you?'

'Well...' I said, covered in confusion. 'Well, she has shown that she cares a little. You know that it's years since I took any interest in a girl. You called it unnatural on my part, remember? Well, they simply did not exist for me, that's true.'

'Delayed adolescence,' muttered Dinesh.

'But Sushila is different. She puts me at ease. She doesn't turn away from me. I love her and I want to look after her. I can only do that by marrying her.'

'All right, but take it easy. Don't get carried away. And don't, for God's sake, give her a baby. Not while she's still at school! I will do what I can to help you. But you will have to be patient. And no one else must know of this or I will be blamed for everything. As it is Sunil knows too much and he's too small to know so much.'

'Oh, he won't tell anyone.'

'I wish you had fallen in love with her two years from now. You will have to wait that long, anyway. Getting married isn't a simple matter. People will wonder why we are in such a hurry, marrying her off as soon as she leaves school. They'll think the worst!'

'Well, people do marry for love you know, even in India. It's happening all the time.'

'But it doesn't happen in our family. You know how orthodox most of them are. They wouldn't appreciate your outlook. You may marry Sushila for love but it will have to look like an arranged marriage!'

Little things went wrong that evening.

First, a youth on the road passed a remark which you resented; and you, most unladylike, but most Punjabi-like, picked up a stone and threw it at him. It struck him on the leg. He was too surprised to say anything and limped off. I remonstrated with you, told you that throwing stones at people often resulted in a fight, then realized that you had probably wanted to see me fighting on your behalf.

Later you were annoyed because I said you were a little absent-minded. Then Sunil sulked because I spoke roughly to him (I can't remember why) and refused to talk to me for three hours, which was a record. I kept apologizing but neither of you would listen.

It was all part of a game. When I gave up trying and turned instead to my typewriter and my unfinished story, you came and sat beside me and started playing with my hair. You were jealous of my story, of the fact that it was possible for me to withdraw into my work. And I reflected that a woman had to be jealous of something. If there wasn't another woman, then it was a man's work or his hobby or his best friend or his favourite sweater or his pet mongoose that made her resentful. There is a story in Kipling about a woman who grew insanely jealous of a horse's saddle because her husband spent an hour every day polishing it with great care and loving kindness.

Would it be like that in marriage, I wondered—an eternal triangle: you, me and the typewriter?

But there were only a few days left before you returned to the plains, so I gladly pushed away the typewriter and took you in my arms instead. After all, once you had gone away, it would be a long, long time before I could hold you in my arms again. I might visit you in Delhi but we would not be able to enjoy the same freedom and intimacy. And while I savoured the salt kiss of your lips, I wondered how long I would have to wait until I could really call you my own.

Dinesh was at college and Sunil had gone roller skating and we were alone all morning. At first you avoided me, so I picked up a book and pretended to read. But barely five minutes had passed before you stole up from behind and snapped the book shut.

'It is a warm day,' you said. 'Let us go down to the stream.'

Alone together for the first time, we took the steep path down to the stream and there, hand in hand, scrambled over the rocks until we reached the pool and the waterfall.

'I will bathe today,' you said; and in a few moments you stood beside me, naked, caressed by sunlight and a soft breeze coming down the valley. I put my hand out to share in the sun's caress but you darted away, laughing, and ran to the waterfall as though you would hide behind a curtain of gushing water. I was soon beside you. I took you in my arms and kissed you while the water crashed down upon our heads. Who yielded—you or I? All I remember is that you had entwined yourself about me like a clinging vine and that a little later we lay together on the grass, on bruised and broken clover, while a whistling thrush released its deep sweet secret on the trembling air.

Blackbird on the wing, bird of the forest shadows, black rose in the long ago of summer, this was your song. It isn't time that's passing by, it is you and I.

⌀

It was your last night under my roof. We were not alone but when I woke in the middle of the night and stretched my hand out, across the space between our beds, you took my hand, for you were awake too. Then I pressed the ends of your fingers, one by one, as I had done so often before, and you dug your nails into my flesh. And our hands made love, much as our bodies might have done. They clung together, warmed and caressed each other, each finger taking on an identity of its own and seeking its opposite. Sometimes the tips of our fingers merely brushed against each other, teasingly, and sometimes our palms met with a rush, would tremble and embrace, separate and then passionately seek each other out. And when sleep finally overcame you, your hand fell listlessly between our beds, touching the ground. And I lifted it up, and after putting it once to my lips, returned it gently to your softly rising bosom.

And so you went away, all three of you, and I was left alone with the brooding mountain. If I could not pass a few weeks without you how was I to pass a year, two years? This was the question I kept asking myself. Would I have to leave the hills and take a flat in Delhi? And what use would it be—looking at you and speaking to you but never able to touch you? Not to be able to touch that which I had already possessed would have been the subtlest form of torture.

The house was empty but I kept finding little things to remind me that you had been there—a handkerchief, a bangle, a length of ribbon—and these remnants made me feel as though you had gone forever. No sound at night, except the rats scurrying about on the rafters.

The rain had brought out the ferns, which were springing up from tree and rock. The murmur of the stream had become an angry rumble. The honeysuckle creeper winding over the front windows was thick with scented blossom. I wish it had flowered a little earlier, before you left. Then you could have put the flowers in your hair.

At night I drank brandy, wrote listlessly, listened to the wind in the chimney and read poetry in bed. There was no one to tell stories to and no hand to hold.

I kept remembering little things—the soft hair hiding your ears, the movement of your hands, the cool touch of your feet, the tender look in your eyes and the sudden stab of mischief that sometimes replaced it.

Mrs Kapoor remarked on the softness of your expression. I was glad that someone had noticed it. In my diary I wrote: 'I have looked at Sushila so often and so much that perhaps I have overlooked her most compelling qualities—her kindness (or is it just her easy-going nature?), her refusal to hurt anyone's feelings (or is it just her indifference to everything?), her wide tolerance (or is it just her laziness?).... Oh, how absolutely ignorant I am of women!'

∽

Well, there was a letter from Dinesh and it held out a lifeline, one that I knew I must seize without any hesitation. He said he might be joining an art school in Delhi and asked me if I would like to return to Delhi and share a flat with him. I had always dreaded the possibility of leaving the hills and living again in a city as depressing as Delhi but love, I considered, ought to make any place habitable...

∽

And then I was on a bus on the road to Delhi.

The first monsoon showers had freshened the fields and everything looked much greener than usual. The maize was just shooting up and the mangoes were ripening fast. Near the larger villages, camels and bullock-carts cluttered up the road and the driver cursed, banging his fist on the horn.

Passing through small towns, the bus driver had to contend with cycle rickshaws, tonga ponies, trucks, pedestrians and other buses. Coming down from the hills for the first time in over a year, I found the noise, chaos, dust and dirt a little unsettling.

As my taxi drew up at the gate of Dinesh's home, Sunil saw me and came running to open the car door. Other children were soon swarming around me. Then I saw you standing near the front door. You raised your hand to your forehead in a typical Muslim form of greeting—a gesture you had picked up, I suppose, from a film.

For two days Dinesh and I went house hunting, for I had decided to take a flat if it was at all practicable. Either it was very hot and we were sweating or it was raining and we were drenched. (It is difficult to find a flat in Delhi, even if one is in a position to pay an exorbitant rent, which I was not. It is especially difficult for bachelors. No one trusts bachelors, especially if there are grown-up daughters in the house. Is this because bachelors are wolves or because girls are so easily seduced these days?)

Finally, after several refusals, we were offered a flat in one of those new colonies that sprout like mushrooms around the capital. The rent was two hundred rupees a month and although I knew I couldn't really afford so much, I was so sick of refusals and already so disheartened and depressed that I took the place and made out a cheque to the landlord, an elderly gentleman with his daughters all safely married in other parts of the country.

There was no furniture in the flat except for a couple of beds but we decided we would fill the place up gradually. Everyone at Dinesh's home—brothers, sister-in-law, aunts, nephews and nieces—helped us to move in. Sunil and his younger brother were the first arrivals. Later the other children, some ten of them, arrived. You, Sushila, came only in the afternoon, but I had gone out for something and only saw you when I returned at teatime. You were sitting on the first-floor balcony and smiled down at me as I walked up the road.

I think you were pleased with the flat; or at any rate, with my courage in taking one. I took you up to the roof and there, in a corner under the stairs, kissed you very quickly. It had to be quick because the other children were close on our heels. There wouldn't be much opportunity for kissing you again. The mountains were far and in a place like Delhi, and with a family like yours, private moments would be few and far between.

Hours later when I sat alone on one of the beds, Sunil came to me, looking rather upset. He must have had a quarrel with you.

'I want to tell you something,' he said.

'Is anything wrong?'

To my amazement he burst into tears.

'Now you must not love me anymore,' he said.

'Why not?'

'Because you are going to marry Sushila and if you love me too much it will not be good for you.'

I could think of nothing to say. It was all too funny and all too sad.

But a little later he was in high spirits, having apparently forgotten the reasons for his earlier dejection. His need for affection stemmed perhaps from his father's long and unnecessary absence from the country.

ᦀ

Dinesh and I had no sleep during our first night in the new flat. We were near the main road and traffic roared past all night. I thought of the hills, so silent that the call of a nightjar startled one in the stillness of the night.

I was out most of the next day and when I got back in the evening it was to find that Dinesh had had a rumpus with the landlord. Apparently the landlord had really wanted bachelors and couldn't understand or appreciate a large number of children moving in and out of the house all day.

'I thought landlords preferred having families,' I said.

'He wants to know how a bachelor came to have such a large family!'

'Didn't you tell him that the children were only temporary and wouldn't be living here?'

'I did, but he doesn't believe me.'

'Well, anyway, we're not going to stop the children from coming to see us,' I said indignantly. (No children, no Sushila!) 'If he doesn't see reason, he can have his flat back.'

'Did he cash my cheque?'

'No, he's given it back.'

'That means he really wants us out. To hell with his flat! It's too noisy here anyway. Let's go back to your place.'

We packed our bedding, trunks and kitchen utensils once more; hired a bullock-cart and arrived at Dinesh's home (three miles distant) late at night, hungry and upset.

Everything seemed to be going wrong.

ᦀ

Living in the same house as you but unable to have any real contact with you (except for the odd, rare moment when we were left alone in the same room and were able to exchange a word or a glance) was an exquisite form of self-inflicted torture: self-inflicted, because no one was forcing me to stay in Delhi. Sometimes you had to avoid me and I could not stand that. Only Dinesh (and, of course, Sunil and some of the children) knew anything about the affair—adults are much slower than children at sensing the truth—and it was still too soon to reveal the true state of affairs and my own feelings to anyone else in the family. If I came out with the declaration that I was in love with you, it would immediately become obvious that something had happened during your holiday in the hill station. It would be said that I had taken advantage of the situation (which I had) and that I had seduced you—even though I was beginning to wonder if it was you who had seduced me! And if a marriage was suddenly arranged, people would say: 'It's been arranged so quickly. And she's so young. He must have got her into trouble.' Even though there were no signs of your having got into that sort of trouble.

And yet I could not help hoping that you would become my wife sooner than could be foreseen. I wanted to look after you. I did not want others to be doing it for me. Was that very selfish? Or was it a true state of being in love?

There were times—times when you kept your distance and did not even look at me—when I grew desperate. I knew you could not show your familiarity with me in front of others and yet, knowing this, I still tried to catch your eye, to sit near you, to touch you fleetingly. I could not hold myself back. I became morose, I wallowed in self-pity. And self-pity, I realized, is a sign of failure, especially of failure in love.

It was time to return to the hills.

∽

Sushila, when I got up in the morning to leave, you were still asleep and I did not wake you. I watched you stretched out on your bed, your dark face tranquil and untouched by care, your black hair spread over the white pillow, your long thin hands and feet in repose. You were so beautiful when you were asleep.

And as I watched, I felt a tightening around my heart, a sudden panic that I might somehow lose you.

The others were up and there was no time to steal a kiss. A taxi was at the gate. A baby was bawling. Your grandmother was giving me advice. The taxi driver kept blowing his horn.

Goodbye, Sushila!

We were in the middle of the rains. There was a constant drip and drizzle and drumming on the corrugated tin roof. The walls were damp and there was mildew on my books and even on the pickle that Dinesh had made.

Everything was green, the foliage almost tropical, especially near the stream. Great stag ferns grew from the trunks of trees, fresh moss covered the rocks and the maidenhair fern was at its loveliest. The water was a torrent, rushing through the ravine and taking with it bushes and small trees. I could not remain out for long, for at any moment it might start raining. And there were also the leeches who lost no time in fastening themselves on to my legs and feasting on my blood.

Once, standing on some rocks, I saw a slim brown snake swimming with the current. It looked beautiful and lonely. I dreamt a dream, a very disturbing dream, which troubled me for days.

In the dream, Sunil suggested that we go down to the stream. We put some bread and butter into an airbag, along with a long bread knife, and set off down the hill. Sushila was barefoot, wearing the old cotton tunic which she had worn as a child, Sunil had on a bright yellow T-shirt and black jeans. He looked very dashing. As we took the forest path down to the stream, we saw two young men following us. One of them, a dark, slim youth, seemed familiar. I said 'Isn't that Sushila's boyfriend?' But they denied it. The other youth wasn't anyone I knew.

When we reached the stream, Sunil and I plunged into the pool while Sushila sat on the rock just above us. We had been bathing for a few minutes when the two young men came down the slope and began fondling Sushila. She did not resist but Sunil climbed out of the pool and began scrambling up the slope. One of the youths, the less familiar one, had a long knife in his hand. Sunil picked up a stone and flung it at the youth, striking him on the shoulder. I rushed up and grabbed the hand that held the knife. The youth kicked me on the shins and thrust me away and I fell beneath him. The arm with the knife was raised over me but I still held the wrist. And then I saw Sushila behind him, her face framed by a passing cloud. She had the bread knife in her hand, and her arm swung up and down, and the knife cut through my adversary's neck as though it were passing through a ripe melon.

I scrambled to my feet to find Sushila gazing at the headless corpse with the detachment and mild curiosity of a child who has just removed the wings from a butterfly. The other youth, who looked like Sushila's boyfriend, began running away. He was chased by the three of us. When he slipped and fell, I found myself beside him, the blade of the knife poised beneath his left shoulder blade. I couldn't push the knife in. Then Sunil put his hand over mine and the blade slipped smoothly into the flesh.

∽

At all times of the day and night I could hear the murmur of the stream at the bottom of the hill. Even if I didn't listen, the sound was there. I had grown used to it. But whenever I went away, I was conscious of something missing and I was lonely without the sound of running water.

I remained alone for two months and then I had to see you again, Sushila. I could not bear the long-drawn-out uncertainty of the situation. I wanted to do something that would bring everything nearer to a conclusion. Merely to stand by and wait was intolerable. Nor could I bear the secrecy to which Dinesh had sworn me. Someone else would have to know about my intentions—someone would have to help. I needed another ally to sustain my hopes; only then would I find the waiting easier.

You had not been keeping well and looked thin, but you were as cheerful, as serene as ever.

When I took you to the pictures with Sunil, you wore a sleeveless kameez made of purple silk. It set off your dark beauty very well. Your face was soft and shy and your smile hadn't changed. I could not keep my eyes off you.

Returning home in the taxi, I held your hand all the way.

Sunil (in Punjabi): 'Will you give your children English or Hindi names?'

Me: 'Hindustani names.'

Sunil (in Punjabi): 'Ah, that is the right answer, Uncle!'

 C∩

And first I went to your mother.

She was a tiny woman and looked very delicate. But she'd had six children—a seventh was on the way—and they had all come into the world without much difficulty and were the healthiest in the entire joint family.

She was on her way to see relatives in another part of the city and I accompanied her part of the way. As she was pregnant, she was offered a seat in the crowded bus. I managed to squeeze in beside her. She had always shown a liking for me and I did not find it difficult to come to the point.

'At what age would you like Sushila to get married?' I asked casually, with almost paternal interest.

'We'll worry about that when the time comes. She has still to finish school. And if she keeps failing her exams, she will never finish school.'

I took a deep breath and made the plunge.

'When the time comes,' I said, 'when the time comes, I would like to marry her.' And without waiting to see what her reaction would be, I continued: 'I know I must wait a year or two, even longer. But I am telling you this so that it will be in your mind. You are her mother and so I want you to be the first to know.' (Liar that I was! She was about the fifth to know. But what I really wanted to say was, 'Please don't be looking for any other husband for her just yet.')

She didn't show much surprise. She was a placid woman. But she said, rather sadly, 'It's all right but I don't have much say in the family. I do not have any money, you see. It depends on the others, especially her grandmother.'

'I'll speak to them when the time comes. Don't worry about that. And you don't have to worry about money or anything—what I mean is, I don't believe in dowries—I mean, you don't have to give me a Godrej cupboard and a sofa set and that sort of thing. All I want is Sushila...'

'She is still very young.'

But she was pleased—pleased that her flesh and blood, her own daughter, could mean so much to a man.

'Don't tell anyone else just now,' I said.

'I won't tell anyone,' she said with a smile.

So now the secret—if it could be called that—was shared by at least five people.

The bus crawled on through the busy streets and we sat in silence, surrounded by a press of people but isolated in the intimacy of our conversation.

I warmed towards her—towards that simple, straightforward, uneducated woman (she had never been to school, could not read or write), who might still have been young and pretty had her circumstances been different. I asked her when the baby was due.

'In two months,' she said. She laughed. Evidently she found it unusual and rather amusing for a young man to ask her such a question.

'I'm sure it will be a fine baby,' I said. And I thought: That makes six brothers-in-law!

ᔕ

I did not think I would get a chance to speak to your Uncle Ravi (Dinesh's elder brother) before I left. But on my last evening in Delhi, I found myself alone with him on the Karol Bagh road. At first we spoke of his own plans for marriage and, to please him, I said the girl he'd chosen was both beautiful and intelligent.

He warmed towards me.

Clearing my throat, I went on. 'Ravi, you are five years younger than me and you are about to get married.'

'Yes, and it's time you thought of doing the same thing.'

'Well, I've never thought seriously about it before—I'd always scorned the institution of marriage—but now I've changed my mind. Do you know whom I'd like to marry?'

To my surprise Ravi unhesitatingly took the name of Asha, a distant cousin I'd met only once. She came from Ferozepur, and her hips were so large that from a distance she looked like an oversized pear.

'No, no,' I said. 'Asha is a lovely girl but I wasn't thinking of her. I would like to marry a girl like Sushila. To be frank, Ravi, I would like to marry Sushila.'

There was a long silence and I feared the worst. The noise of cars, scooters and buses seemed to recede into the distance and Ravi and I were alone together in a vacuum of silence.

So that the awkwardness would not last too long, I stumbled on with what I had to say. 'I know she's young and that I will have to wait for some time.' (Familiar words!) 'But if you approve, and the family approves, and Sushila approves, well then, there's nothing I'd like better than to marry her.'

Ravi pondered, scratched himself, and then, to my delight, said: 'Why not? It's a fine idea.'

The traffic sounds returned to the street and I felt as though I could set fire to a bus or do something equally in keeping with my high spirits.

'It would bring you even closer to us,' said Ravi. 'We

would like to have you in our family. At least I would like it.'

'That makes all the difference,' I said. 'I will do my best for her, Ravi. I'll do everything to make her happy.'

'She is very simple and unspoilt.'

'I know. That's why I care so much for her.'

'I will do what I can to help you. She should finish school by the time she is seventeen. It does not matter if you are older. Twelve years difference in age is not uncommon. So don't worry. Be patient and all will be arranged.'

And so I had three strong allies—Dinesh, Ravi and your mother. Only your grandmother remained and I dared not approach her on my own. She was the most difficult hurdle because she was the head of the family and she was autocratic and often unpredictable. She was not on good terms with your mother and for that very reason I feared that she might oppose my proposal. I had no idea how much she valued Ravi's and Dinesh's judgement. All I knew was that they bowed to all her decisions.

How impossible it was for you to shed the burden of your relatives! Individually, you got on quite well with all of them; but because they could not live without bickering among themselves, you were just a pawn in the great joint family game.

∽

You put my hand to your cheek and to your breast. I kissed your closed eyes and took your face in my hands and touched your lips with mine; a phantom kiss in the darkness of a veranda. And then, intoxicated, I stumbled into the road and walked the streets all night.

I was sitting on the rocks above the oak forest when I saw a young man walking towards me down the steep path. From his careful manner of walking and light clothing, I could tell that he was a stranger, one who was not used to the hills. He was about my height, slim, rather long in the face; good-looking in a delicate sort of way. When he came nearer, I recognized him as the young man in the photograph, the youth of my dream—your late admirer! I wasn't too surprised to see him. Somehow, I had always felt that we would meet one day.

I remembered his name and said, 'How are you, Pramod?'

He became rather confused. His eyes were already clouded with doubt and unhappiness but he did not appear to be an aggressive person.

'How did you know my name?' he asked.

'How did you know where to find me?' I countered.

'Your neighbours, the Kapoors, told me. I could not wait for you to return to the house. I have to go down again tonight.'

'Well then, would you like to walk home with me or would you prefer to sit here and talk? I know who you are but I've no idea why you've come to see me.'

'It's all right here,' he said, spreading his handkerchief on the grass before sitting down on it. 'How did you know my name?'

I stared at him for a few moments and got the impression that he was a vulnerable person—perhaps more vulnerable than myself.

My only advantage was that I was older and therefore better able to conceal my real feelings.

'Sushila told me,' I said.

'Oh. I did not think you would know.'

I was a little puzzled but said, 'I knew about you, of course. And you must have known that or you would hardly have come here to see me.'

'You knew about Sushila and me?' he asked, looking even more confused.

'Well, I know that you are supposed to be in love with her.'

He smote himself on the forehead. 'My God! Do the others know, too?'

'I don't think so.' I deliberately avoided mention of Sunil.

In his distraction he started plucking at tufts of grass. 'Did she tell you?' he asked.

'Yes.'

'Girls can't keep secrets. But in a way I'm glad she told you. Now I don't have to explain everything. You see, I came here for your help. I know you are not her real uncle but you are very close to her family. Last year in Delhi she often spoke about you. She said you were very kind.'

It then occurred to me that Pramod knew nothing about my relationship with you, other than that I was supposed to be the most benevolent of 'uncles'. He knew that you had spent your summer holidays with me—but so had Dinesh and Sunil. And now, aware that I was a close friend of the family, he had come to make an ally of me—in much the same way that I had gone about making allies!

'Have you seen Sushila recently?' I asked.

'Yes. Two days ago, in Delhi. But I had only a few minutes alone with her. We could not talk much. You see, Uncle—you will not mind if I also call you uncle? I want to marry her but there is no one who can speak to her people on my behalf. My own parents are not alive. If I go straight to her family, most probably I will be thrown out of the house. So I want you to help me. I am not well off but I will soon have a job and then I can support her.'

'Did you tell her all this?'

'Yes.'

'And what did she say?'

'She told me to speak to you about it.'

Clever Sushila! Diabolical Sushila!

'To me?' I repeated.

'Yes, she said it would be better than talking to her parents.'

I couldn't help laughing. And a long-tailed blue magpie, disturbed by my laughter, set up a shrill creaking and chattering of its own.

'Don't laugh, I'm serious, Uncle,' said Pramod. He took me by the hand and looked at me appealingly.

'Well, it ought to be serious,' I said. 'How old are you, Pramod?'

'Twenty-three.'

'Only seven years younger than me. So please don't call me uncle. It makes me feel prehistoric. Use my first name, if you like. And when do you hope to marry Sushila?'

'As soon as possible. I know she is still very young for me.'

'Not at all,' I said, 'Young girls are marrying middle-aged men every day! And you're still quite young yourself. But she can't get married as yet, Pramod, I know that for a certainty.'

'That's what I feared. She will have to finish school, I suppose.'

'That's right. But tell me something. It's obvious that you are in love with her and I don't blame you for it. Sushila is the kind of girl we all fall in love with! But do you know if she loves you? Did she say she would like to marry you?'

'She did not say—I do not know...'

There was a haunted, hurt look in his eyes and my heart went out to him. 'But I love her—isn't that enough?'

'It could be enough—provided she doesn't love someone else.'

'Does she, Uncle?'

'To be frank, I don't know.'

He brightened up at that. 'She likes me,' he said. 'I know that much.'

'Well, I like you too but that doesn't mean I'd marry you.'

He was despondent again. 'I see what you mean.... But what is love, how can I recognize it?'

And that was one question I couldn't answer. How do we recognize it?

I persuaded Pramod to stay the night. The sun had gone down and he was shivering. I made a fire, the first of the winter, using oak and thorn branches. Then I shared my brandy with him.

I did not feel any resentment against Pramod. Prior to meeting him, I had been jealous. And when I first saw him coming along the path, I remembered my dream, and thought, 'Perhaps I am going to kill him, after all. Or perhaps he's going to kill me.' But it had turned out differently. If dreams have any meaning at all, the meaning doesn't come within our limited comprehension.

I had visualized Pramod as being rather crude, selfish and irresponsible, an unattractive college student, the type who has never known or understood girls very well and looks on them as strange exotic creatures who are to be seized and plundered at the first opportunity. Such men do exist but Pramod was never one of them. He did not know much about women; neither did I. He was gentle, polite, unsure of himself. I wondered if I should tell him about my own feelings for you.

After a while he began to talk about himself and about you. He told me how he fell in love with you. At first he had been friendly with another girl, a class-fellow of yours but a year or two older. You had carried messages to him on the girl's behalf. Then the girl had rejected him. He was terribly depressed and one evening he drank a lot of cheap liquor. Instead of falling dead, as he had been hoping, he lost his way and met you near your home. He was in need of sympathy and you gave him that. You let him hold your hand. He told you how hopeless he felt and you comforted him. And when he said the world was a cruel place, you consented. You agreed with him. What more can a man expect from a woman? Only fourteen at the time, you had no difficulty in comforting a man of twenty-two. No wonder he fell in love with you!

Afterwards you met occasionally on the road and spoke

to each other. He visited the house once or twice, on some pretext or other. And when you came to the hills, he wrote to you.

That was all he had to tell me. That was all there was to tell. You had touched his heart once and touching it, had no difficulty in capturing it.

Next morning I took Pramod down to the stream. I wanted to tell him everything and somehow I could not do it in the house.

He was charmed by the place. The water flowed gently, its music subdued, soft chamber music after the monsoon orchestration. Cowbells tinkled on the hillside and an eagle soared high above.

'I did not think water could be so clear,' said Pramod. 'It is not muddy like the streams and rivers of the plains.'

'In the summer you can bathe here,' I said. 'There is a pool further downstream.'

He nodded thoughtfully. 'Did she come here too?'

'Yes, Sushila and Sunil and I.... We came here on two or three occasions.' My voice trailed off and I glanced at Pramod standing at the edge of the water. He looked up at me and his eyes met mine.

'There is something I want to tell you,' I said.

He continued staring at me and a shadow seemed to pass across his face—a shadow of doubt, fear, death, eternity, was it one or all of these or just a play of light and shade? But I remembered my dream and stepped back from him. For a moment both of us looked at each other with distrust and uncertainty. Then the fear passed. Whatever had happened between us, dream or reality, had happened in some other existence. Now he took my hand and held it, held it tight, as though seeking assurance, as though identifying himself with me.

'Let us sit down,' I said. 'There is something I must tell you.'

We sat down on the grass and when I looked up through

the branches of the banj oak, everything seemed to have been tilted and held at an angle, and the sky shocked me with its blueness and the leaves were no longer green but purple in the shadows of the ravine. They were your colour, Sushila. I remembered you wearing purple—dark smiling Sushila, thinking your own thoughts and refusing to share them with anyone.

'I love Sushila too,' I said.

'I know,' he said naively. 'That is why I came to you for help.'

'No, you don't know,' I said. 'When I say I love Sushila, I mean just that. I mean caring for her in the same way that you care for her. I mean I want to marry her.'

'You, Uncle?'

'Yes. Does it shock you very much?'

'No, no.' He turned his face away and stared at the worn face of an old grey rock and perhaps he drew some strength from its permanency. 'Why should you not love her? Perhaps, in my heart, I really knew it, but did not want to know—did not want to believe. Perhaps that is why I really came here—to find out. Something that Sunil said...'

'But why didn't you tell me before?'

'Because you were telling me!'

'Yes, I was too full of my own love to think that any other was possible. What do we do now? Do we both wait and then let her make her choice?'

'If you wish.'

'You have the advantage, Uncle. You have more to offer.'

'Do you mean more security or more love? Some women place more value on the former.'

'Not Sushila. I mean you can offer her a more interesting life. You are a writer. Who knows, you may be famous one day.'

'You have your youth to offer, Pramod. I have only a few years of youth left to me—and two or three of them will pass in waiting.'

'Oh, no,' he said. 'You will always be young. If you have Sushila, you will always be young.'

Once again I heard the whistling thrush. Its song was a crescendo of sweet notes and variations that rang clearly across the ravine. I could not see the bird but its call emerged from the forest like some dark sweet secret and again it was saying, 'It isn't time that's passing by, my friend. It is you and I.'

∽

Listen. Sushila, the worst has happened. Ravi has written to say that a marriage will not be possible—not now, not next year; never. Of course he makes a lot of excuses—that you must receive a complete college education ('higher studies'), that the difference in our age is too great, that you might change your mind after a year or two—but reading between the lines, I can guess that the real reason is your grandmother. She does not want it. Her word is law and no one, least of all Ravi, would dare oppose her. But I do not mean to give in so easily. I will wait my chance. As long as I know that you are with me, I will wait my chance.

I wonder what the old lady objects to in me. Is it simply that she is conservative and tradition-bound? She has always shown a liking for me and I don't see why her liking should change because I want to marry her grand-niece. Your mother has no objection.

Perhaps that's why your grandmother objects. Whatever the reason, I am coming down to Delhi to find out how things stand.

Of course the worst part is that Ravi has asked me—in the friendliest terms and in a most roundabout manner—not to come to the house for some time. He says this will give the affair a chance to cool off and die a natural (I would call it an unnatural) death. He assumes, of course, that I will accept the old lady's decision and simply forget all about you. Ravi is yet to fall in love.

∽

Dinesh was in Lucknow. I could not visit the house. So I
sat on a bench in the Talkatora Gardens and watched a
group of children playing gulli danda. Then I recalled that
Sunil's school got over at three o'clock and that if I hurried
I would be able to meet him outside the St Columba's gate.

I reached the school on time. Boys were streaming
out of the compound and as they were all wearing green
uniforms—a young forest on the move—I gave up all hope
of spotting Sunil.

But he saw me first. He ran across the road, dodged a
cyclist, evaded a bus and seized me about the waist.

'I'm so happy to see you, Uncle!'

'As I am to see you, Sunil.'

'You want to see Sushila?'

'Yes, but you too. I can't come to the house, Sunil.
You probably know that. When do you have to be home?'

'About four o'clock. If I'm late, I'll say the bus was too
crowded and I couldn't get in.'

'That gives us an hour or two. Let's go to the exhibition
grounds. Would you like that?'

'All right, I haven't seen the exhibition yet.'

We took a scooter rickshaw to the exhibition grounds
on Mathura Road. It was an industrial exhibition and there
was little to interest either a schoolboy or a lovesick author.
But a cafe was at hand, overlooking an artificial lake, and
we sat in the sun consuming hot dogs and cold coffee.

'Sunil, will you help me?' I asked.

'Whatever you say, Uncle.'

'I don't suppose I can see Sushila this time. I don't want
to hang about near the house or her school like a disreputable
character. It's all right lurking outside a boys' school; but it
wouldn't do to be hanging about the Kanyadevi Pathshala
or wherever it is she's studying. It's possible the family will
change their minds about us later. Anyway, what matters

now is Sushila's attitude. Ask her this, Sunil. Ask her if she wants me to wait until she is eighteen.

'She will be free then to do what she wants, even to run away with me if necessary—that is, if she really wants to. I was ready to wait two years. I'm prepared to wait three. But it will help if I know she's waiting too. Will you ask her that, Sunil?'

'Yes, I'll ask her.'

'Ask her tonight. Then tomorrow we'll meet again outside your school.'

∽

We met briefly the next day. There wasn't much time. Sunil had to be home early and I had to catch the night train out of Delhi. We stood in the generous shade of a peepul tree and I asked,

'What did she say?'

'She said to keep waiting.'

'All right, I'll wait.'

'But when she is eighteen, what if she changes her mind? You know what girls are like.'

'You're a cynical chap, Sunil.'

'What does that mean?'

'It means you know too much about life. But tell me— what makes you think she might change her mind?'

'Her boyfriend.'

'Pramod? She doesn't care for him, poor chap.'

'Not Pramod. Another one.'

'Another! You mean a new one?'

'New,' said Sunil. 'An officer in a bank. He's got a car.'

'Oh,' I said despondently. 'I can't compete with a car.'

'No,' said Sunil. 'Never mind, Uncle. You still have me for your friend. Have you forgotten that?'

I had almost forgotten but it was good to be reminded.

'It is time to go,' he said. 'I must catch the bus today. When will you come to Delhi again?'

'Next month. Next year. Who knows? But I'll come. Look after yourself, my friend.'

He ran off and jumped on to the footboard of a moving bus. He waved to me until the bus went round the bend in the road.

It was lonely under the peepul tree. It is said that only ghosts live in peepul trees. I do not blame them, for peepul trees are cool and shady and full of loneliness.

I may stop loving you, Sushila, but I will never stop loving the days I loved you.

A KNOCK AT THE DOOR

For Sherlock Holmes, it usually meant an impatient client waiting below in the street. For Nero Wolfe, it was the doorbell that rang, disturbing the great man in his orchid rooms. For Poe or Walter de la Mare, that knocking on a moonlit door could signify a ghostly visitor—no one outside!—or, even more mysterious, no one in the house...

Well, clients I have none, and ghostly visitants don't have to knock; but as I spend most of the day at home, writing, I have learnt to live with the occasional knock at the front door. I find doorbells even more startling than ghosts, and ornate brass knockers have a tendency to disappear when the price of brassware goes up; so my callers have to use their knuckles or fists on the solid mahogany door. It's a small price to pay for disturbing me.

I hear the knocking quite distinctly, as the small front room adjoins my even smaller study-cum-bedroom. But sometimes I keep up a pretense of not hearing anything straight away. Mahogany is good for the knuckles! Eventually, I place a pencil between my teeth and, holding a sheet of blank foolscap in one hand, move slowly and thoughtfully toward the front door, so that, when I open it, my caller can see that I have been disturbed in the throes of composition. Not that I have ever succeeded in making any one feel guilty about it; they stay as long as they like. And after they have gone, I can get back to listening to my tapes of old Hollywood operettas.

Impervious to both literature and music, my first caller is usually a boy from the village, wanting to sell me his cucumbers or 'France-beans'. For some reason he won't call them French beans. He is not impressed by the accoutrements of my trade. He thrusts a cucumber into my arms and empties the beans on a coffee-table book which has been sent to me for review. (There is no coffee table, but the book makes a good one.) He is confident that I cannot resist his France-beans, even though this sub-Himalayan variety is extremely hard and stringy. Actually, I am a sucker for cucumbers, but I take the beans so I can get the cucumber cheap. In this fashion, authors survive.

The deal done, and the door closed, I decide it's time to do some work. I start this little essay. If it's nice and gets published, I will be able to take care of the electricity bill. There's a knock at the door. Some knocks I recognize, but this is a new one. Perhaps it's someone asking for a donation. Cucumber in hand, I stride to the door and open it abruptly only to be confronted by a polite, smart-looking chauffeur who presents me with a large bouquet of flowering gladioli!

'With the compliments of Mr B. P. Singh,' he announces, before departing smartly with a click of the heels. I start looking for a receptacle for the flowers, as Grandmother's flower vase was really designed for violets and forget-me-nots.

B. P. Singh is a kind man who had the original idea of turning his property outside Mussoorie into a gladioli farm. A bare hillside is now a mass of gladioli from May to September. He sells them to flower shops in Delhi, but his heart bleeds at harvesting time.

Gladioli arranged in an ice bucket, I return to my desk and am just wondering what I should be writing next, when there is a loud banging on the door. No friendly knock this time. Urgent, peremptory, summoning! Could it be the police? And what have I gone and done? Every good citizen has at least one guilty secret, just waiting to be discovered! I move warily to the door and open it an inch or two. It is a policeman!

Hastily, I drop the cucumber and politely ask him if I can be of help. Try to look casual, I tell myself. He has a small packet in his hands. No, it's not a warrant. It turns out to be a slim volume of verse, sent over by a visiting DIG of police, who has authored it. I thank his emissary profusely, and, after he has gone, I place the volume reverently on my bookshelf, beside the works of other poetry-loving policemen. These men of steel, who inspire so much awe and trepidation in the rest of us, they too are humans and some of them are poets!

Now it's afternoon and the knock I hear is a familiar one, and welcome, for it heralds the postman. What would writers do without postmen? They have more power than literary agents. I don't have an agent (I'll be honest and say an agent won't have me), but I do have a postman, and he turns up every day except when there's a landslide.

Yes, it's Prakash the postman who makes my day, showering me with letters, books, acceptances, rejections, and even the occasional cheque. These postmen are fine fellows, they do their utmost to bring the good news from Ghent to Aix.

And what has Prakash brought me today? A reminder: I haven't paid my subscription to the Author's Guild. I'd better send it off or I shall be a derecognized author. A letter from a reader: would I like to go through her 800-page dissertation on the Gita? Some day, my love.... A cheque, a cheque! From Sunflower Books, for nineteen rupees only, representing the sale of six copies of one of my books during the previous year. Never mind. Six wise persons put their money down for my book. No fresh acceptances, but no rejections either. A postcard from Goa, where one of my publishers is taking a holiday. So the post is something of an anti-climax. But I mustn't complain. Not every knock on the door brings gladioli fresh from the fields. Tomorrow's another day, and the postman comes six days a week.

FROM SMALL BEGINNINGS

And the last puff of the day-wind brought from the
unseen villages, the scent of damp wood-smoke, hot
cakes, dripping undergrowth, and rotting pine cones.
That is the true smell of the Himalayas, and if once it
creeps into the blood of a man, that man will at the
last, forgetting all else, return to the hills to die.

—Rudyard Kipling

On the first clear September day, towards the end of the rains, I visited the pine knoll, my place of peace and power.

It was months since I'd last been there. Trips to the plains, a crisis in my affairs, involvements with other people and their troubles and an entire monsoon had come between me and the grassy, pine-topped slope facing the Hill of Fairies (Pari Tibba to the locals). Now I tramped through late monsoon foliage—tall ferns, bushes festooned with flowering convolvulus—crossed the stream by way of its little bridge of stones—and climbed the steep hill to the pine slope.

When the trees saw me, they made as if to turn in my direction. A puff of wind came across the valley from the distant snows. A long-tailed blue magpie took alarm and flew noisily out of an oak tree. The cicadas were suddenly silent. But the trees remembered me. They bowed gently in the breeze and beckoned me nearer, welcoming me home. Three pines, a straggling oak and a wild cherry. I went among them and acknowledged their welcome with a touch of my hand against their trunks—the cherry's smooth and polished; the pine's patterned and whorled; the oak's rough, gnarled, full of experience. He'd been there longest and the wind had bent his upper branches and twisted a few so that he looked shaggy and undistinguished. But like the philosopher who is careless about his dress and appearance, the oak has secrets, a hidden wisdom. He has learnt the art of survival!

While the oak and the pines are older than me and have been here many years, the cherry tree is exactly seven years old. I know, because I planted it.

One day I had this cherry seed in my hand, and on an impulse I thrust it into the soft earth and then went away and forgot all about it. A few months later I found a tiny cherry tree in the long grass. I did not expect it to survive. But the following year it was two feet tall. And then some goats ate its leaves and a grass cutter's scythe injured the stem and I was sure it would wither away. But it renewed itself, sprang up even faster, and within three years it was a healthy, growing tree, about five feet tall.

I left the hills for two years—forced by circumstances to make a living in Delhi—but this time I did not forget the cherry tree. I thought about it fairly often, sent telepathic messages of encouragement in its direction. And when, a couple of years ago, I returned in the autumn, my heart did a somersault when I found my tree sprinkled with pale pink blossom (the Himalayan cherry flowers in November). And later, when the fruit was ripe, the tree was visited by finches, tits, bulbuls and other small birds, all come to feast on the sour, red cherries.

Last summer I spent a night on the pine knoll, sleeping on the grass beneath the cherry tree. I lay awake for hours, listening to the chatter of the stream and the occasional tonk-tonk of a nightjar, and watching through the branches overhead, the stars turning in the sky, and I felt the power of the sky and earth and the power of a small cherry seed...

And so when the rains are over, this is where I come, that I might feel the peace and power of this place. It's a big world and momentous events are taking place all the time. But this is where I have seen it happen.

This is where I will write my stories. I can see everything

from here—my cottage across the valley; behind and above me, the town and the bazaar, straddling the ridge; to the left, the high mountains and the twisting road to the source of the great river; below me, the little stream and the path to the village; ahead, the Hill of Fairies, the fields beyond; the wide valley below, and then another range of hills and then the distant plains. I can even see Prem Singh in the garden, putting the mattresses out in the sun.

From here he is just a speck on the far hill but I know it is Prem by the way he stands. A man may have a hundred disguises but in the end it is his posture that gives him away. Like my grandfather, who was a master of disguise and successfully roamed the bazaars as fruit vendor or basket maker. But we could always recognize him because of his pronounced slouch.

Prem Singh doesn't slouch, but he has this habit of looking up at the sky (regardless of whether it's cloudy or clear), and at the moment he's looking at the sky.

Eight years with Prem. He was just a sixteen-year-old boy when I first saw him, and now he has a wife and child.

I had been in the cottage for just over a year.... He stood on the landing outside the kitchen door. A tall boy, dark, with good teeth and brown, deep-set eyes; dressed smartly in white drill—his only change of clothes. Looking for a job. I liked the look of him, but—

'I already have someone working for me,' I said.

'Yes, sir. He is my uncle.'

In the hills, everyone is a brother or an uncle.

'You don't want me to dismiss your uncle?'

'No, sir. But he says you can find a job for me.'

'I'll try. I'll make inquiries. Have you just come from your village?'

'Yes. Yesterday I walked ten miles to Pauri. There I got a bus.'

'Sit down. Your uncle will make some tea.'

He sat down on the steps, removed his white keds,

wriggled his toes. His feet were both long and broad, large feet, but not ugly. He was unusually clean for a hill boy. And taller than most.

'Do you smoke?' I asked.

'No, sir.'

'It is true,' said his uncle, 'he does not smoke. All my nephews smoke, but this one, he is a little peculiar, he does not smoke—neither beedi nor hookah.'

'Do you drink?'

'It makes me vomit.'

'Do you take bhang?'

'No, sahib.'

'You have no vices. It's unnatural.'

'He is unnatural, sahib,' said his uncle.

'Does he chase girls?'

'They chase him, sahib.'

'So he left the village and came looking for a job.' I looked at him. He grinned, then looked away, began rubbing his feet.

'Your name is?'

'Prem Singh.'

'All right, Prem, I will try to do something for you.'

I did not see him for a couple of weeks. I forgot about finding him a job. But when I met him again, on the road to the bazaar, he told me that he had got a temporary job in the Survey, looking after the surveyor's tents.

'Next week we will be going to Rajasthan,' he said.

'It will be very hot. Have you been in the desert before?'

'No, sir.'

'It is not like the hills. And it is far from home.'

'I know. But I have no choice in the matter. I have to collect some money in order to get married.'

In his region there was a bride price, usually of two thousand rupees.

'Do you have to get married so soon?'

'I have only one brother and he is still very young. My

mother is not well. She needs a daughter-in-law to help her in the fields and with the cows and in the house. We are a small family, so the work is greater.'

Every family has its few terraced fields, narrow and stony, usually perched on a hillside above a stream or river. They grow rice, barley, maize, potatoes—just enough to live on. Even if their produce is sufficient for marketing, the absence of roads makes it difficult to get the produce to the market towns. There is no money to be earned in the villages, and money is needed for clothes, soap, medicines and for recovering the family jewellery from the moneylenders. So the young men leave their villages to find work, and to find work they must go to the plains. The lucky ones get into the army. Others enter domestic service or take jobs in garages, hotels, wayside tea shops, schools...

In Mussoorie the main attraction is the large number of schools, which employ cooks and bearers. But the schools were full when Prem arrived. He'd been to the recruiting centre at Roorkee, hoping to get into the army; but they found a deformity in his right foot, the result of a bone broken when a landslip carried him away one dark monsoon night; he was lucky, he said, that it was only his foot and not his head that had been broken.

He came to the house to inform his uncle about the job and to say goodbye. I thought: another nice person I probably won't see again; another ship passing in the night, the friendly twinkle of its lights soon vanishing in the darkness. I said 'come again', held his smile with mine so that I could remember him better and returned to my study and my typewriter. The typewriter is the repository of a writer's loneliness. It stares unsympathetically back at him every day, doing its best to be discouraging. Maybe I'll go back to the old-fashioned quill pen and marble inkstand; then I can feel like a real writer, Balzac or Dickens, scratching away into the endless reaches of the night.... Of course, the days and nights are seemingly shorter than they need to be! They must be, otherwise why do we hurry so much and achieve so little, by the standards of the past...

Prem goes, disappears into the vast faceless cities of the plains, and a year slips by, or rather I do, and then here he is again, thinner and darker and still smiling and still looking for a job. I should have known that hillmen don't disappear altogether. The spirit-haunted rocks don't let their people wander too far, lest they lose them forever.

I was able to get him a job in the school. The headmaster's wife needed a cook. I wasn't sure if Prem could cook very well but I sent him along and they said they'd give him a trial. Three days later the Headmaster's wife met me on the road and started gushing all over me. She was the type who gushes.

'We're so grateful to you! Thank you for sending me that lovely boy. He's so polite. And he cooks very well. A little too hot for my husband, but otherwise delicious—just delicious! He's a real treasure—a lovely boy.' And she gave me an arch look—the famous look which she used to captivate all the good-looking young prefects who became prefects, it was said, only if she approved of them.

I wasn't sure that she didn't want something more than a cook and I only hoped that Prem would give every satisfaction.

He looked cheerful enough when he came to see me on his day off.

'How are you getting on?' I asked.

'Lovely,' he said, using his mistress's favourite expression.

'What do you mean—lovely? Do they like your work?'

'The memsahib likes it. She strokes me on the cheek whenever she enters the kitchen. The sahib says nothing. He takes medicine after every meal.'

'Did he always take medicine—or only now that you're doing the cooking?'

'I am not sure. I think he has always been sick.'

He was sleeping in the headmaster's veranda and getting

sixty rupees a month. A cook in Delhi got a hundred and sixty. And a cook in Paris or New York got ten times as much. I did not say as much to Prem. He might ask me to get him a job in New York. And that would be the last I saw of him! He, as a cook, might well get a job making curries off Broadway; I, as a writer, wouldn't get to first base. And only my Uncle Ken knew the secret of how to make a living without actually doing any work. But then, of course, he had four sisters. And each of them was married to a fairly prosperous husband. So Uncle Ken divided his year among them. Three months with Aunt Ruby in Nainital. Three months with Aunt Susie in Kashmir. Three months with my mother (not quite so affluent) in Jamnagar. And three months in the Vet Hospital in Bareilly, where Aunt Mabel ran the hospital for her veterinary husband. In this way, he never overstayed his welcome. A sister can look after a brother for just three months at a time and no more. Uncle K. had it worked out to perfection.

But I had no sisters and I couldn't live forever on the royalties of a single novel. So I had to write others. So I came to the hills.

The hillmen go to the plains to make a living. I had to come to the hills to try and make mine.

'Prem,' I said, 'why don't you work for me?'

'And what about my uncle?'

'He seems ready to desert me any day. His grandfather is ill, he says, and he wants to go home.'

'His grandfather died last year.'

'That's what I mean—he's getting restless. And I don't mind if he goes. These days he seems to be suffering from a form of sleeping sickness. I have to get up first and make his tea...'

Sitting here under the cherry tree, whose leaves are just beginning to turn yellow, I rest my chin on my knees and gaze across the valley to where Prem moves about in the garden. Looking back over the seven years he has been with me, I recall some of the nicest things about him. They come to me in no particular order—just pieces of cinema—coloured slides slipping across the screen of memory...

Prem rocking his infant son to sleep—crooning to him, passing his large hand gently over the child's curly head— Prem following me down to the police station when I was arrested (on a warrant from Bombay, charging me with writing an allegedly obscene short story!), and waiting outside until I reappeared, his smile, when I found him in Delhi, his large, irrepressible laughter, most in evidence when he was seeing an old Laurel and Hardy movie.

Of course, there were times when he could be infuriating, stubborn, deliberately pig-headed, sending me little notes of resignation—but I never found it difficult to overlook these little acts of self-indulgence. He had brought much love and laughter into my life, and what more could a lonely man ask for?

It was his stubborn streak that limited the length of his stay in the headmaster's household. Mr Good was tolerant enough. But Mrs Good was one of those women who, when they are pleased with you, go out of their way to help, pamper and flatter; and who, when they are displeased, become vindictive, going out of their way to harm or destroy. Mrs Good sought power—over her husband, her dog, her favourite pupils, her servant.... She had absolute power over the husband and the dog, partial power over her slightly bewildered pupils; and none at all over Prem, who missed the subtleties of her designs upon his soul. He did not respond to her mothering or to the way in which she tweaked him on the cheeks, brushed against him in the kitchen and made admiring remarks about his looks and physique. Memsahibs, he knew, were not for him. So he kept a stony face and went diligently about his duties. And she felt slighted, put in her place. Her liking turned to dislike. Instead of admiring remarks, she began making disparaging remarks about his looks, his clothes, his manners. She found fault with his cooking. No longer was it 'lovely'. She even accused him of taking away the dog's meat and giving it to a poor family living on the hillside: no more heinous crime could be imagined! Mr Good threatened him with dismissal. So Prem became stubborn. The following day he withheld the dog's food altogether; threw it down the khud where it was seized upon by innumerable strays, and went off to the pictures.

It was the end of his job. 'I'll have to go home now,' he told me. 'I won't get another job in this area. The mem will see to that.'

'Stay a few days,' I said.

'I have only enough money with which to get home.'

'Keep it for going home. You can stay with me for a few days, while you look around. Your uncle won't mind sharing his food with you.'

His uncle did mind. He did not like the idea of working for his nephew as well; it seemed to him no part of his duties. And he was apprehensive that Prem might get his job.

So Prem stayed no longer than a week.

Here on the knoll the grass is just beginning to turn October yellow. The first clouds approaching winter cover the sky. The trees are very still. The birds are silent. Only a cricket keeps singing on the oak tree. Perhaps there will be a storm before evening. A storm like that in which Prem arrived at the cottage with his wife and child—but that's jumping too far ahead...

After he had returned to his village, it was several months before I saw him again. His uncle told me he had taken a job in Delhi. There was an address. It did not seem complete but I resolved that when I was next in Delhi I would try to see him.

The opportunity came in May, as the hot winds of summer blew across the plains. It was the time of year when people who can afford it try to get away to the hills. I dislike New Delhi at the best of times and I hate it in summer. People compete with each other in being bad-tempered and mean. But I had to go down—I don't remember why, but it must have seemed very necessary at the time—and I took the opportunity to try and see Prem.

Nothing went right for me. Of course the address was all wrong and I wandered about in a remote, dusty, treeless colony called Vasant Vihar (Spring Garden) for over two hours, asking all the domestic servants I came across if they could put me in touch with Prem Singh of Village Koli, Pauri Garhwal. There were innumerable Prem Singhs, but apparently none who belonged to Village Koli. I returned to my hotel and took two days to recover from heatstroke before returning to Mussoorie, thanking God for mountains!

And then the uncle gave me notice. He'd found a better paid job in Dehradun and was anxious to be off. I didn't try to stop him.

For the next six months I lived in the cottage without any help. I did not find this difficult. I was used to living alone. It wasn't service that I needed but companionship. In the cottage it was very quiet. The ghosts of long dead residents were sympathetic but unobtrusive. The song of the whistling thrush was beautiful but I knew he was not singing for me. Up the valley came the sound of a flute but I never saw the flute player. My affinity was with the little red fox who roamed the hillside below the cottage. I met him one night and wrote these lines:

As I walked home last night
I saw a lone fox dancing
In the cold moonlight.
I stood and watched—then
Took the low road, knowing
The night was his by right.
Sometimes, when words ring true,
I'm like a lone fox dancing
In the morning dew.

During the rains, watching the dripping trees and the mist climbing the valley, I wrote a great deal of poetry. Loneliness is of value to poets. But poetry didn't bring me much money and funds were low. And then, just as I was wondering if I would have to give up my freedom and take a job again, a publisher bought the paperback rights of one of my children's stories and I was free to live and write as I pleased—for another three months!

That was in November. To celebrate, I took a long walk through the Landour Bazaar and up the Tehri road. It was a good day for walking; and it was dark by the time I returned to the outskirts of the town. Someone stood waiting for me on the road above the cottage. I hurried past him.

If I am not for myself,

Who will be for me?

And if I am not for others,

What am I?

And if not now, when?

I startled myself with the memory of these words of Hillel, the ancient Hebrew sage. I walked back to the shadows where the youth stood and saw that it was Prem.

'Prem!' I said. 'Why are you sitting out here, in the cold? Why did you not go to the house?'

'I went, sir, but there was a lock on the door. I thought you had gone away.'

'And you were going to remain here, on the road?'

'Only for tonight. I would have gone down to Dehra in the morning.'

'Come, let's go home. I have been waiting for you. I looked for you in Delhi but could not find the place where you were working.'

'I have left them now.'

'And your uncle has left me. So will you work for me now?'

'For as long as you wish.'

'For as long as the gods wish.'

We did not go straight home but returned to the bazaar and took our meal in the Sindhi Sweet Shop, hot puris and strong sweet tea.

We walked home together in the bright moonlight. I felt sorry for the little fox dancing alone.

That was twenty years ago, and Prem and his wife and three children are still with me. But we live in a different house now, on another hill.

TALES OF FOSTERGANJ

FOSTER OF FOSTERGANJ

Straddling a spur of the Mussoorie range, as it dips into the Doon valley, Fosterganj came into existence some two hundred years ago and was almost immediately forgotten. And today it is not very different from what it was in 1961, when I lived there briefly.

A quiet corner, where I could live like a recluse and write my stories—that was what I was looking for. And in Fosterganj I thought I'd found my retreat: a cluster of modest cottages, a straggling little bazaar, a post office, a crumbling castle (supposedly haunted), a mountain stream at the bottom of the hill, a winding footpath that took you either uphill or down. What more could one ask for? It reminded me a little of an English village, and indeed that was what it had once been; a tiny settlement on the outskirts of the larger hill station. But the British had long since gone, and the residents were now a fairly mixed lot, as we shall see.

I forget what took me to Fosterganj in the first place. Destiny, perhaps; although I'm not sure why destiny would have bothered to guide an itinerant writer to an obscure hamlet in the hills. Chance would be a better word. For chance plays a great part in all our lives. And it was just by chance that I found myself in the Fosterganj bazaar one fine morning early in May. The oaks and maples were in new leaf; geraniums flourished on sunny balconies; a boy delivering milk whistled a catchy Dev Anand song; a mule train clattered down the street. The chill of winter had gone and there was warmth in the sunshine that played upon old walls.

I sat in a tea shop, tested my teeth on an old bun, and washed it down with milky tea. The bun had been around for some time, but so had I, so we were quits. At the age of forty I could digest almost anything.

The tea shop owner, Melaram, was a friendly sort, as are most tea shop owners. He told me that not many tourists made their way down to Fosterganj. The only attraction was the waterfall, and you had to be fairly fit in order to scramble down the steep and narrow path that led to the ravine where a little stream came tumbling over the rocks. I would visit it one day, I told him.

'Then you should stay here a day or two,' said Melaram. 'Explore the stream. Walk down to Rajpur. You'll need a good walking stick. Look, I have several in my shop. Cherry wood, walnut wood, oak.' He saw me wavering. 'You'll also need one to climb the next hill—it's called Pari Tibba.' I was charmed by the name—Fairy Hill.

I hadn't planned on doing much walking that day—the walk down to Fosterganj from Mussoorie had already taken almost an hour—but I liked the look of a sturdy cherry-wood walking stick, and I bought one for two rupees. Those were the days of simple living. You don't see two-rupee notes any more. You don't see walking sticks either. Hardly anyone walks.

I strolled down the small bazaar, without having to worry about passing cars and lorries or a crush of people. Two or three schoolchildren were sauntering home, burdened by their school bags bursting with homework. A cow and a couple of stray dogs examined the contents of an overflowing dustbin. A policeman sitting on a stool outside a tiny police outpost yawned, stretched, stood up, looked up and down the street in anticipation of crimes to come, scratched himself in the anal region and sank back upon his stool.

A man in a crumpled shirt and threadbare trousers came up to me, looked me over with his watery grey eyes, and said, 'Sir, would you like to buy some gladioli bulbs?' He held up a basket full of bulbs which might have been onions. His chin was covered with a grey stubble, some of his teeth were missing, the remaining ones yellow with neglect.

'No, thanks,' I said. 'I live in a tiny flat in Delhi. No room for flowers.'

'A world without flowers,' he shook his head. 'That's what it's coming to.'

'And where do *you* plant your bulbs?'

'I grow gladioli, sir, and sell the bulbs to good people like you. My name's Foster. I own the lands all the way down to the waterfall.'

For a landowner he did not look very prosperous. But his name intrigued me. 'Isn't this area called Fosterganj?' I asked.

'That's right. My grandfather was the first to settle here. He was a grandson of Bonnie Prince Charlie who fought the British at Bannockburn. I'm the last Foster of Fosterganj. Are you sure you won't buy my daffodil bulbs?'

'I thought you said they were gladioli.'

'Some gladioli, some daffodils.'

They looked like onions to me, but to make him happy I parted with two rupees (which seemed the going rate in Fosterganj) and relieved him of his basket of bulbs. Foster shuffled off, looking a bit like Chaplin's tramp but not half as dapper. He clearly needed the two rupees. Which made me feel less foolish about spending money that I should have held on to. Writers were poor in those days. Though I didn't feel poor.

Back at the tea shop I asked Melaram if Foster really owned a lot of land.

'He has a broken-down cottage and the right-of-way. He charges people who pass through his property. Spends all the money on booze. No one owns the hillside, it's government land. Reserved forest. But everyone builds on it.'

Just as well, I thought, as I returned to town with my basket of onions. Who wanted another noisy hill station?

One Mall Road was more than enough. Back in my hotel room, I was about to throw the bulbs away, but on second thoughts decided to keep them. After all, even an onion makes a handsome plant.

BATHROOM WITH A VIEW

Next morning I found myself trudging down from Mussoorie to Fosterganj again. I didn't quite know why I was attracted to the place—but it was quaint, isolated, a forgotten corner of an otherwise changing hill town; and I had always been attracted to forgotten corners.

There was no hotel or guesthouse in the area, which in itself was a blessing; but I needed somewhere to stay, if I was going to spend some time there.

Melaram directed me to the local bakery. Hassan, the baker, had a room above his shop that had lain vacant since he built it a few years ago. An affable man, Hassan was the proud father of a dozen children; I say dozen at random, because I never did get to ascertain the exact number as they were never in one place at the same time. They did not live in the room above the bakery, which was much too small, but in a rambling old building below the bazaar, which housed a number of large families—the baker's, the tailor's, the postman's, among others.

I was shown the room. It was scantily furnished, the bed taking up almost half the space. A small table and chair stood near the window. Windows are important. I find it impossible to live in a room without a window. This one provided a view of the street and the buildings on the other side. Nothing very inspiring, but at least it wouldn't be dull.

A narrow bathroom was attached to the room. Hassan was very proud of it, because he had recently installed a flush tank and western-style potty. I complimented him on the potty and said it looked very comfortable. But what really took my fancy was the bathroom window. It hadn't been opened for some time, and the glass panes were caked with dirt. But when finally we got it open, the view was remarkable. Below the window was a sheer drop of two or three hundred feet. Ahead, an open vista, a wide valley, and then the mountains striding away towards the horizon. I don't think any hotel in town had such a splendid view. I could see myself sitting for hours on that potty, enraptured, enchanted, having the valley and the mountains all to myself. Almost certain constipation of course, but I would take that risk.

'Forty rupees a month,' said Hassan, and I gave him two months' rent on the spot.

'I'll move in next week,' I said. 'First I have to bring my books from Delhi.'

On my way back to the town I took a short cut through the forest. A swarm of yellow butterflies drifted across the path. A woodpecker pecked industriously on the bark of a tree, searching for young cicadas. Overhead, wild duck flew north, on their way across Central Asia, all travelling without passports. Birds and butterflies recognize no borders.

I hadn't been this way before, and I was soon lost. Two village boys returning from town with their milk cans gave me the wrong directions. I was put on the right path by a girl who was guiding a cow home. There was something about her fresh face and bright smile that I found tremendously appealing. She was less than beautiful but more than pretty, if you know what I mean. A face to remember.

A little later I found myself in an open clearing, with a large pool in the middle. Its still waters looked very deep. At one end there were steps, apparently for bathers. But the water did not look very inviting. It was a sunless place, several old oaks shutting out the light. Fallen off leaves floated on the surface. No birds sang. It was a strange, haunted sort of place. I hurried on.

LATE FOR A FUNERAL

When I said that Fosterganj appeared to be the sort of sleepy hollow where nothing ever happened, it only served to show that appearances can be deceptive. When I returned that summer, carrying books and writing materials, I found the little hamlet in a state of turmoil.

There was a rabies scare.

On my earlier visit I had noticed the presence of a number of stray dogs. The jackal population must have been fairly large too. And jackals are carriers of the rabies virus.

I had barely alighted from the town's only Ambassador taxi when I had to jump in again. Down the road came some ten to fifteen dogs, of no particular breed but running with the urgency of greyhounds, ears flattened, tails between their legs, teeth bared in terror, for close behind them came the dog-catchers, three or four men carrying staves and what appeared to be huge butterfly nets. Even as I gaped in astonishment one of the dogs took a tumble and, howling with fright, was scooped up and dumped in a metal cage on wheels which stood at the side of the road.

The dog chase swept past me, one young man staying behind to secure the trapped canine. Some people have faces that bear an uncanny resemblance to the features of different animals. This particular youth had something of the wolf in his countenance. The dog obviously thought so too, for it whimpered and cowered in a corner of its rusty cage. I am not a great dog-lover but I felt sorry for this frightened creature and put my hand through the bars to try and pat it. Immediately it bared its teeth and lunged at my hand. I withdrew it in a hurry.

The young man laughed at my discomfiture.

'Mad dog,' he said. 'All the dogs are going mad. Biting people. Running all over the place and biting people. We have to round them up.'

'And then what will you do? Shoot them?'

'Not allowed to kill them. Cruelty to animals.'

'So then?'

'We'll let them loose in the jungle—down near Rajpur.'

'But they'll start biting people there.'

'Problem for Rajpur.' He smiled disarmingly—canines like a wolf's.

'If they are mad they'll die anyway,' I said. 'But don't you have a vet—an animal doctor—in this place?'

'Not in Fosterganj. Only in Rajpur. That's why we leave them there.'

Defeated by this logic, I picked up my two suitcases and crossed the empty street to Hassan's bakery. The taxi spedaway; no business in Fosterganj.

∽

Over the next few days, several people were bitten and had to go down to Dehra for anti-rabies treatment. The cobbler's wife refused to go, and was dead within the month. There were many cases in Rajpur, due no doubt to the sudden influx of mad dogs expelled from Fosterganj.

In due course, life returned to normal, as it always does in India, post earthquakes, cyclones, riots, epidemics and cricket controversies. Apathy, or lethargy, or a combination of the two, soon casts a spell over everything and the most traumatic events are quickly forgotten.

'Sab chalta hai,' Hassan, my philosophical landlord, would say, speaking for everyone.

It did not take me long to settle down in my little room above the bakery. Recent showers had brought out the sheen on new leaves, transformed the grass on the hillside from a faded yellow to an emerald green. A barbet atop a spruce tree was in full cry. It would keep up its monotonous chant all summer. And early morning, a whistling-thrush would render its interrupted melody, never quite finishing what it had to say.

It was good to hear the birds and laughing schoolchildren through my open window. But I soon learnt to shut it whenever I went out. Late one morning, on returning from my walk, I found a large rhesus monkey sitting on my bed, tearing up a loaf of bread that Hassan had baked for me. I tried to drive the fellow away, but he seemed reluctant to leave. He bared his teeth and swore at me in monkey language. Then he stuffed a piece of bread into his mouth and glared at me, daring me to do my worst. I recalled that monkeys carry rabies, and not wanting to join those who had recently been bitten by rabid dogs, I backed out of the room and called for help. One of Hassan's brood came running up the steps with a hockey stick, and chased the invader away.

'Always keep a mug of water handy,' he told me. 'Throw the water on him and he'll be off. They hate cold water.'

'You may be right,' I said. 'I've never seen a monkey taking a bath.'

'See how miserable they are when it rains,' said my rescuer. 'They huddle together as though it's the end of the world.'

'Strange, isn't it? Birds like bathing in the rain.'

'So do I. Wait till the monsoon comes. You can join me then.'

'Perhaps I will.'

On this friendly note we parted, and I cleaned up the mess made by my simian visitor, and then settled down to do some writing.

But there was something about the atmosphere of Fosterganj that discouraged any kind of serious work or effort. Tucked away in a fold of the hills, its inhabitants had begun to resemble their surroundings: one old man resembled a willow bent by rain and wind; an elderly lady with her umbrella reminded me of a colourful mushroom, quite possibly poisonous; my good baker-cum-landlord looked like a bit of the hillside, scarred and uneven but stable. The children were like young grass, coming up all over the place; but the adolescents were like nettles, you never knew if they would sting when touched. There was a young Tibetan lady whose smile was like the blue sky opening up. And there was no brighter blue than the sky as seen from Fosterganj on a clear day.

It took me some time to get to know all the inhabitants. But one of the first was Professor Lulla, recently retired, who came hurrying down the road like the White Rabbit in *Alice in Wonderland*, glancing at his watch and muttering to himself. If, like the White Rabbit, he was saying 'I'm late, I'm late!' I wouldn't have been at all surprised. I was standing outside the bakery, chatting to one of the children, when he came up to me, adjusted his spectacles, peered at me through murky lenses, and said, 'Welcome to Fosterganj, sir. I believe you've come to stay for the season.'

'I'm not sure how long I'll stay,' I said. 'But thank you for your welcome.'

'We must get together and have a cultural and cultured exchange,' he said, rather pompously. 'Not many intellectuals in Fosterganj, you know.'

'I was hoping there wouldn't be.'

'But we'll talk, we'll talk. Only can't stop now. I have a funeral to attend. Eleven o'clock at the Camel's Back cemetery. Poor woman. Dead. Quite dead. Would you care to join me?'

'Er—I'm not in the party mood,' I said. 'And I don't think I knew the deceased.'

'Old Miss Gamleh. Your landlord thought she was a flowerpot—would have been ninety next month. Wonderful woman. Hated chokra-boys.' He looked distastefully at the boy grinning up at him. 'Stole all her plums, if the monkeys didn't get them first. Spent all her life in the hill station. Never married. Jilted by a weedy British colonel, awful fellow, even made off with her savings. But she managed on her own. Kept poultry, sold eggs to the hotels.'

'What happens to the poultry?' I asked.

'Oh, hens can look after themselves,' he said airily. 'But I can't linger or I'll be late. It's a long walk to the cemetery.' And he set off in determined fashion, like Scott of the Antarctic about to brave a blizzard.

'Must have been a close friend, the old lady who passed away,' I remarked.

'Not at all,' said Hassan, who had been standing in his doorway listening to the conversation. 'I doubt if she ever spoke to him. But Professor Lulla never misses a funeral. He goes to all of them—cremations, burials—funerals of any well-known person, even strangers. It's a hobby with him.'

'Extraordinary,' I said. 'I thought collecting match-box labels was sad enough as a hobby. Doesn't it depress him?'

'It seems to cheer him up, actually. But I must go too, sir. If you don't mind keeping an eye on the bakery for an hour or two, I'll hurry along to the funeral and see if I can get her poultry cheap. Miss Gamla's hens give good eggs, I'm told. Little Ali will look after the customers, sir. All you have to do is see that they don't make off with the buns and cream-rolls.'

I don't know if Hassan attended the funeral, but he came back with two baskets filled with cackling hens, and a rooster to keep them company.

ENTER A MAN-EATER

Did I say nothing ever happens in Fosterganj?

That is true in many ways. If you don't count the outbreak of rabies, that is, or the annual depredations of a man-eating leopard, or the drownings in the pool.

I suppose I should start with the leopard, since its activities commenced not long after I came to live in Fosterganj.

Its first victim was Professor Lulla, who was on his way

to attend another funeral.

I don't remember who had died. But I remember the cremation was to take place in Rajpur, at the bottom of the hill, an hour's walk from Fosterganj. The professor was anxious not to miss it, although he had met the recipient of the honour only once. Before the sun was up, he was on his way down the mountain trail. At that early hour, the mist from the valley rises, and it obscured the view, so that he probably did not see the leopard as it followed silently behind him, waiting its opportunity, stalking its victim with pleasurable anticipation. The importunate professor might have heard the rattle of stones as the leopard charged; might have had a glimpse of it as it sprang at his throat; might even have uttered a cry, or screamed for help. But there was no one to hear, no witness of the attack.

The leopard dragged the dying man into the kingora bushes and began to gnaw at his flesh. He was still at his meal when, half an hour later, a group of Nepali labourers came down the path, singing and making merry, and frightened the beast away. They found the mangled remains of the professor; two of the party ran back to Fosterganj for help, while the rest stood guard over the half-eaten torso.

Help came in the form of half the population of Fosterganj. There was nothing they could do, as the leopard did not return. But next day they gave the professor a good funeral.

However, a couple of public-spirited citizens were determined to hunt down the leopard before it took a further toll of human life. One of them was our local bank manager, Vishaal, a friendly and amiable sort, who was also a self-confessed disciple of Jim Corbett, the great shikari who had disposed of dozens of man-eaters. Vishaal did not possess a gun, but the bank's chowkidar, a retired Gurkha soldier, did. He had an ancient 12-bore shotgun which he carried about with him wherever he was on duty. The gun hadn't been fired for years—not since it had gone off accidentally when being handled by an inquisitive customer.

Vishaal found a box of cartridges in the bank's safe. They had been there for several years and looked a little mouldy, as did almost everything in Fosterganj, including some of the older residents. 'Stay here more than three years,' philosophized Hassan, 'and unless you have God on your side, your hair goes white and your teeth get yellow. Everyone ends up looking like old Foster—descendent of the kings of Scotland!'

'It must be the water,' I said.

'No, it's the mist,' said Hassan. 'It hangs around Fosterganj even in good weather. It keeps the sun out. Look at my bread. Can't keep a loaf fresh for more than a day, the mould gets to it in no time. And the monsoon hasn't even begun!'

In spite of his bad teeth and ragged appearance, however, Foster—or Bonnie Prince Charlie, as the older residents called him—was fairly active, and it was he who set up a rough machaan in an old oak tree overlooking the stream at the bottom of the hill. He even sold Vishaal an old goat, to be used as bait for the leopard.

Vishaal persuaded me to keep him company on the machaan, and produced a bottle of brandy that he said would see us through the night.

Our vigil began at eight, and by midnight the brandy bottle was empty. No leopard, although the goat made its presence apparent by bleating without a break.

'If the leopard has developed a taste for humans,' I said, 'why should it come for a silly old goat?'

I dozed off for some time, only to be awakened by a nudge from Vishaal, who whispered, 'Something's out there. I think it's the leopard! Shine the torch on it!'

I shone the torch on the terrified goat, and at the same moment a leopard sprang out of the bushes and seized its victim. There was a click from Vishaal's gun. The cartridge had failed to go off.

'Fire the other barrel!' I urged.

The second cartridge went off. There was a tremendous bang. But by then both leopard and goat had vanished into the night.

'I thought you said it only liked humans,' said Vishaal.

'Must be another leopard,' I said.

We trudged back to his rooms, and opened another bottle of brandy.

In the morning a villager came to the bank and demanded a hundred rupees for his goat.

'But it was Foster's goat,' protested Vishaal. 'I've already paid him for it.'

'Not Foster Sahib's goat,' said the villager. 'He only borrowed it for the night.'

A MAGIC OIL

A day or two later I was in the bank, run by Vishaal (manager), Negi (cashier), and Suresh (peon). I was sitting opposite Vishaal, who was at his desk, taken up by two handsome paperweights but no papers. Suresh had brought me a cup of tea from the tea shop across the road. There was just one customer in the bank, Hassan, who was making a deposit. A cosy summer morning in Fosterganj: not much happening, but life going on just the same.

In walked Foster. He'd made an attempt at shaving, but appeared to have given up at a crucial stage, because now he looked like a wasted cricketer finally on his way out. The effect was enhanced by the fact that he was wearing flannel trousers that had once been white but were now greenish yellow; the previous monsoon was to blame. He had found an old tie, and this was strung round his neck, or rather his unbuttoned shirt collar. The said shirt had seen many summers and winters in Fosterganj, and was frayed at the cuffs. Even so, Foster looked quite spry, as compared to when I had last seen him.

'Come in, come in!' said Vishaal, always polite to his customers, even those who had no savings. 'How is your gladioli farm?'

'Coming up nicely,' said Foster. 'I'm growing potatoes too.'

'Very nice. But watch out for the porcupines, they love potatoes.'

'Shot one last night. Cut my hands getting the quills out. But porcupine meat is great. I'll send you some the next time I shoot one.'

'Well, keep some ammunition for the leopard. We've got to get it before it kills someone else.'

'It won't be around for two or three weeks. They keep moving, do leopards. He'll circle the mountain, then be back in these parts. But that's not what I came to see you about, Mr Vishaal. I was hoping for a small loan.'

'Small loan, big loan, that's what we are here for. In what way can we help you, sir?'

'I want to start a chicken farm.'

'Most original.'

'There's a great shortage of eggs in Mussoorie. The hotels want eggs, the schools want eggs, the restaurants want eggs. And they have to get them from Rajpur or Dehradun.'

'Hassan has a few hens,' I put in.

'Only enough for home consumption. I'm thinking in terms of hundreds of eggs—and broiler chickens for the table. I want to make Fosterganj the chicken capital of India. It will be like old times, when my ancestor planted the first potatoes here, brought all the way from Scotland!'

'I thought they came from Ireland,' I said. 'Captain Young, up at Landour.'

'Oh well, we brought other things. Like Scotch whisky.'

'Actually, Irish whisky got here first. Captain Kennedy, up in Simla.' I wasn't Irish, but I was in a combative frame of mind, which is the same as being Irish.

To mollify Foster, I said, 'You did bring the bagpipe.'

And when he perked up, I added: 'But the Gurkha is better at playing it.'

This contretemps over, Vishaal got Foster to sign a couple of forms and told him that the loan would be processed in due course and that we'd all celebrate over a bottle of Scotch whisky. Foster left the room with something of a swagger. The prospect of some money coming in—even if it is someone else's—will put any man in an optimistic frame of mind. And for Foster the prospect of losing it was as yet far distant.

I wanted to make a phone call to my bank in Delhi, so that I could have some of my savings sent to me, and Vishaal kindly allowed me to use his phone.

There were only four phones in all of Fosterganj, and there didn't seem to be any necessity for more. The bank had one. So did Dr Bisht. So did Brigadier Bakshi, retired. And there was one in the police station, but it was usually out of order.

The police station, a one-room affair, was manned by a Daroga and a constable. If the Daroga felt like a nap, the constable took charge. And if the constable took the afternoon off, the Daroga would run the place. This worked quite well, as there wasn't much crime in Fosterganj—if you didn't count Foster's illicit still at the bottom of the hill (Scottish hooch, he called the stuff he distilled); or a charming young delinquent called Sunil, who picked pockets for a living (though not in Fosterganj); or the barber who supplemented his income by supplying charas to his agents at some of the boarding schools; or the man who sold the secretions of certain lizards, said to increase sexual potency—except that it was only linseed oil, used for oiling cricket bats.

I found the last mentioned, a man called Rattan Lal, sitting on a stool outside my door when I returned from the bank.

'Saande-ka-tel,' he declared abruptly, holding up a small bottle containing a vitreous yellow fluid. 'Just one application, sahib, and the size and strength of your valuable member will increase dramatically. It will break down doors, should doors be shut against you. No chains will hold it down. You will be as a stallion, rampant in a field full of fillies. Sahib, you will rule the roost! Memsahibs and beautiful women will fall at your feet.'

'It will get me into trouble, for certain,' I demurred. 'It's great stuff, I'm sure. But wasted here in Fosterganj.'

Rattan Lal would not be deterred. 'Sahib, every time you try it, you will notice an increase in dimensions, guaranteed!'

'Like Pinocchio's nose,' I said in English. He looked puzzled. He understood the word 'nose', but had no idea what I meant.

'Naak?' he said. 'No, sahib, you don't rub it on your nose. Here, down between the legs,' and he made as if to give a demonstration. I held a hand up to restrain him.

'There was a boy named Pinocchio in a far-off country,' I explained, switching back to Hindi. 'His nose grew longer every time he told a lie.'

'I tell no lies, sahib. Look, my nose is normal. Rest is very big. You want to see?'

'Another day,' I said.

'Only ten rupees.'

'The bottle or the rest of you?'

'You joke, sahib,' and he thrust a bottle into my unwilling hands and removed a ten-rupee note from my shirt pocket; all done very simply.

'I will come after a month and check up,' he said. 'Next time I will bring the saanda itself! You are in the prime of your life, it will make you a bull among men.' And away he went.

᪣

The little bottle of oil stood unopened on the bathroom shelf for weeks. I was too scared to use it. It was like the bottle in *Alice in Wonderland* with the label DRINK ME. Alice drank it, and shot up to the ceiling. I wasn't sure I wanted to grow that high.

I did wonder what would happen if I applied some of it to my scalp. Would it stimulate hair growth? Would it stimulate my thought processes? Put an end to writer's block?

Well, I never did find out. One afternoon I heard a clatter in the bathroom and looked in to see a large and sheepish-looking monkey jump out of the window with the bottle.

But to return to Rattan Lal—some hours after I had been sold the aphrodisiac, I was walking up to town to get a newspaper when I met him on his way down.

'Any luck with the magic oil?' I asked.

'All sold out!' he said, beaming with pleasure. 'Ten bottles sold at the Savoy, and six at Hakman's. What a night it's going to be for them.' And he rubbed his hands at the prospect.

'A very busy night,' I said. 'Either that, or they'll be looking for you to get their money back.'

'I come next month. If you are still here, I'll keep another bottle for you. Look there!' He took me by the arm and pointed at a large rock lizard that was sunning itself on the parapet. 'You catch me some of those, and I'll pay you for them. Be my partner. Bring me lizards—not small ones, only big fellows—and I will buy!'

'How do you extract the tel?' I asked.

'Ah, that's a trade secret. But I will show you when you bring me some saandas. Now I must go. My good wife waits for me with impatience.'

And off he went, down the bridle path to Rajpur.

The rock lizard was still on the wall, enjoying its afternoon siesta.

It did occur to me that I might make a living from breeding rock lizards. Perhaps Vishaal would give me a loan. I wasn't making much as a writer.

FAIRY GLEN PALACE

The old bridle path from Rajpur to Mussoorie passed through Fosterganj at a height of about five thousand feet. In the old days, before the motor road was built, this was the only road to the hill station. You could ride up on a pony, or walk, or be carried in a basket (if you were a child) or in a doolie (if you were a lady or an invalid). The doolie was a cross between a hammock, a stretcher and a sedan chair, if you can imagine such a contraption. It was borne aloft by two perspiring partners. Sometimes they sat down to rest, and dropped you unceremoniously. I have a picture of my grandmother being borne uphill in a doolie, and she looks petrified. There was an incident in which a doolie, its occupant and two bearers, all went over a cliff just before Fosterganj, and perished in the fall. Sometimes you can see the ghost of this poor lady being borne uphill by two phantom bearers.

Fosterganj has its ghosts, of course. And they are something of a distraction.

Writing is my vocation, and I have always tried to follow the apostolic maxim: 'Study to be quiet and to mind your own business.' But in small-town India one is constantly drawn into other people's business, just as they are drawn towards yours. In Fosterganj it was quiet enough, there were few people; there was no excuse for shirking work. But tales of haunted houses and fairy-infested forests have always intrigued me, and when I heard that the ruined palace half way down to Rajpur was a place to be avoided after dark, it was natural for me to start taking my evening walks in its direction.

Fairy Glen was its name. It had been built on the lines of a Swiss or French chalet, with numerous turrets decorating its many wings—a huge, rambling building, two-storeyed, with numerous balconies and cornices and windows; a hodge-podge of architectural styles, a wedding-cake of a palace, built to satisfy the whims and fancies of its late owner, the Raja of Ranipur, a small state near the Nepal border. Maintaining this ornate edifice must have been something of a nightmare; and the present heirs had quite given up on it, for bits of the roof were missing, some windows were without panes, doors had developed cracks, and what had once been a garden was now a small jungle. Apparently there was no one living there anymore; no sign of a caretaker. I had walked past the wrought-iron gate several times without seeing any signs of life, apart from a large grey cat sunning itself outside a broken window.

Then one evening, walking up from Rajpur, I was caught in a storm.

A wind had sprung up, bringing with it dark, overburdened clouds. Heavy drops of rain were followed by hailstones bouncing off the stony path. Gusts of wind rushed through the oaks, and leaves and small branches were soon swirling through the air. I was still a couple of miles from the Fosterganj bazaar, and I did not fancy sheltering under a tree, as flashes of lightning were beginning to light up the darkening sky. Then I found myself outside the gate of the abandoned palace.

Outside the gate stood an old sentry box. No one had stood sentry in it for years. It was a good place in which to shelter. But I hesitated because a large bird was perched on the gate, seemingly oblivious to the rain that was still falling.

It looked like a crow or a raven, but it was much bigger than either—in fact, twice the size of a crow, but having all the features of one—and when a flash of lightning lit up the gate, it gave a squawk, opened its enormous wings and took off, flying in the direction of the oak forest. I hadn't seen such a bird before; there was something dark and malevolent and almost supernatural about it. But it had gone, and I darted into the sentry box without further delay.

I had been standing there some ten minutes, wondering when the rain was going to stop, when I heard someone running down the road. As he approached, I could see that he was just a boy, probably eleven or twelve; but in the dark I could not make out his features. He came up to the gate, lifted the latch, and was about to go in when he saw me in the sentry box.

'Kaun? Who are you?' he asked, first in Hindi then in English. He did not appear to be in any way anxious or alarmed.

'Just sheltering from the rain,' I said. 'I live in the bazaar.' He took a small torch from his pocket and shone it in my face.

'Yes, I have seen you there. A tourist.'

'A writer. I stay in places, I don't just pass through.'

'Do you want to come in?'

I hesitated. It was still raining and the roof of the sentry box was leaking badly.

'Do you live here?' I asked.

'Yes, I am the raja's nephew. I live here with my mother. Come in.' He took me by the hand and led me through the gate. His hand was quite rough and heavy for an eleven- or twelve-year-old. Instead of walking with me to the front steps and entrance of the old palace, he led me around to the rear of the building, where a faint light glowed in a mullioned window, and in its light I saw that he had a very fresh and pleasant face—a face as yet untouched by the trials of life.

Instead of knocking on the door, he tapped on the window. 'Only strangers knock on the door,' he said. 'When I tap on the window, my mother knows it's me.'

'That's clever of you,' I said.

He tapped again, and the door was opened by an unusually tall woman wearing a kind of loose, flowing gown that looked strange in that place, and on her. The light was behind her, and I couldn't see her face until we had entered the room. When she turned to me, I saw that she had a long reddish scar running down one side of her face. Even so, there was a certain, hard beauty in her appearance.

'Make some tea—Mother,' said the boy rather brusquely.
'And something to eat. I'm hungry. Sir, will you have
something?' He looked enquiringly at me. The light from
a kerosene lamp fell full on his face. He was wide-eyed,
full-lipped, smiling; only his voice seemed rather mature for
one so young. And he spoke like someone much older, and
with an almost unsettling sophistication.

'Sit down, sir.' He led me to a chair, made me
comfortable. 'You are not too wet, I hope?'

'No, I took shelter before the rain came down too heavily.
But you are wet, you'd better change.'

'It doesn't bother me.' And after a pause, 'Sorry there
is no electricity. Bills haven't been paid for years.'

'Is this your place?'

'No, we are only caretakers. Poor relations, you might
say. The palace has been in dispute for many years. The
raja and his brothers keep fighting over it, and meanwhile
it is slowly falling down. The lawyers are happy. Perhaps
I should study and become a lawyer some day.'

'Do you go to school?'

'Sometimes.'

'How old are you?'

'Quite old, I'm not sure. Mother, how old am I?' he
asked, as the tall woman returned with cups of tea and a
plate full of biscuits.

She hesitated, gave him a puzzled look. 'Don't you know?
It's on your certificate.'

'I've lost the certificate.'

'No, I've kept it safely.' She looked at him intently,
placed a hand on his shoulder, then turned to me and said,
'He is twelve,' with a certain finality.

We finished our tea. It was still raining.

'It will rain all night,' said the boy. 'You had better
stay here.'

'It will inconvenience you.'

'No, it won't. There are many rooms. If you do not mind the darkness. Come, I will show you everything. And meanwhile my mother will make some dinner. Very simple food, I hope you won't mind.'

The boy took me around the old palace, if you could still call it that. He led the way with a candle-holder from which a large candle threw our exaggerated shadows on the walls.

'What's your name?' I asked, as he led me into what must have been a reception room, still crowded with ornate furniture and bric-a-brac.

'Bhim,' he said. 'But everyone calls me Lucky.'

'And are you lucky?'

He shrugged. 'Don't know...' Then he smiled up at me. 'Maybe you'll bring me luck.'

We walked further into the room. Large oil paintings hung from the walls, gathering mould. Some were portraits of royalty, kings and queens of another era, wearing decorative headgear, strange uniforms, the women wrapped in jewellery—more jewels than garments, it seemed—and sometimes accompanied by children who were also weighed down by excessive clothing. A young man sat on a throne, his lips curled in a sardonic smile.

'My grandfather,' said Bhim.

He led me into a large bedroom taken up by a four-poster bed which had probably seen several royal couples copulating upon it. It looked cold and uninviting, but Bhim produced a voluminous razai from a cupboard and assured me that it would be warm and quite luxurious, as it had been his grandfather's.

'And when did your grandfather die?' I asked.

'Oh, fifty-sixty years ago, it must have been.'

'In this bed, I suppose.'

'No, he was shot accidentally while out hunting. They said it was an accident. But he had enemies.'

'Kings have enemies.... And this was the royal bed?'

He gave me a sly smile; not so innocent after all. 'Many

women slept in it. He had many queens.'
    'And concubines.'
    'What are concubines?'
    'Unofficial queens.'
    'Yes, those too.'
    A worldly-wise boy of twelve.

A BIG BLACK BIRD

I did not feel like sleeping in that room, with its musty
old draperies and paint peeling off the walls. A trickle of
water from the ceiling fell down the back of my shirt and
made me shiver.

    'The roof is leaking,' I said. 'Maybe I'd better go home.'
    'You can't go now, it's very late. And that leopard has
been seen again.'

    He fetched a china bowl from the dressing-table and
placed it on the floor to catch the trickle from the ceiling.
In another corner of the room a metal bucket was receiving
a steady patter from another leak.

    'The palace is leaking everywhere,' said Bhim cheerfully.
'This is the only dry room.'

    He took me by the hand and led me back to his own
quarters. I was surprised, again, by how heavy and rough
his hand was for a boy, and presumed that he did a certain
amount of manual work such as chopping wood for a daily
fire. In winter the building would be unbearably cold.

    His mother gave us a satisfying meal, considering the
ingredients at her disposal were somewhat limited. Once
again, I tried to get away. But only half-heartedly. The boy
intrigued me; so did his mother; so did the rambling old
palace; and the rain persisted.

    Bhim the Lucky took me to my room; waited with the
guttering candle till I had removed my shoes; handed me
a pair of very large pyjamas.

    'Royal pyjamas,' he said with a smile. I got into them

and floated around.

'Before you go—' I said. 'I might want to visit the bathroom in the night.'

'Of course, sir. It's close by.' He opened a door, and beyond it I saw a dark passage. 'Go a little way, and there's a door on the left. I'm leaving an extra candle and matches on the dressing-table.'

He put the lighted candle he was carrying on the table, and left the room without a light. Obviously he knew his way about in the dark. His footsteps receded, and I was left alone with the sound of raindrops pattering on the roof and a loose sheet of corrugated tin roofing flapping away in a wind that had now sprung up.

It was a summer's night, and I had no need of blankets; so I removed my shoes and jacket and lay down on the capacious bed, wondering if I should blow the candle out or allow it to burn as long as it lasted.

Had I been in my own room, I would have been reading—a Conrad or a Chekhov or some other classic—because at night I turn to the classics—but here there was no light and nothing to read.

I got up and blew the candle out. I might need it later on.

Restless, I prowled around the room in the dark, banging into chairs and footstools. I made my way to the window and drew the curtains aside. Some light filtered into the room because behind the clouds there was a moon, and it had been a full moon the night before.

I lay back on the bed. It wasn't very comfortable. It was a box-bed, of the sort that had only just begun to become popular in households with small bedrooms. This one had been around for some time—no doubt a very early version of its type—and although it was covered with a couple of thick mattresses, the woodwork appeared to have warped because it creaked loudly whenever I shifted my position. The boards no longer fitted properly. Either that, or the box-bed had been overstuffed with all sorts of things.

After some time I settled into one position and dozed off for a while, only to be awakened by the sound of someone screaming somewhere in the building. My hair stood on end. The screaming continued, and I wondered if I should get up to investigate. Then suddenly it stopped—broke off in the middle as though it had been muffled by a hand or piece of cloth.

There was a tapping at the pane of the big French window in front of the bed. Probably the branch of a tree, swaying in the wind. But then there was a screech, and I sat up in bed. Another screech, and I was out of it.

I went to the window and pressed my face to the glass. The big black bird—the bird I had seen when taking shelter in the sentry box—was sitting, or rather squatting, on the boundary wall, facing me. The moon, now visible through the clouds, fell full upon it. I had never seen a bird like it before. Crow-like, but heavily built, like a turkey, its beak that of a bird of prey, its talons those of a vulture. I stepped back, and closed the heavy curtains, shutting out the light but also shutting out the image of that menacing bird.

Returning to the bed, I just sat there for a while, wondering if I should get up and leave. The rain had lessened. But the luminous dial of my watch showed it was two in the morning. No time for a stroll in the dark—not with a man-eating leopard in the vicinity.

Then I heard the shriek again. It seemed to echo through the building. It may have been the bird, but to me it sounded all too human. There was silence for a long while after that. I lay back on the bed and tried to sleep. But it was even more uncomfortable than before. Perhaps the wood had warped too much during the monsoon, I thought, and the lid of the old box-bed did not fit properly. Maybe I could push it back into its correct position; then perhaps I could get some sleep.

So I got up again, and after fumbling around in the dark for a few minutes, found the matches and lit the candle.

Then I removed the sheets from the bed and pulled away the two mattresses. The cover of the box-bed lay exposed. And a hand protruded from beneath the lid.

It was not a living hand. It was a skeletal hand, fleshless, brittle. But there was a ring on one finger, an opal still clinging to the bone of a small index finger. It glowed faintly in the candlelight.

Shaking a little (for I am really something of a coward, though an inquisitive one), I lifted the lid of the box-bed. Laid out on a pretty counterpane was a skeleton. A bundle of bones, but still clothed in expensive-looking garments. One hand gripped the side of the box-bed; the hand that had kept it from shutting properly.

I dropped the lid of the box-bed and ran from the room—only to blunder into a locked door. Someone, presumably the boy, had locked me into the bedroom.

I banged on the door and shouted, but no one heard me. No one came running. I went to the large French window, but it was firmly fastened, it probably hadn't been opened for many years.

Then I remembered the passageway leading to the bathroom. The boy had pointed it out to me. Possibly there was a way out from there.

There was. It was an old door that opened easily, and I stepped out into the darkness, finding myself entangled in a creeper that grew against the wall. From its cloying fragrance I recognized it as wisteria.

A narrow path led to a wicket-gate at the end of the building. I found my way out of the grounds and back on the familiar public road. The old palace loomed out of the darkness. I turned my back on it and set off for home, my little room above Hassan's bakery.

Nothing happens in Fosterganj, I told myself. But something had happened in that old palace.

THE STREET OF LOST HOMES

'What did you want to go there for?' asked Hassan, when I knocked on his door at the crack of dawn.

'It was raining heavily, and I stopped near the gate to take shelter. A boy invited me in, his mother gave me something to eat, and I ended up spending the night in the raja's bedroom.' I said nothing about screams in the night or the skeleton in the bed.

Hassan presented me with a bun and a glass of hot sweet tea.

'Nobody goes there,' he said. 'The place has a bad name.'

'And why's that?'

'The old raja was a bad man. Tortured his wives, or so it was said.'

'And what happened to him?'

'Got killed in a hunting accident, in the jungles next to Bijnor. He went after a tiger, but the tiger got to him first. Bit his head off! Everyone was pleased. His younger brother inherited the palace, but he never comes here. I think he still lives somewhere near the Nepal border.'

'And the people who still live in the palace?'

'Poor relations, I think. Offspring from one of the raja's wives or concubines—no one quite knows, or even cares. We don't see much of them, and they keep to themselves. But people avoid the place, they say it is still full of evil, haunted by the old scoundrel whose cruelty has left its mark on the walls.... It should be pulled down!'

'It's falling down of its own accord,' I said. 'Most of it is already a ruin.'

ᔕ

Later that morning I found Hassan closing the doors of the bakery.

'Are you off somewhere?' I asked.

He nodded. 'Down to Rajpur. My boys are at school

and my daughter is too small to look after the place.'

'It's urgent, then?'

'That fool of a youth, Sunil, has got into trouble. Picking someone's pocket, no doubt. They are holding him at the Rajpur thana.

'But why do you have to go? Doesn't he have any relatives?'

'None of any use. His father died some time back. He did me a favour once. More than a favour—he saved my life. So I must help the boy, even if he is a badmash.'

'I'll come with you,' I said on an impulse. 'Is it very far?'

'Rajpur is at the bottom of the hill. About an hour's walk down the footpath. Quicker than walking up to Mussoorie and waiting for a bus.'

I joined him on the road, and together we set off down the old path.

We passed Fairy Glen—the ruin where I had passed the night. It looked quite peaceful in the April sunshine. The gate was closed. There was no sign of the boy or his mother, my hosts of the previous night. It would have been embarrassing to meet them, for I had left in an almighty hurry. There was no sign of the big black bird, either. Only a couple of mynas squabbling on the wall, and a black-faced langur swinging from the branch of an oak.

I had some difficulty in keeping up with Hassan. Although he was over forty and had the beginnings of a paunch, he was a sturdy fellow, and he had the confident, even stride of someone who had spent most of his life in the hills.

The path was a steep one, and it began to level out only when it entered the foothills hamlet of Rajpur. At that time Rajpur was something of a ghost town. Some sixteen years earlier, most of its inhabitants, Muslims like Hassan, had fled or been killed by mobs during the communal strife that followed the partition of the country.

Rajpur had yet to recover. We passed empty, gutted

buildings, some roofless, some without doors and windows. Weeds and small bushes grew out of the floors of abandoned houses. Successive monsoons had removed the mud or cement plaster from the walls, leaving behind bare brickwork which was beginning to crumble. The entire length of the street, where once there had been a hundred homes pulsating with life and human endeavour, now stood empty, homes only to jackals, snakes, and huge rock lizards.

Hassan stopped before an empty doorway. Behind it an empty courtyard. Behind it a wall with empty windows.

'I lived here once,' he said. 'My parents, younger brother, sister, my first wife...all of us worked together, making bread and buns and pastries for the rich folk in the houses along the Dehra road. And in one night I lost everyone, everything—parents, brother, sister, wife.... The fire swept through the mohalla, and those who ran out of their houses were cut down by swords and kirpans.'

I stopped and put a hand on his shoulder.

'It's hard for me to talk about it. Later, perhaps...' And he moved on.

The street of lost homes gave way to a small bazaar, the only visible sign of some sort of recovery. A young man from a nearby village ran the small dhaba where we stopped for tea and pakoras. He was too young to have any memories of 1947. And in India, town and countryside often appear to have completely different histories.

Hassan asked me to wait at the dhaba while he walked down to the local thana to enquire after Sunil.

'A thana is no place for a respectable person like you,' he said.

'In Delhi, the prisons are full of respectable people,' I said.

'But not respected anymore?'

'Well, some of them don't seem to be too bothered. They get bail, come out with a swagger, and drive home in their cars.'

'And what are their crimes?'

'The same as Sunil's. They pick pockets, but in a big way. You don't see them doing it. But carry on, I'll wait here for you.'

The dhak, or flame of the forest, was in flower, and I sat on a bench taking in the sights and sounds of summer's arrival in the valley. Scarlet bougainvillea cascaded over a low wall, and a flock of parrots flung themselves from one tall mango tree to another, sampling the young unripe fruit.

'Will there be a good crop this year?' I asked the young dhabawala.

'Should be, if the parrots and monkeys leave any for us.'

'You need a chowkidar,' I said, and thought of recommending Sunil. But Hassan came back without him.

'No magistrate in court today. We'll try again tomorrow. In the meantime he gets board and lodging at government expense. He doesn't have to pick any pockets.'

'He will, if he gets a chance. It's an incurable disease.'

EYE OF THE LEOPARD

We did not return by way of the ruined and deserted township. Hassan wished to avoid it. 'Bad memories,' he said.

We cut across a couple of fields until we reached a small stream which came down the ravine below Fosterganj. Hassan knew it well. He went there to bathe from time to time. A narrow path took us upstream.

'How did you escape?' I asked, still curious about the events of 1947.

Hassan continued to walk, looking straight ahead. He did not turn his face to me as he spoke. 'I was late returning from Mussoorie. The houses were already ablaze. I began running towards ours, but the mob cut me off. Most of them Sikhs, wanting revenge—they had lost homes and loved ones in the Punjab—there was madness everywhere—hate and greed and madness. Gandhi couldn't stop it. Several men caught hold of me and flung me to the ground. One stood over me with his sword raised. That's when Bhai Saheb— Sunil's father—appeared as if out of nowhere. "What are you doing?" he cried. "That's my nephew. Don't touch him, or my entire village will be up in arms against you!" The attackers left me and moved on to other targets. Of course it was all over with my people. Sunil's father kept me in his village, not far from here, until the killing stopped. Sooner or later it had to stop. It exhausts itself. A few hours of madness and we spend years counting the cost.'

∽

After almost an hour of walking upstream, slipping on moss-covered boulders and struggling up the little-used pathway, we came to a pool, a catchment area where the water was still and deep.

'We'll rest here awhile,' said Hassan. 'Would you like to bathe?'

It was a warm day, and down there in the ravine there was no breeze. I stripped to my underwear and slipped into the pool.

After some time Hassan joined me. He was a well-built man. Birthing and raising so many children had worn out his consumptive wife, but he was in fine shape—strong in the chest and thighs; he had the build of a wrestler.

I was enjoying the water, swimming around, but Hassan was restless, continually looking up at the hillside and the overhanging branches of the trees that grew near the water. Presently he left the pool and began striding up a grassy knoll as though in search of something—as though he sensed the presence of danger. If you have faced danger once, you will know when it comes again.

'What are you looking for?' I called.

'Nothing,' he replied. 'Just looking around.' And he went further up the path.

I swam around a little, then pulled myself up on a flat boulder, and sat there in the sun, contemplating a thicket of ferns. A long-tailed magpie squawked and flew away in a hurry. The sun was in my eyes. I turned my back to it, and looked up into the yellow eyes of a leopard crouching on the rocks above me.

I wanted to shout, but couldn't. And perhaps it was better that I remained silent. Was it the man-eater? There was no way of knowing, but it seemed likely.

For what seemed an age, I looked at the leopard and the leopard stared at me. In fact, it was only a matter of seconds; but each second was an hour to me.

The leopard came forward a little and snarled. Perhaps he was puzzled that I made no sound and did not run. But he sank down, his forepaws spreading to get a grip on the rocks. His tail began to twitch—a sure signal that he was about to spring. His lips drew back and the sun shone on his canines and the dark pink of his gums.

Then I saw Hassan appear just behind the crouching beast. He held a large rock in his hands—it was bigger than a football. He raised his arms and brought the rock down with all his might on the leopard's head.

The leopard seemed to sag. Its paws scrabbled in the dust. Blood trickled from its ears. Hassan appeared again, with an even bigger rock, and he brought it down with such force that I heard the animal's skull crack. There was a convulsive movement, and then it was still.

ొ

We returned to Fosterganj and told everyone that the man-eater was dead. A number of people went down to the stream to fetch the carcass. But Hassan did not join them. He was behind with his work, and had to bake twenty to thirty loaves of bread for delivery the next morning. I tried to help him, but I am not much good at baking bread, and he told me to go to bed early.

Everyone was pleased that the leopard had been killed. Everyone, that is, except Vishaal, the bank manager, who had been hoping to vanquish it himself.

AN EVENING WITH FOSTER

> *Keep right on to the end of the road,*
> *Keep right on to the end.*
> *If your way be long*
> *Let your heart be strong,*
> *And keep right on to the end.*
> *If you're tired and weary*
> *Still carry on,*
> *Till you come to your happy abode.*
> *And then all you love*
> *And are dreaming of,*
> *Will be there—*
> *At the end of the road!*

The voice of Sir Harry Lauder, Scottish troubadour of the 1930s, singing one of his favourites, came drifting across the hillside as I took the winding path to Foster's cottage.

On one of my morning walks, I had helped him round up some runaway hens, and he had been suitably grateful.

'Ah, it's a fowl subject, trying to run a poultry farm,' he quipped. 'I've already lost a few to jackals and foxes. Hard to keep them in their pens. They jump over the netting and wander all over the place. But thank you for your help. It's good to be young. Once the knees go, you'll never be young again. Why don't you come over in the evening and split a bottle with me? It's a homemade brew, can't hurt you.'

I'd heard of Foster's homemade brew. More than one person had tumbled down the khad after partaking of the stuff. But I did not want to appear standoffish, and besides, I was curious about the man and his history. So towards sunset one summer's evening, I took the path down to his cottage, following the strains of Harry Lauder.

The music grew louder as I approached, and I had to knock on the door several times before it was opened by my bleary-eyed host. He had already been at the stuff he drank, and at first he failed to recognize me.

'Nice old song you have there,' I said. 'My father used to sing it when I was a boy.'

Recognition dawned, and he invited me in. 'Come in, laddie, come in. I've been expecting you. Have a seat!'

The seat he referred to was an old sofa and it was occupied by three cackling hens. With a magnificent sweep of the arm Foster swept them away, and they joined two other hens and a cock-bird on a book-rack at the other end of the room. I made sure there were no droppings on the sofa before subsiding into it.

'Birds are finding it too hot out in the yard,' he explained. 'Keep wanting to come indoors.'

The gramophone record had run its course, and Foster switched off the old record player.

'Used to have a real gramophone,' he said, 'but can't get the needles any more. These electric players aren't any good. But I still have all the old records.' He indicated a pile of 78 rpm gramophone records, and I stretched across and sifted through some of them. Gracie Fields, George Formby, The Street Singer…music hall favourites from the 1930s and 40s. Foster hadn't added to his collection for twenty years.

He must have been close to eighty, almost twice my age. Like his stubble (a permanent feature), the few wisps of hair on his sunburnt head were also grey. Mud had dried on his hands. His old patched-up trousers were held up by braces. There were buttons missing from his shirt, laces missing from his shoes.

'What will you have to drink, laddie? Tea, cocoa or whisky?'

'Er—not cocoa. Tea, maybe—oh, anything will do.'

'That's the spirit. Go for what you like. I make my own whisky, of course. Real Scotch from the Himalaya. I get the best barley from yonder village.' He gestured towards the next mountain, then turned to a sagging mantelpiece, fetched a bottle that contained an oily yellow liquid, and poured a generous amount into a cracked china mug. He poured a similar amount into a dirty glass tumbler, handed it to me, and said, 'Cheers! Bottoms up!'

'Bottoms up!' I said, and took a gulp.

It wasn't bad. I drank some more and asked Foster how the poultry farm was doing.

'Well, I had fifty birds to start with. But they keep wandering off, and the boys from the village make off with them. I'm down to forty. Sold a few eggs, though. Gave the bank manager the first lot. He seemed pleased. Would you like a few eggs? There's a couple on that cushion, newly laid.'

The said cushion was on a stool a few feet from me. Two large hens' eggs were supported upon it.

'Don't sit on 'em,' said Foster, letting out a cackle which was meant to be laughter. 'They might hatch!'

I took another gulp of Foster's whisky and considered the eggs again. They looked much larger now, more like goose eggs.

Everything was looking larger.

I emptied the glass and stood up to leave.

'Don't go yet,' said Foster. 'You haven't had a proper drink. And there's dinner to follow. Sausages and mash! I make my own sausages, did you know? My sausages were famous all over Mussoorie. I supplied the Savoy, Hakman's, the schools.'

'Why did you stop?' I was back on the sofa, holding another glass of Himalayan Scotch.

'Somebody started spreading a nasty rumour that I was using dog's meat. Now why would I do that when pork was cheap? Of course, during the war years a lot of rubbish went into sausages—stuff you'd normally throw away. That's why they were called "sweet mysteries". You remember the old song? "Ah! Sweet Mystery of Life!" Nebon Eddy and Jeanette Macdonald. Well, the troops used to sing it whenever they were given sausages for breakfast. You never knew what went into them—cats, dogs, camels, scorpions. If you survived those sausages, you survived the war!'

'And *your* sausages, what goes into them?'

'Good, healthy chicken meat. Not crow's meat, as some jealous rivals tried to make out.'

He frowned into his china mug. It was suddenly quieter inside. The hens had joined their sisters in the backyard; they were settling down for the night, sheltering in cardboard cartons and old mango-wood boxes. Quck-quck-quck. Another day nearer to having their sad necks wrung.

I looked around the room. A threadbare carpet. Walls that hadn't received a coat of paint for many years. A couple of loose rafters letting in a blast of cold air. Some pictures here and there—mostly racing scenes. Foster must have been a betting man. Perhaps that was how he ran out of money.

He noticed my interest in the pictures and said, 'Owned a racehorse once. A beauty, she was. That was in Meerut, just before the war. Meerut had a great racecourse. Races every Saturday. Punters came from Delhi. There was money to be made!'

'Did you win any?' I asked.

'Won a couple of races hands down. Then unexpectedly she came in last, and folks lost a lot of money. I had to leave town in a hurry. All my jockey's fault—he was hand in glove with the bookies. They made a killing, of course! Anyway, I sold the horse to a sporting Parsi gentleman and went into the canteen business with my Uncle Fred in Roorkee. That's Uncle Fred, up there.'

Foster gestured towards the mantelpiece. I expected to see a photograph of his Uncle Fred but instead of a photo I found myself staring at a naked skull. It was a well-polished skull and it glistened in the candlelight.

'That's Uncle Fred,' said Foster proudly.

'That skull? Where's the rest of him?'

'In his grave, back in Roorkee.'

'You mean you kept the skull but not the skeleton?'

'Well, it's a long story,' said Foster, 'but to keep it short, Uncle Fred died suddenly of a mysterious malady—a combination of brain fever, blood-pressure and Housemaid's Knee.'

'Housemaid's Knee!'

'Yes, swollen kneecaps, brought about by being beaten too frequently with police lathis. He wasn't really a criminal, but he'd get into trouble from time to time, harmless little swindles such as printing his own lottery tickets or passing forged banknotes. Spent some time in various district jails until his health broke down. Got a pauper's funeral—but his cadaver was in demand. The students from the local medical college got into the cemetery one night and made off with his cranium! Not that he had much by way of a brain, but he had a handsome, well-formed skull, as you can see.'

I did see. And the skull appeared to be listening to the yarn, because its toothless jaws were extended in a grin; or so I fancied.

'And how did you get it back?' I asked.

'Broke into their demonstration room, naturally. I was younger then, and pretty agile. There it was on a shelf, among a lot of glass containers of alcohol, preserving everything from giant tapeworms to Ghulam Qadir's penis and testicles.'

'Ghulam Qadir?'

'Don't you know your history? He was the fellow who blinded the Emperor Shah Alam. They caught up with him near Saharanpur and cut his balls off. Preserved them for posterity. Waste of alcohol, though. Have another drink, laddie. And then for a sausage. Ah! Sweet Mystery of Life!'

After another drink and several 'mystery' sausages, I made my getaway and stumbled homewards up a narrow path along an open ridge. A jackal slunk ahead of me, and a screech-owl screeched, but I got home safely, none the worse for an evening with the descendant of Bonnie Prince Charlie.

WHO'S BEEN SLEEPING IN MY BED?

There was a break in the rains, the clouds parted, and the moon appeared—a full moon, bathing the mountains in a pollen-yellow light. Little Fosterganj, straddling the slopes of the Ganga-Yamuna watershed, basked in the moonlight, each lighted dwelling a firefly in the night.

Only the Fairy Glen palace was unlit, brooding in the darkness. I was returning from an evening show at the Realto in Mussoorie. It had been a long walk, but a lovely one. I stopped outside the palace gate, wondering about its lonely inhabitants and all that might have happened within its walls. I wanted to see them again, but not at night—not with strange birds flapping around and skeletons hidden in the box-beds. Old skeletons, maybe; but what were they doing there?

I reached Hassan's bakery around midnight, and mounted the steps to my room. My door was open. It was never locked, as I had absolutely nothing that anyone would want to take away. The typewriter, which I had hired from a shop in Dehradun, was a heavy machine, designed for office use; no one was going to carry it off.

But someone was in my bed.

Fast asleep. Snoring peacefully. Not Goldilocks. Nor a bear.

I switched on the light, shook the recumbent figure. He started up. It was Sunil. After giving him a beating, the police had let him go.

'Uncle, you frightened me!' he exclaimed.

He called me 'Uncle', although I was only some fifteen or sixteen years older than him. Call a tiger 'Uncle', and

he won't harm you; or so the forest-dwellers say. Not quite
how it works out with people approaching middle age. Being
addressed as 'Uncle' didn't make me very fond of Sunil.

'I'm the one who should be frightened,' I said. 'A
pickpocket in my bed!'

'I don't pick pockets any more, Uncle. I've turned a new
leaf. Don't you know that expression?' Sunil had studied
up to Class 8 in a 'convent school'.

'Well, you can turn out of my bed,' I said. 'And return
that watch you took off me before you got into trouble.'

'You *lent* me the watch, Uncle. Don't you remember?
Here!' He held out his arm. 'Take it back.' There were two
watches on his wrist; my modest HMT, and something far
more expensive.

I removed the HMT and returned it to my own wrist.

'Now can I have my bed back?' I asked.

'There's room for both of us.'

'No, there isn't, it's only a khatiya. It will collapse under
our combined weight. But there's this nice easy chair here,
and in the morning, when I get up, you can have the bed.'

Reluctantly, Sunil got off the bed and moved over to
the cane chair. Perhaps I'd made a mistake. It meant that
Sunil would be awake all night, and that he'd want to talk.
Nothing can be more irritating than a room companion
who talks all night.

I switched off the light and stretched out on the cot. It
was a bit wobbly. Perhaps the floor would have been better.
Sunil sat in the chair, whistling and singing film songs—
something about a red dupatta blowing in the wind, and
telephone calls from Rangoon to Dehradun. A romantic soul,
Sunil, when he wasn't picking pockets. Did I say there's
nothing worse than a companion who talks all night? I
was wrong. Even worse is a companion who sings all night.

'You can sing in the morning,' I said. 'When the sun
comes out. Now go to sleep.'

There was silence for about two minutes. Then: 'Uncle?'

'What is it?'

'I have to turn over a new leaf.'

'In the morning, Sunil,' I turned over and tried to sleep.

'Uncle, I have a *project*.'

'Well, don't involve me in it.'

'It's all seedha-saadha, and very interesting. You know that old man who sells saande-ka-tel—the oil that doubles your manhood?'

'I haven't tried it. It's an oil taken from a lizard, isn't it?'

'A big lizard.'

'So?'

'Well, he's old now and can't go hunting for these lizards. You can only find them in certain places.'

'Maybe he should retire and do something else, then. Grow marigolds. Their oil is also said to be good for lovers.'

'Not as good as lizard oil.'

'So what's your project?' He was succeeding in keeping me awake. 'Are you going to gather lizards for him?'

'Exactly, Uncle. Why don't you join me?'

∽

Next morning Sunil elaborated on his scheme. I was to finance the tour. We would trek, or use a bus where there were roads, and visit the wooded heights and rocky slopes above the Bhagirathi river, on its descent from the Gangotri glacier. We would stay in rest-houses, dharamsalas, or small hotels. We would locate those areas where the monitors, or large rock lizards, were plentiful, catch as many as possible and bring them back alive to Fosterganj, where our gracious mentor would reward us to the tune of two hundred rupees per reptile. Sunil and I would share this bonanza.

The project, if any, did not interest me. I was extremely sceptical of the entire scheme. But I was bored, and it sounded like it could be fun, even an adventure of sorts, and I would have Sunil as guide, philosopher and friend. He could be a lovely and happy-go-lucky companion—provided he kept his hands out of other people's pockets and did not sing at night.

Hassan was equally sceptical about the success of the project. For one thing, he did not believe in the magical properties of saande-ka-tel (never having felt the need for it); and for another, he did not think those lizards would be caught so easily. But he thought it would be a good thing for Sunil, something different from what he was used to doing. The young man might benefit from my 'intellectual' company. And in the hills, not many folks had money in their pockets.

And so, with the blessings of Hassan, and a modest overdraft from Vishaal, our friendly bank manager, I packed a haversack with essentials (including my favourite ginger biscuits as prepared by Hassan) and set out with Sunil on the old pilgrim road to Tehri and beyond.

Sunil had brought along two large baskets, as receptacles for the lizards when captured. But as he had no intention of carrying them himself—and wisely refrained from asking me to do so—he had brought along a twelve-year-old youth from the bazaar—a squint-eyed, hare-lipped, one-eared character called Buddhoo, whose intelligence and confidence made up for his looks. Buddhoo was to act as our porter and general factotum. On our outward journey he had only to carry the two empty baskets; Sunil hadn't told him what their eventual contents might be.

It was late July, still monsoon time, when we set out on the Tehri road.

In those days it was still a mule-track, meandering over several spurs and ridges, before descending to the big river. It was about forty miles to Tehri. From there we could get a bus, at least up to Pratap Nagar, the old summer capital of the hill state.

ON THE TRAIL OF THE LIZARD

That first day on the road was rather trying. I had done a certain amount of walking in the hills, and I was reasonably fit. Sunil, for all his youth, had never walked further than Mussoorie's cinemas or Dehra's railway station, where the pickings for his agile fingers had always been good. Buddhoo, on the other hand, belied his short stature by being so swift of foot that he was constantly leaving us for behind. Every time we rounded a corner, expecting to find him waiting for us, he would be about a hundred yards ahead, never tiring, never resting.

To keep myself going I would sing either Harry Lauder's 'Keep right on to the end of the road,' or Nelson Eddy's 'Tramp, tramp, tramp'.

> *Tramp, tramp, tramp, along the highway,*
> *Tramp, tramp, tramp, the road is free!*
> *Blazing trails along the byways...*

Sunil did not appreciate my singing.

'You don't sing well,' he said. 'Even those mules are getting nervous.' He gestured at a mule-train that was passing us on the narrow path. A couple of mules were trying to break away from the formation.

'Nothing to do with my singing,' I said. 'All they want are those young bamboo shoots coming up on the hillside.'

Sunil asked one of the mule-drivers if he could take a ride on a mule; anything to avoid trudging along the stony path. The mule-driver agreeing, Sunil managed to mount one of the beasts, and went cantering down the road, leaving us far behind.

Buddhoo waited for me to catch up. He pointed at a large rock to the side of road, and sure enough, there, resting at ease, basking in the morning sunshine, was an ungainly monitor lizard about the length of my forearm.

'Too small,' said Buddhoo, who seemed to know

something about lizards. 'Bigger ones higher up.'

The lizard did not move. It stared at us with a beady eye; a contemptuous sort of stare, almost as if it did not think very highly of humans. I wasn't going to touch it. Its leathery skin looked uninviting; its feet and tail reminded me of a dinosaur; its head was almost serpent like. Who would want to use its body secretions, I wondered. Certainly not if they had seen the creature. But human beings, men especially, will do almost anything to appease their vanity. Tiger's whiskers or saande-ka-tel—anything to improve their sagging manhood.

We did not attempt to catch the lizard. Sunil was supposed to be the expert. And he was already a mile away, enjoying his mule-ride.

An hour later he was sitting on the grassy verge, nursing a sore backside. Riding a mule can take the skin off the backside of an inexperienced rider.

'I'm in pain,' he complained. 'I can't get up.'

'Use saande-ka-tel,' I suggested.

Buddhoo went sauntering up the road, laughing to himself.

'He's mad,' said Sunil.

'That makes three of us, then.'

COMPANIONS OF THE ROAD

By noon we were hungry. Hassan had provided us with buns and biscuits, but these were soon finished, and we were longing for a real meal. Late afternoon we trudged into Dhanolti, a scenic spot with great views of the snow peaks; but we were in no mood for scenery. Who can eat sunsets? A forest rest house was the only habitation, and had food been available we could have spent the night there. But the caretaker was missing. A large black dog frightened us off.

So on we tramped, three small dots on a big mountain,

mere specks, beings of no importance. In creating this world, God showed that he was a Great Mathematician; but in creating man, he got his algebra wrong. Puffed up with self-importance, we are in fact the most dispensable of all his creatures.

On a long journey, the best companion is usually the one who talks the least, and in that way Buddhoo was a comforting presence. But I wanted to know him better.

'How did you lose your ear?' I asked.

'Bear tore it off,' he said, without elaborating.

Brevity is the soul of wit, or so they say.

'Must have been painful,' I ventured.

'Bled a lot.'

'I wouldn't care to meet a bear.'

'Lots of them out here. If you meet one, run downhill. They don't like running downhill.'

'I'll try to remember that,' I said, grateful for his shared wisdom. We trudged on in silence. To the south, the hills were bleak and windswept; to the north, moist and well-forested. The road ran along the crest of the ridge, and the panorama it afforded, with the mountains striding away in one direction and the valleys with their gleaming rivers snaking their way towards the plains, gave me an immense feeling of freedom. I doubt if Sunil felt the same way. He was preoccupied with tired legs and a sore backside. And for Buddhoo it was a familiar scene.

A brief twilight, and then, suddenly, it grew very dark. No moon; the stars just beginning to appear. We rounded a bend, and a light shone from a kerosene lamp swinging outside a small roadside hut.

It was not the pilgrim season, but the owner of the hut was ready to take in the odd traveller. He was a grizzled old man. Over the years the wind had dug trenches in his cheeks and forehead. A pair of spectacles, full of scratches, almost opaque, balanced on a nose long since broken. He'd lived a hard life. A survivor.

'Have you anything to eat?' demanded Sunil.

'I can make you dal-bhaat,' said the shopkeeper. Dal and rice was the staple diet of the hills; it seldom varied.

'Fine,' I said. 'But first some tea.'

The tea was soon ready, hot and strong, the way I liked it. The meal took some time to prepare, but in the meantime we made ourselves comfortable in a corner of the shop, the owner having said we could spend the night there. It would take us two hours to reach the township of Chamba, he said. Buddhoo concurred. He knew the road.

We had no bedding, but the sleeping area was covered with old sheepskins stitched together, and they looked comfortable enough. Sunil produced a small bottle of rum from his shoulder bag, unscrewed the cap, took a swig, and passed it around. The old man declined. Buddhoo drank a little; so did I. Sunil polished off the rest. His eyes become glassy and unfocused.

'Where did you get it?' I asked.

'Hassan Uncle gave it to me.'

'Hassan doesn't drink—he doesn't keep it, either.'

'Actually, I picked it up in the police station, just before they let me go. Found it in the havildar's coat pocket.'

'Congratulations,' I said. 'He'll be looking forward to seeing you again.'

The dal-bhaat was simple but substantial.

'Could do with some pickle,' grumbled Sunil, and then fell asleep before he could complain any further.

∽

We were all asleep before long. The sheepskin rug was reasonably comfortable. But we were unaware that it harboured a life of its own—a miniscule but active population of fleas and bugs—dormant when undisturbed, but springing into activity at the proximity of human flesh and blood.

Within an hour of lying down we were wide awake

When God, the Great Mathematician, discovered that in making man he had overdone things a bit, he created the bedbug to even things out.

Soon I was scratching. Buddhoo was up and scratching. Sunil came out of his stupor and was soon cursing and scratching. The fleas had got into our clothes, the bugs were feasting on our blood. When the world as we know it comes to an end, these will be the ultimate survivors.

Within a short time we were stomping around like Kathakali dancers. There was no relief from the exquisite torture of being seized upon by hundreds of tiny insects thirsting for blood or body fluids.

The tea shop owner was highly amused. He had never seen such a performance—three men cavorting around the room, scratching, yelling, hopping around.

And then it began to rain. We heard the first heavy raindrops pattering a rhythm on the tin roof. They increased in volume, beating against the only window and bouncing off the banana fronds in the little courtyard. We needed no urging. Stripping off our clothes, we dashed outside, naked in the wind and rain, embracing the elements. What relief! We danced in the rain until it stopped, and then, getting back into our clothes with some reluctance, we decided to be on our way, no matter how dark or forbidding the night.

We paid for our meal—or rather, I paid for it, being the only one in funds—and bid goodnight and goodbye to our host. Actually, it was morning, about 2 a.m, but we had no intention of bedding down again; not on those sheepskin rugs.

A half-moon was now riding the sky. The rain had refreshed us. We were no longer hungry. We set out with renewed vigour.

Great lizards, beware!

TAIL OF THE LIZARD

At daybreak we tramped into the little township of Chamba,
where Buddhoo proudly pointed out a memorial to soldiers
from the area who had fallen fighting in the trenches in
France during the First World War. His grandfather had been
one of them. Young men from the hills had traditionally
gone into the army; it was the only way they could support
their families; but times were changing, albeit slowly. The
towns now had several hopeful college students. If they did
not find jobs they could go into politics.

The motor road from Rishikesh passed through Chamba,
and we were able to catch a country bus which deposited
us at Pratap Nagar later that day.

Pratap Nagar is not on the map, but it used to exist once
upon a time. It may still be there, for all I know. Back in
the days of the old Tehri Raj it had been the raja's summer
capital. There had even been a British resident and a tiny
European population—just a handful of British officials and
their families. But after Independence, the raja no longer
had any use for the place. The state had been poor and
backward, and over the years he had spent more time in
Dehradun and Mussoorie.

We were there purely by accident, having got into the
wrong bus at Chamba.

The wrong bus or the wrong train can often result
in interesting consequences. It's called the charm of the
unexpected.

Not that Pratap Nagar was oozing with charm. A
dilapidated palace, an abandoned courthouse, a dispensary
without a doctor, a school with a scatter of students and
no teachers, and a marketplace selling sad-looking cabbages
and cucumbers—these were the sights and chief attractions
of the town. But I have always been drawn to decadent,
decaying, forgotten places—Fosterganj being one of them—
and while Sunil and Buddhoo passed the time chatting to

some of the locals at the bus stand—which appeared to be the centre of all activity—I wandered off along the narrow, cobbled lanes until I came to a broken wall.

Passing through the break in the wall I found myself in a small cemetery. It contained a few old graves. The inscriptions had worn away from most of the tombstones, and on others the statuary had been damaged. Obviously no one had been buried there for many years.

In one corner I found a grave that was better preserved than the others, by virtue of the fact that the lettering had been cut into an upright stone rather than a flat slab. It read:

Dr Robert Hutchinson
Physician to His Highness
Died July 13, 1933
of Typhus Fever
May his soul rest in peace.

Typhus fever! I had read all about it in an old medical dictionary published half a century ago by *The Statesman* of Calcutta and passed on to me by a fond aunt. Not to be confused with typhoid, typhus fever is rare today but sometimes occurs in overcrowded, unsanitary conditions and is definitely spread by lice, ticks, fleas, mites and other micro-organisms thriving in filthy conditions—such as old sheepskin rugs which have remained unwashed for years.

I began to scratch at the very thought of it.

I remembered more: 'Attacks of melancholia and mania sometimes complicate the condition, which is often fatal.'

Needless to say, I now found myself overcome by a profound feeling of melancholy. No doubt the mania would follow.

I examined the other graves, and found one more victim of typhus fever. There must have been an epidemic. Fortunately for my peace of mind, the only other decipherable epitaph told of the missionary lady who had fallen victim to an earthquake in 1905. Somehow, an earthquake seemed less sinister than a disease brought on by bloodthirsty bugs.

While I was standing there, ruminating on matters of life and death, my companions turned up, and Sunil exclaimed: 'Well done, Uncle, you've already found one!'

I hadn't found anything, being somewhat short-sighted, but Sunil was pointing across to the far wall, where a great fat lizard sat basking in the sun.

Its tail was as long as my arm. Its legs were spread sideways, like a goalkeeper's. Its head moved from side to side, and suddenly its tongue shot out and seized a passing dragonfly. In seconds the beautiful insect was imprisoned in a pair of strong jaws.

The giant lizard consumed his lunch, then glanced at us standing a few feet away.

'Plenty of fat around that fellow,' observed Sunil. 'Full of that precious oil!'

The lizard let out a croak, as though it had something to say on the matter. But Sunil wasn't listening. He lunged forward and grabbed the lizard by its tail. Miraculously, the tail came away in his hands.

Away went lizard, minus its tail.

Buddhoo was doubled up with laughter. 'The tail's no use,' he said. 'Nothing in the tail!'

Sunil flung the tail away in disgust.

'Never mind,' I said. 'Catch a lizard by its tail—make a wish, it cannot fail!'

'Is that true?' asked Sunil, who had a superstitious streak.

'Nursery rhyme from Brazil,' I said.

The lizard had disappeared, but a white-bearded patriarch was looking at us from over the wall.

'You need a net,' he said. 'Catching them by hand isn't easy. Too slippery.'

We thanked him for his advice; said we'd go looking for a net.

'Maybe a bedsheet will do,' Sunil said.

The patriarch smiled, stroked his flowing white beard,

and asked: 'But what will you do with these lizards? Put them in a zoo?'

'It's their oil we want,' said Sunil, and made a sales pitch for the miraculous properties of saande-ka-tel.

'Oh, that,' said the patriarch, looking amused. 'It will irritate the membranes and cause some inflammation. I know—I'm a nature therapist. All superstition, my friends. You'll get the same effect, even better, with machine oil. Try sewing-machine oil. At least it's harmless. Leave the poor lizards alone.'

And the barefoot mendicant hitched up his dhoti, gave us a friendly wave, and disappeared in the monsoon mist.

TREMORS IN THE NIGHT

Not to be discouraged, we left the ghost town and continued our journey upriver, as far as the bus would take us. The road ended at Uttarkashi, for the simple reason that the bridge over the Bhagirathi had been washed away in a flash flood. The glaciers had been melting, and that, combined with torrential rain in the upper reaches, had brought torrents of muddy water rushing down the swollen river. Anything that came in its way vanished downstream.

We spent the night in a pilgrim shelter, built on a rocky ledge overlooking the river. All night we could hear the water roaring past below us. After a while, we became used to the unchanging sound; it became like a deep silence, and made our sleep deeper. Sometime before dawn, however, a sudden tremor had us trembling out of our cots.

'Earthquake!' shouted Sunil, making for the doorway and banging into the wall instead.

'Don't panic,' I said, feeling panicky.

'It will pass,' said Buddhoo.

The tremor did pass, but not before everyone in the shelter had rushed outside. There was the sound of rocks falling, and everyone rushed back again. 'Landslide!'

someone shouted. Was it safer outside or inside? No one could be sure.

'It will pass,' said Buddhoo again, and went to sleep. Sunil began singing at the top of his voice: 'Pyar kiya to darna kya—Why be afraid when we have loved'. I doubt Sunil had ever been in love, but it was a rousing song with which to meet death.

'Chup, beta!' admonished an old lady on her last pilgrimage to the abode of the gods. 'Say your prayers instead.'

The room fell silent. Outside, a dog started howling. Other dogs followed his example. No serenade this, but a mournful anticipation of things to come; for birds and beasts are more sensitive to the earth's tremors and inner convulsions than humans, who are no longer sensitive to nature's warnings.

A couple of jackals joined the chorus. Then a bird, probably a nightjar, set up a monotonous croak. I looked at my watch. It was 4 a.m, a little too early for birds to be greeting the break of day. But suddenly there was a twittering and cawing and chattering as all the birds in the vicinity passed on the message that something was amiss.

There was a rush of air and a window banged open.

The mountain shuddered. The building shook, rocked to and fro.

People began screaming and making for the door.

The door was flung open, but only a few escaped into the darkness.

Across the length of the room a chasm opened up. The lady saying her prayers fell into it. So did one or two others. Then the room and the people in it—those who were on the other side of the chasm—suddenly vanished.

There was the roar of falling masonry as half the building slid down the side of the mountain.

We were left dangling in space.

'Let's get out of here quickly!' shouted Sunil.

We scrambled out of the door. In front of us, an empty

void. I couldn't see a thing. Then Buddhoo took me by the hand and led me away from the crumbling building and on to the rocky ledge above the river.

The earth had stopped quaking, but the mountain had been shaken to its foundations, and rocks and trees were tumbling into the swollen river. The town was in darkness, the power station having shut down after the first tremor. Here and there a torch or lantern shone out of the darkness, and people could be heard wailing and shouting to each other as they roamed the streets in the rain. Somewhere a siren went off. It only seemed to add to the panic.

At 5 a.m, the rain stopped and the sky lightened. At six it was daybreak. A little later the sun came up. A beautiful morning, except for the devastation below.

THE MOUNTAINS ARE MOVING

'I think I'll join the army,' announced Sunil three days later, when we were back in Fosterganj. 'Do you think they'll take me?'

Sunil had been impressed by the rescue work carried out by the army after the Uttarkashi earthquake.

'Like a flash,' I said. 'Provided you keep your fingers out of the brigadier's pockets.'

∽

In those early hours of the morning, confusion had prevailed in and around Uttarkashi. Houses had crumbled from the tremors and aftershocks, or been buried under the earth and rocks of a number of landslides. Survivors were wandering around in a daze. Many lay crushed or trapped under debris. It would take days, weeks for the town to recover.

At first there were disorganized attempts at rescue, and Sunil, Buddhoo and I made clumsy attempts to extricate people from the ruins of their homes. A township built between two steep mountains, and teetering along the banks

of a moody river, was always going to be at risk. It had
happened before, it would happen again.

A little girl, dusty but unhurt, ran to me and asked,
'Will there be school today?'

'I don't think so,' I said.

A small boy was looking for his mother; a mother was
searching for her children; several men were digging in the
rubble, trying to extricate friends or family members.

And then a couple of army trucks arrived, and the rescue
work moved more swiftly, took on a certain momentum.
The jawans made all the difference. Many were rescued
who would otherwise have perished.

But the town presented a sad spectacle. A busy marketplace
had vanished; a school building lay in ruins; a temple had
been swallowed up by a gaping wound in the earth.

On the road we met the bearded patriarch, the one we
had encountered two days earlier.

'Did you find your lizards?' he asked. But we had
forgotten about lizards.

'What we need now are kitchen utensils,' he said. 'Then
we can prepare some food for those who need it.'

He was, it appeared, the head of a social service
organization, and we followed him to his centre, a shed
near the bus stand, and tried to make ourselves useful. A
doctor and nurse were at work on the injured.

I have no idea how many perished, or were badly injured
in that earthquake, I was never any good at statistics. Old
residents told me that the area was prone to such upheavals.

'Men come and go,' I said, 'but the mountains remain.'

'Not so,' said an old-timer. 'Out here, the mountains
are still on the move.'

∽

As soon as the buses were running again, Sunil and I returned
to Fosterganj. Buddhoo remained behind, having decided to
join the patriarch's aid centre. We missed his good-natured

company, even his funny hare-teeth smile. He promised to meet us again. But till the time I left Fosterganj, we were still waiting for him to turn up. I wonder what became of him. Some of the moving forces of our lives are meant to touch us briefly and then go their way.

A GHOST VILLAGE

On our way back, the bus broke down, as buses were in the habit of doing in those good old days. It was shake, rattle and roll for most of the journey, or at least part of the journey, until something gave way. Occasionally a bus went out of control and plunged over a cliff, taking everyone with it; a common enough occurrence on those hill roads.

We were lucky. Our bus simply broke its axle and came to rest against a friendly deodar tree.

So we were walking again.

Sunil said he knew of a short cut, and as a result we got lost, just the two of us, everyone else having kept to the main road.

We wandered over hill and dale, through a forest of oak and rhododendron, and then through some terraced fields (with nothing in them) and into a small village which appeared to be inhabited entirely by monkeys. An unfriendly lot of the short-tailed rhesus clan, baring their teeth at us, making guttural sounds and more or less telling us to be off.

There were about fifteen houses in the village, and all of them were empty—except for the monkeys and a colony of field rats. Where were all the people?

Going from house to house, we finally found an old couple barricaded inside a small hut on the outskirts of the village. They were happy to see us. They hadn't seen another human for over a month.

Prem Singh and his wife Chandni Devi were the only people still living in the village. The others had gone away—most of them to towns or cities in the plains, in search of employment, or to stay with friends or relatives; for there was nothing to sustain them in the village. The monkeys by day and the wild boars by night had ravaged the fields. Not a leaf, nor an edible root, remained. Prem Singh and his wife were living on their small store of rice and lentils. Even so, the wife made us tea and apologized that there was no milk or sugar.

'We too will leave soon,' she said. 'We will go to our son in Ludhiana. He works in a factory there.'

And that was what the others had done—gone wherever an earning member of the family had settled.

As it was growing dark, and the couple had offered us the occupancy of a spare room, we decided to stay the night.

An eerie silence enveloped the hillside. No dogs barked. They were no match for the monkeys. But we were comfortable on our charpais.

Just before daybreak Sunil had to go outside to relieve himself. The nearest field would do, he said; they were all empty anyway. I was still asleep, dreaming of romantic encounters in a rose garden, when I was woken by shouts and a banging of the door, and Sunil rushed in bare-bottomed and out of breath.

'What happened?' I asked, somewhat disoriented by this ridiculous interruption of my love dream.

'A wild pig came after me!' he gasped. 'One of those with tusks. I got up just in time!'

'But it got your pants, it seems,' I said.

When the sun came up, we both ventured into the field but there was no sign of a wild pig. By now the monkeys were up and about, and I had a feeling that they had made off with Sunil's pants. Prem Singh came to the rescue by giving him an old pair of pyjamas, but they were much too tight and robbed Sunil of his usual jaunty ebullience. But he had to make to do with them.

The whole situation had provided Prem Singh and his wife with much needed comic relief. In their hopeless predicament they could still find something to laugh at. Sunil invited them to visit his village, and we parted on friendly terms.

And so we limped back to Fosterganj without any lizards, and Sunil without pants; but we had learnt something during the week's events. Life in the hills and remote regions of the country was very different from life in the large towns and cities. And already the drift towards the cities had begun. Would the empty spaces be taken over again by the apes, reptiles and wild creatures? It was too early to tell, but the signs were there.

Meanwhile, Sunil was still intent on joining the army, and no sooner were we back in Fosterganj than he was off to the recruiting centre in Lansdowne. Would they take him, I wondered. He wasn't exactly army material. But then, neither was Beetle Bailey.

SOME PEOPLE DON'T AGE

As usual, nothing was happening in Fosterganj. Even the earthquake had barely touched it. True, part of Foster's old cottage had collapsed, but it was going to do that anyway. He simply moved into the remaining rooms without bothering about the damaged portion. In any case, there was no money for repairs.

Passing that way a couple of times, I heard the strains of Sir Harry Lauder again. At least the gramophone was still intact!

Hassan had a Murphy radio and had heard about the Uttarkashi earthquake and its aftermath, so he was relieved to see that I was back.

There was a rumour going around that Fairy Glen had been sold, and that it was going to be pulled down to make way for a grand hotel. I wondered what would happen to its occupants, the young-old boy and his equally intriguing mother. And would skeletons be turning up all over the place, now that it was to be dismantled? Or had I imagined that skeletal hand in the box-bed? In retrospect, it seemed more and more like a nightmare.

I dropped in at the bank and asked Vishaal if the rumours were true.

'There's something going on,' he admitted. 'Nothing certain as yet, because there's more than one owner—a claimant in Nepal, another in Calcutta and a third in Mauritius! But if they come to some agreement there's a hotel group that's interested.'

'Who would want to come to Fosterganj?' I mused.

'Oh, you never know. They say the water here has healing properties.'

'Well, I certainly get diarrhoea pretty frequently.'

'That's because it's pumped up from the dhobi ghat. Don't drink the tap water. Drink the water from upstream.'

'I walked upstream,' I said, 'and I arrived at the burning ghat.'

'Oh, that. But it isn't used much,' said Vishaal. 'Only one or two deaths a year in Fosterganj.'

'They can put that in the brochure, when they build that hotel. But tell me—what will happen to those people living in the palace? They're caretakers, aren't they?

'The boy and his mother? Poor relatives. They'll be given some money. They'll go away.'

I thought it would be charitable on my part to warn the boy and his mother of the impending sale—if they did not know about it already. Quixotic rather than charitable. Or perhaps I just needed an excuse to see them again.

But unwilling to meet skeleton or big black bird, I went there during the day.

It was early September, and the monsoon was beginning to recede. While the foliage on the hillside was still quite lush, autumn hues were beginning to appear. The Virginia creepers, suspended from the oak trees, were turning red. Wild dahlias reared their heads from overhanging rocky outcrops. In the bank manager's garden, chrysanthemums flounced around like haughty maharanis. In the grounds of Fairy Glen, the cosmos had spread all over the place and was just beginning to flower. In the late monsoon light, the old palace looked almost beautiful in its decadence; a pity it would have to go. We need these reminders of history, even though they be haunted, or too grand for their own good.

The boy was out somewhere, but the mother—if, indeed, she was his mother—was at the back of the building, putting out clothes to dry. She smiled when she saw me. The smile spread slowly across her face, like the sun chasing away a shadow, but it also lit up the scar on her cheek.

She asked me to sit down, offered me tea. I declined the tea but sat down on the steps, a bench and a couple of old chairs being festooned with garments.

'At last I can dry some clothes. After so many days the sun has finally come out.'

Although the boy usually spoke in English, she was obviously more at home in Hindi. She spoke it with a distinct Nepali lilt.

'Well, you haven't seen the sun for days,' I said, 'and I haven't seen the dhobi for weeks. I'm down to my last shirt.' She laughed. 'You should get married.'

It was my turn to laugh. 'You mean marry a washerwoman? Wives don't wash clothes anymore.'

'But mothers do.' And then she surprised me by adding, 'Wives can also be mothers.'

'There are washing machines now, in England and America,' I said. 'They'll be here soon enough. Expensive, of course. But new things are always expensive. We'll also have television soon.'

'What's that?'

'Radio with pictures. It's in Delhi already. A bit boring but it might catch on. Then you won't have to go to the cinema.'

'I don't go to the cinema. Not since my husband died.

He took me once—six or seven years ago. I forget the name of the film, but an actress called Madhubala was in it. She was very pretty.'

'Just like you,' I said.

She looked away. 'I'm not young.'

'Some people don't age. Your son—some say that he's much older than he looks.'

She did not reply, and just then the boy himself appeared, whistling cheerfully and bowing to me as he approached.

'It is good to see you again,' he said. 'The last time you were here, you left in a hurry.'

'I'm sorry, but that was a very creepy room you put me in. There was something in the box-bed. My imagination, probably.'

'A skeleton, probably. Grandfather stored them all over the palace. He didn't like burial grounds or cremations. And in the old days, if you were rich and powerful you could do as you liked.'

'It's the same today,' I said. 'Although not so openly. But I heard the property is being sold, to be pulled down—a hotel will come up. Did you know?'

'If it's true—' a shadow crossed his face, and for a few seconds he looked much older. 'If it's true, then...' He did not complete what he wanted to say.

'If it happens,' said his mother, 'then we will have to leave. To Nepal, perhaps. Or to Nabha. I have a cousin there. We are Sirmauris on my mother's side.'

'We are not going anywhere,' said the boy, glowering. The brightness had gone from his face. No one likes the thought of being thrown out of a house which has been a home for most of one's life. When I was a boy, my mother and stepfather were constantly being evicted from one house after another. Their fault, no doubt, but I grew up feeling that the world was a hostile place full of rapacious landlords.

'I'll try to find out more,' I said, getting up to leave. 'Vishaal, the bank manager, will know.'

MORNING AT THE BANK

When I called on Vishaal at the bank a day or two later, he was busy with a couple of customers. This was unusual. Busy days in the bank, let alone in Fosterganj, were rare indeed.

The cashier brought in another chair, and I joined the tea party in Vishaal's office. No secrets in Fosterganj. Everyone knew what everyone else had in their accounts, savings or otherwise.

One of the clients was Mr Foster.

He had first presented Vishaal with a basket of eggs, with the proviso that they be distributed among the staff.

'I should have brought sweets,' said Foster, 'but for sweets I'd have to trudge up to Mussoorie, while the eggs are courtesy my hens. Courtesy your bank, of course.'

'We appreciate them,' said Vishaal. 'We'll have omelettes in the lunch break. So how are the hens doing?'

'Well, a fox got two of them, and a jackal got three, and your guard got my rooster.'

Vishaal looked up at the guard who was standing just outside the door, looking rather stupid.

'Gun went off by mistake,' said the guard.

'It's not supposed to go off at all,' said Vishaal. 'You could kill somebody. It's only for show. If someone holds up the bank, we give them the money. It's all insured.'

The second customer looked interested. A lean, swarthy man in his sixties, he played with the knob of his walnutwood walking stick and said, 'Talking of insurance, do you know if the Fairy Glen was insured?'

'Don't think so,' said Vishaal. 'It's just a ruin. What is there to insure?'

'It's full of interesting artifacts, I'm told. Old pictures, furniture, antiques... I'm going there today. The owners have asked me to list anything that may be valuable, worth removing, before they hand over the place to the hotel people.'

'So it's really going?' I asked.

'That's right,' he said. 'The deal is all but sealed.'

'And the present occupants?'

'Just caretakers. Poor relatives. I believe the woman was the old raja's keep—or one of them, anyway. They'll have to go.'

'Perhaps the hotel can find some work for them.'

'They want vacant possession.' He got up, twirling his walking stick. 'Well, I must go. Calls to make.'

'You can use our phone,' said Vishaal. 'The only other public phone is at the police outpost, and it's usually out of order. And if you like, I can send for the local taxi.'

'No, I'll call from Mussoorie. I shall enjoy walking back to town. But I might want that taxi later.'

He strode out of the bank, walking purposefully through the late monsoon mist. He was one of the world's middlemen, a successful commission agent, fixing things for busy people. After some time they make themselves indispensable.

Mr Foster was quite the opposite. No one really needed him. But he needed another loan.

'No more chickens,' said Vishaal. 'And you haven't built your poultry shed.'

'Someone stole the wire netting. But never mind the chickens, I've another proposition. Mr Vishaal, sir, what about aromatherapy?'

'What about it? Never heard of such a thing.'

'It's all the rage in France, I hear. You treat different ailments or diseases with different aromas. Calendula for headaches, roses for nervous disorders, gladioli for piles—'

'Gladioli don't have an aroma,' I said.

'Mine do!' exclaimed Foster, full of enthusiasm. 'I can cover the hillside with gladioli. And dahlias too!'

'Dahlias don't have an aroma, either.' I was being Irish again.

'Well then, nasturtiums,' said Foster, not in the least put out. 'Nasturtiums are good for the heart.'

'All right, go ahead,' said Vishaal. 'What's stopping you? You don't need a loan to grow flowers.'

'Ah, but I have to distil the aroma from them.'

'You need a distillery?'

'Something like that.'

'You already have one. That rhododendron wine you made last year wasn't bad. Forget about aromas. Stick to wine and spirits, Mr Foster, and you'll make a fortune. Now I'm off for lunch.'

The bank shut its doors for lunch, and we went our different ways: Vishaal to his rented cottage, Foster to his dilapidated house and poultry farm, and I to Fairy Glen to warn my friends of trouble that lay in store for them.

MORNING AT THE POOL

Over the next two days the assessor, let's call him Mr Middleman, was busy at Fairy Glen, notebook in hand, listing everything that looked as though it might have some value: paintings, furnishings, glassware, chinaware, rugs, carpets, desks, cupboards, antique inkwells, an old grandfather clock (home to a colony of mice, now evicted), and a nude statue of Venus minus an arm. Two or three rooms had been locked for years. These were opened up by Mr Middleman who proceeded to explore them with enthusiasm. Small objects, like silver hand-bowls and cutglass salt cellars, went into his capacious pockets.

The boy and his mother watched all this activity in silence. They had been told to pack and go, but in reality they had very little to pack. The boy had handed over a bunch of keys; he wasn't obliged to do any more.

On the second day, when he had finished his inventory, Mr Middleman said he would be back the next day with a truck and some workmen to help remove all that he had listed—box-beds included. The boy simply shrugged and walked away; his mother set about preparing dinner, the kitchen still her domain. They were in no hurry.

It was almost dark when Mr Middleman set out on his walk back to town. The clouds had parted, and a full moon was coming up over Pari Tibba, Fairy Hill. In the moonlight a big black bird swooped low over the ravished building.

Pockets bulging with mementoes, Mr Middleman strode confidently through the pine forest, his walking stick swinging at his side. A village postman, on his way home, passed him in the gathering darkness. That was the last time Mr Middleman was seen alive.

His body was discovered early next morning by some girls on their way to school. It lay at the edge of the pond, where the boys sometimes came for a swim. But Mr Middleman hadn't been swimming. He was still in his clothes and his pockets were still bulging with the previous day's spoils. He had been struck over the head several times with the clubbed head of his walking stick. Apparently it had been wrenched from his hands by a stronger person, who had then laid into him with a fury of blows to the head. The walking stick lay a few feet away, covered with blood.

AN INSPECTOR CALLS

From then on, events moved quickly.

A jeepful of policemen roamed up and down Fosterganj's only motorable road, looking for potential killers. The bank, the bakery and the post office were centres of information and speculation.

Fosterganj might have had its mad dogs and professor-eating leopards; old skeletons might pop up here and there; but it was a long time since there'd been a proper murder. It was reported in the Dehradun papers (both Hindi and English) and even got mentioned in the news bulletin from All India Radio, Najibabad.

When I walked into Vishaal's small office in the bank, I found him chatting to a police inspector who had come down from Mussoorie to investigate the crime. One of his suspects was Sunil, but Sunil was far away in Lansdowne, making an earnest attempt to enlist in the Garhwal Rifles. And Sunil would have cleaned out the victim's pockets, the only possible motivation being robbery.

The same for Mr Foster, who was also one of the inspector's suspects. He wouldn't have left behind those valuable little antiques. And in any case, he was a feeble old man; he would not have been able to overcome someone as robust as Mr Middleman.

The talk turned to the occupants of Fairy Glen. But the inspector dismissed them as possible suspects: the woman could never have overpowered the assessor; and her son was just a boy.

I could have told him that the boy was much stronger than he looked, but I did not wish to point the finger of suspicion in his direction; or in any direction, for that matter. Mr Middleman was an outsider; his enemies were probably outsiders too.

After the inspector had gone, Vishaal asked: 'So—who do you think did it?'

'I, said the sparrow, with my bow and arrow, I killed Cock Robin!'

'Seriously, though.'

'I, said the fly, with my little eye, I saw him die.' Vishaal raised his hands in exasperation. I decided to be serious. 'We'll know only if there was a witness,' I said. 'Someone who saw him being attacked. But that's unlikely, if it happened after dark. Not many people use that path at night.'

'True. More than one person has fallen into that pond.'

Indeed, before the day was over, the inspector had fallen into the pond. He had been looking for clues at the water's edge, peering down at a tangle of reeds, when he heard an unusually loud flapping of wings. Looking up, he saw a big black bird hovering above him. He had never seen such a bird before. Startled, he had lost his footing and fallen into the water.

A constable dragged him out, spluttering and cursing. Along with the reeds and water weeds that clung to him was a mask made of cloth. It was a small mask, made for a boy.

The inspector threw it away in disgust, along with a drowned rat and a broken cricket bat that had come to the surface with him. Empty a village pond, and you will come up with a lot of local history; but the inspector did not have time for history.

The only person who seemed unperturbed by the murder was Hassan; he had seen people being killed out of feelings of hate or revenge. But here the reasons seemed more obscure.

'Such men make enemies,' he said. 'The go-betweens, the fixers. Someone must have been waiting for him.' He shrugged and went back to his work.

Hassan, a man who loved his work. He loved baking, just as some of us love writing or painting or making things. Most of the children were off to school in the morning, and his wife would be busy washing clothes or cleaning up the mess that children make. The older boys would take turns making deliveries, although sometimes Hassan did the rounds himself. But he was happiest in the bakery, fashioning loaves of bread, buns, biscuits and other savouries.

The first condition of happiness is that a man must find joy in his work. Unless the work brings joy, the tedium of an aimless life can be soul-destroying.

Something that I had to remember.

A FIRE IN THE NIGHT

It was late evening the same day when I encountered the boy from the palace.

I was strolling through the forest, admiring the mushrooms that had sprung up in damp, shady places. Poisoned, no doubt, but very colourful. Beware of nature's show-offs: the banded krait, the scarlet scorpion, the beautiful belladonna, the ink-squirting octopus. Even so, history shows human beings to be the most dangerous of nature's show-offs. Inimical to each other, given over to greed and insatiable appetites. Nature strikes when roused; man, out of habit and a perverse nature.

The boy still had some of the animal in him, which was what made him appealing.

'I've been looking for you, sir,' he said, as he stepped out of the shadows.

'I did not see you,' I said, startled.

'They've been looking for me. The police. Ever since that fellow was killed.'

'Did *you* kill him?'

I could see him smile even though it was dark. 'Such a big man? And why bother? They will take the palace anyway.'

He fell into step with me, holding my hand, leading the way; he knew the path and the forest better than I did. They would not find him easily in these hills.

'My mother has a favour to ask of you, sir.'

'Yes?'

'Will you keep something for her?'

'If it's not too big. I can't carry trunks and furniture around. I'm a one-suitcase person.'

'It's not heavy. I have it with me.' He was carrying a small wooden case wrapped in cloth. 'I can't open it here. It contains her jewellery. A number of things. They are all hers, but they will take them from us if they get a chance.'

'They?'

'The owners. The old king's family. Or their friends.'

'So you are going away?'

'We have to. But not before—' He did not finish what he was going to say. 'You will keep them for us?'

'For how long? I may leave Fosterganj before the end of the year. I will run out of money by then. I'll have to return to Delhi and take up a job.'

'We will get in touch with you. We won't be far.'

'All right, then. Give me the case. I'll have to look inside later.'

'Of course. But don't let anyone else see it. I'll go now. I don't want to be seen.'

He put the wrapped-up box in my hands, embraced me—it was more of a bear hug, surprising me with its intensity—and made off into the darkness.

ᴄᴐ

I returned to my room with the box, but I did not open it immediately. The door of my room did not fasten properly, and anyone could have walked in. It was only eight o'clock. So I placed the box on a shelf and covered it with my books. No one was going to touch them. Books gather dust in Fosterganj.

Vishaal had asked me over for a drink, and it was past ten when I started walking back to my room again.

Hassan and family were out on the road, along with some other locals. They were speculating on the cause of a bright rosy glow over the next ridge.

'What's happening?' I asked.

'Looks like a fire,' said Hassan. 'Down the Rajpur road.'

'It may be the Fairy Glen palace,' I said.

'Yes, it's in that direction. Let's go and take a look. They might need help.'

Fosterganj did not have a fire engine, and in those days Mussoorie did not have one either, so there was little that anyone could do to put out a major fire.

And this was a major fire.

One section of the palace was already ablaze, and a strong wind was helping the fire to spread rapidly. There was no sign of the boy and his mother. I could only hope that they were safe somewhere, probably on the other side of the building, away from the wind-driven flames.

A small crowd had gathered on the road, and before long half the residents of Fosterganj were watching the blaze.

'How could it have started?' asked someone.

'Probably an electrical fault. It's such an old building.'

'It didn't have electricity. Bills haven't been paid for years.'

'Then maybe an oil lamp fell over. In this wind anything is possible.'

'Could have been deliberate. For the insurance.'

'It wasn't insured. Nothing to insure.'

'Plenty to insure, the place was full of valuables and antiques. Furniture, mostly. All gone now.'

'What about the occupants—that woman and her boy?'

'Might be gone too, if they were sleeping.'

'Perhaps they did it.'

'But why?'

'They were being forced out, I heard.'

And so the speculation continued, everyone expressing an opinion, and in the meantime the fire had engulfed the entire building, consuming everything within—furniture, paintings, box-beds, skeletons, carpets, curtains, grandfather clock, a century's accumulated finery, all reduced to ashes. Most of the stuff had already outlived its original owner, who had himself been long since reduced to ashes. His heirs had wished to add to their own possessions, but possession is always a fleeting, temporary thing, and now there was nothing.

Towards dawn the fire burnt itself out and the crowd melted away. Only a shell of the palace remained, with here and there some woodwork still smouldering among the blackened walls. I wandered around the property and the hillside, looking for the boy and his mother, but I did not really expect to find them.

As I set out for home, something screeched in the tallest tree, and the big black bird flew across the road and over the burnt-out palace before disappearing into the forest below.

A HANDFUL OF GEMS

After an early breakfast with Hassan, I returned to my room and threw myself down on my bed. Then I remembered the case that the boy had left with me. I got up to see if it was still where I had hidden it. My books were undisturbed.

So I took the case down from the shelf, placed it on the bed, and prepared to open it. Then I realized I had no key. There was a keyhole just below the lid, and I tried inserting the pointed end of a pair of small scissors, but to no avail; then a piece of wire from the wire netting of the window, but did no better with that. Finally I tried the open end of a safety pin which I had been using on my pyjama jacket; no use. Obviously I was not meant to be a locksmith, or a thief.

Eventually, in sheer frustration, I flung the box across the room. It bounced off the opposite wall, hit the floor, and burst open.

Gemstones and jewellery cascaded across the floor of the room.

When I had recovered from my astonishment and confusion, I made sure the door was shut, then set about collecting the scattered gems.

There were a number of beautiful translucent red rubies, all aglow in the sun that streamed through the open window. I spread them out on my counterpane. I did not know much about gemstones, but they looked genuine enough to me. Presumably they had come from the ruby mines of Burma.

There was a gold bracelet studded with several very pretty bright green emeralds. Where did emeralds come from? South America, mostly. Supposedly my birthstone; but I'd never been able to afford one.

A sapphire, azure, sparkling in a silver neck-chain. A sapphire from Sri Lanka? And a garnet in a ring of gold. I could recognize a garnet because my grandmother had one. When I was small and asked her what it was, she said it was a pomegranate seed.

So there I was, with a small fortune in my hands. Or may be a large fortune. I had never bothered with gemstones before, but I was beginning to get interested. Having them in your hands makes all the difference.

Where should I hide them? Sooner or later someone would disturb my books. I looked around the room; very few places of concealment. But on my desk was a round biscuit tin. One of Hassan's boys used to keep his marbles in it; I had given him more marbles in exchange for the tin, because it made a handy receptacle for my paper-clips, rubber bands, erasers and such like. These I now emptied into a drawer. The jewels went into the biscuit tin—rubies, emeralds, sapphire, garnet—just like marbles, only prettier.

But I couldn't leave that biscuit tin lying around. One of the boys might come back for it.

On the balcony were several flowerpots; two were empty; one was home to a neglected geranium, another to a moneyplant that didn't seem interested in going anywhere. I put the biscuit tin in an empty pot, and covered it with the geranium, earth, roots and all, and gave it a light watering. It seemed to perk up immediately! Nothing like having a fortune behind you.

I brought the pot into my room, where I could keep an eye on it. The plant would flourish better indoors.

All this activity had sharpened my appetite, and I went down to the bakery and had a second breakfast.

FOSTER MAKES A SALE

In our dear country sensational events come and go, and excitement soon gives way to ennui.

And so it was in Fosterganj. Interest in the murder and the fire died down soon enough, although of course the police and the palace owners continued to make their enquiries.

Vishaal tried to liven up the hillside, spotting another

leopard in his back garden. But it was only a dog-lifter, not a man-eater, and since there were very few dogs to be found in Fosterganj after the last rabies scare, the leopard soon moved on.

A milkman brought me a message from Foster one morning, asking me to come and see him.

'Is he ill?' I asked.

'Looks all right,' said the milkman. 'He owes me for two months' supply of milk.'

'He'll give you a laying hen instead,' I said. 'The world's economy should be based on exchange.'

'That's all right,' said the milkman. 'But his hens are dying, one by one. Soon he won't have any left.'

This didn't sound too good, so I made my way over to Foster's and found him sitting in his small patch of garden, contemplating his onions and a few late gladioli.

'No one's buying my gladioli, and my hens are dying,' he said gloomily. An empty rum bottle lay in the grass beside his wobbly cane chair. 'Sorry I can't offer you anything to drink. I've run out of booze.'

'That's all right,' I said. 'I don't drink in the daytime. But why don't you sell onions? They'll fetch a better price than your gladioli.'

'They've all rotted away,' he said. 'Too much rain. And the porcupines take the good ones. But sit down—sit down, I haven't been out for days. Can't leave the hens alone too long, and the gout is killing me.' He removed a slipper and displayed a dirty bare foot swollen at the ankles. 'But tell me—how's the murder investigation going?'

'It doesn't seem to be going anywhere.'

'Probably that boy,' said Foster. 'He's older than he looks. A strange couple, those two.'

'Well, they are missing. Disappeared after the fire.'

'Probably started it. Well, good luck to them. We don't want a flashy hotel in the middle of Fosterganj.'

'Why not? They might buy your eggs—and your gladioli.'

'No, they'd go to town for their supplies.'

'You never know…. By the way, when did Fosterganj last have a murder? Or was this the first?'

'Not the first by any means. We've had a few over the years. Mostly unsolved.'

'The ones in the palace?'

'The disappearing maharanis—or mistresses. Very mysterious. No one really knows what happened to them, except they disappeared. Any remains probably went in that fire. But no one really bothered. The raja's life was his own business, and in those days they did much as they wanted. A law unto themselves.'

A large white butterfly came fluttering up to Foster and sat on his ear. He carried on speaking.

'Then there was that school principal, down near Rajpur. Fanthorne, I think his name was. Suspected his wife of infidelity. Shot her, and then shot himself. Nice and simple. Made it easy for the police and everyone concerned. A good example to all who contemplate murder. Carry out the deed and then turn yourself in or blow your brains out. Why leave a mess behind?'

'Why, indeed. Apart from your brains.'

'Of course you can also hang yourself, if you want to keep it clean. Like poor old Kapoor, who owned the Empire. It went downhill after Independence. No one coming to Mussoorie, no takers for the hotel. He was heavily in debt. He tried setting fire to it for the insurance, but it was such a sturdy old building, built with stones from the riverbed, that it wouldn't burn properly! A few days later old Kapoor was found hanging from a chandelier in the ballroom.'

'Who got the hotel?'

'Nobody. It passed into the Receiver's hand. It's still there, if you want to look at it. Full of squatters and the ghost of old Kapoor. You can see him in the early hours, wandering about with a can of petrol, trying to set fire to the place.'

'Suicide appears to have been popular.'

'Yes, it's that kind of place. Suicidal. I've thought of it once or twice myself.'

'And how would you go about it?'

'Oh, just keep boozing until I pass out permanently.'

'Nice thought. But don't do it today—not while I'm here.'

'I was coming to that—why I asked you to come over. I was wondering if you could lend me a small sum—just to tide me over the weekend. I'm all out of rations and the water supply has been cut too. Have to fill my bucket at the public tap, after all those washerwomen. Very demeaning for a sahib!'

'Well, I'm a little short myself,' I said. 'Not a good time for writers. But I can send you something from the bakery, I have credit there.'

'Don't bother, don't bother. You wouldn't care to buy a couple of hens, would you? I'm down to just three or four birds.'

'Where would I keep them? But I'll ask Hassan to take them off you. He'll give you a fair price.'

'Fine, fine. And there's my furniture. I could part with one or two pieces. That fine old rocking chair—been in the family for a century.'

I had seen the rocking chair on my previous visit, and had refrained from sitting in it, as it had looked rather precarious.

'I would laze in it all day and get no work done,' I said.

'What about Uncle Fred's skull? It's a real museum piece.'

'No, thanks. It's hardly the thing to cheer me up on a lonely winter's evening. Unlike your gramophone, which is very jolly.'

'Gramophone! Would you like the gramophone?' The white butterfly jumped up a little, as excited as Foster, then settled back on his ear.

'Well, it only just occurred to me—but you wouldn't want to part with it.'

'I might, if you made me a good offer. It's a solid HMV 1942 model. Portable, too. You can play it on a beach in Goa or a mountaintop in Sikkim. Springs are in good condition. So's the handle. Four hundred rupees, and you get the records free. It's a bargain!'

How do you bargain with a Scotsman? Foster's urgent need of money overrode his affection for the ballads of Sir Harry Lauder. I offered him two hundred, which was all the money I had on me. After a good deal of haggling we settled on three hundred. I gave him two and promised to pay the rest later.

In good spirits now, Forster suddenly remembered he had some booze stashed away somewhere after all. We celebrated over a bottle of his best hooch, and I stumbled home two hours later, the gramophone under one arm and a box of records under the other.

That night I treated myself to Sir Harry Lauder singing 'Loch Lomond', Dame Clara Buck singing 'Comin' through the Rye', and Arthur Askey singing 'We have no bananas today'. Hassan's children attended the concert, and various passers-by stopped in the road, some to listen, others to ask why I couldn't play something more pleasing to the ear. But everyone seemed to enjoy the diversion.

TREASURE HUNT

The nights were getting chilly, and I needed another blanket. The rains were over, and a rainbow arched across the valley, linking Fosterganj to the Mussoorie ridge. A strong wind came down from Tibet, rattling the rooftops.

I decided to stay another month, then move down to Rajpur.

∽

Someone had slipped a letter under my door. I found it there early one morning. Inside a plain envelope was a slip of paper with a few words on it. All it said was: 'Chakrata. Hotel Peak View. Next Sunday'.

I presumed the note was from the boy or his mother. Next Sunday was just three days away, but I could get to Chakrata in a day. It was a small military cantonment half way between Mussoorie and Simla. I had been there as a boy, but not in recent years; it was still a little off the beaten track.

I did not tell Hassan where I was going, just said I'd be back in a day or two; he wasn't the sort to pry into my affairs. I stuffed a change of clothes into a travel bag, along with the little box containing the jewels. Before hiding it, I had taped the lid town with Sellotape. It was still under the geranium, and I removed it carefully and returned the plant to its receptacle, where it would now have a little more freedom to spread its roots.

I took a bus down to Dehradun, and after hanging around the bus station for a couple of hours, found one that was going to Chakrata. It was half empty. Only a few village folk were going in my direction.

A meandering road took us through field and forest, and then we crossed the Yamuna just where it emerged from its mountain fastness, still pure and unpolluted in its upper reaches. The road grew steeper, more winding, ascending through pine and deodar forest, and finally we alighted at a small bus stop, where an old bus and two or three ponies appeared to be stranded. A deserted church and a few old graves told me that the British had once been present here.

There was only one hotel on the outskirts of the town, and it took me about twenty minutes to get to it, as I had to walk all the way. It stood in a forest glade, but it did provide a view of the peaks, the snow-capped Chor range being the most prominent.

It was a small hotel, little more than a guesthouse, and I did not notice any other residents. There was no sign of a manager, either; but a gardener or handyman led me to the small reception desk and produced a register. I entered my name and my former Delhi address. He then took me to a small room and asked me if I'd like some tea.

'Please,' I said. 'And something to eat.'

'No cook,' he said. 'But I'll bring you something from the market.' And he disappeared, leaving me to settle down in my room.

I needed a wash, and went into the bathroom. It had a nice view, but there was no water in the tap. There was a bucket half filled with water, but it looked rather murky. I postponed the wash.

I settled down in an armchair, and finding it quite comfortable, immediately fell asleep. Being a man with an easy conscience I've never had any difficulty in falling asleep.

I woke up about an hour later, to find the cook-gardener-caretaker hovering over me with a plate of hot pakoras and a pot of tea. He had only one eye, which, strangely, I hadn't noticed before. I recalled the old proverb: 'In the country of the blind the one-eyed man is king.' But I'd always thought the antithetical was true, and a more likely outcome, in the country of the blind, would be the one-eyed man being stoned to death. How dare he be different.

My one-eyed man seemed happy to talk. Not many tourists came to Chakrata; the intelligence department took a strong interest in visitors. In fact, I could expect a visit from them before the day was out.

'Has anyone been asking for me?' I asked. 'A young man accompanied by his mother?'

'They were here last week. Said they were from Nepal. But they left in a hurry. They did not take your name.'

'Perhaps they'll be back. I'll stay tonight—leave in the morning. Will that be all right?'

'Stay as long as you like. It's ten rupees a day for the room and two rupees for a bucket of water. Water shortage.'

'And it's been raining for three months.'

'But we are far from the river,' he said. And then he

left me to my own devices.

It was late evening when he appeared again to inform me that there were people in the hall who wanted to see me. Assuming that the boy and his mother had arrived, I said, 'Oh, show them in,' and got up from the armchair to receive them.

Three men stepped into the room. They were total strangers.

One of them asked to see my passport.

'I don't have one,' I said. 'Never left the country.'

'Any identification?'

I shook my head. I'd never been asked for identification. This was 1961, and border wars, invasions, insurrections and terrorist attacks were all in the future. We were free to travel all over the country without any questions being asked.

One of the three was in uniform, a police inspector. The second, the man who had spoken to me, was a civilian but clearly an official. The third person had some personal interest in the proceedings.

'I think you have something to deliver,' he said. 'Some stones belonging to the royal family.'

'You represent the royal family?' I asked.

'That is correct.'

'And the people who looked after the property?'

'They were servants. They have gone missing since the fire. Are you here to meet them?'

'No,' I said. 'I'm a travel writer. I'm writing a book on our hill stations. Chakrata is one of them.'

'But not for tourists,' said the official. 'This is purely a military station now.'

'Well, I have yet to see a soldier. Very well camouflaged.'

'Soldiers are not deployed here. It is a scientific establishment.'

I thought it better to leave it at that. I had come to the place simply to deliver some gemstones, and not as a spy; I said as much.

'Then may we have the stones?' said the third party. 'You will then be free to leave, or to enjoy the hospitality of this hotel.'

'And if I don't hand them over?'

'Then we may have to take you into custody,' said the inspector. 'For being in possession of stolen property.' And without further ado, he picked up my travel bag, placed it on a table, and rummaged through the contents. With three men standing over me, and the gardener in the background, there was no point in trying to be a hero.

The biscuit tin was soon in his hands. He shook it appreciatively, and it responded with a pleasing rattle. He tore off the tape, pressed open the lid and emptied the contents on the table.

Some thirty or forty colourful marbles streamed across the table, some rolling to the ground, others into the hands of the inspector, who held them up to the light and exclaimed, 'But these are not rubies!'

'My marble collection,' I said. 'And just as pretty as rubies.'

THE GREAT TRUCK RIDE

What had happened, quite obviously, was that Hassan's children, or at least one of them, had seen me secrete the box in the geranium pot. Wanting it back, they had unearthed it while I was out, removed the gemstones and replaced them with their store of marbles.

But what on earth had they done with the jewels? Hidden them elsewhere, perhaps. Or more likely, being still innocent children, they had seen the gems as mere rubbish and thrown them out of my window, into the ravine.

If I got back safely, I'd have to search the ravine.

But I was still in Chakrata, and my interlocutors had told me not to leave before morning. They were still hoping that the boy and his mother, or someone on their behalf, might have followed me to Chakrata.

The three gentlemen left me, saying they'd be back in the morning. I was left with the one-eyed gardener.

'When does the first bus leave for Dehradun?' I asked.

'At ten tomorrow.'

'Are there no taxis here?'

'Who would want a taxi? There is nothing to see. The best view is from your window.'

I gave him five rupees and asked him to bring me some food. He came back with some puris and a potato curry, and I shared it with him. He became quite chatty, and told me the town hadn't been off-bounds in the past, but security had been tightened since some border intrusions by the Chinese. Relations with China had soured ever since the Dalai Lama and his followers had fled to India two years previously. The Dalai Lama was still living in Mussoorie. Chakrata was, in a way, a lookout point; from here, the passes to the north could be better monitored. I'd come to the wrong place at the wrong time.

'I'm no spy,' I said. 'I'll come some other time to enjoy the scenery. I'll be off in the morning.'

'If they let you go.'

That sounded ominous.

The gardener-caretaker left me in order to lock up for the night, and I lay down on my bed in my clothes, wondering what I should do next. I was never much good in an emergency, and I was feeling quite helpless. Without friends, the world can seem a hostile place.

After some time I heard the door being bolted from outside. I'd been locked in.

I hate being locked into rooms. Once, as a small boy, I broke an expensive vase, and as punishment my grandmother locked me in the bathroom. I tried kicking the door open, and when that didn't work, I got hold of a water jug, smashed open a window, and climbed out; only to receive further punishment, by way of being sent to bed without any dinner.

And now I did more or less the same thing, but I waited for an hour or two, to give the gardener time to retire for the night. Then I unlatched the window—no need to break any glass—and peered out into the night.

The moon was a melon, just coming up over the next mountain. There was a vegetable patch just below the window. A cluster of cucumbers stood out in the mellow light. As I did not want to be encumbered with things to carry, I abandoned my travel bag and its meager contents; I would survive without pyjamas and a tattered old sweater. I climbed out on the window ledge and dropped into the vegetable patch, avoiding the cucumbers but pitching forward into a clump of nettles.

The nettles stung me viciously on the hands and face, and I cursed in my best Hindustani. The European languages have their strengths, but for the purposes of cursing out loud you can't beat some of the Indian languages for range and originality.

It took about twenty minutes for the pain of the nettle stings to subside, and by then my linguistic abilities were exhausted. But the nettles had given greater urgency to my flight, and I was soon on the motor road, trudging along at a good pace. I was beginning to feel like a character in a John Buchan novel, always on the move and often in the wrong direction. All my life had been a little like that. But I wouldn't have known any other way to live.

I knew I had to go downhill, because that was the way to the river. After walking for an hour, I was hoping someone would come along and give me a lift. But there would be few travellers at that late hour. Jackals bayed, and an owl made enquiring sounds, but that was all...

And then I heard the approach of heavy vehicles—not one, but several—and a convoy of army trucks came down the road, their headlights penetrating the gloom and leaving no corner of the road in shadow.

I left the road and stood behind a walnut tree until they had passed. I had no intention of taking a lift in an army truck; I could end up at some high-altitude border post, abandoned there in sub-zero temperatures.

So I returned to the road only when the last truck had gone round the bend, then continued to tramp along the highway, sore of foot but strong of heart. Harry Lauder would have approved.

Something else was coming down the road. Another truck. An old one, rattling away and groaning as it changed gear on a sudden incline. The army wouldn't be using an old wreck. So I stood in the middle of the road and waved it to a stop. An elderly Sardarji, older than the truck, looked out of his cabin window and asked me where I was headed.

'Anywhere,' I said. 'Wherever you're going.'

'Herbertpur,' he said. 'Get in the back.'

Herbertpur was a small township near the Timli Pass, on the old route to Dehradun. Herbert had been a tea-planter back in the 1860s or thereabouts. The family had died out, but the name remained.

I would have liked to sit up front, but Sardarji already had a companion, his assistant, about half my age and fair of face, who showed no signs of making way for me. So I made my way to the back of the truck and climbed into its open body, expecting to find it loaded with farm produce. Instead, I found myself landing in the midst of a herd of goats.

There must have been about twenty of them, all crammed into the back of the truck. Before I could get out, the truck started, and I found myself a fellow traveller with a party of goats destined for a butcher's shop in Herbertpur.

I must say they tried to make me welcome. As the truck lurched along the winding road, we were thrown about a good deal, and I found myself in close contact with those friendly but highly odorous creatures.

Why do we eat them, I wonder. There can be nothing

tougher than the meat of a muscular mountain goat. We should instead use them as weapons of offence, driving herds of goats into enemy territory, where they will soon consume every bit of greenery—grass, crops, leaves—in a matter of minutes. Sometimes I wonder why the Great Mathematician created the goat; hardly one of nature's balancing factors.

But I was the intruder, I had no right to any of their space. So I could not complain when a kid mistook me for its mother and snuggled up to me, searching for an udder. When I thrust it away, a billy goat got annoyed and started butting me on the rump. Fortunately for me, two female goats came to my rescue, coming between me and the aggressive male.

By the time we reached Herbertpur it was two in the morning, and I was feeling like a serving of rogan josh or mutton keema, two dishes that I resolved to avoid if ever I saw a menu again.

When I scrambled out of that truck, I was smelling to high heaven. The goats were bleating, as though they missed me. I thanked Sardarji for the lift, and he offered to take me further—all the way to Saharanpur. The goats, he said, would soon be unloaded, and replaced by a pair of buffaloes.

I decided to walk.

There was a small canal running by the side of the road.

There was just one thing I wanted in life. A bath.

I jumped into the canal, clothes and all, and wallowed there until daylight.

RUBIES IN THE DUST

I was back in Fosterganj that same evening, but I waited near the pool until it was dark before returning to my room. My clothes were in a mess, and I must have looked like the Creature from the Black Lagoon or an explorer who had lost his way in the jungle. After another bath, this time with good old Lifebuoy soap, I changed into my last pair of pyjamas, and slept all through the night and most of the next day, only emerging from my room because hunger had overcome lassitude. Hassan fed me on buns, biscuits and boiled eggs while I gave him an edited account of my excursion. He did not ask any questions, simply told me to avoid areas which were in any way under surveillance. Sage advice.

Over the next week, nothing much happened, except that the days grew shorter and the nights longer and I needed a razai at night.

I inspected all the flowerpots, emptying them one by one, just in case the marble players had switched the hiding place of the gemstones. The children watched me with some amusement, and I had to pretend that I was simply repotting the geraniums and begonias. It was the season for begonias; they flamed scarlet and red and bright orange, challenging the autumn hues of dahlias and chrysanthemums. Early October was a good time for flowers in Fosterganj. Vishaal's wife had created a patch of garden in front of the bank; the post office veranda had been brightened up; and even Foster's broken-down cottage was surrounded by cosmos gone wild.

I searched the ravine below the bakery, in case the gems had been thrown down from my window. I found broken bottles, cricket balls, old slippers, chicken bones, the detritus that accumulates on the fringes of human habitations; but nothing resembling jewellery.

And then one morning, as I was returning from a walk in the woods, I encountered the poor woman who was sweeping the road. This chore was usually carried out by her husband, but he had been ill for some time and she had taken over his duties. She was a sturdy woman, plain-looking, and dressed in a faded sari. Even when sweeping the road she had a certain dignity—an effortless, no-fuss dignity that few of us possess.

When I approached, she was holding something up to the light. And when she saw me, she held it out on her palm, and asked, 'What is this stone, Babuji? It was lying here in the dust. It is very pretty, is it not?'

I looked closely at the stone. It was not a pebble, but a ruby, of that I was certain.

'Is it valuable?' she asked. 'Can I keep it?'

'It may be worth something,' I said. 'But don't show it to everyone. Just keep it carefully. You found it, you keep it.'

'Finder's keepers', the philosophy of my school days. And whom did it belong to, anyway? Who were the rightful owners of those stones? There was no way of telling.

And what was their real worth? We put an artificial value on pretty pebbles found in remote places. Just bits of crystals, poor substitutes for marbles. Innocent children know their true worth. Nothing more than the dust at their feet.

The good lady tied the stone in a corner of her sari and lumbered off, happy with her find. And I hoped she'd find more. Better in her hands than in the hands of princes.

SUNIL IS BACK

Out of the blue, Sunil arrived. There he was, lean and languid, sitting on the bakery steps, waiting for me to return from my walk.

'I thought you'd joined the army,' I said.

'They wouldn't take me. I couldn't pass the physical. You have to be an acrobat to do some of those things, like climbing ropes or swinging from trees like Tarzan.'

'All out of date,' I said. 'They need less brawn and more brain.'

He followed me up the steps to my room and stretched himself out on the cot. He reminded me of a cat, sleek and utterly self-satisfied.

'So what else happened?' I asked.

'Well, the colonel was a nice chap. He couldn't enlist me, but he gave me a job in the mess room. You know, keeping the place tidy, polishing the silver, helping at the bar. It wasn't hard work, and sometimes I was able to give myself a rum or a vodka on the quiet. Lots of silver trophies on the shelves. Very tempting, but you can't do much with those things, they are mostly for show.'

'What made you leave?'

'Ivory. There were these elephant's tusks mounted on the wall, you see. Huge tusks. They'd been there for years. The elephant had been shot by a colonel-shikari about fifty years ago, and the tusks put on display in the mess. All that ivory! Very tempting.'

'You can't just pocket elephant tusks.'

'Not pocket them, but you can carry them off. And I knew how to get into that mess room in the middle of the night without anyone seeing me.'

'So did you get away with them?'

'Perfectly. I had a rug in which I hid the tusks, and I'd tied them up with a couple of good army belts. I took the bus down to Kotdwar without any problem. No one was going to miss those tusks—not for a day or two, anyway.'

'So what went wrong?'

'Things went wrong at the Kotdwar railway station. I was walking along the platform with the rug on my shoulder, looking for an empty compartment, when a luggage trolley bumped into me. I dropped the rug and it burst open. The tusks were there for all to see. A couple of railway police were coming down the platform, so I took off like lightning. Ran down the platform until it ended, then crossed the railway lines and hid in a sugarcane field. Later, I took a ride on a bullock-cart until I was well away from the town. Then I borrowed a bicycle and rode all the way to Najibabad.'

'Where's the cycle?'

'Left it outside the police station just in case the owner came looking for it.'

'Very thoughtful of you. So here you are.'

He smiled at me. He was a rogue. But at least he'd stopped calling me uncle.

ᢒ

It was only later that day—towards evening, in fact—that Sunil spotted the gramophone in a corner of my room.

'What's this you've got?' he asked.

'Mr Foster's gramophone. It plays music.'

'I know that. My grandfather has one. He plays old Saigal records.'

'Well, this one has old English records. You won't care for them. I bought the gramophone and the records came with it.'

Sunil lost no time in placing the gramophone on the table, opening it, and putting a record on the turntable. But the table was stuck.

'It's fully wound,' said Sunil. 'There's something jammed inside.'

'It was all right when I went away. The kids must have been fooling around with it.'

'Have you a screwdriver?'

'No, but Hassan will have one. I'll go and borrow it.'

I left Sunil fiddling about with the gramophone, and went downstairs, and came back five minutes later with a small screwdriver. Sunil took it and began unscrewing the upper portion of the gramophone. He opened it up; revealing the springs, inner machinery, the emerald bracelet, garnet broach and sapphire ring.

Sunil immediately slipped the ring on to a finger and said, 'Very beautiful. Did it come with the gramophone?'

SAPPHIRES ARE UNLUCKY

'Sapphires are unlucky,' I told him. 'You have to be very special to wear a sapphire.'

'I'm lucky,' he said, holding his hands to the light and admiring the azure stone in its finely crafted ring. 'It suits me, don't you think? And where did all this treasure come from?'

There was no point in making up a story. I told him how the jewels had come into my possession. Even as I did, I wondered who had put the jewellery in the gramophone. One of the children, I presumed—only a child would recognize the value of jewels but not of gemstones. I thought it best not to tell Sunil this. I did not mention the rubies, either. I did not want him hunting all over Fosterganj for them, and interrupting games of marbles to check if the children were playing with rubies.

'Those two won't be back,' he said, referring to the palace boy and his mother. 'They will be wanted for theft, arson and murder. But others may be after these pretty pebbles.'

'I know,' I said, and told him about my visitors in Chakrata.

'And you will get visitors here as well. I think we should go away for some time. Come to my village. Not the one near Rajpur. I mean my mother's village in Bijnor, on the other side of the Ganga. It's an out-of-the-way place, far from the main highways. Strangers won't be welcome.'

'Will I be welcome?'

'With me, you will always be welcome.'

∽

I allowed Sunil to take over. I wasn't really interested in the stones, they were more trouble than they were worth. All I wanted was a quiet life, a writing pad, books to read, flowers to gaze upon, and sometimes a little love, a little kiss.... But Sunil was fascinated with the gems. Like a magpie, he was attracted to all that glittered.

He transferred the jewels to a small tin suitcase, the kind that barbers and masseurs used to carry around. It was seldom out of his sight. He told me to pack a few things, but to leave my books and the gramophone behind; we did not want any heavy stuff with us.

'You can't carry a palace around,' he said. 'But you can carry the king's jewels.'

'Take that sapphire off,' I said. 'Unless it's your birthstone, it will prove to be unlucky.'

'Well, I don't know my date of birth. So I can wear anything I like.'

'It doesn't suit you. It makes you look too prosperous.'

'Seeing it, people won't suspect that I'm after their pockets.'

He had a point there. And he wasn't going to change his ways.

You have to accept people as they are, if you want to live with them. You can't really change people. Only a chameleon can change colour, and then only in order to deceive you.

If, like Sunil, you have a tendency to pick pockets, that tendency will always be there, even if one day you become a big corporate boss. If, like Foster, you have spent most of your life living on the edge of financial disaster, you will always be living on the edge. If, like Hassan, you are a single-minded baker of bread and maker of children, you won't stop doing either. If, like Vishaal, you are obsessed with leopards, you won't stop looking for them. And if, like me, you are something of a dreamer, you won't stop dreaming.

GANGA TAKES ALL

'Ganga-maiki jai!'

The boat carrying pilgrims across the sacred river was ready to leave. Sunil and I scrambled down the river bank and tumbled into it. It was already overloaded, but we squeezed in amongst the pilgrims, mostly rural folk who had come to Hardwar to visit the temples and take home bottles of Ganga water—in much the same way that the faithful come to Lourdes, in France, and carry away the healing waters of a sacred stream. People are the same everywhere.

In those days there was no road bridge across the Ganga, and the train took one to Bijnor by a long and circuitous route. Sunil's village was off the beaten track, some thirty miles from the nearest station. The easiest way to get there was to cross the river by boat and then take an ekka, or pony-cart, to get to the village.

The boat was meant to take about a dozen people, but for a few rupees more the boatmen would usually take in more than the permitted number. When we set off, there must have been at least twenty in the boat—men, women and children.

'Ganga-maiki jai!' they chanted, as the two oarsmen swung into the current.

For a time, all went well. In spite of its load, the boat made headway, being carried a little downstream but in the general direction of its landing place. Then halfway across the river, where the water was deep and strong, the boat began to wobble about and water slopped in over the sides.

The singing stopped, and a few called out in dismay. There was little one could do, except urge the oarsmen on.

They did their best, straining at the oars, the sweat pouring down their bare bodies. We made some progress, although we were now drifting with the current.

'It doesn't matter where we land,' I said, 'as long as we don't take in water.'

I had always been nervous in small boats. The fear of drowning had been with me since childhood: I'd seen a dhow go down off the Kathiawar coast, and bodies washed ashore the next day.

'Ganga-maiki jai!' called one or two hardy souls, and we were about two-thirds across the river when water began to fill the boat. The women screamed, the children cried out.

'Don't panic!' I yelled, though filled with panic. 'It's not so deep here, we can get ashore.'

The boat struck a sandbank, tipped over. We were in the water.

I was waist-deep in water, but the current was strong, taking me along. The menfolk picked up the smaller children and struggled to reach the shore. The women struggled to follow them.

Two of the older women were carried downstream; I have no idea what happened to them.

Sunil was splashing about near the capsized boat. 'Where's my suitcase?' he yelled.

I saw it bobbing about on the water, just out of his reach. He made a grab for it, but it was swept away. I saw it disappearing downstream. It might float for a while, then sink to the bottom of the river. No one would find it there. Or some day the suitcase would burst open, its contents carried further downstream, and the emerald bracelet be washed up among the pebbles of the riverbed. A fisherman might find it. In older times he would have taken it to his king. In present times he would keep it.

We struggled ashore with the others and sank down on the sand, exhausted but happy to be alive.

Those who still had some strength left sang out: 'Ganga-maiki jai!' And so did I.

Sunil still had the sapphire ring on his hand, but it hadn't done him much good.

END OF THE ROAD

We stayed in Sunil's village for almost a month. I have to say I enjoyed the experience, in spite of the absence of modern conveniences. Electricity had come to the village—which was surprising for that time—and in our room there was a ceiling fan and an old radio. But sanitation was basic, and early in the morning one had to visit a thicket of thorn bushes, which provided more privacy than the toilets at the bus stop. Water came from an old well. It was good sweet water. There were pigeons nesting in the walls of the well, and whenever we drew up a bucket of water the pigeons would erupt into the air, circle above us, and then settle down again.

There were other birds. Parrots, green and gold, settled in the guava trees and proceeded to decimate the young fruit. The children would chase them away, but they would return after an hour or two.

Herons looked for fish among the hyacinths clogging up the village pond. Kingfishers swooped low over the water. A pair of Sarus cranes, inseparable, treaded gingerly through the reeds. All on fishing expeditions.

The outskirts of an Indian village are a great place for birds. You will see twenty to thirty species in the course of a day. Bluejays doing their acrobatics, sky-diving high above the open fields; cheeky bulbuls in the courtyard; seven sisters everywhere; mynas quarrelling on the veranda steps; scarlet minivets and rosy pastors in the banyan tree; and at night, the hawk cuckoo or brain fever bird shouting at us from the mango-tope.

Almost every village has its mango-tope, its banyan tree, its small temple, its irrigation canal. Old men smoking hookahs; the able-bodied in the fields; children playing gulli-danda or cricket. An idyllic setting, but I did not envy my hosts. They toiled from morn till night—ploughing, sowing, reaping, always with an eye on the clouds—and then having to sell, in order to buy...

Sunil's uncle urged him to stay, to help them on the farm; but he was too lazy for any work that required physical exertion. Towns and cities were his milieu. He was fidgety all the time we were in the village. And when I told him it was time for me to start working, looking for a job in Delhi, he did not object to my leaving but instead insisted on joining me. He too would find a job in Delhi, he said. He could work in a hotel or a shop or even start his own business.

And so I found myself back in my old room in dusty Shahdara in Delhi, and within a short time I'd found work with a Daryaganj publisher, polishing up the English of professors who were writing guides to Shakespeare, Chaucer and Thomas Hardy.

Sunil had friends in Delhi, and he disappeared for long periods, turning up only occasionally, when he was out of pocket or in need of somewhere to spend the night.

And then one of his friends came by to tell me he'd been arrested at the New Delhi railway station. He'd been back to his old ways, relieving careless travellers of their cash or wristwatches. He was a skilful practitioner of his art, but he'd grown careless.

The police took away the sapphire ring, and of course he never saw it again. It must have brought a little affluence but not much joy to whoever flaunted it next.

Denied bail, Sunil finally found himself lodged in a new, modern jail that had come up at a village called Tihar, on the old Najafgarh road. As a boy I'd gone fishing in the extensive Najafgarh Jheel, but now much of it had been filled in and built over. The herons and kingfishers had moved on, the convicts had moved in.

Sunil had been there a few months when at last I was able to see him. He was looking quite cheerful, not in the least depressed; but then, he was never the despondent type. He was working in the pharmacy, helping out the prison doctor. He had become popular with the inmates, largely due to his lively renderings of Hindi film songs.

Our paths had crossed briefly, and now diverged. I knew we would probably not see each other again. And we didn't. What became of him? Perhaps he spent many more months in jail, making up prescriptions for ailing dacoits, murderers, embezzlers, fraudsters and sexual offenders; and perhaps when he came out, he was able to start a chemist's shop. Unlikely, but possible. In any case, he would have made

Delhi his home. The big city would have suited him.

Fosterganj was a far cry from all this, and I was too busy to give it much thought. And then one Sunday, when I was at home, I had a visitor.

It was Hassan.

He had come to Delhi to attend a relative's marriage and he had got my address from the publisher in Daryaganj. Having given up any hope of seeing me again in Fosterganj, he'd brought along my books, typewriter, and the gramophone.

He spent all morning with me, bringing me up to date on happenings in Fosterganj.

Vishaal had been transferred, getting a promotion, and taking over a branch in the heart of Madhya Pradesh. Mowgli country! Leopard country! Vishaal would be happy there.

'And how's old Foster?' I asked.

'Not too good. He says he won't last long, and he may be right. He wants to know if you'll accept his uncle's skull as a gift.'

'Tell him to gift it to the Mussoorie municipality. I believe they are starting a museum in the Clock Tower. But thanks for bringing the gramophone down. I could do with a little music.'

Hassan then told me that the hotel was now coming up on the site of the old palace. It would be a posh sort of place, very expensive.

'What are they calling it?' I asked.

'Lake View Hotel.'

'But there isn't a lake.'

'They plan to make one. Extend the old pool, and feed it with water from the dhobi ghat. Fosterganj is changing fast.'

'Well, as long as it's good for business. Should be good for the bakery.'

'Oh, they'll have their own bakery. But I'll manage. So many workers and labourers around now. Population is going up. So when will you visit us again?'

'Next year, perhaps. But I can't afford Lake View Palaces.'

'You don't need to. Your room is still there.'

'Then I'll come.'

∽

Over the next three or four years I lost touch with Fosterganj. My life changed a little. I found companionship when I was least expecting it, and I became a freelance writer for a travel magazine. It was funded by a Parsi gentleman who was rumoured to own half of Bombay. I saw no evidence of the wealth in the cheques I received for my stories, but at least I got to travel a lot, zipping around the country by train, bus and, on one occasion, a dilapidated old Dakota of the Indian Airlines.

The forests of Coonoor; the surge of the sea at Gopalpur; old settlements on the Hooghly; the ghats of Banaras; the butterflies of the Western Ghats; the forts of Gwalior; the sacred birds of Mathura; the gardens of Kashmir—all were grist to my mill, or rather to the portable typewriter which had taken the place of the clumsy old office machine. How could Fosterganj's modest charms compare with the splendours that were on offer elsewhere in the land?

So Fosterganj was far from my thoughts—until one day I picked up a newspaper and came across a news item that caught my attention.

On the outskirts of the hill station of Nahan a crime had been committed. An elderly couple living alone in a sprawling bungalow had been strangled to death. The police had been clueless for several weeks, and the case was almost forgotten, until a lady turned up with information about the killer. She led them to a spot among the pines behind the bungalow, where a boy was digging up what looked like a small wooden chest. It contained a collection of valuable gemstones. The murdered man had been a well-known jeweller with an establishment in Simla.

The accused claimed that he was a minor, barely fifteen. And certainly he had looked no older to the police. But the woman told them he was only a few years younger than her, and that she was nearly fifty. She confessed to being his accomplice in similar crimes in the past; it was always gems and jewellery he was after. He had been her lover, she said. She had been under his domination for too long.

I looked at the photograph of the man-boy that accompanied the report. A bit fuzzy, but it certainly looked like Bhim the Lucky. Who else could it have been?

The next few mornings I scanned the papers for more information on the case. There was a small update, which said that a medical test had confirmed the accused was in his forties. And the woman had disappeared.

Then there was nothing. The newspapers had moved on to other scandals and disasters.

I felt sorry for the woman. We had met only twice, but I had sensed in her a fellow feeling, a shared loneliness that was on the verge of finding relief. But for her it was not to be. I wondered where she was, and what she would do to forget she had given many years of her life for a love that had never truly existed.

I never saw her again.

∽

Not the happiest memory to have of Fosterganj. When I look back on that year, I prefer to think of Hassan and Sunil and Vishaal, and even old Foster (long gone), and the long-tailed magpies flitting among the oak trees, and the children playing on the dusty road.

And last winter, when I was spending a few weeks in a bungalow by the sea—far from my Himalayan haunts—I remembered Fosterganj and thought: I have written about moonlight bathing the Taj and the sun beating down on the Coromandel Coast—and so have others—but who will celebrate little Fosterganj?

And so I decided to write this account of the friends I made there—a baker, a banker, a pickpocket, a hare-lipped youth, an old boozer of royal descent, and a few others—to remind myself that there had been such a place, and that it had once been a part of my life.

THE GARDEN OF DREAMS

It wasn't so long ago that I found myself in Kathmandu, the colourful capital of Nepal, attending one of those literary festivals that have caught on in countries where books are still written, published and sometimes read. I had a day or two to myself and I was wandering about in the streets looking for quaint corners—for I am a collector of quaint corners—when I came across a walled enclosure, a long high wall with just an entrance, a heavy door over which was painted the following legend: 'Garden of Dreams'.

Naturally I was curious. If there was a garden it was behind that wall. And since it had advertised itself, presumably it was open to the public.

On the pavement, not far from the entrance, sat an old woman who was selling trinkets, costume jewellery and semi-precious stones.

'Mother,' I said, for she seemed older than me, 'What's in that garden of dreams?'

'Flowers,' she said, 'And running water. And dreams.'

Her face was furrowed with the passage of time but she had a cheerful, winning smile and her forearms were covered with the colourful bangles, her fingers with rings of onyx and jade.

'I suppose I can go in,' I said.

'It will open any minute,' she said. 'But first, why don't you buy something? A bracelet for your lady-love?'

'I don't have a lady-love.' But I bought a tiny mirror from her. It was ringed with different coloured stones and crowned with a gaudily painted wooden parrot. As I pocketed my purchase, the door to the garden opened and the old lady said, 'You can go in now and look for your dream.'

There was no one at the door and I couldn't see anyone in the garden, although there were signs of activity at the other end, where a couple of gardeners were pruning a rose bush.

There were roses everywhere—lush golden roses, and pink lollipops, and roses that opened like a woman's labia, and roses that shone in the early morning sun, and some that still held dewdrops between their petals.

I had the garden to myself for almost half an hour and in that time I followed little paths that meandered between beds of crimson poppies, scented petunias of every shade, carpets of multi-coloured phlox, pansies with their funny faces that looked like Oliver Hardy's larkspur, wallflowers, snapdragons...

There was a small waterfall at one end of the garden and it fed a small stream that ran in and out of the spaces between the flower beds. Here and there you could cross the stream by means of small bridges. They gave the garden a distinct Japanese or Oriental look.

I sat down on a bench and tried to take it all in. I am a sensualist by nature, but here there was so much to absorb—colour, fragrance, sunshine and shade, the flow of water, the pattern of leaves, the twitter of small birds, the passage of a butterfly.... And presently other people were trickling into the garden—some Japanese tourists, laden with cameras; a stout Indian lady in a pink sari, accompanied by a brood of children; a bearded, bespectacled artist with a sketch pad; an English-looking woman lurking beneath a large hat.

The woman in the hat stopped beside me and said, 'Lovely garden, isn't it? So very English...'

'They say the late Rana was inspired by a garden he saw in France,' I commented.

'But French gardens are so formal, aren't they? And this one has something of everything. Even a bit of the willow pattern plate. Was that Chinese or Japanese?'

'Probably a bit of both,' I said. 'Let's just say it's uniquely Nepalese!'

The lady in the hat moved on and the woman in the pink sari plonked herself down on the bench. She was soon joined by two of her noisy children and I made way for them and strolled across to the far end of the garden. Here a fountain was playing and in the pool surrounding it there were several goldfish. Nearby there was a girl on a swing. She could have been sixteen or twenty-six, I couldn't guess her age, she was young and pretty but she was also quite adult in her poise and manner. She made me think of *Alice in Wonderland*. She was dressed all in green, but there was a purple hibiscus in her hair.

'Do you like goldfish?' she asked.

'I do,' I said. 'There is something very restful about them. I can watch them for hours. How they silently glide around in their watery world.'

'And they don't bark,' she said. 'Or make any noise at all.'

I laughed. 'Do you come here often?'

'Quite often,' she said. 'It's your first visit, isn't it?'

'Yes and I'm only here for a day or two. This garden belonged to a princess, I'm told. Does anyone live there now, in the old palace?'

'Sometimes the princess comes. But she's very old now—she doesn't come down from her tower.'

'And you—are you a princess too?'

She laughed and I noticed that her eyes were dark like hazelnuts. There were silver anklets on her feet and a daisy chain around her throat.

'No,' she said, 'I'm just a—' She broke off and looked away and there was a touch of sadness on her face. 'I do all sorts of things,' she said, sounding quite cheerful again. 'Have you seen the birds?'

'You mean the sparrows?'

'No, the aviary. There are lots of small birds. Come, I'll show you.'

She jumped off the swing and beckoned and I found

myself by her side, holding her hand.

Had she taken my hand or had I taken hers? I wasn't sure. It was just something that had happened.

The touch of her hand sent a strange thrill through my entire person. It wasn't like any hand that I'd ever held. It was a young hand, the palms soft and the fingers strong; but it was also the hand of her ancestors and I felt that it had stories to tell. It was also taking something out of me. I felt younger, even reckless. I clung to her hand as though I was clinging to life itself; I did not want to let go.

A variety of small, colourful birds flitted about the spacious aviary, some on swings, some on the branches of a small blossoming plum tree. Plum blossoms were flung far and wide. There was a great amount of birdsong, if you could call it that. Really just twittering and chirping, like a bunch of cocktail party humans having a gossip session. A pair of lovebirds appeared to be enamoured of each other; they kept kissing each other with their tiny beaks.

'See, they are making love!' exclaimed my companion, her hand pressing into mine. Her hazel eyes were excited. I was tempted to kiss her but at that moment the large hatted lady loomed over us and we became self-conscious.

'Sexy little creatures, aren't they?' she said. 'Just like a couple of teenagers.'

She was obviously referring to the lovebirds, for I was no teenager; but my companion led me away, still holding me by the hand.

She took me into a shady arbour, and we sat there for some time, and she told me her name, Kiran, and that she lived close by and came to the garden almost every day. I did not ask her too many questions. Conscious that I was much older than her and that she knew nothing about me, I did not want to frighten her off with too much familiarity. A gazelle will come to you if you are very still but if you move towards it, the beautiful creature will dart away. And this was a gazelle I was talking to.

She asked me questions and I told her about myself, that I worked for an Indian publishing firm and that I was in Kathmandu for a few days—with just a day or two to go.

'Will you come again tomorrow?' she asked.

'If you like,' I said, 'And then perhaps you can show me the marketplace. It's close by, isn't it?'

'Yes, quite close. But I like it here in the garden.' She had released my hand and I felt that something was going from me. And then the lady in the pink sari barged in with her kids, and the spell was broken.

She walked with me as far as the garden door. I looked back at the tall, old building behind the garden.

'Do you live there?' I asked.

She nodded, smiling wistfully.

'It looks very old,' I said. 'So you really are a princess?'

She laughed and her dark eyes lit up in the sunshine. 'I am anything I want to be.'

'Till tomorrow, then,' I said.

'Till tomorrow...'

And so we parted. Out on the street I bought another trinket, and the old lady noticed that I looked happy and she gave me a toothless grin and asked, 'Did you find your dream?'

'Better than a dream,' I said and made my way back to the hotel where I had a meeting with local publishers.

∽

I forget how I spent the rest of that day. I kept thinking about the girl in the garden. We had struck up a good rapport and I wanted to see her again and take our friendship forward.

So next morning, after breakfast, I sallied forth to the garden of dreams.

She wasn't there.

I walked around the garden several times. I hung about near the pool and the aviary and sat on a bench for at least an hour. Visitors came and went. Tourists from China and Japan; talking, admiring. Loud-voiced Americans. Some quiet, reserved Africans. A writer from India came up to me and thrust a folder into my hands. 'For you to publish,' he said. 'It will sell in millions!' He must have followed me into the garden. I promised to read his masterpiece.

Then I paced about, studying rose bushes, herbaceous borders, lovebirds. No one came.

It was getting on to noon when I gave up and left the garden.

No, I did not buy any trinkets.

The old woman looked up at me and said, 'No good dream today?'

I shook my head and said, 'Yesterday I met a girl in the garden. She said her name was Kiran. She was to meet me again today. She was a princess, I think. Do you know her?'

The old woman shook her head. 'There is no princess living here. Kiran? I do not know the name. Perhaps she could not come today. Why not try tomorrow?'

'But I must leave tomorrow.'

'It is sad, then. She means much to you, this girl?'

'I think so.'

She nodded wisely. 'Many hearts have been broken in the garden of dreams.' And she said no more.

∽

I wandered the streets of Kathmandu. I wasn't looking for anyone. I just couldn't stand being alone in my hotel room or in the company of writers and publishers.

Towards evening I passed the garden of dreams. The door was shut, the walls were too high to see anything. I supposed she did not want to see me again. That overture of friendship, the pressure of her hand, the tenderness in her eyes, her every gesture had spoken of liking, if not of love. Perhaps it meant nothing after all. Just a way of passing the time.... And here I was, a middle-aged moron, fretting like an adolescent who had just fallen in love!

My plane was to leave at noon.

There was time for one last visit to the garden, albeit a hurried one.

It was far too early. The street was deserted. The garden door was locked from within. The old lady with her wares was yet to arrive. The sun was only just coming up.

Further along the street, where the garden enclosure ended, someone was sweeping the pavement using a long-handled broom. Fallen leaves and plastic waste were being swept into an imposing heap—all so symbolic of the new century.

I approached the early morning sweeper. Perhaps he could help me.

It wasn't a 'he'. The person, dressed in a uniform of sorts, turned to me when I spoke and I was shocked into silence; for it was none other than Kiran.

She was as surprised as I was. She dropped the broom. A look of panic crossed her face and then vanished just as quickly.

'You are here—so early—it does not open till ten.'

'I came to see you, not the garden,' I said. 'And you promised to meet me yesterday.'

'I could not come. I was sent into town on some work. My father works for the old king's family. But as you can see, I am not a princess. That was just a game.' She gave me an enigmatic smile.

'So let the game continue,' I said and held out my hand.

She took it, held it for a moment, then let it fall. 'You are a good person,' she said simply.

'And you are a princess,' I said, 'and I want to see you again. But my plane leaves shortly. If I come again in a few months' time, will you be here?'

'In the garden or outside?' Her good humour was returning.

'Near the aviary. Where the lovebirds sing.'

'They don't sing,' she said, laughing. 'They kiss each

other all the time.'

Well, I didn't kiss her, although I longed to do so. The street was filling up, people were staring at us. There were no cell phones then, but I gave her my home address and asked her to write to me. Then I rushed back to the hotel, collected my bag, sent for a taxi and headed for the airport.

Soon the garden and Kiran were just a dream.

∽

But it was a dream that wouldn't go away.

The monsoon rains came and went and an autumn breeze swept across the hills and knocked over the windows of my hilltop home. There was no word from Kiran. Perhaps she did not write letters. Perhaps she did not write at all!

On my desk was the little mirror I'd bought from the old lady outside the garden. It sparkled in the morning sun; it glowed at the time of sunset. A little bird—just a sparrow— flew in at the open window—examined the wooden parrot, pecked at the mirror and flew away. Sometimes I thought I saw someone in the mirror—just a figure, a slight figure in green, but she was always walking away. Mirrors can play tricks.

And this planet, this earth and its hidden fires, can be cruel.

An earthquake struck the Himaal.

It ran through the heart of Nepal, razing towns, villages, palatial buildings and humble dwellings. Thousands perished. Thousands lost their homes, their living, their loved ones. These sudden horrific natural calamities almost always strike the poorest, most vulnerable countries—Haiti, Mozambique, small island nations, landlocked mountain lands, Nepal...

As the news came through on my television, I feared the worst. Would Kiran have survived? And what of other friends and associates? I phoned them, made enquires, but news trickled through very slowly. People were too busy salvaging what was left of their homes. And many slept in the open as aftershocks ran through the country, bringing down structures already weakened by the earth's convulsions.

And then there was a period of quiet as things began to settle. Normalcy could not return, but the resilient people of this small nation went about rebuilding their homes and shattered lives.

There was no news of Kiran or the garden or the old lady on the street. They were not people who normally made the news. I would have to visit Kathmandu again, to see if the garden and its occupants were still there.

But before I could do that I had a visitor.

The steps to my room are steep and uneven and I was struggling up them after a visit to the bazaar when I noticed someone sitting on the top step, a backpack by her side.

It was Kiran. She looked tired and weak, but more beautiful than ever.

'I've come to see you,' she said.

'For a long, long time, I hope.' And I took her by the hand and led her into my home, my garden of books.

And that was how Kiran came into my life.

If you meet her, she will tell you about the garden of dreams (it's still there) and the old lady on the street (she's still there) and the lovebirds and the goldfish and the little stream. And perhaps she will take you there some day; for she is a girl who can make dreams come true.